Lizzie's Legacy

Book Four
'The Lizzie Series'

J. Robert Whittle

By J. Robert Whittle

The Lizzie Series

Lizzie: Lethal Innocence

Lizzie: Lethal Innocence – *Audio Book*
Narrated by J. Robert Whittle
(CD/Tape/MP3)
Lizzie's Secret Angels
Streets of Hope
Lizzie's Legacy

Victoria Chronicles

Bound by Loyalty
Loyalty's Reward

Moonbeam Series

Leprechaun Magic
(with Joyce Sandilands)
Leprechaun Magic – *Audio Book* (CD)
Narrated by Joyce Sandilands

3 On A Moonbeam
(by Joyce Sandilands)
3 On A Moonbeam – *Audio Book* (CD)
Narrated by Joyce Sandilands and Shayla

Lizzie's Legacy

❧❧❧

J. Robert Whittle

Whitlands Publishing Ltd.
4444 Tremblay Drive
Victoria, BC Can. V8N 4W5
Tel: 250-477-0192

www.whitlands.com
www.jrobertwhittle.com
email: info@whitlands.com

Original cover artwork by Barbara Porter
Cover design by Jim Bisakowski
Back cover photo by Terry Seney

Library and Archives Canada Cataloguing in Publication

Whittle, J. Robert (John Robert), 1933-
    Lizzie's legacy / J. Robert Whittle.

(The Lizzie series ; bk. 4)
ISBN 0-9734383-0-4

    I. Title. II. Series: Whittle, J. Robert (John Robert),
1933- . Lizzie series ; bk. 4.

PS8595.H4985L593 2004   C813'.54   C2004-
905629-8

Printed and bound in Canada by
Friesens, Altona, MB

iv

To Linda, Dave, Heather,
and all my 5 a.m. coffee pals
who keep me thinking with their
lively chatter and encouragement.

Acknowledgements

How can one express the sentiment of 'thank you' in different words or phrases so as not to trivialize the expression of gratitude? As the years go by, I have said these words so many, many times to you, my readers—at markets, craft shows, on the telephone, in emails .... your support, making two of my novels Canadian bestsellers over the past six remarkable years has been immense, and carries me forward.

I do not know if this volume will see the last of my favourite character, a girl after my own heart, a girl of my imagination and my life. Lizzie has become real to so many people including myself. I may not be able to let her rest if her fans demand it—that I should have enough time in this life to revisit dockland and continue her story.

My life, as many of you realize, is very full these days and there seems little time for writing until winter sets in—which I await with eagerness. This Lizzie is my 7th published novel, however, there are still several completed, unpublished, manuscripts waiting on my computer.

In 2004, we made the decision to hire a distributor. As has happened so often, fate stepped in and we met Tony Lawrence of Meluki Book Marketing. Thanks to Tony, all our books are now available through both Canadian and United States distribution houses. See www.whitlands.com for up to date information.

Many tell us they have heard about our books—on radio, television and in newspapers across North America and in England. With distribution, we hope our books will now be discovered in your local bookstores—if not, please ask for them.

Again, thanks to our hard-working team who makes this all possible: Barbara Porter, a gifted artist for her rendering of Lizzie's world; Jim Bisakowski for turning Barbara's art into another great cover; Deborah Wright, our ever-supportive friend and proofreader; Tara Poilieve, our invaluable office assistant, and not to forget, my editor and partner in life, Joyce, without whose encouragement and assistance none of this would be possible.

Joyce and I hope you enjoy this Lizzie as much as we have.

J. Robert 'Bob' Whittle, October 2004
robert@jrobertwhittle.com

Main Characters (in order of appearance)

Lizzie Short – 18-year-old partner in TLS Co.
Quon Lee – Lizzie's friend, partner in TLS Co.
Abe Kratze – Jewish tailor
Captain Johann Davis – captain of government ship, *Falcon*
One-Eyed Jack – first mate on *Falcon*
Charley Mason – TLS engineer and dockmaster
Nathan Goldman – Jewish businessman, cousin to Abe Kratze
Dan and Wick – gypsy bodyguards to Nathan Goldman
Tom Legg (Pegleg) – retired mariner and informant
Olivera "Oly" O'Mara – bakery lad, adopted son of Captain Davis
Bill Johnson – Yorkshire baker
Connie Johnson – baker's wife
Clem Radcliff – baker's helper
Sam Benson – foundry owner
Arthur Miller – wool merchant, son-in-law of Sam Benson
Captain Roland Hall – cavalry officer
Lady Penelope Sutton – print shop owner
Margaret (Daisy) Sutton – daughter of Lady Sutton
Gabriel Flood – partner in print shop, former army officer
Fred Monk – printer, former monk
Cuthbert Dunbar – printer, former owner of print shop
Willie O'Rourke – 5-year-old son of Ada and Mick
Ada Mason-O'Rourke – TLS bookkeeper, mother of Willie
Martha Johnson – Joe's Yorkshire housekeeper and cook
Joe Todd – Lizzie and Quon's adopted father and business partner
Mick O'Rourke – Ada's husband, TLS yard foreman
Richard Byrd – lumber merchant and councilman
Angus McClain – Scottish brewery manager
Tom Jackson – architect and councilman
Ned Cabin – TLS office clerk

Main Characters (cont'd)

Billy – bake shop lad, former street waif
Tom Day – bake shop lad, handicapped ex-sailor
Clara Spencer – seamstress working for Abe Kratze
Grey and Green Grim – Charley Mason's helpers
Zak and Dominic Zorba – unsavoury characters
Jake (Stormy) Newton – actor
Judge Aurelius Harvey – judge and councillor
Admiral Jones – admiralty officer and councillor
Captain Harry Roach – captain of *Black Otter*
Alyse Byrd – daughter of Sam Benson, wife of Richard
Barnsby – butler at Byrd home
Captain Ben Thorn – captain of *Restitution*
Walter Groves – wine cellarman at Bishop's Palace
Jacob Tide – Bishop
Percy (Tip) Palmer – new minister
Patrick Sandilands – Scottish captain and rag merchant
John Watson – TLS brewery maltster
Willy Dent – Lizzie's childhood friend
Captain McHoule – captain of Australian ship *Goose*
William Toppit – council clerk
Sir. John Hope – Scottish lawyer, Patrick's uncle
Minnie Harris – owner of Dawson Shipping Co.
Alexander Harris – businessman and son of Minnie Harris
Jeb Dark – local gypsy leader
Sir Nowles Compton – chairman of Jewish Merchant's Assoc.
Albert Potter – artist and councillor
Captain Riley – soldier

Chapter 1 - 1808

Lizzie and Quon stood together in the morning sunshine. Arms linked, holding back threatening tears, they waved goodbye to the orphans. Once again mounted with their friend, Jeb Dark and his gypsies, the children were being spirited back to the safety of the Hertfordshire farm.

A few tears escaped, running slowly down Lizzie's cheek as small arms gave a last sad wave before the wagons disappeared onto the heath. She quickly brushed them away, wiping her hand on her old grey dress, then turning she dug her fingers deeply into Quon's arm.

Ten wonderful days had slipped by with the children as the centre of their world—business problems were swept aside as each revelled in the time spent together. There were trips on the Thames, buggy rides through London and joyous days picking flowers on the heath. Often Quon was by her side; other times, he took the boys and they did things only boys could enjoy.

It's hard to realize these are the same children who suffered so cruelly at the hands of the orphanage caretakers only a few years ago, she thought. That day when told of the hopeless situation at the orphanage, Lizzie, despite her young age, acted instantly. She and the nine youngsters quickly discovered a bond she could never have imagined possible. They became her personal charges, her angels, when surviving life itself had become impossible for their starving and battered bodies. She knew she had to help and fully intended these children to have meaningful lives.

Drover's Lane seemed empty without the children's laughter. *There is much work to be done,* she told herself sharply. A gleam of fire came into her eyes and she slipped her slim arm over Quon's shoulder. He looked adoringly up at her and as if reading her mind, they moved off silently down Water Lane. He knew there were plots to hatch and the council meeting—where Lizzie had applied to be the first woman councilman—was less than 10 days away.

Nearing the tailor's shop, Lizzie stopped. Looking over at her partner her eyes danced with mischief. She stood for a moment and looked down the street past rumbling drays and the bustle of activity to the Thames' docks, marvelling that so much of this was theirs. She smiled and took

Quon's arm, pulling him into Abe's shop. They noted the absence of Clara, his seamstress, and found him sitting alone at his table. He glanced up over wire-framed spectacles and put his needle and thread to one side.

"I heard a rumour, girl," he growled.

Smiling, Lizzie took a seat at the table.

"I have a question, old friend," she said softly, ignoring his statement. "Where do we find the Benson Foundry?"

"Benson Foundry?" Abe repeated, scratching his wispy beard with long, bony fingers. "Big chimney, always smoking, half a mile north of here. Can't miss it." He looked at her curiously.

"Who runs it?"

"Old Sam Benson."

"What's he like?"

The tailor's eyebrows raised a little and his face grew dark. "Hard and cruel … crafty as a box full of monkeys!" he replied harshly.

Quon's fingers tapped an unnoticed message on his partner's shoulder in their private sign language—a holdover from the days when Quon could barely speak English. She touched his hand in a silent reply as the tailor again picked up his sewing.

"He's always in his office at noon," Abe muttered offhandedly, and the youngsters stood up knowing it was time to leave.

As they stepped out into the sunshine, one of the young newsboys from the *Observer* was passing.

"*Falcon*'s back in port, Miss Lizzie," called the street urchin.

Changing direction, she and Quon cut through the back streets down to the busy government dock. They could see their friend leaning over the upper deck rail even from that distance.

Captain Davis, the gruff captain of the government ship, *Falcon*, frowned as he watched them approach, dodging the milling traffic of Dock Street just like they had done as youngsters years ago. *She hasn't changed much,* he mused, *always busy and scheming up something. She's a young woman now but you'd be hard-pressed to know it by the way she dresses.* He had been expecting them. They reached the dock and at a run crossed the expanse of warehouse facilities, busy with sailors unloading his cargo.

"YOU GOT 'EM?" Lizzie yelled up at him.

Glowering, Davis turned away from the rail. Snatching his pipe from his teeth, he walked toward his cabin.

"BRING 'EM ABOARD, SAILOR," he bellowed.

"We got 'em, lass." First Mate, One-Eyed Jack spoke in low tones, rubbing the empty socket under his eyepatch, as they passed him on their way up the gangway. "Captain and crew of *My Belle* are already in jail."

"Thanks, Jack," she replied, grinning as they turned to run across the deck. They could already hear the sound of the captain's pacing as he stormed about inside his cabin.

"COME IN!" boomed the familiar voice as Jack tapped on the door. Standing in the shadows of the dimly lit room, the captain continued to pace even as they entered.

Lizzie took her usual seat in front of the desk and reached absent-mindedly for the heavy brass paperweight. Picking it up, her fingers toyed with the object as she waited for the usual tirade.

"Well, lass," he hissed, in an abnormally quiet tone, coming to stand opposite them. "We caught the dogs red-handed! We found not one cannon but two hidden in the bales of wool, just as you said." He placed his hands on the desk and leaned menacingly toward them.

"And now?" she said, her voice emotionless.

"Now they hang 'em!" Davis said excitedly.

"Miller will be arrested?" she asked calmly, setting the paperweight back down on the table.

"This is treason, girl!" his voice thundered as he moved away into the shadows, causing a shiver to run up Quon's spine. "Miller and Benson are dead men."

"Well, that won't help me get on council, will it?" retorted the girl, looking up at him with a frown.

"It might," returned the scowling Davis, stepping out of the shadows, "if my report gives you credit for the information that caught 'em."

"How?"

"By bringing you to the attention of the authorities."

Picking up the paperweight again, she brought it down on the desk with a crash. Davis' eyebrows flicked upwards.

"We don't need that kind of attention!" she replied shrilly. "With our dock at Sheppey loaded with contraband goods, you'd have some explaining to do, Mister Davis!"

The captain began to pace back and forth again.

"I need to get on that council for the future of all the Olivera O'Mara's in dockland," she continued.

"My Oly?" Davis snarled, coming back to stand at the desk. "What the hell's he got to do with this?"

"What would Oly be without Billy and Tom?" Lizzie questioned, the paperweight again rising off the desk. "And how many youngsters are out there who need a helping hand and I can do it if I get on council. Well, Mister Davis, you might not care, but I do." Leaping to her feet, she crashed the paperweight down again.

Davis shook his head in frustration, snatching up the paperweight and putting it out of her reach. Many times in the past, he had felt the stinging lash of Lizzie's tongue as she stirred his usually well-hidden feelings, but she was also responsible for bringing little Olivera to him ... a child who had changed his life. Yes, Lizzie knew just what to say to tug on the heartstrings of this gruff old seadog.

"Damn you, girl," he hissed, tugging fiercely on his beard. Pushing a chair out of the way, he stomped over to the wall cabinet. Scowling, he muttered to himself as he sloshed liquor into a tankard. He put the bottle down. Eyes blazing with fury, he emptied the liquid down his throat.

"We go Wizzy," Quon hissed under his breath, tugging on her sleeve and nervously edging toward the door.

"And you go to hell, you old goat!" Lizzie called back at him as she followed Quon, slamming the cabin door behind her.

"Wait!" One-Eyed Jack was frowning as she stomped across the deck toward him. "The captain had no choice, lass."

"I thought to scare 'em Jack, not hang 'em," she snapped. "I needed an advantage to force Miller to support my application for council."

Jack smiled ruefully and shrugged his shoulders as Lizzie and Quon hurried down the gangway.

"Well dumplin," she said as they walked toward the TLS Company docks—a company Lizzie, Quon and their adopted dad, Joe Todd, owned. "We certainly won't get Mister Miller's support for council now will we, but neither can he vote against me!"

A group of soldiers ran by and Lizzie watched them curiously, then noticing others moving between the dockworkers.

"What're the soldiers doing, lad?" she asked an old sailor.

"Rumour has it ther searching fer Miller, the wool merchant," he grunted, not taking his eyes off the soldiers.

Turning onto the TLS dock, they found Charley Mason, the TLS dockmaster. He quickly confirmed the rumour, adding his own condemnation of Miller's deeds. Being an ex-navy man, he had very little sympathy for traitors.

"Here comes Nathan," Charley chuckled. "Ask him, he'll know more about what's happening."

Nathan Goldman's gypsy driver slowly manoeuvred the high-stepping gray along the busy dock and the buggy drew up in front of them. Lizzie grinned up at Dan and Wick, the Jewish trader's gypsy bodyguards, then shot a question at the salesman through the open window of the buggy.

"What's happening, Nathan?"

"They're searching for a traitor," he snapped pompously, making no effort to leave the conveyance. "Will this trouble affect our supply?" he asked. They could hear his silver-topped cane tapping irritably on the floor.

"Affect our supply of what?" she asked.

"Continental cheese and wine."

"Why should it?" Charley inquired. "Coastal shipping won't be under scrutiny."

"Fool!" Nathan sneered, leaning out of the window. "Captain Davis will be watched."

"Captain Davis," Lizzie laughed sarcastically, "will be a hero! They'll probably make him an admiral and give the old goat a medal!"

Quon's fingers moved silently on her arm. She looked over and grinned at the scowling trader and nodded. Quon slapped the gray's rump and the startled horse jerked forward sending Nathan tumbling backwards onto his seat. He screamed abuse at Dan, who laughed aloud as he quickly pulled back on the reins to keep the horse still.

Nathan babbled his dismay but quickly fell silent when Lizzie opened the carriage door and climbed into the buggy.

"Don't you ever stop grumbling?" she hissed in his face.

"I was only trying to help," he whined as Quon joined them.

"You could help by riding us to the Benson Foundry."

"Sam Benson's foundry?" he asked fearfully.

"Yes."

"But why would you want to go there? Rumours say it was a Benson cannon Captain Davis found on that wool ship." The trader's face twitched nervously. "I'm not going near that place."

Lizzie pressed her lips together. She didn't feel like arguing with Nathan and she wasn't about to tell him what she knew.

As the buggy slowly turned into Dock Street, Lizzie signalled to Quon and, before Nathan could blink, the door opened and they had jumped out. Dan waved as they ran to the side of the road out of the traffic. They made their way over to *The Robin* coaching house, where they could usually find their one-legged informant. They eavesdropped on conversations as they searched for Tom Legg among the patrons. Following the direction of her partner's pointing hand, she saw him.

Eyes almost closed, he looked like he would fall from his barrel perch at any moment. Soldiers, who listened attentively as he talked, surrounded the little man. He wobbled dangerously close to falling but one of the soldiers caught him, putting him upright. At a nearby table, three men sat quietly listening.

"He's drunk," Lizzie muttered in disgust but, noticing the interest of the three men whom she recognized as local captains, she moved closer. Quon was right beside her.

"By George, the rumour can't be true," a highborn-sounding voice at another table declared, "Arthur Miller is Benson's son-in-law. They're men of honour. It just can't be true."

"Ther'll be the devil to pay," a rasping voice added, "if it is."

"I wouldn't want to be Davis, if old Sam Benson gets annoyed," said one of the captains.

Lizzie shuddered and looked over at Quon to see if he had heard. He had. Beginning to move away, her fingers gripped Quon's arm but she stopped when she heard the captain's name mentioned again.

"Davis won't live long enough to testify!" insisted the rasping voice. "You mark my words, Sam has the ears of Admiral Jones and Judge Harvey. He'll use his influence to his advantage."

Frowning, Lizzie and Quon made their way through the stableyard, dodging the urgent activity of stable hands, snorting horses and a stagecoach coming to a rumbling stop. A clock in the distance struck the noon hour. As they emerged into Mast Lane, the familiar sound of young Olivera's high-pitched laughter and the rattle of his bread cart's iron-rimmed wheels, reached their ears. As he came around the corner, they were amazed at his new position. Instead of sitting in the front, he was standing like a charioteer.

"Lizzie!" the Portuguese lad squealed excitedly as the partners pushed open the gate to the baker's yard, "Uncle Davis is back!"

"Ah know, lad," she grinned as he jumped down and ran to hug her. "Have you seen him yet?"

"Pies are hot, don't burn yer fingers," Bill Johnson warned Quon as the Chinese lad ran by him and into the bake house. "Too late!" he chuckled, when he heard Quon's squeal of pain.

"We've had soldiers here, Liz," Bill told her quietly. "Ther lookin fer a man named Miller."

"I know."

"What's it all about, lass?"

"Captain Davis caught his ship out at sea with cannon barrels hidden in bales of wool."

"Ee by gum, that's serious," the Yorkshireman gasped. "Did yer hear that Clem?" he shouted to his helper. "That Miller fella has committed treason."

"Big trouble, he'll rot in prison," Clem gasped, dumping an armload of fresh bread on Oly's cart.

"Nay lad," Bill exclaimed, "they'll hang im!"

Eyes flashing, Olivera leapt up from the table.

"You not hurt my Uncle Johann!" he exclaimed defiantly, showering Quon and Lizzie with pie crumbs.

"No, no lad," assured the baker, "it's not yer Uncle Johann we're talkin about."

The lad's eyes flashed over to Lizzie for confirmation as he sat back down on the bench beside her. She hugged him again, reassuring him with a smile and his head dropped onto her shoulder.

"Oly scared," he whimpered.

"Come on, son," the baker gently coaxed. "Billy and Tom will be wonderin where ye've got to, lad."

Oly finished his drink then slowly got up and went over to his pony, speaking to him quietly. He picked up the lead rope and tugged but the pony stood still as a rock. He tugged again with the same result. Dropping the rope, he turned around to face the baker.

"Ah know, ah know," Bill laughed, walking toward a covered wooden crate. "He wants one of me blasted apples. Deary me, even the pony thinks I should feed him!" He tossed an apple to Olivera and the lad took a bite before giving it to the animal, who devoured it with obvious relish.

Oly led the pony out of the yard as the voice of Connie, the baker's wife, rang from the bake house door, reminding them all there was work to be done.

"Come on, dumplin," said Lizzie, pulling on her partner's arm, "let's go look for a foundry."

Just as old Abe had told them, the big chimney, belching black smoke, rose high above the rooftops. As they got nearer, the ever-increasing smell of sulphur hung in the air.

Travelling along unfamiliar streets where every building looked old, worn and grimy, they arrived at a wall and faced imposing iron gates with the words *Benson Foundry* etched above. Peering through the gates, they watched as horses strained at heavily loaded drays and workmen scurried around the yard to the noisy clanging and banging of a prosperous foundry at work.

"What do you want, girl?" a sweating workman growled irritably when he saw the girl walking purposely toward him.

"Mister Benson's office, please sir?" she asked sweetly.

Frowning, he pointed with a blackened hand through the swirling dust to a coal-streaked stone building at the end of the yard. Offering no further information, he turned abruptly away.

"Friendly folk, ain't they?" she muttered, feeling her partner's reassuring hand on her arm.

Sam Benson was staring contentedly out of his office window surveying the day's activity when he noticed the arrival of the curious, nondescript couple.

"Now, who might they be?" he wondered thoughtfully, rising to his feet and adjusting the folds of his silk cravat.

Creaking loudly, the opening of the heavy oak door alerted Jacob Hardy, Benson's longtime bookkeeper, in the outer office. Hunched over a high desk, he raised his head slightly and peered silently at the two visitors through wire-framed spectacles. Setting his quill upright in the inkwell, he smoothed the few hairs on his shiny, balding head and coughed to clear his throat.

"Something you need, young lady?" Hardy's voice rumbled.

"Mister Benson, please sir," Lizzie said softly, in mock humility.

Stool legs scraped harshly on the bare wooden floor. The clerk eased himself to an upright position and, shuffling slowly on wobbly legs, went across the room to knock timidly on Sam Benson's office door.

"A person to see you, sir," he called, without opening the door.

"SEND HER IN, HARDY."

He knew we were here, Quon's fingers tapped on her arm.

"Go in," Hardy mumbled disinterestedly, making no effort to open the door for them.

Quon stepped forward to open the door, allowing his partner to pass, then falling in behind her. He quietly closed the door as his eyes took in the dull, sparsely furnished room. He noted a single, small bookcase, a modest, unpolished desk, three wooden chairs and a well-stocked liquor cabinet with the doors slightly ajar.

"Who are you?" Benson snapped, neglecting to offer them a seat as he tipped back in his chair, eyes flicking from one to the other.

He hasn't heard the rumour yet, Lizzie thought to herself.

"My name is Lizzie Short, sir. I'm your new council member!" she replied boldly, yet keeping her voice low.

"LIKE HELL YOU ARE!" the foundry owner exploded. "A WOMAN ON COUNCIL—I'D DIE BEFORE I WOULD LET THAT HAPPEN!"

"May I sit down?" she asked calmly.

"NO! STAND! I know who you are. You're that trash from Slaughter Lane."

Quon's eyes flashed as he leapt toward the desk. "MY WIZZY, YOU PIG!" he exclaimed, crashing a fist on the desk under the foundry owner's nose.

Arms flailing wildly, Sam Benson's sudden movement sent his chair crashing backwards against the wall. Desperately trying to keep his balance, he clawed at the desk, scattering papers and sending a glass inkpot spinning across its surface and onto the floor, leaving a black stain in its path.

Lizzie took a step backward, making no attempt to stop her partner's assault on the owner. Suddenly, the door burst open and another, younger man entered.

"YOU!" he bellowed at the girl. Seeing Sam on the floor and his chair toppled over, he advanced on Lizzie, viciously swinging his riding crop.

Although not absolutely sure of the identity of this man, both Quon and Lizzie were correct in thinking he was Benson's son-in-law, Arthur Miller.

Like a springing tiger, Quon blocked the charging wool merchant's action in a single bound. Taking a stinging blow on his forearm, the Chinese boy swung his fist into Miller's flabby middle.

"Run Wizzy!" he cried as Miller's body crashed to the floor.

"Not this time, dumplin," she chuckled, glancing out the window into the yard. She picked up a book from the desk and hurled it at the cowering foundry owner, hitting him on the head, as he tried to stand up.

Benson cursed, his hand going to the slightly bleeding gash on his forehead.

Lizzie picked up another book and glowered. "Help seems to have arrived, gentlemen."

To prove her point, a commotion erupted in the outer office.

"STOP!" shouted Hardy's voice on the other side of the door.

However, the door flew open and, with sabres drawn, a cavalry captain and three soldiers spilled into the room. Sunlight, filtering through the dirty, multi-paned window, flashed menacingly off their weapons.

"Put the book down, miss!" the captain ordered with a hint of amusement on his lips as he noted the small trickle of blood on Benson's face. "I think the fight is over."

"Arrest them!" Benson demanded, scrambling to his feet. "They're trash from dockland."

"And who might you be, sir?" asked the captain.

"I'm Samuel Benson, the owner of this foundry."

"Arrest him!" declared the captain and his men moved forward to take Benson in hand. Ignoring the exclamations of protest from the foundry owner as the soldiers dragged him away, he turned to Arthur Miller, still sitting on the floor and cowering against the wall as he watched his father-in-law led away.

"You're Miller aren't you?" the captain snarled, prodding the wool merchant coldly with the tip of his sabre, "a cowardly traitor who sells cannon to our enemies. I should save England the cost of a hanging and deal with you right now!" He raised his sabre above his head.

"NO!" Lizzie shouted in alarm, leaping in front of the captain.

A slow smile spread across Captain Rolly Hall's face. He was a man who'd fought many battles, faced danger and death in countless campaigns, and lived for the thrill of a cavalry charge. He couldn't resist having a bit of fun with this sorrowful excuse for a human being, but he did recognize courage and leadership—this young woman was definitely unusual and seemed to possess both.

"Who are you, young lady?" he asked, lowering his sabre.

"I'm Lizzie Short. I believe no man should be condemned without a fair trial, sir!"

"An admirable sentiment," the captain chuckled, "but I think there be more depth in your meaning than this miserable dog deserves."

Turning toward the window, Captain Hall noticed that a crowd of noisy foundry workers now packed the yard and his men were attempting to keep them in control.

"Get on your feet, scoundrel. A welcoming party awaits!" he growled sarcastically.

Once again, he prodded Miller with his sabre and the wool merchant pulled himself reluctantly to his feet. As he did so, he glanced out the window, gasping when he saw Benson, now in chains, being led out into the yard.

By the time they, too, reached the yard, a horse and open-backed cart had been confiscated and a loudly protesting Sam Benson was being assisted, none too gently, aboard. Miller was also chained and thrown roughly in beside him.

He looked up at his father-in-law and mumbled, "Shut up, Sam!"

As if bringing the foundry owner to his senses, Benson's head dropped limply to his chest and he went silent.

Surrounded by the mounted cavalry, a soldier climbed aboard the cart and took up the reins. The crowd, now chanting loudly, pushed forward threatening to overpower the guards.

"TRAITOR! TRAITOR! TRAITOR!"

"WHAT ABOUT OUR JOBS?"

"WE HAVE FAMILIES TO FEED!"

"I think we should escort you and your friend out of here, Miss Short, and rather quickly," announced Captain Hall, as a worried frown crossed his face. "You can ride pillion with two of my men. The sergeant will assist you," he said, flicking his eyes at the soldier standing beside him.

Grasping Lizzie's elbow, the young sergeant ushered her toward three mounted soldiers waiting at the bottom of the steps. She recognized them as the same three who had come into the office. The sergeant cupped his hands and assisted her up behind one of the men. When she turned to look for Quon, he was climbing unaided up behind one of the other soldiers. He gave her an almost imperceptible nod.

Immediately, the captain gave the signal and the small group moved ahead to lead the strange-looking cavalcade out of the foundry yard. The shouts of the angry workers followed them.

Winding slowly through the narrow streets, from her seat Lizzie watched the suspicious glances of passing draymen and women who protectively gathered their children to them, or ran inside, slamming doors. Men hid around corners, nervously puffing on pipes.

Why are these people so frightened of the soldiers? she wondered. "You can let us off here, sir," she said aloud.

The rider signalled the soldier beside him and the two horses reined in as the rest of the group proceeded up the road. Captain Hall noticed what was happening and turned his mount back to join them. He dismounted to assist, but the young people were already on the ground.

"Good day, Miss Short. Perhaps we will meet again." He saluted before riding off.

"Foundry dead now, Wizzy?" Quon asked, frowning deeply as they watched the captain and his men gallop off.

J. Robert Whittle

"No."

"Who boss man now?"

"I don't know."

Her partner's questions had set a train of thoughts rushing through her head. Who would run the foundry now Benson was gone? Would scores, perhaps hundreds, of ordinary people be put out of work? Worriedly she quickened the pace, using back lanes to avoid traffic.

"Daisy Sutton will know," she exclaimed, when they stopped to catch their breath.

Several young street urchins, hired as newspaper vendors, scurried past with arms full of newspapers, yelling, "TRAITORS SOUGHT! TRAITORS SOUGHT!"

Slowing to a walk as they turned into Brown's Yard, they saw a crowd of people had gathered around the newspaper office. Nathan's buggy stood in front of the door.

"I think we need larger premises," Lady Penelope Sutton sighed when Lizzie appeared in her office doorway.

"And more printing presses," Nathan added pompously. "Business is growing."

Pulling Lizzie around to face him, Quon's arms spun wildly. "Ask him, Wizzy," he insisted.

"He wants to know," his partner began, looking at Nathan, "who would run the foundry if Sam Benson died."

"Benson's dead?" Nathan gasped, staggering back against the work table.

The Stanhope Press squeaked to a stop and everyone listened intently.

"No, not yet," she replied, saying each word very deliberately.

"He's ill?" Penny whispered.

"No."

"What a stupid thing to say," the trader ranted. "What the devil …?"

"Answer the question," Lizzie snapped abruptly, glaring at Nathan.

"One of his sons-in-law, of course."

There was a moment of silence as they all waited for Lizzie to continue but running feet sounded and Daisy burst into the office.

"They caught them, they caught them!" she repeated excitedly.

Frustration showed on Nathan's face but he said nothing.

"I talked to Captain Roland Hall," Daisy said breathlessly. "He showed me the prisoners."

"Rolly Hall!" Gabriel whooped. "Why, I haven't seen him in years. I wondered if he had signed up again. He was still in France when I returned to England."

"Daisy," Lady Sutton interrupted, "I hope you weren't in any danger."

"No mother, I was at the dock with Charley when the cavalry troop came by."

"And you talked to the soldiers?"

"Oh mother," Daisy took her mother's hand, "this is dockland. Real people live here. I talk to anyone."

Unable to bear the suspense any longer, Nathan turned to the reporter and spluttered out his question. "Well, who did they capture, Miss Margaret? Who were they? Give us a name, girl."

"Sam Benson, the foundry owner and his son-in-law, Arthur Miller," Lizzie said casually. "Captain Davis caught them shipping cannon barrels to the enemy, hidden in bales of wool. We were there not half an hour ago when the army came to arrest them at the foundry."

"You did go there ...," Nathan mumbled, looking curiously at Lizzie.

Lady Sutton sat down heavily on a chair, her face growing pale as she whispered, "They'll hang them."

"And so they should," Gabriel growled fiercely.

"Careful, lad," Fred Monk muttered. "I can understand your feelings, but don't judge a man too harshly."

"There will have to be a trial first," Daisy sighed. "Just think of the disgrace."

"Yes, a trial," Lizzie added, beginning to raise her voice, "a real trial, not the sham we get when Judge Harvey sends widows and orphans to Australia for being hungry. You lot think the war is over on the continent, don't you?" her voice softened. "Well, it's not. It's here in dockland fighting the shame of being poor and that nobody cares what happens to them."

"Me care, Wizzy," Quon murmured, putting his arm around her.

"You really care about dockland, don't you love?" Penny Sutton whispered. "Someday you'll be a great statesman and changes will be made."

"No, ah hardly think that's likely," Fred chuckled, "but she could be the first great stateswoman!"

In a sudden burst of energy, Lady Sutton clapped her hands and took control. She ordered her daughter to begin writing an account of Benson's and Miller's arrest and, Fred to start laying out a new print bed, while Gabriel, her partner, was given the task of stripping down and cleaning the

Stanhope printer.

"But what about me?" old Cuthbert, the former owner of the shop whined, looking hurt.

"Cuthbert, you can mix 10 gallons of ink," Penny chuckled, "we're going to spread this news all over dockland in the morning."

Lizzie winked at her partner as she turned toward the door, a tingle of excitement touching her thoughts. One never knew what strange, unexpected things could happen in dockland.

Chapter 2

As the partners walked toward home, Quon chuckled when the church clock struck six.

"Wate again," he muttered.

"Yes, we're late again," was the even quieter reply.

"WIZZY," young Willie yelled, spilling his plate as he leaped up from the table.

"Willie O'Rourke, you little monkey," his mother reacted, "come back here."

Already safely nestled in Lizzie's arms, the five-year-old was totally oblivious to his mother's anger, as he planted a kiss on the girl's mouth.

"Leave him be," Martha whispered, "ah'll clean up the mess. We should all be welcomed home like that."

"But he has to learn some manners," Ada sighed.

"Let him be a child first," Joe growled, "he'll be a long time grown up." He lay down his fork. "I never had a childhood and neither did them two," he nodded toward Lizzie and Quon, "but I'm damned sure young Willie's going to have one."

A dampness touched Ada's eyes as she toyed with her food. In another five or six months Willie would have a sister or brother to shower his love upon and she knew this special family, which had adopted the two of them, would enjoy another little one in the house.

Captain Davis, who had joined them for dinner, looked over at Eva. "Those small arms are a statement of fact, lass. Those two are bonded for life."

Glancing at Davis, Charley Mason's eyebrows jumped, surprised at the quietly spoken statement from the usually harsh and dour captain.

Willie's squeals again shattered the silence that had settled over the cottage. Quon's tickling fingers had him bouncing around in Lizzie's arms as he called for Martha's help.

"Me big hungry, Mum," announced Quon, smiling at Martha as he took the squirming boy from Lizzie and returned him to his chair.

Smiling, Ada noticed the touch of pink that coloured Martha's cheeks as she handed a plate to the young man. Then the expression changed to

J. Robert Whittle

one of concern when she saw the bruises on his outstretched arm.

"You've bin hurt, lad," she murmured.

"Miller's whip." Through a mouthful of bread, Quon's reply was barely discernible.

"You were there?" asked Mick.

"Yes, we were," Lizzie admitted, taking her place at the table. "There was hardly anything to it, soldiers arrived right after us and took them away."

"I instigated the arrest," Captain Davis growled. "We extracted the information from the crew. You shouldn't have gone there, it was a foolhardy thing to do."

"You did too much," Lizzie grunted, stopping to swallow her mouthful. "I only wanted 'em scared. That's two councillors gone now and still no advantage to us—a wasted effort!"

"Damn you, girl, are you never satisfied?" Davis responded, crashing his fist onto the table making plates and cutlery jump. "We caught two traitors!"

Willie, startled by the noise, leapt for the safety of his grandfather's lap.

"You heathen!" Martha squealed, smashing her big wooden spoon over the captain's knuckles. "Behave yerself or go."

Sheepishly, Davis pushed his chair back and rose, fumbling for words as he rubbed his sore hand.

"Sorry folks," he exclaimed. "I meant no disrespect, but that young woman sorely boils my temper at times."

"Sit down, you old goat," Lizzie chuckled. "Now you've scared everybody to death, I've got something to tell you."

Captain Davis sat back in his chair. From the very first moment he'd met her, Lizzie Short had been a thorn in his side, always able to annoy him to distraction; she could wind up his temper to the point of explosion. Her craftiness and initiative scared the tough old seafarer, perhaps because he had begun to recognize his feelings of concern for the girl. Those feelings were not unlike the ones he felt for Oly and the orphaned bread boys who had become like sons to him.

"Dumplin and me think you might be in danger," she continued, interrupting his thoughts. "We heard two gentlemen talking at the ale house; they said you wouldn't live to testify against Benson. So would you please be careful. Take One-Eyed Jack with you wherever you go."

"My lads are here," Charley interrupted, struggling to pick up his

16

crutches from the floor. Labouriously, the engineer came to his feet and began to shuffle toward the door. Partway, he stopped. "You listen to her, captain. Benson's family are going to be right peeved with you. Never no telling what they might get up to."

Everyone in the room listened to Charley's warning and several nodded their heads in agreement. Soon afterward, the group began to leave with Mick and Ada being the first, gathering up their son who peered suspiciously over his father's shoulder at Captain Davis.

❧☙

Down the Thames, in an army barracks near the Tower of London, Sam Benson and Arthur Miller languished alone in their musty and cold jail cells, their fate to be decided by the high court.

With damning evidence from captain and crew—caught red-handedly by the *Falcon* and Captain Davis in mid-channel—their future looked terribly limited. All hope now centred on Richard Byrd, husband of Sam's youngest daughter, Alyse. Not quite a man of action, Byrd drew his attitude of power from a reputation as a cruel, oppressive employer, and many of his associates feared his senseless, blazing temper.

Drinking with cronies at an out-of-town inn, a whispered rumour from a coachman alerted him to the disastrous situation. Urging more speed from his driver, the coachman's words … *Sam Benson … treason*, rolled over and over in his brain.

Arriving at the Benson mansion, his temper erupted when confronted by soldiers confining the family members who had gathered. An officer smugly assumed the responsibility of relating the whole sordid story, insisting Byrd accompany them to the army barracks warning him that no interference would be tolerated.

At the barracks, he felt the cold hand of disgrace as they treated him with contempt and kept him under close guard. They questioned him about the business and the smuggled cannons, roughly brushing his demands aside when he asked to see the two men. When released, he stormed outside yelling abuse at his driver who had arrived to escort him back to the family estate. The lumber merchant's wild, staring eyes warned of imminent danger as demented thoughts coursed through his brain.

Arriving back at the Benson home, he had little stomach for niceties and ordered Sam's aged mother, his wife and daughters, including his own wife, Alyse, to depart immediately to Sam's country estate. Ignoring their protests, he demanded the servants aid the women with their packing.

Finally alone, he sat down at the desk in his father-in-law's study and listened as the sound of the carriages faded in the distance. He poured another glass of scotch whisky then sat back in the leather chair cursing under his breath.

It's Captain Davis who has caused all this trouble, his brain whispered. *He must be silenced.* His logic obscured by worry and drink, Richard Byrd was headed on a pathway of doom.

ဆာၢၷ

Morning found Lizzie and Quon eagerly eavesdropping on the arguments that raged on every street corner. The news of treason had spread through dockland like wildfire fuelled by Daisy Sutton's startling and graphic account in that morning's newspaper.

Moving slowly along familiar streets and alleys, the young partners made their way toward the old corn mill. Now owned by TLS, it bustled with activity. Renovations, under the watchful eye of Angus McClain, their brewery manager, were complete and its conversion into bulk grain storage was proving exceedingly useful; Charley's steam engine-run conveyor belt was proving even more valuable than originally thought.

Quon touched Lizzie's elbow and pointed to the doorway in which Lefty, the one-armed ex-soldier, who often acted as the TLS messenger, had appeared and was now hurrying away from.

Calling his name brought Lefty limping over to join them. "Where have you been?" she asked abruptly, "and why are you limping?"

"Oh, just me rheumatism, is all—it's the dampness in the morning. I been to tell Joe that gent's comin to see him."

"What gent?"

"The architect man Mister Goldman sent me," Lefty muttered, struggling to fill his stubby clay pipe with one hand.

"Here, let me do that for you, Lefty," Lizzie offered, taking the pipe from him. She reached into his pocket for the loose tobacco, stuffed some into the pipe, tamped it down, and handed it back. Quon produced a light.

Puffing happily, Lefty waved his thanks and ambled away.

"I wonder what an architect is?" asked Lizzie, although not expecting an answer from her partner.

"HEY, YOU TWO," Joe shouted from an upper-floor window, "come up here."

Dust-laden air made them cough as they climbed the stairs to where Joe and Angus McClain were waiting.

"It's splitting," said Angus, pointing upward to the huge centre beam with his pipe stem. "We need Charley."

"He doesn't have time, we have an architect coming. This must be him now," Joe muttered, peering out of the open window. "UP HERE, LAD," he shouted to someone in the yard below.

The man waved his cane in acknowledgement and made his way into the building. A little overweight, the architect struggled up the stairs, red-faced and out of breath by the time he arrived at their side.

"Tom Jackson, sir," he introduced himself, holding out his hand to Joe.

Quon Lee's fingers moved onto Lizzie's arm, their movement causing her to glance quickly in his direction. She winked at him, a wisp of a smile playing about her lips. Then, as Joe made introductions, the merry twinkle in his eyes didn't go unnoticed by the two when he referred to Jackson as architect and councillor.

"So you're Lizzie Short," Jackson chuckled, "but you're so young."

"What did you expect, councillor?" she replied cheekily, "a wrinkled old granny."

"Well no, but someone a mite older than you," he replied, unflustered by the girl's brashness. "My Uncle Ned talks about you with a reverence akin to worship. I just naturally thought you were somewhat older."

"Your Uncle Ned who?" she asked, suspiciously.

"Cabin," Jackson replied.

"Our Ned's your uncle?"

"Yes, my mother is Ned's sister."

Lizzie's eyes hardened and Quon's fingers could feel the tension building in her slender body as a grin of anticipation spread across both Joe's and Angus' faces.

"And you're going to try to keep me off council, are you?" Lizzie snapped.

Taking his time to answer, the architect held her gaze; and their eyes locked.

"No, I'm going to vote for you and so is Albert Potter, we discussed it only this morning," he murmured.

"Why?" she asked, not allowing her voice to soften as her memory went back to the day she first met Albert Potter—an artist who lived near the bread shop.

"Because Uncle Ned financed my education and I respect his opinion. He thinks you're the uncrowned princess of dockland, the way you give jobs to every broken-down sailor that comes your way. I've heard Billy, at the bread shop, shouting your praises from his barrel. I want to be there when you tackle council!"

Lizzie slipped her hand into the pocket of her coat and her fingers touched Albert's thimble.

"And what are Albert Potter's reasons?" she asked.

"Oh," Tom chuckled, "Billy has promised to find Albert's lucky thimble for him if he supports you."

"I thank you, sir." Lizzie curtsied, adding, "I hope you are a man of your word." She went over to Joe and gave him a peck on the cheek. "See you at dinner, old luv," she said, nodding at the others.

Not sure if he'd been insulted, the architect watched her move away. *This Lizzie Short certainly has an air of confidence and a quick mind. Perhaps too quick for the council's liking!* Then, hearing the urgent note in Joe Todd's voice, his mind returned to the task at hand.

"She's a very good-looking young lady," he remarked aloud as his eyes strayed upward to view the cracked beam, "somebody should tame that girl."

"Ach man, get on with yerr worrk," Angus growled irritably, "an keep yerr thoughts to yerrsen."

Leaving the dusty yard, Lizzie heard the familiar rumbling that told her Quon was hungry, but she said nothing as they headed up Goat Hill toward the cottage. Quon spit the dust from his mouth and grinned. Crossing Drover's Lane, they noticed young Willie happily at play with the gypsy children. A sigh escaped her lips as she thought of their youngsters, whom she had hugged only yesterday. *I wonder how long it will be before we see them again?* she thought.

Quon, feeling very sure he knew what she was thinking, took her arm and gently steered her toward the garden gate. He, too, felt the pain of separation from their young charges.

Martha's stew quickly supplied renewed energy and her comic chatter in broad Yorkshire always brought smiles to their faces.

Taller than Quon, Lizzie's arm rested easily on his shoulder as they strolled up the lane to the TLS office after their meal. Nathan's buggy stood outside with Wick tending the horse. Through the open door, they heard the trader complaining about an urgent delivery.

"Everything sounds normal to me, dumplin," she commented, as Wick tipped his hat and winked at them.

Suddenly, Mick appeared at the door holding the little man by his coat collar. "Sure hoy be tired of listenin to yer whinin," he hissed in the trader's ear. "Go home to yer mother, boyo."

"Did you see that, Miss Lizzie?" Nathan complained, hastily throwing the package he was holding into the carriage. "That stupid Irishman threw me out."

"Nathan," she sighed, "I don't want to hear your problems today."

"Nobody values me around here," he grumbled as he scrambled into the buggy. "I've a good mind to never come back," he continued, as the gypsy climbed aboard and waved to the youngsters.

"Aye, and you might grow to six feet tall," she called after the fast departing buggy, "but that won't happen real soon either!" Shaking her head, she smiled when laughter greeted them as they walked into the office.

Mick had tears running down his face and Ada rocked back and forth on her chair. Old Ned Cabin was trying hard not to laugh as his pipe wobbled between his teeth.

"Do you know what that was all about?" Ada gasped. "Mick made him deliver a rush order of cheese and Nathan loathes the smell of it, says it lingers for days in his buggy!"

"Hm, so that's what he had in his package," Lizzie mused. When things settled down, she raised the subject of her meeting Tom Jackson. She thanked Ned for his kind comments, explaining she had no idea that the councilman was his nephew. "Is he a big landowner?"

"No, but he represents a number of foreign investors," Ned replied, offering no further information.

Sounds of running feet and a loud knock on Mick's outside door brought instant silence as the foreman sprang to his feet and opened the door. A ragged street lad was revealed gripping a note in his dirty hand.

"What is it, son?" Mick asked the wild-eyed boy.

"It's from Miss Daisy, sir." The lad offered the note at arm's length, obviously eager to see it delivered and be off.

Mick took the piece of paper but Lizzie jumped up and went toward the lad pulling a half-penny out of her pocket.

"Here lad, take this and thank you for the delivery."

"No, mum," he whispered, nervously backing away. "Miss Daisy said not to tek any money." Spinning on his heel, he was gone.

"My word, Captain Davis has been hurt—badly it seems," said Mick reading the note. "It says a horse and carriage ran over him in Dock Street … on purpose."

"Where is he now?" asked Lizzie, her voice cracking with emotion.

"It doesn't say."

"Get the flag, dumplin, and call the Chinese doctors," Lizzie snapped. "Then alert the gypsy women to get ready for him and meet me at the printing shop."

Mick, Ada and Ned watched as Lizzie took control, as she so often did. Her sudden burst of orders sent Quon scurrying away without question.

"What do you want us to do?" Mick asked.

"Nothing yet … except ask our drivers if they know who did this," she called over her shoulder as she followed Quon outside.

"Hoy feel so helpless," the Irishman muttered dejectedly.

"I know, love," Ada consoled him, "but the general who planned the Zarauz raid is in control and nothing will stop her. I saw that flash in her eyes when you read the note. Heaven help anybody that gets in her way … and Lord help the man who did this."

Chapter 3

Taking shortcuts through several alleys and narrow snickets, Lizzie raced for the newspaper office. She was gasping for breath when she arrived at the open doorway.

"Billy's bread shop," Gabriel redirected her. "Daisy's there waiting for you."

Taking a deep breath, Lizzie picked up her skirts and headed in the direction of the bread shop. The air was strangely devoid of the sound of Billy's voice which always rang through the streets this time of day. When Lizzie arrived, she noticed Billy's empty platform and the group of inquisitive people standing in front of the store were speaking in whispers.

"He's dun for," growled One-Eyed Jack, slumped in the doorway.

Lizzie pushed past him.

There, on a bed in the tiny back room, lay the unconscious figure of Captain Davis. His skin was pale and ghostlike; blood frothed from his lips. His head was a mass of dirt, blood and already swelling bruises; and his clothes were dirty, torn and blood-stained. One arm lay across his chest, obviously broken, and his right leg was twisted grotesquely.

Billy and Daisy knelt beside him trying to hold back their tears. Lizzie looked down at the pitiful sight of the adversary who had become one of her dearest friends. Immediately, she began to scream orders jolting everyone out of their stupor.

"HE'S NOT DEAD YET AND WE'RE NOT GOING TO LET HIM DIE. DO YOU ALL HEAR?" She looked around at each of them with the urgency of desperation. "Then let's get busy."

A stretcher was fashioned by One-Eyed Jack and Billy and, with everyone helping, they carefully moved the unconscious captain. Quon arrived with two of the TLS men in a dray. They loaded the limp body into the back as carefully as they could. Lizzie climbed up beside him, grateful he was unconscious—in her mind, she willed him to live.

As they were leaving, Nathan and Wick arrived on the scene.

"FOLLOW US!" she cried, then lowering her voice she looked at the group who had gathered around the dray. "Go back to the *Falcon,* Jack, and the rest of you, it's business as normal ... and no one is to say

J. Robert Whittle

anything. Let's go!" she urged and the dray moved forward.

"Faster, faster," Lizzie urged, as they swept up past the TLS office.

Ada's worried face peered through the open window, watching them disappear in a cloud of dust. Going as fast as they dared, they drove past the rag yard and into the gypsy camp, narrowly avoiding a collision with a rag cart.

As soon as the dray came to a halt, they transferred their patient to a long box-like crib, made ready by the women. Lizzie sighed with relief when she realized her friend was still breathing. She looked back to see the trader's carriage pulling up behind them. Nathan had already opened the door and was preparing to exit as Wick jumped down to assist him.

"What is happening, Miss Lizzie? Is it Captain Davis?" he asked excitedly.

"Yes Nathan, it is Captain Davis." She proceeded to quickly explain what had happened, answering several of the trader's questions. "We need to find out who's responsible for this, Nathan. I need your help."

Quon slipped in beside Lizzie and his hand slid reassuringly onto hers. She squeezed his fingers, looking off into the distance.

"I know dumplin, you're always there when I need you," she whispered, suddenly realizing her eyes were watching a man's figure run across the holding paddock toward them. It was Mick.

"Murphy, oh Murphy," he gasped, running up to join them. "Is the old fella alive?"

"Barely, but he's in good hands now," Lizzie answered, her eyes holding the Irishman's gaze. "When the Chinese doctors arrive, show them straight up here, Mick."

"That hoy will, luv," Mick assured her, "hoy'll be tellin all the draymen to be watchin for 'em." He turned away then stopped, "And just what will you be up to, moy darlin?"

"Why lad we're going to find out who did this," she said in a low voice, adding, "and when I've done with him, he'll wish he were dead."

"You be careful, lass, or you'll not get to that council meeting."

Without waiting for her answer, Mick turned on his heel and strode away. He knew she would need some protection but she had Quon and who else could they trust with Jeb and, most of his men, gone away to the farm with the children.

A sudden yell from Tiny, his yard foreman, waving from the paddock, told Mick he was needed in the office. With delivery problems to deal with, thoughts of Lizzie's safety were momentarily driven from his mind.

24

Watching from her window, Ada saw her husband's hunched shoulders and faltering stride. Her fingers instinctively traced a line around her lips as she waited for the news.

Puffing hard on his pipe, Ned also recognized the signs of worry and frustration in his workmates. Blowing a thick cloud of smoke upwards, he turned to Ada. "Stop yer worrying lass, Lizzie has more friends out there than any of us know about."

"Here they come," she said, dropping heavily into her chair.

Ned came over to join her at the window. Hurrying up the lane, Lizzie and Quon waved to them but continued on by.

"WHERE ARE YOU GOING?" she called after them.

"THE PRINTERS," Lizzie called back over her shoulder, "WE'LL BE HOME FOR SUPPER."

No words were spoken as they dodged pedestrians and traffic in Pump Street, their thoughts centred on one thing. Rounding the corner at Brown's Yard, they saw a group of street lads standing around Daisy in The Print Shop doorway. They couldn't hear what she was saying and, although exhausted, they quickened their pace.

"Now go and find out what you can, lads," were her parting words as she handed out the bundles of newspapers.

Quon heard and grabbed Lizzie's arm.

Like rabbits, the boys raced off, each going a different way down a street or ducking into an alley until they had all quickly disappeared. Lifting her head, Daisy flicked a wisp of hair from her brow. Her young, pretty face frowned with worry when she saw her friends.

"Will the captain live?" she asked as they followed her into the shop to join her mother and the others.

"Tell me what you know," asked Lizzie, directing her question at Daisy.

"Almost nothing," she replied wearily, helplessly shrugging her shoulders, "except it happened in Dock Street at one o'clock—a gentleman's coach with a driver and one gentleman passenger—it all happened so quickly."

Quon's hands spoke and everyone watched, waiting for the translation.

"He wants to know if anyone noticed the horse?"

"I never thought of asking," Daisy said helplessly.

"Fred made you two more copies of that letter from Judge Harvey," Lady Sutton murmured, changing the subject and going over to her desk. She returned with some papers. "Do you want to take them now, Lizzie?"

Lizzie looked down at the pieces of paper—forged copies of a damning letter from Judge Harvey's past—and nodded expressionless. She glanced them over quickly before folding them carefully and handing them to Quon. He deposited them in his deep pocket. She turned for the door. There was an awkward silence, so she simply waved goodbye.

The church clock began striking five bells as she and Quon moved off down the street back toward the bread shop; glancing at each other, they tried to smile when they heard Billy's voice in the distance.

"Him tough," Quon muttered, frowning when the shouting suddenly stopped, "but Oly ...."

He left the rest unsaid as they quickened their pace to a run, and were soon in sight of the shops. As they feared, there stood the pony and cart loaded with bread but no sign of the bread lads. Mary, the butcher's wife, was serving customers at the counter across the street and noticed Lizzie and Quon hurry into the bake shop. She shook her head as she served a customer. *Poor lads, I hope the captain will be all right.*

Looking around the empty shop, Lizzie and Quon heard the muffled sound of sobbing coming from the back room. *Oly!* Going toward the heartbreaking sounds, they found all three lads holding each other like brothers as little Olivera sobbed in Tom Day's arms.

"Hey, you three! Come on, act like men now," she feigned anger but tried to smile. "There's work to be done."

Olivera lifted his head. Tears had stained his dusty face as thoughts of his beloved uncle overwhelmed his young mind. Flopping over on the bed away from Tom, he struggled to get the words out.

"But Uncle Johann's dead," he sobbed.

Sitting down beside him Lizzie took him in her arms. "No, he isn't," she whispered, "he's hurt bad, but he is *not* dead and he's *not* going to die."

"Can we see him, Miss Lizzie?" the boy snivelled.

"In a day or two, lad," her arms tightened comfortingly around him and she wiped his face with a cloth Billy handed her. "After the doctors have been and he's a bit stronger, we'll take you to see him." She spoke confidently and hoped with all her heart what she was saying was the truth of it.

The three lads listened carefully and knew, that of anyone, Lizzie would have everything under control. Their absolute faith in her gave them the confidence and assurance they needed. Billy's leadership showed clearly, as he returned outside and climbed back onto the barrel, urging his partners to unload the bread cart and make the last ship delivery of the day. He was obviously tired and his voice had lost some of its sparkle as he called to late shoppers.

It was just after six when Lizzie and Quon said weary goodbyes and started for home.

"Need a ride?" Nathan's voice called as his buggy pulled up beside them before they had gone a block.

Gratefully accepting, they slowly climbed inside. As she settled into the seat, she became aware that the trader was eager to talk.

"That flag at the cottage, the red one with the big white dot, what's that all about?" he asked.

"We sent for the Chinese doctors," Lizzie said slowly.

"With a flag?"

"Yes." Her voice came in a whisper. "I want to know who did it, Nathan."

"An enemy no doubt—someone with a grudge against our sweet-tempered captain," he said sarcastically.

Lizzie's eyes bored fiercely into the trader, her back stiffening as she waited for his next comment.

"And that," he continued, "could be one of a hundred people."

Quon touched her arm in warning as her lips tightened.

"But it's more likely to be something very recent," Nathan concluded.

The boy's fingers danced excitedly on her arm.

"He wouldn't dare, would he?" the girl replied.

Nathan watched the youngsters' eyes lock, staring at each other with an unwavering intensity. It was their strange, silent way of transferring thoughts and it sent shivers down his back.

The carriage stopped at the cottage gate. They alighted and Nathan solemnly touched his cap ordering his driver to continue. Lizzie and Quon slowly walked arm-in-arm to the cottage door. It was open and a low murmur of voices emanated from within.

Lizzie stopped before climbing the steps, her hand grasping Quon's arm. "We have to find a way, dumplin. We can't let him get away with this!" Lizzie hissed venomously, watching her partner nod.

Pans rattled as they walked through the doorway. Two plates of hot food appeared in the housekeeper's hands.

"You need to eat, luvs," Martha coaxed gently.

The usual group was there at the table including One-Eyed Jack. All eyes turned expectantly toward them watching silently as they moved to their places and sat down. They all knew Martha didn't like business being discussed while her meal was being consumed so their questions would have to wait.

"Has anybody checked on Davis in the last couple of hours?" Lizzie asked, breaking the silence as she finally put her fork down.

"Hoy have," Mick ventured eagerly. "He'll live, the old devil is screaming blue murder up there already."

"Are you going to tell us what is happening?" Ada murmured.

"It's my fault," Jack chastised himself. "I should have seen it comin."

Leaning forward in his chair, Joe tapped his pipe on the hearth, a sure sign he was about to say something important.

"If you lot just shut up for a minute, she'll tell yer," he growled.

"Well, this is the situation," Lizzie began, but suddenly there was a knock at the open door.

"Cum in," Martha called to the young gypsy woman who stood wringing her hands in the doorway.

"Miss Lizzie, come quick," she said nervously. "Two China men at camp."

"Come on, Mick," Lizzie yelped, leaping from her chair, "we're going to need yer."

"'Am coming, too," said Jack, pushing his chair away from the table.

"No, yer not!" Lizzie snapped as the Irishman followed Quon out of the door, "you're captain of the *Falcon* now, Jack; get that vessel out of the harbour after dark and nobody will be the wiser. We're playing for time now."

"Go," Charley snapped, "ah'll see he does it, lass."

Racing past the slaughterhouse and rag yard, she could hear the screaming of a man in pain. Running as hard as she could, Lizzie arrived at the gypsy camp.

"Get these heathens away from me!" Davis yelled when he saw them.

Specks of foaming blood on his lips alarmed her and Lizzie dropped onto her knees beside him—taking his good hand, she squeezed it, noticing how hot it was.

"SHUT UP, YOU OLD FOOL," she screamed in his face, "they're here to help you."

The sound of her voice had a strange effect on the injured man. His head rolled slowly to one side as he tried to focus his pain-laden eyes on the girl. He began to whimper Olivera's name over and over again.

Lizzie sat down on the ground resting her head on the edge of the crib and talked to him in a soothing tone. It wasn't long until he thankfully slipped back into the painless oblivion of unconsciousness.

Speedily, Doctors Fung and Chew went back to work. The broken arm was set quickly with efficient fingers, cuts were stitched, and ribs pulled back into place. The twisted leg was straightened and held by strong bindings and only then did an involuntary groan escape the captain's swollen lips.

"We done, Miss Wizzy," Doctor Fung stated as they packed up their implements and prepared to leave. "We come back in two week, gypsies look after him now."

Mick, Lizzie and Quon had stood back and watched in wonder as the doctors performed their work. Davis' broken body was now covered in numerous wraps; his leg and arm, encased in long sticks and fast-hardening mud, looked enormous. It was not the first time they had experienced the medical talents of these two Chinese doctors, for they had saved Quon's life in Hertfordshire not many months before.

"He'll be needin some watching," Mick growled. "That old devil will be as mad as a tick on a dog's back when he wakes up."

"We have a way to keep him asleep," said the gypsy woman as she led them back to the gate. "You want we keep him here, missy?"

"That would solve a lot of problems," Lizzie replied.

"Pony cart coming at full speed!" one of the gypsy lads called. Pointing up the track they saw Oly's bread cart flying toward them.

It pulled up beside them and Tom Day hauled back on the reins. Olivera, in his urgency, tumbled off onto the grass, bouncing hard before leaping to his feet and racing over to them. Mick caught him and held him.

"Steady lad," said the big Irishman, dropping to his knees. He took the young lad in his arms. "Yer uncle is goin to be fine, Oly."

"I couldn't stop him, Miss Lizzie, and I wanted to come with him," explained Tom, the eldest of the bakery lads and a former sailor who had lost a leg in battle.

"Uncle! Uncle!" Olivera cried in panic. "Where are you?" Legs and arms flailing, he fought to free himself from Mick's grasp.

"OLY!" Lizzie's voice cut through the noisy confusion with an air of authority. "Stop that blubbering and act like a man!"

Weakly, Olivera sagged onto Mick's broad shoulder. Quon went over and gently took the boy from the Irishman. Oly was still small for his age, being malnourished when Tom and Billy had found him eating scraps from *The Robin*'s refuse pile several years before. At the time, they had estimated his age to be about six and taking pity on the lad had asked Lizzie if they could keep him. She agreed, becoming especially interested when she realized he could act as a translator for Captain Davis in some dealings with a Portuguese sea captain. The temporary, close association of the little lad and the captain had cemented a lasting relationship, which earlier this year had grown to include the other boys.

"Be stlong, little man," Quon whispered. "Wizzy and Quon are here. We look after your uncle."

"Can we see him, miss?" Tom pleaded. "He's ours you know; we need to see him."

A single tear found its way down Lizzie's cheek and her heart missed a beat. The bond between the hard-working lads of doubtful origin and the bad-tempered captain was so strong she knew it would help him survive.

She gave Tom's arm an encouraging squeeze. He thanked her with a half-smile, reaching into the cart for his crutch. Quon let Oly down and he came to Lizzie's side and placed his small hand in hers. Now ready, they all followed the gypsy woman through the camp back to where Captain Davis lay sleeping.

Awed by the sight of his injured uncle, Olivera stared at the still figure on the blanket. His legs buckled and he flopped onto his knees beside the bed.

"Uncle Johann," the boy choked, "please don't die, we need yer."

Silent tears ran down Lizzie's face and she turned away, going to stand beside Quon. He put his arm around her and they watched the tender scene until wiping her tears, Lizzie moved back toward the bed.

"That's enough Oly," she whispered, "he will get better but he needs to rest."

"Who done it, miss?" asked Tom.

"Don't know yet, lad, but we'll find out."

"If I had both me legs, I'd go find him meself!" he muttered bitterly.

"It's all right, Tom. We'll find it out soon enough," she vowed.

Walking back to the cottage, they watched the pony cart disappear into Slaughter Lane, its youngest occupant huddled against the other.

"Sure it makes a man want to be killin somebody," Mick growled suddenly.

Deep in thought, Lizzie proffered no reply as they walked in silence, her thoughts racing over the events of the day. *Could Richard Byrd be that stupid to run Davis down?* she wondered. *Didn't they have enough trouble in the Benson family already?*

Joe's eyes fluttered open when he heard the door creak. He turned in his chair and looked over at Lizzie.

"He'll recover," she said, answering his unspoken question.

"Hoy'll tell you at home, luv," Mick cut short his wife's query. Scooping young Willie from Joe's knee, he followed his wife out of the door into the twilight of the warm summer evening.

"It's bad, isn't it lass?" Martha asked when they had gone.

"Yes, he's pretty broken up, but the Chinese doctors say he'll be all right. He'll get good care from the gypsies," she replied, going to sit on the floor against the old man's knees. Together they stared into the red embers of the fire as Joe stroked her long, soft auburn hair.

Quon sat down at the table and removed his boots.

"I'll find him," she promised herself quietly, cocking her head to watch as Quon's fingers began to tap on the table. Frowning, she gave no indication of wanting to translate the message and went back to staring into the fire.

It was still not yet dark when Martha suggested bed and began to turn out the lamps. They exchanged good nights and the cottage quickly fell into its night time quietness.

Chapter 4

Fully clothed, Lizzie and Quon lay on her bed looking out the window and listening to the moaning of cattle as darkness overtook dockland. Through the slightly open door, they could hear Joe and Martha snoring contentedly in their rooms.

"Ready?" Lizzie whispered in the darkness.

Answered by the touch of Quon's hand, they crept silently down the stairs, easing open the squeaky front door. Moonlight bathed the rooftops of dockland as the almost round sphere slid across the evening sky, flitting in and out of clouds as it went.

Moving quickly up Drover's Lane, they skirted the gypsy camp staying well away so as not to alarm the dogs. The soft grass of the heath dulled their footsteps as a church clock struck 11. They picked their way carefully when darkness came upon them, moving more quickly each time the moon reappeared. They walked without conversation for almost 20 minutes before the roof top of the Sutton mansion appeared.

"There it is," Lizzie muttered, altering her direction.

Clouds again covered the moon as they scrambled over a stone wall and walked cautiously down a tree-lined avenue that separated the grand houses of the rich. A fortunate shaft of moonlight illuminated the tall, stone gate posts and the brass name plate which read BYRD.

"Careful now," she whispered, as they moved around the high front wall and found the gardener's gate standing open.

Sniffing the air, Quon gripped the girl's hand, leading her through the pitch blackness of shrubbery and trees. Suddenly, an owl hooted irritably at the disturbance and Lizzie froze—the hair on the back of her neck standing on end.

"Stables and carriage house over there," Quon hissed, tugging on her hand.

Stooping low, they entered the stable and, with fumbling hands, found a lantern on the windowsill. Feeling around, Quon soon found some matches. The sudden glow disturbed the horses who snorted in alarm. They scrambled to their feet, stamping when the light moved away toward the connecting door of the carriage house.

Slipping quietly between the lined-up carriages, the partners checked every iron-rimmed wheel until at last they found what they were seeking— one with dry blood-stained spokes and wheel.

Morning came too soon for Lizzie and Quon, awakened by Martha's constant calling that breakfast was waiting. Joe eyed them suspiciously as they yawned uncontrollably over breakfast, but said nothing.

Water Lane was already a hubbub of activity when they stopped at the tailor's shop. Abe stood on his step gazing at the docks, shielding his eyes from the rising sun with a thin, bony hand.

"Is Davis dead?" he asked abruptly without turning his head.

"No."

"Thought so," the old tailor mumbled, "because the *Falcon* must have left in the night."

If Abe is fooled and we can keep Nathan from talking, Lizzie thought, *no one will suspect that One-Eyed Jack is captaining the* Falcon. But her presumptuous thoughts were soon shattered when the trader's buggy appeared, trotting briskly up the hill.

"Good morning, folks," he grinned, making no attempt to leave the buggy.

"Have you told anyone about Captain Davis?" Lizzie's tone had an ominous ring as she watched Nathan's expression change to one of discomfort.

The tailor listened intently, his hands knotted together in anticipation.

"Well yes, but only the truth of the matter," Nathan's voice faltered as he looked at her curiously.

Quon's hands suddenly burst into wild gyrations, startling Abe so that he stumbled backwards into his doorway.

"And the truth of the matter, Mister Goldman, is ...," Lizzie repeated, "Captain Davis sailed aboard the *Falcon* before dawn."

"No, that can't be," Nathan gasped.

"Well Mister Blabberer, *that*'s what you're going to tell folks."

"They'll think me a fool for changing my story," the trader pouted stubbornly, as his cousin, totally confused at the strange conversation, shuffled off into his shop and banged the door.

Stepping closer to him, Lizzie hissed fiercely, "Go tell Lady Sutton and Gabriel that I want them to print a little story in the newspaper." She paused for a moment, her eyes shooting sparks at the recoiling trader. "Tell them to say it was Captain Johns who was hurt and the driver has been identified by respectable witnesses."

"But that's not true," Nathan whimpered as he shrank back into the corner of the buggy. "I don't know of a Captain Johns."

"It's all right, Nathan, he doesn't exist. It's only bait to flush the culprit out!"

The trader's eyes flicked instantly to Quon whose hands were again spinning wildly.

"What's he saying?"

"He says you're a smart man," Lizzie translated, "you'll know how to make it sound like the truth."

"Yes, yes, I understand perfectly, my dear." Nathan sat up straight, and took a deep breath as his fingers gripped tightly on his cane. "I knew you and I would work out a plan to expose the rogue."

Shaking her head, Lizzie felt Quon's hand on the small of her back as they watched the buggy disappear into Chandler Lane. Glancing over her shoulder, she saw a smartly dressed merchant entering the tailor's doorway and they followed him inside. Moving silently behind the clothing racks, she put her finger to her lips when Clara glanced up from her work and saw them. Startled, the seamstress frowned as the girl ducked behind the table just as the merchant began to speak.

"Are my breeches ready, Mister Kratze?" the customer growled. "What's this rumour of Captain Davis being killed on the street?"

"Lies," Abe whined as he wrapped the parcel. "He sailed the *Falcon* out before dawn."

"Blasted rumour mongers," the customer grumbled clinking coins into the outstretched hand. "I shall inform my friends to pay no heed to the idle talk of fools."

"That's what we need," Lizzie whispered in her partner's ear as Clara watched wide-eyed.

Grumbling to himself, the tailor shuffled over to his stove. The young partners waited until the man had left and they, too, disappeared quietly outside. Standing on the sidewalk, Quon suddenly pointed up the street. Oly and the pony cart were heading across Water Lane toward the bakery. Sitting on the corner of the cart, its driver—a usually bright and happy lad—was hunched over in misery.

"The Print Shop," Lizzie muttered, watching his hands spin. Frowning, she stopped. "You think Tom Legg might know something?"

Changing direction, they headed for the coaching house. Drawing closer, they heard his raucous laughter rising above the noise. It was still only mid-morning and the peg-legged old mariner was already tipsy. "He's drunk already," she hissed.

Squaring his shoulders, Quon marched up to the swaying figure sitting astride the barrel and removed the tankard of ale from his hand. Startled, Tom's face twisted in anger until Lizzie's voice cut through his haze.

"Useless drunkard!" she snapped harshly, "a man was hurt in Dock Street yesterday and I want to know who done it."

"I knows who done it, miss," Tom slobbered. "A penny gets his name."

"Who?"

"A penny first."

"Help him remember, dumplin," Lizzie sighed.

Quon moved fast. Snatching the ever-present shepherd's crook from the old mariner's hand, he prodded him in the belly.

"CALL HIM OFF, LASS," Tom screamed, as he fell from the barrel and scrambled around to sit looking up at her. "It wer the Byrd man."

"Bird man?"

"Aye, Rich-Rich-Richard Byrd," the mariner struggled with the words.

"How do yer know?" she asked, watching the mariner cower again as Quon began to raise the shepherd's crook.

"A cabby recognized Miller's driver."

"And who was hurt?"

"Some said it was Captain Davis," he whined, "but it couldn't be cos the *Falcon* sailed at first light."

Fear had driven the haze from Tom Legg's brain and his eyes now focused clearly on the young woman in front of him. She nodded to her partner and Quon flicked a penny that rattled onto the cobblestones in front of him. Quon lowered the crook offering it back to the mariner and he scrambled after the penny.

"No, it weren't Davis, it was Captain Toby Johns," she stated convincingly as they turned to leave. "With their uniforms on, they look the spitting image of each other."

Quon's eyes twinkled as he glanced at his partner. The rumour was started and Tom Legg would spread it through the drinking fraternity at all the taverns in dockland. By evening, it would be taken as fact and Captain Davis' name would be dropped from the accounts of the accident.

Lunch time found them entering the open doorway of the newspaper office and Gabriel's voice rose in greeting over the squealing and clunking of the Stanhope Press. Daisy and her mother were deep in conversation looking at an article for the morning edition on their work table. Two thin and ragged street waifs stood patiently waiting at the counter.

"Miss Daisy," one of them called over the counter, reaching up to deposit a handful of coins onto its ink-stained surface.

Daisy pushed a wisp of hair off her face and came beaming toward them, winking coyly at her friends as she focused her attention on the newspaper lads.

"That's right, boys," she said cheerfully, counting out the 10 pennies and pushing half back to the grubby, waiting hands. "Now tell me your news."

"Talk on the street, miss, says it weren't Captain Davis that got run over," the boys told her eagerly, "it were Captain Johns ... an he died!"

"And what about Benson and Miller?" she asked.

"Folks are angry, miss, they want a hangin."

Thanking them profusely, Daisy handed them each 10 more newspapers before they hurried away.

"How's Davis?" Gabriel asked as the printing press squeaked to a stop.

"Mad as hell, I bet," Lizzie replied, shrugging her shoulders. "We haven't seen him yet today."

"You heard what the lad said, how did that rumour get started?" Lady Sutton asked. "Several of the lads have been in to tell us it was a Captain Johns that got run over."

"You can count on rumours to move speedily in dockland, it seems," replied Lizzie, raising her eyebrows and grinning. "Did Nathan come in this morning?"

"He did," Daisy nodded, "but who is Captain Johns?"

Ignoring the question, Lizzie posed one of her own.

"Did you write anything about the accident yet?"

"Read it for yourself." Lady Sutton frowned as she offered a sheet of hand-written copy to the girl. "Cuthbert was just going to typeset it."

VISITING CAPTAIN KILLED IN STREET BY PROMINENT CITY MERCHANT, it read in glaring large print. Then it went on to say that the culprit would be found and named in the *Dockland Observer* if he didn't come forward and own up. *We know who you are coward!* it ended.

Without taking his eyes from the paper, Quon's fingers tapped out a message on the counter, causing a wicked smile to curl the corner of Lizzie's mouth.

"That's fine," she murmured, "now Fred, can you add a picture of a man strapped to a cannon?"

The former monk's eyes danced with glee, wiping his ink-stained hands on a much-used rag before finding a piece of paper and quickly sketching the scene with a piece of charcoal. "Will that do?" he asked, chuckling at his own picture.

"A bigger man, fatter face and beaverskin top hat," Lizzie instructed, watching Fred skilfully adjust the picture.

"You know who did it, don't you?" Gabriel growled.

Quon's stomach rumbled, causing Daisy to giggle as he tugged on Lizzie's sleeve.

"Me big hungry, Wizzy."

"Well," Gabriel snapped, "are you going to tell us?"

"No," she replied, flashing them a smile before turning for the door.

Lady Sutton hooked her arm affectionately over her daughter's shoulder and shook her head at Gabriel's frustration.

"Stop fuming, you silly ass, and think," Penny Sutton admonished her partner. "She's told you it's a wealthy man by depicting the beaver skin hat and she knows something that could ruin him because he's stretched over a loaded cannon. That's danger, m'boy. This man will go crazy imagining everybody knows his identity."

"And what good will that do?" Gabriel growled.

"Why that's easy," the white-haired, diminutive lady sighed, as she went to sit down. "It's Lizzie's way of punishing him forever."

"I like her sense of justice." Fred Monk's eyes twinkled as he rubbed his whiskers. "Let's do it! Cuthbert, set that print tray up," he called.

Down the street, Lizzie and Quon were coming within the range of Billy's voice as he once again shouted his wares from his barrel-top perch. Their eyes met as they slowed and stopped, listening carefully. He was yelling news of docking ships and their cargoes mixed in amongst his advertising.

"Dumplin," Lizzie whispered, as they quickened their pace. "Billy's just given me an idea."

A passing coach slowed to listen, occupants craning their necks to hear the young man's words. Meanwhile, Billy's ever-watchful eyes scanned the passing shoppers winking mischievously at Lizzie as they arrived.

"Billy, come inside," she said quietly, motioning with a slight nod.

Another voice yelled as they were about to enter the bread shop. Looking back, they saw Oly on the pony cart trotting down the hill toward them. Billy grinned at the look of surprise on Lizzie's face when she heard Oly's squeaky call, "NEW BREAD, LADIES," he shouted, "JUST BAKED IT MESELF!"

"He's trying to copy me," Billy laughed. "Can I help him unload miss?"

"Course you can. Dumplin's hungry; he wants a bag of tripe from Sid Brown."

Quon's arms flew into wild gyrations jumping back from the doorway.

"NO! No twipe!" he exclaimed, his face contorting with revulsion as he stormed off to the butcher's shop next door.

"Ah don't think he liked that suggestion, Miss Lizzie!" the bread lad chuckled.

Quon reappeared with a meat pie in his hand followed by Sid Brown, the butcher, in his blood-splattered apron.

"Need a lift with that cider barrel, lad?" the amiable, ruddy-faced butcher asked, quickly swinging the barrel to the ground and disappearing back into his store.

"How's uncle, miss?" Oly tugged urgently on Lizzie's sleeve, his eyes looking sad.

"Get me a meat pie, too, will you Billy," she said, handing him a coin. When they were alone, she slid her arm over the Portuguese boy's shoulder and led him into the bread shop's back room. "Now sit down and listen."

Billy returned and silently handed her the pie. Between mouthfuls, she told them her plan.

I want you both to begin shouting something new," she began. "Everybody knows there was an accident yesterday, but they're not sure who was hurt. So I want you to tell them it was Captain Toby Johns and he died."

"But it wor Uncle Johann," Oly cried, looking up at her with a confused expression.

Lizzie could see the tears brimming in his eyes.

"Yes, ah know, lad," she said gently, "but we're going to fool 'em into thinking it were somebody else."

"Why?" Billy asked.

"So *Falcon* can sail as normal and your uncle will keep his job."

"I want to know who done it," Billy mumbled stubbornly.

Oly nodded his head vigorously.

"We already know who did it, lads," Lizzie whispered, "and he'll suffer, I promise you, but we have to do it my way. Now off you go back to work. You let us worry about your uncle."

The partners threaded their way through the back alleys until they reached Dock Street, often standing close to people so they could eavesdrop on their conversations. The rumour appeared to be spreading like wildfire among the waterfront gentry and businessmen. Captain Toby Johns had become real. They also heard other snippets of information as men talked of the traitors, Benson and Miller, and laughed at the rumour that a woman had put her name up for council.

"She doesn't stand a chance, those men will eat her alive. Why Benson stands more chance of beating the hangman!" a shipowner laughingly advised his friends. "Judge Harvey has a vicious tongue; she'll be in tears before they can accomplish anything!"

"Ridiculous state of affairs we've come to," another pompous voice interceded. "Women have no valid opinions; I say the vote will be seven to none against her."

"Don't you bet on it," Lizzie whispered as Quon's fingers tightened on her arm in warning, pulling her gently past the group.

It was almost three o'clock when they turned into the TLS dock. Passing the hissing steam engine unloading another grain ship, the strong smell of cheese bit into their nostrils. Farther along, Charley sat on his high seat watching. Standing by the cart was the familiar figure of Daisy Sutton.

"Now just what are you doing here?" Lizzie startled the newswoman, knowing she had become sweet on the engineer.

"Gathering news," Daisy blushed, "and spreading a rumour."

"This is our first full load of Dutch cheese," Charley explained. "It's from the Van Horn lumber deal and Ben's on his way up the Thames with another load of grain."

Daisy reached up and touched the dockmaster's hand.

"You will come for supper, won't you, Charley?" she asked quietly. "I'll send a carriage for you."

"No, no," Charley objected. "I must work late tonight."

"He'll come," Lizzie interjected with a wink, "he's just stubborn."

Slowly turning his head, Charley slapped his crippled legs in silent frustration, his eyes meeting Lizzie's then turning to watch the figure of Daisy disappear off the dock.

"I'm not going to supper at Sutton Manor, Liz," he muttered.

"Oh shut up whining, Charley," Lizzie snapped. "She needs a friend; it's just a shame she's picked a selfish fool like you who only cares about himself."

The dockmaster appeared stunned by her outburst. He clenched his hand into a fist and rapped it silently on the side of his cart, hidden from view.

"That's a lie," he hissed. "I do care about her."

"Then why punish her by not going for supper?"

"All right, all right, ah'll go," the dockmaster capitulated, his face growing red. "Are you happy now?"

"I don't care one way or the other," Lizzie shot back flippantly. "When's Ben due in?"

"Early tide."

"You'll make him aware of what's going on with the *Falcon* and Captain Davis?" she asked coldly but not waiting for an answer, she took Quon's arm and they quickly moved away.

She noticed the strong aroma of cheese as they followed a loaded dray along the dock. Quon's head twitched violently and his hands began talking with agitated urgency. Lizzie watched him and a smug smile spread across her face.

"Dumplin, sometimes it's quicker to push than to coax!"

Men were cleaning the deck of the empty grain ship as they passed the grain dock. The steam engine was quietly chugging in the background—occasionally letting off steam—only some of many noises in the busy dock area.

Escaping the smell finally, they crossed busy Dock Street to the front of the coaching house where drinkers were noisily quenching their summertime thirst. Threading their way between tables, they followed the sound of Tom Legg's drunken laughter.

"Av news, missy," cried the old mariner, choking on a mouthful of ale. He banged his crook on the ground to keep himself steady, as glazed eyes focused on the young partners. "A penny for old Tom, me deary," he pleaded.

Silently, Lizzie flicked a coin at the one-legged mariner and he quickly tucked it away in his money bag.

"Wallace Dawson's back in town, we seen im," he mumbled.

"Dawson's dead, you fool," Lizzie snorted impatiently.

Slowly, Tom's eyes closed, his head dropping onto his chest as he slipped from the barrel with a thud. Ale from the tankard, still gripped firmly in his hand, spilled over his dirty shirtfront as he flopped onto his side and began to snore.

Lizzie shook her head. *Is this what's in store for all these poor men who fought so hard for this country?* she thought. *They need their self-*

respect back. Docklands is a scrap heap for battered sailors like him. Would I be able to change that if I got on council?

There was silence between them as she and Quon went through the back alley and up Mast Lane to the bakery. Bill's rotund figure watched from his bake house, frowning when he saw the slumped shoulders and bowed head of his usually effervescent friend.

"What's up, lass?" he called, "yer look like all't winds gone outa yer sails."

"It's useless, Bill," she moaned, "everywhere you look there's another heartache happening in this part of London."

"Nar look eer, lass," Bill growled, "yer doin yer best, luv, don't give up on us now."

Quon's hands suddenly burst into action, then reaching for her hand he raised it to his lips and kissed her fingers.

"What did he say?" Bill whispered reverently.

Slowly, she squared her shoulders, brushed her hair to one side and ruffled Quon's hair.

"He says I'm not to worry, he's always there."

"Want some pie?" Clem Radcliffe shouted from inside the bake house.

The two bakers sat quietly watching Lizzie and Quon eat their pie and a glass of buttermilk, their eyes locked together. Finally, wiping the milk and crumbs from her mouth, she jumped to her feet.

"Give me a hug, Bill," she grinned, her despondent mood gone, "then we're off!"

The startled baker responded easily to her command; one he did not often receive from this girl. Taking the pretty 18-year-old in his arms for the first time in some years, he couldn't help but think about the day that a little 9-year-old waif had appeared at their door. Lizzie wasn't asking for a handout, she had said she desperately needed to make some money so she could feed herself and an invalid she was looking after. *So much has happened since Joe's accident,* thought Bill, *and now it's Davis she's worried about.* He stood with Clem and watched them run up the road in the direction of Goat Hill.

"I wonder what that was all about?" mused Clem.

"Ye'd do right not t'even pass it through yer mind!" chirped the Yorkshireman.

Slowing, the twosome walked up the hill. At the top, they again broke into a run passing the cottage and continuing on up Drover's Lane to the gypsy camp. Cattle were coming in and gypsy drovers were everywhere

41

but none of them looked familiar. It was too early for Jeb to be back. Leaping the fence, they cut across the empty holding paddock. The camp was alive with noise as they made their way to the place where they had last seen Captain Davis.

"We moved him," a gypsy woman shouted, waving them over to a shelter and a small campfire set off to one side.

Inside, they gazed down at the still-pale, unmoving figure of the captain. A young gypsy girl they recognized was gently mopping his brow with a wet cloth. She looked up and smiled. "The fever is down this afternoon."

"Good, I wonder if he knows we're here?" Lizzie whispered.

"Yes, he does," the woman murmured, "his body's asleep but his mind is awake and free from pain."

"You mean he can hear me?"

"Yes."

"Can he talk to me?"

"Not with words," she said, settling onto her knees and taking Captain Davis' undamaged hand. "Ask him a question and watch his fingers."

"Can you hear me, captain?" Lizzie asked. "It's Lizzie."

She felt Quon's hand grip her elbow when a finger on Davis' hand slowly rose and fell.

"He hear," Quon whispered.

Sinking to her knees, Lizzie stared at the patient's face. "Do you know who ran you down, Captain Davis?"

The finger slowly moved again.

Quon's hand tightened on her shoulder. "Test him, Wizzie," he whispered.

She nodded. She had to know for sure whether the answers Davis was giving were muscle reflexes or was he really answering her questions.

Thinking hard, she deliberately asked a lie. "Is *Falcon* a coal barge, captain?" The finger never moved. She altered the question and asked, "Or is *Falcon* a government ship?" Immediately the finger twitched, then lifted and fell.

Leaning over, she kissed him gently on the cheek then murmured in his ear. "It was the lumber merchant, Richard Byrd that ran you down, wasn't it?" Again, the finger strained, lifting as a sigh whispered from his lips and the finger slowly settled onto the gypsy woman's hand.

"That's enough for now, Miss Lizzie," the gypsy gently insisted.

Satisfied Captain Davis had the best of care, they made their way slowly home. They both knew their problems were far from over. Richard Byrd's cowardly act could not possibly go unpunished.

"We need a lookalike," Lizzie muttered, as they reached the cottage, "somebody we could pass off as Davis."

"Yer late!" was the housekeeper's welcome as they entered. She rose and went to the hearth to fill two plates with stew. "We saw yer go past almost an hour ago—bin to visit Captain Davis, av yer?"

Lizzie sat down and picked up her fork. She looked up and nodded.

"Well," Ada prodded gently, "is he conscious yet?"

"He's in good hands," Lizzie sighed, before filling her mouth, hoping to forestall any further questions.

"Charley's late, too," Martha observed with concern. "He's working too hard."

The youngsters' eyes met and Lizzie began to giggle.

"He ain't workin," she said, watching Willie try to copy Quon's finger-tapping on the table.

Ada looked up at the girl. "Well, where is he?" she asked, genuinely concerned about the brother of her late husband.

"Courting!"

The effect of Lizzie's one-word statement silenced the room. Everyone waited expectantly assuming she would give the name of the woman, but none came. Instead, Lizzie turned on her most innocent expression and filled her mouth with potatoes.

"Well, who then?" Ada demanded.

"Daisy Sutton, I'll wager!" Mick offered, raising an eyebrow. "Sure and begorra, I think that lass is sweet on our lad—she certainly admires his intelligence. That's a beginnin'!"

Quon grinned, nodding vigorously. "Wizzy done it," he announced proudly, "Wizzy bump him!"

A smile of understanding strayed across the bookkeeper's face while the others threw Lizzie a silent, puzzled query.

"So young lady, you pushed him into it did you?" Ada chuckled.

"He just needed a gentle nudge," Lizzie smiled disarmingly.

Mick burst out laughing as Quon rolled his eyes and a titter of amusement ran around the table. Even Willie joined in by clapping his hands.

"Ee just think of it, Joe," Martha sighed, "Lady Sutton's daughter and our Charley."

$\mathcal{C}hapter$ 5

For the first time in a month Charley called the Grim brothers to take him home at five o'clock. No questions were asked as he left the dock, though men scratched their heads in surprise.

"Wait for me," he ordered the twins, as he struggled through the doorway and went inside his humble home.

Washed and shaved, he reappeared in less than 20 minutes. The Grim brothers gasped at the sight of the dockmaster, resplendent and handsome in his naval uniform. Shoulders pressed back, his boyish good looks and twinkling eyes almost disguised the two walking sticks that supported him.

"Take me back to the dock, boys. The Sutton coach will be coming to pick me up there."

Outwardly, Charley Mason showed confidence and authority, a man in charge of his destiny, but inwardly his stomach squirmed and rumbled— the knowledge of his crippled legs haunting him. There would never be dancing in his lifetime and walking with sticks was painful and slow. He felt like an oddity away from the dock and wished he'd never allowed Lizzie to persuade him to accept the Sutton's hospitality. It had been many months since he had been to the Sutton home, managing to keep Daisy's advances to a minimum until today.

Back on the dock, nervous anticipation kept him glancing up as he busied himself overseeing the men loading an outgoing cargo. His blood racing, he finally caught sight of the Sutton coach coming slowly toward him. A swift, low whistle brought the Grim boys who lifted him down from the cart.

Fighting the pain of moving unaided, he struggled toward the coach. The coachman greeted him as he opened the door and awkwardly helped him inside. Charley sighed as he settled into the soft leather seat. He glanced out at his beloved dock through the open window as the coach rumbled into motion.

Leaving the congested streets, they moved quickly to the better class area, travelling along tree-lined avenues past the mansions of the wealthy to the vale where the Sutton estate was situated. Charley fiddled with his walking sticks, his mind racing with near panic when the driver turned and drove through the big iron gates.

"You're looking very handsome tonight, sir," Daisy murmured, as she came to the door of the coach to meet him. Moving quickly to help him alight, she staggered under his weight as he awkwardly manoeuvred himself down the single step.

"I can manage," he said in frustration, wobbling forward to greet Lady Sutton in the doorway.

Lady Sutton kissed him on the cheek and, grinning at her daughter, led the way toward the dining room. Knowing how difficult it was for their visitor, they tried to make small talk as they settled Charley into his chair and Daisy brought him his favourite drink.

"You remembered," Charley murmured, looking into her face as she handed it to him. "Thank you, Daisy." He couldn't help but think how pretty she was looking tonight. *I suppose I should tell her so,* he thought.

At that moment, the kitchen maid appeared.

"Yes Jane, you may serve dinner right away. I'm sure Mister Mason is as hungry as we are, after such a busy day." The maid disappeared and an uncomfortable silence settled over the room.

"Is Gabriel not joining us tonight?" asked Charley, as two of the kitchen staff and Jane appeared carrying covered tureens, a roast on a large platter and a pitcher of gravy.

"No, he's working late at the newspaper office with Fred," Penny explained. "We have a newspaper to get out for tomorrow morning."

The atmosphere relaxed as Charley savoured his meal and they found themselves talking about Lizzie as they often did when together. Charley admitted for the first time, with alarming frankness not portrayed before, that Lizzie Short had employed him when life had held no future. Now, even more, his fierce loyalty to the girl was blatantly obvious.

"We know, dear boy," said Penny, "we too, have much to thank that young woman for."

Supper ended with the clinking of wine glasses and a toast to the TLS Company. As the staff appeared to clear the dinner dishes, the diners moved into the comfort of the drawing room. Daisy produced the book of De Vinci inventions and came to sit beside him on the couch. Together, they balanced it on their knees and scanned the pages.

"Look at that," Charley pointed excitedly to a rolling clay mould, "we could adapt that to print your newspapers."

"How?" Daisy asked eagerly.

Lady Sutton smiled slightly as she watched, listening to the argument that ensued between these two intelligent young people. She enjoyed it immensely when they fought each other's thoughts with hotly held opinions. Charley's creative mind was at work, his impediment forgotten, and Penelope Sutton was pleased to see him feeling more comfortable in their home.

"Then let's try it," Daisy was challenging him when her mother brought her mind back to the goings-on in the room. "Let's see if it works."

"No, it needs steam," he exclaimed. "Steam is the answer."

"Children, children," Lady Sutton interrupted, "you're arguing like brother and sister. Come, come now, it's after 10 and we all have work in the morning."

Silenced by her mother's interruption, Daisy closed the book and reached for Charley's hand. Gazing at him with her startlingly beautiful blue eyes, she whispered, "Can I be your sister, Mister Mason?"

"W-why yes, you certainly may, D-Daisy," Charley's voice wavered, as he fought to answer the unexpected question. "You certainly may," he repeated, feeling a rush of relief.

A low morning mist hovered over the Thames on Thursday, spreading its damp, eerie fingers through the waterfront streets as Lizzie and Quon made their way down the hill to Abe's shop. They found him standing on his doorstep staring into the fog, looking almost ghost-like in the haze.

"What are you watching?" she asked.

"Not watching," the tailor snorted. "I'm listening."

"To what?"

"That infernal machine on your dock."

Straining their ears, they could hear the rhythmic thumping and hissing of the steam engine.

"Something's wrong," Abe mumbled, "that thing sounds different this morning."

Visions of another boiler explosion, like the one that had caused the earlier downfall of this engine, flashed though Lizzie's brain, and she grabbed Quon's arm.

"We'd better go see," she called to the surprised tailor, setting off at a run.

They arrived out of breath and quickly found Charley and two of his men standing beside the engine.

"What's wrong?"

"Nothing's wrong, we're putting a new drive belt on," he snapped, his eyes never wavering from the job at hand. "Go away!"

Quon tugged on her arm pointing over to Dock Street. Frowning, she followed him across the waterfront road to the coaching house where a street lad stood handing out the *Observer* to travellers alighting from a coach.

Several more men were standing off to the side reading the newspapers; their chuckles were loud enough to hear as they turned to Fred's drawing. After a silence, when they were no doubt reading Daisy's scathing account of the accident, further comments were heard.

"Who the devil is that fellow?" one local merchant growled. "There should be a way to stop this paper printing such accusations."

Lizzie grinned. They were achieving their purpose. That scoundrel, Richard Byrd, would soon be aware of the talk. *He'll sweat and worry*, she told herself, *then try to bluff it out*. A strange feeling lurked in the back of her mind. *That lumber merchant will find a way to cause more trouble before we are finished. I just know it.*

Unknown to the partners, Byrd was already aware of the latest edition of the newspaper. As he stood at the window of his dockside office, he read the caption on the cartoon and glowered. The timid knock of his clerk sounded on the door. His blood raced through bulging veins, panic clutching at his throat. Have the authorities already come for him? Cold sweat ran down the back of his neck as the door opened slightly.

"Judge Harvey to see you, sir," the clerk announced in such a quiet voice that Byrd had to strain to hear.

Pushing roughly past the clerk, Judge Harvey framed the doorway.

"Damn you, Byrd," the judge fumed, "what the devil's got into you?"

Fearing the worst, Richard Byrd's shoulders dropped as he struggled to find an excuse for running a man down with his coach. Facing the angry judge so early in the day had not been part of his plan. He sat down and desperately tried to find his voice.

"You are not going to vote that woman onto council, you fool!" hissed his visitor, showering the wool merchant with spittle.

Byrd's heart jumped. *He doesn't know about the accident. Someone has informed him that I'm thinking about voting Lizzie Short onto council.* The puzzle of who that person might be was soon cleared up by the judge's next blast.

"Bishop Tide says it's progress!" Judge Harvey's eyes bulged as he ranted. "I say that women should keep their place—interfering in men's

47

work, damnit man, you can't be serious!" Spent of his pent-up energy, he flopped into a nearby chair.

Relief swept though Byrd's body. His friend, the bishop, had made the excuses cleverly supporting Lizzie in the guise of a noble action, thus retaining a measure of respect for his actions.

"We feel she should be given the chance to serve this community," Byrd lied.

"Idiot," replied the judge. "We never served anyone but ourselves and I sir, shall make the meeting hell for her."

ಬಂಛ

All morning Lizzie and Quon roamed the streets hearing the same topic of conversation everywhere they went. It seemed everyone who had read the *Observer* was eager to learn the identity of the man strapped over the cannon, and also the fate of the traitors.

At one point, Quon stopped, his face blank and unmoving.

"What is it, dumplin?" she asked, watching his hands whirl. "Yer right," she whispered, "the *Observer* office will be in danger if they're going to hound the man who ran over Captain Davis." They found themselves at the top of Long Lane, not far from the cottage; across Slaughter Lane was the little church of St. John. A coach standing at the churchyard gate roused their curiosity. The driver, whose back was to them, was watching two figures deep in conversation on the graveyard path.

"I wonder whose coach that is?" she asked. "Do you recognize either of those men?"

Quon shook his head. "Too far to see."

He pointed to a dray coming toward them. Darting behind it, they both managed to get closer for a look.

"It's Richard Byrd talking to the minister," she hissed in Quon's ear.

They left the protection of the dray and ducked down a snicket on the opposite side of the road out of sight. Watching from the corner of a building, they noticed the conversation become more animated. It appeared the men were angry with each other as they waved walking sticks threateningly at each other.

"I wonder what that's all about?" Lizzie muttered.

As the lumber merchant turned to leave, more heated words were exchanged between the men. The minister must have said something pertinent because Byrd spun around to face him again. He spat out a parting comment, waved his stick one last time and strode off toward the carriage. The minister trudged down the path past the church.

"Wizzy," Quon whispered urgently, his finger pointing toward a mound of dirt beside a newly dug grave. The outline of the gravedigger's head was just visible as he, too, eavesdropped.

Watching the minister walk away and Byrd's coach disappear in traffic, they sneaked across the lane into the churchyard. Noiselessly, they darted from gravestone to gravestone until they drew closer to the new grave. The gravedigger was again throwing shovels of dirt into the air. They could hear him grumbling to himself as he worked.

Then the dirt stopped flying. They waited a few seconds and when nothing happened, they cautiously moved over to the mound and peered over. The gravedigger was sitting down smoking his pipe—the strong odour of smoking tobacco wafted by them.

Lizzie looked over at Quon wondering if they should go talk to the old man when he began talking to himself again.

"Cum back after dark tomorra night at ten, he sez. Meet me by Sarah Langton's monument. I'll find someone to burn the place down, he sez," the gravedigger muttered, smoke belching into the air. "But ah'll tell on 'em that's what ah'll do," he spluttered, in evil delight. He lapsed into silence again sending a fresh cloud of smoke into the air.

Quon's stomach rumbled and Lizzie grabbed his arm. They heard the old man scramble to his feet, mumbling to himself as he threw his shovel out of the hole. They ducked quickly behind a nearby monument just as his bearded head peered around the pile of dirt. His eyes darted nervously about, then fastened on another monument nearby.

"Are you wandering out of yer grave again, Sarah?" he asked loudly, throwing a ball of clay at the huge marble tombstone. Then he climbed labouriously out of the hole, grunting heavily, and hurried off up the path. He was still muttering to himself as he closed the gate and went into the street.

Lizzie pressed her finger to her lips and they walked nonchalantly away. Luck, and the ranting of an old man, had presented them with a new plan for dealing with the likes of Richard Byrd. Puzzling for an answer to the threat, Lizzie was sure the target of the two men's anger was the newspaper office. The *Observer* had promised to unmask Byrd and they had already seen *his* anger.

We'll stop them somehow, she told herself silently. Grinning as her partner's stomach rumbled again, they headed home for lunch.

Not a sound could be heard coming from the open cottage doorway as they closed the gate behind them and walked up the path. Entering, Martha motioned for quiet pointing to Willie asleep in Joe's chair, his favourite wooden toy clutched in his hand.

"Feed him," Lizzie mouthed silently, pointing to her companion.

After lunch, they were on their way up the track to Ada's office when Nathan's buggy swept past them with a friendly hail from Dan. The trader offered no acknowledgement when he saw them, even turning away as they passed.

Now what's wrong with him? Lizzie thought as the coach stopped outside the office and they saw Nathan storm angrily inside leaving the door open behind him.

No sooner had he entered than his voice could be heard yelling his demands. Almost instantly, outside the back door, the call bell began to ring furiously, alerting Mick that he was needed.

"Ned's bell velly useful sometime!" grinned Quon. "Mick come qlick."

"I SHALL NOT BE TREATED IN THIS MANNER," Nathan was protesting as the partners arrived at the door.

Trying hard to hide the smile on her face, Ada swung her chair around to look out the window, she would let Ned deal with their rude visitor.

"Don't you ever talk to Mrs. O'Rourke like that again, you pompous shrimp!" Ned threatened, pounding on his desk as Lizzie came to stand between them, but Nathan continued his ranting.

"QUIET, Mister Goldman!" her voice rang ominously.

"Just look at me," the slightly more-subdued trader retorted, spinning around to face the girl.

The sight was certainly worthy of a smile, Lizzie decided, quickly glancing over at Ada who sat with her hand over her mouth. The front of Nathan's suit was covered with a white substance. Upon closer examination, it appeared to be flour, giving him a ghost-like appearance from spats to chin and totally covering his fuzzy, mutton-chops. Quon stifled a chuckle behind her and Lizzie couldn't control her giggle anymore.

"Why lad, you look like a ghost," she exclaimed. "Who did that to you?"

"It's ruined," he whined, gingerly touching his shirtfront making flour dust billow from the garment. "I'll not deal with Sam Firth again."

"Sam Firth!" Lizzie murmured. "He did this?"

At that moment, Mick raced in through the back door, stopping suddenly and grinning when he saw the trader.

"Mother 'o Murphy, it's a ghost!" the Irish foreman declared. "Are ye tryin to scare us to death now, Nathan?"

"No sympathy," Nathan moaned, "no sympathy here." Looking around, he moved toward a chair.

"DON'T SIT DOWN!" Ada ordered. "Go shake yourself outside first, we don't need the chair covered in flour dust, too."

Reluctantly, Nathan turned toward the door, followed outside by Quon.

"Why he do this, Mister Nathan?"

Beginning to boil again, the trader snapped, "Firth's mill has run out of grain and he wanted to jump the order list."

"And you wouldn't let him," Lizzie purred, standing in the doorway.

"No, I wouldn't," the trader replied, glancing slyly at the girl, "that wouldn't be fair, would it now?"

Quon's fingers tapped a message on his partner's arm.

"I know, I know," she replied.

Suspecting Nathan's motives, Ada, Mick and Ned came to the door to watch the bantering of the friendly rivals. Grinning, they soon realized what they already suspected ... Lizzie's logic was ferreting out the truth.

"You offered him a deal, didn't you?" she whispered, her eyes flashing danger signals as they fastened on Nathan. "You asked for a premium for instant delivery."

"Well ... well," the trader blustered dejectedly, "it's a common business practice and more profit for us."

For a moment, Lizzie ignored his answer as her mouth twisted into a cold smile. "Mick, send a messenger to Sam Firth telling him we can supply him with 10 tons of grain."

"Today?" Mick cocked an eyebrow.

"Well, I want at least some of that grain on its way today," she replied.

Nathan hung his head and kicked at a stone as the foreman strode away to arrange the delivery. Ned turned back to the office shaking his head.

"I don't quite see why you're so angry, Nathan," Ada murmured.

"Think of it like this, lad," Lizzie said flatly. "How many men work for Sam Firth? 10? 20? How many, Nathan?"

"Thirty with the draymen," he mumbled.

"Thirty men out of a job, 30 wives and 90 children all going hungry for the sake of an extra shilling in profit. Is that good business, Nathan?" she asked, looking at him sharply.

She's serious, thought Ada, *but she's got something else up her sleeve. I can feel it.*

"However," the girl continued, "you've just given me an idea. Do you think you could find me someone who looks like Captain Davis, Mister Goldman?"

Ada watched the trader's expression as Lizzie's lecture took a sudden change in direction. Lips pressed firmly together, Nathan's stubby fingers briskly rubbed through his mutton-chop whiskers sending flour in all directions. Ada sighed and went back to her desk.

"I hardly think that will be very difficult," he replied, already making his plan.

The dull rattle of a fully loaded dray took their attention.

"Ada, me luv," called Mick, through the open window, "better come book out that grain to Sam Firth. The first load is ready."

The mere mention of the miller's name changed the trader's mood again causing him to pout as the bookkeeper turned toward the door.

"I don't agree with you, girl," he hissed, his eyes squinting as he observed Quon's fingers tapping on Lizzie's arm.

Glancing back, Ada saw Lizzie's back straighten. *He still hasn't learned when to leave it alone,* she mused, stopping in the doorway.

"Listen Mister Goldman, just try to think past the little extra profit we will make," Lizzie was saying. "Otherwise, we would lose the sales from 30 families because they had no money. How would you like to try going hungry for a few weeks?"

Shoulders drooping, Nathan finally returned to his buggy, stopped by Wick who set about brushing the flour off his boss. At the window, Ada watched the two gypsies raise a hand in farewell to the youngsters. Their gentle smiles told her that Lizzie's practical and simple logic had impressed someone, but then all the gypsies loved Lizzie.

"Would you have thought of that?" Ada asked her husband when he returned to the office.

"No luv," he muttered, "ah wouldn't."

Nathan's silver-tipped cane touched Dan's back and the buggy moved off up the track. Sighing, Ada watched them leave. She sat down on the wide window ledge and watched the youngsters set off in the same direction. *When those two are together, nothing changes,* she thought, as Lizzie draped her arm over Quon's shoulder. Watching them walk up the slaughterhouse track, Ada rested her chin on her hand and shook her head.

"If I ever saw two people who belong to each other," she muttered, "it's those two."

"What yer say?" Ned grumbled, barely lifting his eyes from the papers on his desk. "Talk up if yer want me to hear!"

Ada took no notice of him as she turned back to her desk and opened an accounts book.

Passing the ever-busy rag yard, Lizzie and Quon waved to Tiny as he moved between the drays that were loading. A bit farther down the roadway, they ducked through a fence by the holding pens. Cattle and sheep moved out of their way as gypsy guard dogs began to howl a warning.

Met by a gypsy woman, they were again escorted to Davis' makeshift tent. Quon gripped her arm when they saw him, wide awake but resting on a pile of pillows and being spoon-fed by a young girl.

"So you've found time to visit me av yer?" he asked breathlessly, but with some of his irritable sparkle still intact.

"We just called to see if you were dead yet," Lizzie chuckled.

"Damn you, Lizzie Short!" he thundered abruptly seeming to find more energy. His uninjured arm rose partway, then flopped back down on the blankets, as if he meant to accentuate the words but didn't quite have the strength. "Ah'll live to keel haul that bastard or wrap him in chains and send him to Davy Jones' locker!" He began to sputter and cough, closing his eyes in pain.

"Please miss," whispered the gypsy woman, "don't excite him."

Quon's fingers tapped a message on her arm.

"Ask him yourself," she replied sharply.

"What does he say?" Davis growled, glaring at Quon and causing him to move instinctively behind her.

"He wants to know if the pain is gone?" She leaned closer to the old sea dog. "And if you shout one more time you old heathen, I'll kick yer bad leg."

Eyes narrowing, Davis grinned through bruised lips.

"And you'd do it, too!" he muttered. "Tell the lad, no, it still hurts like hell. Now go away."

"He very angry," said the gypsy woman as they walked back through the wagons.

"You would be, too," Lizzie chuckled, "if somebody ran over you with a coach. But he's strong and being mad will help him get better; he's too bad-tempered to die."

J. Robert Whittle

Halfway down Drover's Lane, they noticed Joe and young Willie sitting on the fence at the corner.

"He wanted to come meet yer, lass," Joe explained as the boy jumped off the fence and into her arms.

Lizzie groaned. "My gosh, Willie, you're getting very big ... and heavy!" she declared. "Yer home early today, luv," she commented, looking sideways at Joe. She lifted the boy into position with his legs around her waist. "Is everything all right?"

"It was too hot to work and Angus told me to take the rest of the afternoon off," he grunted. "He said an old fella shouldn't work so hard on a hot day!"

Willie hugged Lizzie and she tousled his hair. "I agree with him, old luv, you deserve a holiday."

"How's the captain doing?" he asked.

"He's doing better than I expected," she admitted, feeling Willie's arms tighten around her neck and pretending to be choked.

"My Wizzy," the boy whispered, planting a sloppy kiss on her cheek and peeking mischievously over her shoulder at Quon.

"No!" declared Quon, darting forward to tickle the boy. "My Wizzy!"

Wriggling wildly, Lizzie struggled to keep him from falling.

"Stop that, you torment!" she admonished her partner. "He's heavy! I'm going to have to put you down anyway, Willie. Quon and I still have something to do before supper."

"What's that, luv?" asked Joe.

"We need to talk to Penny Sutton—we'll explain later." With that, she grabbed Quon's arm and they were out of earshot before Joe could even think about asking any more questions.

At the *Observer* office, they found Penny talking to Gabriel in her office. As the partners entered, the owners appeared relieved to see them.

"We're glad you're here. The street lads have picked up another rumour," Gabriel growled, coming out to meet them. "The talk is that somebody is going to get burned out tonight. We thought you would know what to do."

"Who's going to get burned?"

"Us!" Penny blurted out. She wiped a dirty hand on her black apron, brushed some hair off her face and came to join them.

Lizzie noticed the lines of worry on their faces.

"Billy says," said Daisy, coming from the back, "that the word is out

54

and the fire starters were drinking at *Swans* ale house near the bread shop, just 10 minutes ago!"

Quon's hands went wild and he swung on his partner.

"Yes, yes," she muttered, "yer right."

"Dumplin says you should sleep here tonight, Gabriel, and get four or five of the street lads to stay with you."

"They can't protect us," Gabriel snorted, "they're only youngsters."

"They're not going to fight for you," Lizzie snapped, "they're going to listen. They've got ears like cats and anybody coming close at night will be heard and they'll warn you."

"They'll need blankets," said Lady Sutton.

"We've lots of them in the rag shed. Daisy, go tell one of our draymen to drop some off."

As she hurried out of the door, the young reporter was heard to exclaim, "My, this is exciting!"

Quon was talking urgently to Lizzie, first with signs and then by tugging on her arm, pulling her toward the door.

"We hurry, Wizzy," he urged.

"We've things to do," she explained to the others, "and he's right, we need to hurry."

$$Chapter\ 6$$

Running hard, Lizzie and Quon were soon within range of Billy's voice. Dodging the slow walkers, they threaded their way to the front of the bake shop.

"Do you know where Tom Legg is Billy?" she called interrupting his patter.

"Over at *Swans*," he replied, hardly missing a beat as he yelled out his news.

Off they raced again, only slowing to catch their breath when they saw the ale house ahead and heard the raucous laughter of the one-legged sailor in the crowded forecourt.

Making their way through the group of jostling men, they found Tom sitting happily in his transport—the wheelbarrow his mates often borrowed from *The Robin*.

Two pennies, jingling in Lizzie's hand, drew Tom's attention as Quon's quick movement relieved him of his shepherd's crook.

"Missy," he slurped in surprise, "you have need of me?"

"I need only names," she hissed in a whisper. "Point out the fire starters to me."

Fear clouded the mariner's eyes though his fingers twitched in their eagerness to have the coins that rattled in the girl's hand. His brain, dulled by the ale, quickly made his choice. Finger raised, he pointed to two weasel-faced men sitting inside near the door.

"Zak and Dom Zorba," he slobbered, almost tipping the wheelbarrow as he snatched at the coins.

Keeping hidden amongst the patrons, Lizzie and Quon studied the two diminutive dark-skinned men, their big gold earrings and colourful waistbands making them easily identifiable. Lizzie smiled as the one with long hair rose from his seat and staggered toward the back lane and the outhouse.

Zakariah and Dominic Zorba were strangers to the young partners. Elusive and cunning, they roamed the Thames waterfront in search of easy pickings—kidnapping, thieving from the docks and starting fires for unscrupulous merchants. They came and went like shadows, their identities known only to a few.

"They dlunk," Quon whispered.

"Run back to the bread shop," she ordered. "Tell Billy we need Oly and his pony cart and 10 of the street kids."

Quon's face twisted into a frown, her reasoning escaping him. His hands and arms gesticulated in a tirade of questions.

"Over there," she pointed, "I want them to lay a trap in that blind alley where everyone throws their garbage. We'll take those two rogues out of circulation!"

A few minutes later, there was a strange silence in the distance as the voice of the bread lad stopped its ringing call. *He's talking to Quon,* she thought. Then suddenly, a high-pitched urgent whistle screamed through the streets.

"SOMFINS AMISS!" Tom yelled to his mates. Although his brain was dulled by drink, he too had heard Billy's distinctive call of distress.

Moving quickly to the back door, Lizzie looked around for what she needed. Finding a short plank, she crept closer and silently wedged the wood under the latch of the outhouse door. Then she went inside the ale house. Glancing out the window and across the street, she could see the entrance to the alley. A group of curious onlookers had already gathered and she could see Quon with Billy and several of the street lads.

Now! she thought.

Dom Zorba's eyes narrowed when the unfamiliar, yet beautiful, smiling girl, moved quickly toward him. His inborn suspicious nature should have screamed a warning but she took him by surprise. Stopping in front of his table, she smiled disarmingly, then swept his friend's full tankard of ale off the table, sloshing it in his face.

"WHAT THE 'ELL!" he shouted, wiping the froth from his eyes, but he was too late, she had disappeared. Wiping his face with his sleeve, he took chase just in time to see her disappear out the front door.

The chase was on. Pushing past startled drinkers, he ran outside and saw her running across Chandler Street between the traffic. He followed. *I'll get her,* he thought. *I'm a good runner and she has all those skirts cumbering her.* Even though he wasn't from this part of London, he had recently checked out the backstreets with his brother. They often needed to have a quick route of escape after their dirty deeds. A wicked-looking knife now gleamed in his hand as he darted behind a dray and followed her toward the blind alley.

"I gotcha now, girl," he snarled savagely.

J. Robert Whittle

"Not yet, yer don't!"

The sound of Lizzie's voice was drowned out as the street urchins rose from amid the putrid mess. Dom howled in surprise as they hurled handfuls of stinking garbage at him. Struggling to keep his balance on the slippery cobbles, Dominic Zorba screamed abuse as garbage hit him in the face and body. Finally, unable to keep his balance he reeled, falling heavily. His knife bounced out of his hand as 10 screaming street kids pounced on him.

"Tie him up and leave him here and one of you stay with him." Lizzie's voice cut through the noise. Bending down to retrieve the knife, she hid it behind her back. "When you're done, follow me!"

Cursing violently, the rogue was trussed up and left lying in the alley. One of the boys ran back to stuff the sleeve of a dirty shirt into his mouth.

Obediently following her orders, the group raced up the narrow lane to Chandler and around to the back of the tavern. Even before they reached the rear entrance, they could hear another loud commotion. Someone appeared to be trapped in the outhouse.

Quon smiled and shook his head. *My Wizzy, smart girl!*

Lizzie grabbed his arm and gathered the boys around them.

"It's his partner in there. When I take that plank away from the door," she whispered, "he'll come flying out. Billy, have you got some more rope?"

Quon held up a length of rope he was carrying.

"Good. Tie him up just like the other one and throw him on Oly's pony cart." She pointed behind them where Oly now waited.

Lizzie was right. Things happened mighty fast as the second of the Zorba brothers came hurtling out of the door, bouncing on the cinder-strewn lane. The boys were after him instantly. Confused and reeling, he went careening into the wheel of the waiting bread cart, knocking himself out.

"Now what do we do with him, Miss Lizzie?" Billy chuckled.

"Go with the cart and get the other one from the alley," Lizzie replied, grinning with satisfaction. "You can dump 'em both in the stable behind the bread shop, for the time being."

Billy beckoned for the boys to follow him and they ran off to carry out her orders while she and Quon sat down on a stone wall to catch their breath. She was just about to speak when the church clock struck five bells, reminding them the day was fast slipping away.

"Come on, we need to get back to the printers," she exclaimed.

58

When they entered the shop, they found that Lady Sutton had heeded their warning as blankets were stacked all over the office floor.

"Go home, Penny," Lizzie urged her friend, noting the tired and sad expression in her eyes.

"No," she whispered stubbornly. Straightening her back and squaring her shoulders, she continued, "I refuse to run at the first sign of danger."

"Me neither," Daisy added, linking arms with her mother. "I'm staying, too."

"See what you've done," Gabriel chuckled, "you've turned these two into fighters." His eyes darted from Lizzie to the Sutton women. "I shall be proud to stand alongside them."

Shuffling his feet noisily, Fred Monk distracted them as he stepped out from behind the press. He grinned as he rubbed his face with an ink-stained hand leaving streaks of black on his cheeks.

"Well now," he smiled, "I'll not be staying. I'm just going to wander outside with me Bible."

"Your Bible?" Daisy snorted.

"Yes love," Fred chuckled, "and if anybody comes close, I shall introduce them to Christianity by beating them over the head with the good book!"

The former monk's humorous approach drew a spontaneous giggle from Lizzie and Quon as they backed out of the door. Feeling sure the danger had now gone that the Zorba brothers were safely locked away, they didn't feel as worried about their friends. They wished everyone good night, saying they would see them in the morning.

As they went toward home, Quon made it plain he thought Lizzie should have told them that the danger was over.

"No," she argued, "don't yer see, dumplin, how quickly they all became a family wanting to take care of each other. Leave 'em," she laughed, "it's an exercise in togetherness, they'll be like you and me after tonight."

Hands on hips, Quon stopped dead in the street. "Wike you and me?" he grimaced, failing to understand the similarity.

"Inseparable, my little dumplin," she whispered. Her eyes full of adoration, she giggled as she pinched his cheek. "We always look after each other."

"Wizzy mine," the Chinese boy's voice croaked. He could feel his face turning red and turned away.

"Well, come on, ya little turd," she laughed, running ahead, "we'd better get home for supper before Martha sends Mick out after us."

That evening, not surprisingly, Captain Davis was the topic of conversation.

"Ah sure, he still looks poorly and has a fever," Mick informed them, "but mercifully he was sleeping when hoy called to see him. Those gypsies are takin mighty good care of him."

"They're good people," Joe added, removing his pipe.

Elbows resting on the table, Ada's hands cupped her chin and a worried expression came into her eyes.

"That council meeting's bothering me, Liz," she whispered. "Nathan says all dockland is abuzz with rumours. It seems there's talk that the meeting will be changed to Wednesday. Have you heard anything?"

"No, but we'll find out tomorrow and don't you worry about anything." Lizzie's tone turned cold. "We have a few secret weapons yet to use."

"Tom Jackson and Albert Porter are going to support her," Joe interceded. "I heard Tom say so at the mill."

"That still leaves four against two," Ada sighed, "now that Miller's gone."

"No," Charley interrupted, "the minister doesn't have a vote."

Joe sat bolt upright grabbing his hot pipe in his hand and making a face before he lay it down on the edge of the hearth.

"Yes he does," he argued. "King George gave it to 'em by royal decree."

Further conversation stopped and eyes moved to the door as the sound of footsteps hurrying up the garden path were heard. It was Nathan. He was puffing as he stood at the open door.

"Come in, lad," Martha invited him cordially.

"BRING HIM IN," Nathan shouted over his shoulder before stepping into the room.

All eyes watched the doorway unsure of what was happening. Then there were more footsteps.

"My gawd!" Joe gasped. Having picked up his hot pipe, it now slipped from his hand onto the table with a clatter. Framed in the doorway stood the almost perfect double of Captain Davis.

"Your servant, ma'am," the man greeted them cockily. Although obviously younger than Davis, Lizzie saw immediately how he could be easily mistaken for the captain's twin brother. He talked more slowly than the captain and had an unusual accent. "My name is Stormy Newton. I'm an actor."

Quon's fingers tapped wildly on the table.

"Yes, yes," Lizzie said impatiently, covering his hand. "I can see."

"You were serious, weren't you?" said Ada, a look of astonishment on her face as she turned to Lizzie.

Lizzie grinned but kept her eyes on the actor.

"I may need you for up to two months—are you available, Mister Newton?"

"Yes ma'am, if the terms are right."

"Terms?" Nathan snapped. "You're an out-of-work actor with no prospects."

"A man has his pride," Newton drawled, turning for the door.

"Stay!" Lizzie's voice cracked through the silence stopping the actor in mid-stride. His eyes flicked over to Dan, Nathan's gypsy, who was blocking the doorway.

"As I said, I have need of an acting job for the next eight weeks." She turned to Nathan. "You can go now, Mister Goldman."

Pouting and grumbling, Nathan went outside meeting the Grim brothers as they arrived for Charley.

"Do you want us to stay?" Mick asked Lizzie quietly.

"No, if he'll agree, I want him to impersonate Captain Davis," Lizzie chuckled. "Have you any dinner left, Martha? Perhaps Mister Newton could use a meal if he's been out of work."

Suspicion filled the actor's eyes as he turned back toward the table. Unsure of the situation, he hesitated, having some doubts about accepting work from these strangers. But his stomach was twisting in painful emptiness. He watched the woman named Martha as she took the lid off a big steaming pot over the fire, picked up a plate, and turned to face him. Not having eaten since early the day before, he shrugged his shoulders and moved toward the table and stood behind a chair.

"Find Willie, would you, dear," said Ada, turning to her husband.

"He's bin playin in his room," said Martha, loading the plate with food. "Sit," she sharply ordered the newcomer, sliding the plate of food onto the table under his nose.

Yawning, Ada gathered their coats and waited near the door. Mick appeared with the sleeping boy in his arms. Wiping her hands on her apron, Martha stopped him, lovingly moving a curl from Willie's brow before gently kissing his cheek.

"Good night, little man," she whispered as she went outside with them.

Newton was already filling his face but he was also watching the scene

61

taking place around him while he considered the offer the girl had made. Realizing now that she was serious, he could hardly believe his luck—a job offer for two months and a free meal were a heaven-sent opportunity. And this family was looking more normal to him all the time … and nice, too.

Penniless, he had wandered the streets looking for work for days and sheer chance had led him to Nathan. The actor, who had only recently arrived from America, felt quite elated as he silently downed his meal.

Leaving Boston on a clipper ship less than three months before, he had vowed to make his reputation in the theatres of London, not having been very successful at home. Alas, he had soon felt the bitter disappointment of rejection. His ego had suffered enormously when Drury Lane theatre owners gave him neither time nor consideration.

What would this job entail? he wondered, glancing cautiously at the two young people across the table. Mister Goldman had warned him of the girl, but who was this strange young Asian whose fingers appeared to tap messages on the table.

"Are you ready to hear my proposition, mister?" Lizzie purred, watching her partner's fingers.

He nodded, looking at her without turning his head. He raised an eyebrow in expectation.

"My terms are easy," she continued, "eight shillings for two months work and you do exactly what I tell you."

"Mister Goldman told me I'm to impersonate a Captain Davis."

"Mister Goldman talks too much."

"And the clothes I am to wear?"

"We will provide them," she replied, her attention again drawn to the fingers rapping urgently on the table. "We will require your services starting tomorrow night."

"Could you make me an advance?" the actor whispered, looking slightly uncomfortable. "I'm temporarily short of money."

"No," said Lizzie calmly, "but you may eat at the rag yard cook shack if you can stand the smell. It's up by the slaughterhouse. We'll meet you there at eight tomorrow night."

Frowning into the fireplace, Martha glanced over at Joe. Lizzie's hardness had surprised her, knowing the girl's kindness to unfortunate people, yet she was pleased with her offer. *What is she up to now?* Lizzie never did anything without a good reason.

Newton's eyes narrowed. He felt a surge of animosity toward this beautiful girl who was obviously much younger than his 32 years. She had so easily made the decision to refuse his request. He wondered if she had ever experienced hunger—surely not. He wished he'd never left Boston where the taverns would always pay for a dramatic recitation, no matter how badly delivered.

There was no 'good night' spoken, nor handshake as he left, just a sullen nod of heads before he disappeared into the night.

"Ah don't much care for that one," Martha grumbled.

"That young man is hurting," Lizzie said softly, "and he's not too sure about me giving him orders."

Chapter 7

At half-past five the next afternoon, knife and fork hovering above his half-empty plate, Stormy Newton's eyes flicked up to the doorway of the cook shack as Lizzie and Quon stepped inside. Two drivers, just leaving, respectfully murmured a greeting as they allowed the partners to pass.

"So you found the eating place, my friend?" Lizzie said cheerfully, slipping onto the bench facing the actor. "Carry on eating and listen."

Stormy dropped his eyes onto his plate—the uncomfortable feeling of having this beautiful young woman dictate his duties were setting his nerves on edge. *Why have they come early? Are they checking up on me?* His needs had thrown them together although he hated the thought of following the orders of a woman.

"We'll be leaving from here in a few hours," she said.

"An acting part, ma'am?" he muttered, shovelling the last of the food into his mouth and pushing the empty plate roughly aside. "I shall need time to prepare myself."

"You pompous ass," Lizzie exploded, "you will prepare when I tell you or we won't need your services; why don't you just go and starve somewhere else!"

"Who the devil …?" Stormy began, his voice rising theatrically as he jumped to his feet. Then he caught sight of the knife in Quon's hand. A shadow of fear moved across his eyes as the colour drained quickly from his face. Settling back onto the seat, he tried to speak but no sound came.

"Now we start again," Lizzie announced. "Your real name, sir?"

"J-Jake Newton."

Heavy footsteps sounded moments before the huge body of Tiny, the yard foreman, filled the doorway. The actor visibly flinched and his shoulders sagged.

"You need me, Miss Lizzie?" Tiny's eyes scrutinized the stranger and his voice echoed through the empty building.

Grinning, the girl shook her head. "Not at the moment, Tiny."

The foremen removed himself, but not before taking a long curious look at their guest. Lizzie swung her eyes across the table committing her full attention to the actor.

"You ain't got much backbone, lad," she hissed. "Let's find you some suitable clothes so you look the part."

Jake could hardly believe his ears. Quietly sighing with relief and trying desperately not to appear obvious, he squeezed his hands together under the table. Even though this girl had seen through his bravado, she was giving him a second chance. He quickly decided that he had better use it wisely.

"I-I thought you didn't want me," he whined. "I assure you …."

"Save your voice, m'lad," Lizzie interrupted, her patience wearing thin. She turned to Quon. "Find him some clothes, dumplin."

Leaving them, Quon went around the corner to the rag shed. Dark pants, great coat and a heavy blue sweater were gleaned from the many bins but no cap could be found. Holes, tears and smell ignored, Quon gathered them up and returned to the cook shed. There he dropped them onto the table in front of Jake Newton.

Nose twitching at the vile odour, the actor showed his dismay picking delicately at the garments with the tips of his fingers.

"We must have a cap," Lizzie muttered.

Jake's eyes settled on Quon, as the Chinese man's actions sent a silent message to his partner.

Nodding, a smile brushed her lips. "You wait here," she instructed, "we'll be back at nine. In the meantime, I suggest you and those clothes become friends."

"Yes, ma'am," the actor muttered solemnly, having no intention of waiting around for them for the next three hours. Besides, he still wasn't sure he wanted to work for these people—it sounded mighty dangerous—and that smell! Resting his elbows on the table, Jake's chin settled into cupped hands and his mind wandered. He craved the limelight, cheering crowds and the adoration of fans—things he'd always envied but had only experienced minimally. Thinking of the engagement he had agreed to do for these people, his mind suddenly took a different tact. *There must be a profit to be made by revealing Lizzie's plans of this charade, but to whom?* And what were his chances of escape if he double-crossed her? He heard voices out in the yard. They seemed to be coming toward him. Jake's pulse beat faster and his eyes searched for an escape route.

"Better get changed, lad," a gruff voice spoke from the end of the cook shack as a burly stranger wearing a sailor's cap stepped through the door.

Jake felt a cold shudder run down his back when the light from the man's oil lantern glinted off the hook he had in place of a hand. Instinct

65

told him to run but courage deserted him. Realizing his opportunity to escape had passed, he glanced nervously around, then slowly proceeded to undress. Shaking each piece of the horrible-smelling items, he carefully examined them before putting each one on. *I wouldn't be surprised to find dead animals in here*, he thought.

"Yer a dead ringer fer Captain Davis that's fer sure, mister," the man exclaimed, watching him curiously. "Nobody could tell yer apart, if ye had his hat on."

ඝාලාශ

Lizzie and Quon returned home for supper and after the meal was completed, Charley announced that Billy had found out that, indeed, the council meeting was now on Wednesday.

"If they thought they were going to get rid of me so easily, they have another think coming," Lizzie declared obstinately. Then, excusing themselves, she and Quon headed off to the gypsy camp.

Looking in on a sleeping Captain Davis, the gypsy woman assured them that, "He'll be a different man in a week, you'll see, Miss Lizzie."

"We need to find his cap," Lizzie whispered, and the woman pointed to the sea chest in the corner. A flick of the girl's hand sent Quon to find the distinctive headwear. Then, hat in hand, they raced over to the bake shop to enlist Bill Johnson's help for the next step of their plan.

"We need a shovel full of flour, Bill," she gasped at the startled baker, surprised to see them this late in the day.

"Just 'elp yersen," he muttered, nodding toward a pile of sacks in the corner.

Selecting several, they thanked him and left without any explanation. Bill watched them go. *Ther up to somethin, that's for sure!"*

Over at the stableyard, they found Lefty, the old sailor who had lost a leg many years before. Lefty often acted as a night watchman for TLS and they were able to acquire a lantern and a bucket from him.

"Right, we're ready now," she sighed as they made their way toward the cook shack. She knew they still had lots of time before they needed to be at the graveyard for the minister and Richard Byrd's 10 o'clock meeting.

Meanwhile, Jake had grown impatient, frustrated with his inability to escape. His fingers set to drumming on the table as he waited, earning him a black stare from the man who he now realized had been left to guard him.

"Where the devil are they?" Jake snapped, taking his timepiece, a gift from his uncle upon leaving America, from his pocket.

"They're here now, sir," growled the man with the hook, glancing outside into the growing dusk.

"About time, too!" Jake leapt to his feet to greet them, ready to use his acting skills to lash out at them. His eyes widened in terror as the guard swung his hooked hand just under his nose.

"Wouldn't want that pretty face of yers messed up now, would yer? Ya better mind yer manners, dog," he snarled.

Deflated, Jake sat back down on the bench.

"Right, mister actor man," Lizzie said solemnly as she came through the door. "Your moment of truth has arrived and we had better see the performance of a lifetime from you. We'll tell you what we need you to do as we walk."

Up the lane at the upstairs apartment of Mick and Ada O'Rourke, Ada had noticed the comings and goings of the two young people from their parlour window.

"Look, look!" she called to Mick. "Lizzie and Quon have just left the cook shack with that actor."

Mick had designed their apartment above the TLS offices for just such a moment—giving an unrestricted view of the slaughterhouse track.

"Hoy'd swear on a stack a Bibles," Mick chuckled, "that the man with them were Captain Davis, if hoy didn't know better."

"Where do you think they're going?" Ada murmured, "it'll soon be dark."

Mick slipped his arm around her waist pulling his wife closer.

"Ah sure hoy'll not be worrying about them very long," he whispered amorously, "with Willie in bed and a beautiful woman loyk you in me arms, darlin."

"Stop it," Ada whispered in mock annoyance. "I want to know where they're going at this time of night. They might be getting into some danger and Jeb's not here to help."

"All right, all right, yer nosy little devil," Mick chuckled, reaching for his cap. "Ah'll follow 'em if it will ease yer mind." He opened the door and grinned back at her.

"And don't let them see you!" she warned.

Shadows melted into dusk soon after the sun dropped out of sight behind the western horizon. Mick kept them in sight, sticking to the shadows as he followed as close as he dared. He lost sight of the trio after they went through the churchyard gate.

Where the devil have they gone? he puzzled, listening intently as he peered over the wall. It was barely light and they were nowhere in sight. He knew they couldn't have gone far. *Are they waitin for dark behind one of the monuments? What is that lass gettin herself into now?* A cold chill of apprehension clawed at his skin. Cautiously, he climbed over the wall into the churchyard and hid behind a large monument.

Ten minutes went by, then 12. He was getting cold. *What are they waitin for? I hope she knows what she's doin!*

A short time later, Mick thought he heard the sound of footsteps on gravel coming from the direction of the church. They stopped. It was so dark in the churchyard by now, he could hardly see a thing. The sound of an approaching carriage swung his attention back to the road. The carriage slowed and stopped outside the gate.

Seconds passed and the gate squeaked open. A lantern burst into life over by the church, its eerie glow giving him a direction. The light disappeared and the footsteps moved quickly on the pathway over to his left, then stopped, or were they walking on the grass? Mick wondered as he moved forward, stealthily moving around monuments and gravestones, being careful not to trip and alert them to his presence. He heard a whispered voice from not far away but couldn't make out what it said.

Who are they? he thought.

"Minister, is that you?" a gruff voice hissed from nearby.

"Here, you fool," came the muffled reply from over by the church.

"Oww!" Byrd's voice wailed, as he stumbled over a gravestone. "Where are you, man?"

His voice trailed off as an eerie glow suddenly shone upwards from a half-dug grave nearby and the ghostly figure of Captain Davis rose slowly from the ground.

Mick blinked with surprise. A chill ran down his spine and he flattened his body against a large cross. *The actor! That's what she's up to!*

"You killed me, you dog!" the ghostly apparition moaned. "I will have my revenge. You will never escape the wrath of the dead!"

A bone-chilling scream rent the air as the man lurched among the gravestones trying to make his escape. The ghost disappeared and the light was quickly extinguished. Running footsteps told Mick the minister was also leaving, returning the way he had come. Bumps and exclamations marked their progress toward the perimeter walls. Then, galloping hooves, and all went quiet again.

Looking around the stone, Mick saw the lighted lantern pop out of the ground, quickly followed by Lizzie, Quon, and the actor. *They were hiding in a newly dug grave,* he thought to himself, sighing with relief as the light was extinguished.

"Let's get out of here," he heard Lizzie say.

Mick cut cautiously back across the graveyard, feeling ahead of him with outstretched hands. His efforts were well rewarded when he beat the trio back to the perimeter wall. He climbed over and waited, concealed by bushes, listening to them approach. The sound of the gate opening and whispers—they would be beside him in a few seconds.

"Pay me now," he heard an unfamiliar voice demand as the footsteps stopped, "and I'll be on my way!"

"We're not finished with you yet," Lizzie whispered.

"I think you are. Now, I say!" Jake hissed, seeing his opportunity. "I have a gun, give me your purse."

Quon's hand reached for his partner in the dark, tapping out a sharp message on her arm.

"NOW!" she shouted, leaping to one side as Quon swung the lantern with all his might to where he estimated the actor's kneecaps would be. His guess was right, judging by the screams, as the actor fell to the ground.

"LIZZIE!" Mick cried in anguish. Throwing caution to the wind, he leapt toward the moaning voice, his strong hands finding Jake's hair in the dark.

"Where's the gun, boyo?" he hissed. "Drop it or I'll crush yer head!"

"I don't have a gun," Jake cried desperately. "I don't have a gun!"

"Hold onto him, Mick," Lizzie sighed with relief, "we'll deal with the turd later. We have to find the captain's hat."

"Ah'll kill him," Mick gasped, "when I find his throat!"

"Don't!" she snapped. "I still need him."

Somewhat subdued, yet still fearful for his life, Jake Newton pleaded for mercy as the edge of the rising moon cast dull fingers of light on the road. Mick's rough hands pulled the actor to his feet with a violent surge of power.

"Here hat!" cried Quon.

"Now what?" Mick growled menacingly.

"To the dock!"

Lizzie had made an instant decision even though not completely sure why. She led the way down Long Lane passing the boys' bake shop. Rowdy drinkers still revelled at coaching houses and taverns along the way. Stumbling along, Jake limped and moaned in pain, his unsure future running wild in his brain as the lantern-lit dock area came into sight. Nearing the TLS dock, raucous laughter mixed with the hiss of Charley's resting steam engine as it released pent-up steam. Two night watchmen moved boldly to intercept them, raising their lanterns to identify the intruders.

"Miss Lizzie and Quon, what …!" one of them gasped, stepping sharply backwards as their eyes focused on the unrecognizable figure covered in white dust.

"Chain this dog to the steam engine, boys," she ordered, receiving her partner's suggestion, tapped out on her hand. A quiet chuckle escaped her lips as she added, "Close to the steam valve!"

Shuddering, as the terror of this new situation struck him, Jake resisted wildly, his pain forgotten as he fought to escape Mick's grip. Slowly, they inched closer to the hissing monster and Mick dropped him beside it. Realizing the hopelessness of the situation, his body flopped limply to the wooden deck as a merciful faint blacked out his mind.

"Wot's he bin up to, miss?" asked one of the watchmen.

Wrists bound, they quickly shackled him in place; lanterns held aloft enabled them to watch his reaction upon waking. A few minutes later, the actor's head slowly rolled from side to side, eyes bulging in fear, as the steam valve released its hissing pressure a mere foot away.

"Lock him in the brig of the training ship when Charley gets here in the morning," Lizzie ordered curtly.

"He'll go crazy," Mick ventured as they left the dock, "and what the devil were you playing ghosts in the churchyard with the minister for?"

"Scaring Richard Byrd *and* the minister," she exclaimed, wishing she could see his face in the dark. *How did Mick know? He must have followed them and been watching.*

"Well girl, you sure accomplished that!"

At the cottage gate, they handed the bucket, lantern and flour sacks to Mick. Lizzie gave him a quick hug.

"Thanks Mick," she murmured as they parted ways.

"Av yer been down at Johnson's bakery, love?" Martha inquired, noting the white dust clinging to their clothes. "Yer awful late."

"I hope we didn't worry you. You both should have gone to bed; we had something that had to be done," Lizzie replied, looking innocently at

Quon and going to give Joe a hug.

"Don't get too tired, lass. It's yer big day on Wednesday—that's not too many days away," Joe murmured. "Are yer ready for them, lass?" He puffed anxiously on his pipe. "They'll not let you in easy, yer know."

"I'm all right, old lad," Lizzie sighed, avoiding the discussion as she settled to her knees at his feet. The confident air she portrayed to the old man, however, was not quite what she felt inside knowing that others were secretly planning her downfall.

∞∞

In a more prestigious area of London, the two most powerful men in dockland sat in Judge Harvey's study. Glasses had already been filled several times as a union was rekindled and plans were laid.

Across the room, Admiral Jones' eyes flicked suspiciously over at his host. The dark wood interior of the judge's study, lit by two oil lamps, lent an ominous feeling to the meeting.

"So parliament thinks this turn of events is progress, do they Aurelius?" he growled.

Dropping his eyes to the expensive carpet-laid floor, Judge Harvey left the statement unanswered.

"You fool, if we allow this," continued the admiral, "then others will follow."

"Who is this creature, Lizzie Short?" the judge snarled. A cunning twist tugged at his lips as he watched the admiral's temper rise.

"Oh, she's a clever one; she's already got enough support to walk into council."

"I won't allow it!" Harvey pounded the chair arm. "No woman will ever sit on my council."

"She has to be stopped," Admiral Jones agreed. "Why she's even inciting other women to rebel."

"Rebel?" the judge's voice whispered as he remembered Lady Sutton's vicious verbal attack the day he had attended at the printer's shop. "You mean she's behind Penny Cross at the *Dockland Observer?*"

"I do, and Minnie Harris at Crowther's shipping office."

"Damnit, I wish Benson and Miller were here."

"They're dead men, traitors caught red-handed. There will be no help from them, I fear. I've seen Davis' report."

A smile tugged at the judge's lips as he slurped noisily on his liquor. "We could let her in," he chuckled, "then make her life a misery." Feeling pleased with himself, he grabbed the decanter and filled their glasses again, slopping liquor onto the shiny surface of his well-oiled desk. "To the destruction of Lizzie Short!" he growled, raising his glass in a gleeful toast.

As they gulped down their drinks, the union was sealed. Although each had a sneaking distrust of the other, these men bore no long-time allegiances when their personal power was at stake.

There was one more stop for Admiral Jones to make this night and, as he left the judge's mansion, he secretly gave instructions to his coachman.

"To *The Keg*," he hissed, as he climbed inside the carriage and the coachman closed the door behind him.

Arriving at the dockland tavern frequented by captains of ill-repute and night-roaming ruffians, he entered and was greeted by the owner, Shep Bower, who seated him discreetly in the darkest corner.

"You have a need, governor?" asked the wily owner, delivering a half pint of rum to the shadowy figure.

"Ship, cannon and a gunner," rumbled the admiral's voice, "and a captain with guts!"

Once a crewman on a ship bound for the Caribbean, captained by this same admiral, tavern-owner, Shep Bower, knew better than to ask further questions. The vicious cunning of this man, who took pleasure in hearing the screams of sailors left to drown after looting their sinking vessel, was legendary. His secret, hidden well in the distant past, had enabled his rise to power as admiral in charge of custom ships patrolling the war-torn shipping lanes of the English Channel. It had more recently procured a seat for him on the Dockland Council as the official representative of the British Navy.

Feeling the challenge of progress in Lizzie's application for a seat on council and, having no patience for the judge's approach to the problem, the admiral reverted to his natural instinct of inflicting hurt and fear to protect his power. *I'll ruin the TLS Company by sinking their ships one by one,* he schemed. A movement took his attention and he watched a shadowy figure approach his dark corner.

"'Arry Roach, yer oner," a voice rasped hoarsely, "captain of the *Black Otter*."

He reached for a chair then stopped as the hair on his neck prickled a warning. In the darkness, the admiral's hidden lips twisted into a snarl.

"Stand, you filthy dog!" he hissed.

"Cannon, ship and gunner." Harry stood with hands on hips and snarled back at the stranger. "I have all three. Have you gold, sir?" Straining his eyes to pierce the gloom, he tried to make out the face in the corner. *Who the devil are you?* Harry's mind was churning. *Maybe I should take your gold and throw you in the river!* he thought gleefully.

Seeing the glint of a pistol, Roach changed his mind abruptly, then heard the sound of an ominously cold chuckle.

"Cross me, sailor," the stranger hissed, "and I'll tie yer to me anchor and keel haul yer!"

Captain Roach hesitated. The threat had a familiar ring to it. Back in the depths of his memory, he had heard those exact words spoken once before.

The voice continued, "Sink the vessel I choose and there's fifty golden guineas waiting for you."

"Done," Harry sneered. "Now show me yer gold!"

A bag clinked onto the table, its shape, size and sound giving every indication what the man said was true. Twitching violently, Captain Harry Roach struggled to control his urge to grab the bag. "N-name her," he moaned, "and I'll send her to Davy Jones' locker."

"*Restitution* owned by Lady Sutton."

"That ship's captained by Ben Thorn. She runs grain for the TLS and is unarmed. She'd be a sitting duck," Harry muttered in disgust.

"Fifty golden guineas and no survivors!" whispered the shadowy figure.

"Hand over the gold then."

"After the deed is done. Now go, you dog!" dismissed the voice.

Roach grumbled under his breath as he returned to his mates, his evil mind puzzling over the conversation. *Now why would anybody want to sink a grain ship, and why did he want his identity to be a mystery?* Suddenly realizing he didn't know how to contact the man, he turned back then stopped, frowning at the now-empty seat.

"Who would keel haul a dead body?" he snarled at his companions as the threat buzzed in his head.

"You!" one sailor muttered, causing a roar of raucous laughter from his fellow crewmen.

Across town at the stately home of Richard Byrd, his wife, Alyse, was sitting at her writing desk in the parlour making the day's notation in her journal. As Sam Benson's eldest daughter, she had been trained from a young age to be meticulous, and keeping a diary was a favourite pastime since being a child. Born to a life of wealth and privilege, a child was often wanting for enjoyment and writing a diary had filled that need for young Alyse. In recent days, her husband, obviously in trouble himself, and fearful of reprisals after her father's arrest, had forbidden her to stay in London, but she was having none of that. She didn't want to be stuck out there in the country with her sisters, when she could be quite comfortable right here!

Suddenly, she heard the sound of a coach drawing noisily up to the door. Their butler burst into the room.

"Quick, come quick, ma'am," he wailed. "The master has gone off his head. He says he's seen the ghost of Captain Davis!"

"Don't be a fool, man." Alyse Byrd closed her diary and stood up quickly. Her sleeve caught the edge of her glass, spilling the drink over the desk. Rescuing her diary, she put it safely away and locked the drawer. Retrieving her hanky, tucked into the sleeve of her lace-trimmed blouse, she wiped it across her wet dress.

"Have the maid clean this up, Barnsby.

"She's asleep, ma'am, I'll do it."

"Where is that idiot husband of mine?"

"He's in the coach, ma'am."

By the time Alyse reached the front door, the two coachmen were helping her husband into the house. The men each took an arm and helped their pathetic-looking employer to a chair in the parlour.

"Whisky!" she snapped vehemently, sniffing her husband's breath as he gazed at her with glazed eyes, muttering incoherently. "Take him up to bed. He'll sleep it off."

The noise caused the household to wake and soon candles flickered into life as two maids and the housekeeper appeared in their nightshirts, hastily covered with robes. The men whisked the moaning lumber merchant away and up the stairs to his bedroom. The female servants followed at their heels and, when Barnsby had cleaned up the mess on the desk, Alyse was alone once again.

With no one to turn to, she sat down in her favourite armchair and stared vacantly into the dying embers of the fire contemplating the events of the last two days. She had known something like this was inevitable and now serious trouble had come at last to the Benson family. Their fortunes, built by a cruel and domineering grandfather, were now evaporating in the disgrace of treason. Over the past two days, many of her friends had shunned her and servants were no doubt whispering behind her back. With her father and brother-in-law locked in prison awaiting trial, this was the last straw—a husband gone crazy, imagining ghosts.

Alyse had inherited some of her grandfather's traits and bullying servants, as well as her younger sisters, had easily become a method of hiding her boredom. Her air of harshness and cruel insensibility turned her from a demanding youngster into a bitter over-powering wife. Now, she searched her mind for answers and remembered something her father had often said, "One man's downfall is another man's gain."

At this moment, however, hatred and worry were Alyse's only thoughts and, as the liquor took its toll, her eyes closed. Suddenly, they flicked open. *It could all be mine! With father gone and a husband who's demented, I shall turn this to my advantage. I will be mistress of Highgate Hall!* A smile tugged at her narrow lips and her head fell back onto the overstuffed chair.

Chapter 8

The future, for Admiral William Thomas Jones, was not looking good. Having contracted with the disreputable Captain Roach to sink Lady Sutton's ship, now on its way back up the Thames loaded with grain, he might well have taken a contract with the devil.

Drinking heavily, Captain Roach inadvertently talked of his mission while recruiting extra crewmen. Two of the *Observer* street urchins, asleep in a nearby doorway, were awakened by loud voices as Roach bragged that the *Restitution* would soon be blasted out of the water by the *Black Otter*'s guns.

"An unarmed sitting duck!" he drunkenly proclaimed, before stumbling back toward his ship.

As dawn broke over dockland the next morning, the two young street urchins begged an early morning crust from the bread shop boys and told Tom and Billy what they had overheard.

"Run and tell the *Observer*," Billy coaxed, "an ah'll give yer a big loaf each when ye've done it. Tell 'em to find out where the *Black Otter*'s berthed."

Within the hour, a small army of Daisy's newspaper vendors were searching the docks for Roach's ship. Already at work, Charley Mason, obeying Lizzie's orders, locked the frightened and, now half-crazed actor, in the brig of the training ship for safekeeping.

Lizzie and Quon left home at first light after gobbling down breakfast and receiving a thorough scolding from Martha. They understood she was worried about them and tried to reassure her, to no avail. Finally, when she turned her back to clear up the dishes, they hurried outside. They spent only a moment with Abe as they passed, explaining they had things to do.

"No time for old Abe this morning," he whined, his eyes trying to discern the unusual movement down at the dock as the youngsters raced away down the hill.

Spotting the dockmaster's cart, they dodged the traffic as a street waif with an armful of newspapers stopped to talk to Charley. After what appeared to be a short conversation, the engineer pointed toward Tower Bridge. By the time they came on the scene, the lad had disappeared.

"What did he want?" Lizzie asked the dockmaster.

"He was looking for *Black Otter*."

"Why?"

"I don't know," Charley growled irritably, and then changed the subject. "What are you going to do with that actor fella?"

"Have him taken out to the *Falcon*. Jack will know what to do with him."

The dockmaster nodded, one hand pensively rubbing his chin.

"That might be difficult," Charley replied, "*Falcon* could be anywhere."

Quon's hands went wild, spinning and twisting as Lizzie watched intently.

"Dumplin says they'll be patrolling the channel. Ben will know how to find them and he gets back any day. I think he's right."

Charley's eyes narrowed. "We'll find them." His whisper was almost inaudible as he turned to watch a heavily loaded vessel slowly manoeuvring into the docks.

"I believe your answer has just arrived. That's the *Restitution* just coming in," he muttered, "but she'll have to wait to be unloaded. I'll tell Ben to meet you at the cottage at lunch time ... if that's all right?" Without waiting for a reply, Charley now focused his attention on the incoming ship, waving his stick as he shouted orders at the dock workers.

"We go, Wizzy," said Quon, tugging on her sleeve.

She nodded.

As they headed toward the road, they picked their way between stacks of outgoing cargo, working men, and loaded drays leaving with deliveries. Lizzie grinned as they passed the steam engine, hissing fiercely as workmen struggled to keep pace with its never-ending moving belt, laden with cargo, as it unloaded another vessel.

At Dock Street, an opening in traffic sent them scurrying across the busy road to the coaching house.

"Tom not here," Quon muttered, cocking an ear toward the noisy drinking establishment.

"Yes, he is," Lizzie corrected him, pointing through the mêlée.

Sure enough, there was the usually noisy old mariner sitting silent in a corner. His eyes stared unseeing straight ahead.

Something's wrong, thought Lizzie.

Tom Legg's eyes were sad and watery as he nodded a silent greeting to the pair. His tankard of ale was sitting on the barrel top untouched and his companions were nowhere in sight.

"He's gone," the mariner whispered haltingly. "He's gone."

"Who's gone?" she asked.

"Captain Billy."

"I'm sorry, Tom. Was he an old shipmate?" she asked.

"No, me cat!" he said sadly.

Pulled aside by her partner's grip on her arm, Lizzie patted the old man's back and turned away. *Strange*, she thought, *people don't seem to affect this old warrior, but a cat sends him into mourning!*

She had no way of knowing Captain Billy *was* a cat of distinction, a seafaring friend who had accompanied Tom on many a voyage. This was a cat that had ridden into battle on a mighty man-o-war and survived the blast of Spanish cannon, but age and time had taken its toll. Captain Billy's life had slipped quietly away while sleeping on the old mariner's knee the night before.

Leaving the stableyard, Lizzie and Quon headed for the Johnson bakery. Almost there, they caught a glimpse of Oly and the pony cart as it entered Bill's yard just ahead of them.

"The fire starters!" Lizzie moaned, remembering they were locked in the stable at the bread shop. "What are we going to do with them?"

Quon grinned as his hands performed a spinning dance.

"We can't do that!" she giggled, "you'd better think of something else dumplin.'"

"Miss Lizzie," Olivera's voice came from the bake house yard. "We brought the bad men over here to Mister Bill."

The baker and his helper watched with amusement from the doorway as the partner's eyes swung around taking in the yard.

"Well, where are they?" Lizzie asked in alarm.

"There," Clem replied, beginning to laugh as he pointed to two large barrels standing in the corner. "Bill's pickled 'em!"

"Aye lass," the Yorkshire baker chuckled. "I remembered what old Joe did to Stroud's men a few years back when he poured a gallon of rum into a barrel then dropped a man inside, hammering on the lid. We never heard another peep outa them sailors and these two have gone awful quiet."

"Now what are you going to do with them?" Lizzie asked.

The Yorkshireman shrugged his massive shoulders and looked blankly at his helper—his mind hadn't looked that far ahead.

"Maybe drop them in the river," he suggested half-heartedly.

"No, Bill," Lizzie smiled, "get the bread lads to take them down to *The*

Robin, and leave them outside in the yard."

"Just leave the barrels in the yard?" asked Clem, rubbing his forehead.

Grabbing the girl's arm, Quon spun her around to face him. Arms waving, he grimaced, holding his nose.

"Yes, dumplin, that might be even better," she said, agreeing with whatever he had said.

"Did he say they stink of garbage, luv?" Bill chuckled, looking over at the barrels. "Cos he's right, they stink something fierce but they'll now have a familiar smell about them!"

Clem slapped his leg and began to laugh again.

"No, he said to tip them out onto the manure heap, next to the stables!" Lizzie replied ruefully.

"Ugh, they'll stink even worse then," declared Clem making a face and shuddering. "They'll be the laughing stock of dockland."

"And leave!" Bill added, cocking an eyebrow at Lizzie before turning away. "Cum on Clem, let's load the cart. They'll help themselves to pie."

Oly was quietly listening to the exchange. He went over to the table to sit down but his gaze turned to the barrels. Then he quickly turned away. His young face was set with grim lines of worry and his fingers toyed restlessly with a spoon. Quon brought pie and cream to the table and served a piece to each of them. Oly lifted his sad eyes, looking over at the only mother he had ever known.

"Eat your pie, lad," Lizzie said gently. "Uncle Davis will soon be better and don't you worry none about those men—we haven't hurt them, but they'll have a big headache and won't be planning any trouble in dockland for a long time."

Oly tried to smile, but he had little enthusiasm for talking or eating. He seemed eager to be on his way again once the pony cart was loaded.

"We'll get rid of them barrels, lass," the baker assured her, "you don't need to be involved." Watching the fast-disappearing cart, he quietly added, "By gum that lad's fretting for Captain Davis."

"He'll be all right, Bill," Lizzie muttered, standing up to leave. "He's growing up awful fast, just like the rest of us did. Come on dumplin, we have work to do."

Waving goodbye to the men, they made their way out to the road. Two hours later, their business complete, they were on their way home. Up ahead, they recognized the figure of Captain Ben Thorn striding hurriedly toward the cottage. *Charley's told him*, she thought to herself.

Ben had almost reached the doorway and gone inside when they caught

J. Robert Whittle

up to him.

"Where the devil is he?" they heard him ask in a frustrated tone.

"He's in good hands," Lizzie snapped from behind him. "Eat first and then we'll take you to see him."

"Now!" Ben insisted sharply.

"Later!" Lizzie snapped back, her eyes flashing a warning. "Ain't nothin you can do that hasn't been done, Ben."

"But *Falcon*'s out at sea, I saw her down the coast as we entered the Thames."

"Yes, and we have everybody fooled. They think Captain Davis is aboard."

Ben shook his head, unable to comprehend the implications of Lizzie's charade. Settling reluctantly onto a chair, he glanced over at Joe calmly eating his lunch. He looked up at Martha as she slid a plate of food in front of him. She smiled encouragingly and he picked up his fork.

Over lunch, Lizzie explained what they were doing to protect the captain and his job. "We started a rumour that it was Captain Toby Johns who had been injured in the accident and later died. After the *Observer* reported the details, it seems to have become accepted as fact."

"But who's Toby Johns? Should I know him?" asked Ben, a puzzled look again appearing on his well-tanned, handsome face.

"He doesn't exist," Lizzie smiled shrewdly. "I made him up."

Cocking an eyebrow, Ben chewed hard to clear his mouth.

"Yer a devious one, lass, only you would think like that."

"That's not all of it, lad," added Joe as an involuntary chuckle escaped the old man's lips. He pushed his empty plate away and accepted the recharged pipe Martha held out for him. He puffed gently when the housekeeper applied a lighted splinter to the tobacco. Slowly sliding his chair back, the old man stood up and moved toward the open door. Hesitating a moment, he watched as young Willie raced past with his gypsy friends. They all called out a greeting and Joe waved back. He turned back to the mariner. "Grab tight to yer whiskers Ben, she's at it again!"

Ben's fork dropped noisily onto the empty tin plate and, with the back of his weathered hand, he slowly wiped the remnants of food from his mouth as his gaze fell on Lizzie.

"What the devil are you up to this time, lass?" he growled.

Quon's fingers beat a rapid tattoo on the table. Frowning, Ben's eyes flicked his way, then flashed back to Lizzie, who nodded as a smile spread

80

across her face.

"You're right, dumplin," she said softly, "we should show him." She stood up and beckoned Ben to follow.

Muttering a thank you to Martha, Ben stomped out after them. He followed them down Water Street to the dock where they threaded their way through all the activity to Charley's cart.

"WHERE'S THE PRISONER, CHARLEY?" she shouted up to him.

Hardly shifting his gaze, the dockmaster gave a piercing whistle and the Grim boys arrived at his side as if by magic. Quick orders brought a grin to the boys' faces and they gestured for the visitors to follow. At the end of the dock, the Grims pointed to a ship and left them. Ben led the way up the gangplank and they found their way to the brig. There were only a few sailors about but no one bothered with them.

"Who you got in there?" Ben muttered, peering through the bars into the dim light. Jake was sitting on a barrel looking unkempt and perplexed. "Good God, it's the captain!" he gasped.

"No it ain't," said Lizzie, grinning.

Looking harder at the figure of Jake Newton, Ben searched the man's face and noted his size. He scratched his beard in amazement. The prisoner certainly looked like Captain Davis as he scowled from the back of the cell. His hooded eyes radiated the same hostility Ben had seen from Davis many times.

"Yer planning to use this man to impersonate Captain Davis?" he asked, chuckling at the cleverness of the situation.

"That's right, Ben, and you're going to deliver him to Jack on *Falcon*. Now let's go see the real Captain Davis."

"When am I going to get out of here?" asked Jake, coming to his feet as they turned to leave. His eyes were sad and she knew he now regretted his actions.

"It won't be long now, Jake. You know, if you hadn't been so stupid, you would have been treated much better. Are you getting fed all right?"

"Yes, ma'am." He turned his back and went to sit down again.

As they left the ship, Ben asked why the man seemed to be so resigned to his fate. "Why I'd be screaming blue murder," he commented.

"Well, we did have some trouble with the lad earlier, and we had to use a bit of persuasion to shut him up, that's all," Lizzie replied offhandedly.

Ben looked upward and shook his head in disbelief. Waving to Charley as they passed, Lizzie gestured to them to hurry and they made their way back up the hill. She only slowed when they reached Drover's Lane where she let Ben stop to catch his breath.

"I'm not as young as I used to be, lass. Where the devil are we going?" he panted. "I'll need to visit the office while I'm here."

"Later," she retorted. "You'll see, it's not far now."

On they walked past the stable block, rag yard and stock pens, before turning into the noisy gypsy camp.

"Don't tell me he's here with the gypsies?" the mariner groaned.

Ignoring the question, Quon led them through the wagons and squealing children to the shelter.

Ducking under the cover, Ben stared in amazement at the scene in front of him. A gypsy girl was spoon-feeding a man he barely recognized as the captain he had served under on the *Falcon*.

"That's enough," the captain whispered when he saw his visitors. "Well, Mister Thorn," he hissed, "what thinks yer now?"

"I'll get you out of here, sir," Ben growled, "just give me a day or two to make some arrangements."

"Leave it alone, sailor," Davis thundered. "Tend to yer own obligations, man. I vouch that wench has it all in hand by now."

"But I can't leave you here with these heathens, sir. You need proper care."

"Heathens, you say?" the captain's voice grew angry. "I'll have the lash put to yer back if you don't treat these people with respect, Mister Thorn. They're friends of mine and I'm getting excellent care!"

Quon's fingers touched Lizzie's elbow and she reached up and squeezed his hand. The wild-tempered captain had not only accepted the bread lads, but he also now claimed the gypsies as his friends.

Ben shook his head but reconsidered voicing his thoughts anymore.

Just then, the old gypsy granny shuffled into the shelter. "You go now," she slobbered, splashing tobacco juice from drooping lips and angrily poking at Ben with her stick.

"And you, girl," Davis exclaimed, setting his gaze on Lizzie, "need to change your ways and act like a woman!"

Backing out of the shelter, Ben stopped and straightened, waiting for Lizzie to follow. *I wonder what caused that little tirade,* he thought. Looking around him, he saw many gypsy women moving in and out of their gaily painted homes on wheels, children playing happily and, somewhere in the background, a fiddler brushed the air with a lively tune.

"Kinda peaceful ain't it," Lizzie muttered, pushing past him.

Hardly a word passed between them but Ben could see Lizzie was both puzzled and angered by the captain's harsh comment, as they walked down the rough track to the office. Twice he noticed Quon's hands make silent comments but neither drew any response from the girl.

"What's wrong?" Ada asked, noticing the girl's stormy expression as they all trooped into the office.

"That miserable old seadog," Lizzie retorted, "says I need to act like a woman! What does he mean?"

The bookkeeper tried to suppress her smile and had to turn away. She wanted to help, but wasn't sure how to approach the subject. Ben interrupted her thoughts saving her from having to answer.

"Do you have my next orders ready, Ada," he asked, twiddling his hat nervously.

"Eager to be off, are you Ben?" Ada asked, smiling.

Tapping Lizzie on the shoulder to draw her attention, Quon's hands spun again; staring hard at her as this time, he waited for an answer.

"Dumplin says not to forget your passenger, Ben," Lizzie muttered.

"I won't, I'll have Charley move him to the *Restitution* when I get back to the ship," he growled, glancing at the order papers and money pouch in Ada's outstretched hand. "It appears we leave at first light. Charley must think he can get that grain off and reloaded mightly fast with that fancy machine of his."

Turning to go, he stopped and looked out the window as Nathan's buggy pulled up. It wasn't long before the trader's hurrying footsteps sounded on the steps and the door was flung open. Ben caught it just before it banged off the wall.

"Urgent order, Ada," exclaimed the out-of-breath trader, apparently not worried about whether he was interrupting anything important. "Two sides of beef to the *Jester Tavern* in Arthur Street. They need the order right away." He handed the order sheet over to her.

"We don't supply the *Jester Tavern*," she replied, scanning the paperwork.

"New account, cash on delivery," Nathan replied, turning his attention to the mariner. "Hello Ben, did you come in today?"

"Aye and loaded to the gunnels."

"It's a bit dull being master of a grain ship, isn't it?" Nathan persisted.

"Dull as dishwater," Ben sighed and, nodding to Ada, pulled the door closed behind him.

The trader's eyes now swept over to Lizzie. He seemed in no hurry and eager to talk. "You're very quiet, girl," he said, "has the cat got your

J. Robert Whittle

tongue today?"

"She's thinking," Ada chuckled. "Captain Davis has given her something else to think about."

Frowning at the bookkeeper, Nathan looked back at Lizzie and his stick began to tap the floor. "What was that?"

"Mind yer own business!" the girl snapped. "Go tend to yer customers."

"Ho ho," Nathan chuckled. "Our captain must have touched a sore point, did he, girl?"

"Not really," Ada said softly, "he just told her the truth."

Lizzie's back stiffened, her eyes flashed on the bookkeeper. Recognizing the signs, Nathan raised his eyebrows and made a quick exit.

Lizzie watched him leave, then slowly turned back to face Ada. Seeing the look on the girl's face, the bookkeeper had a sudden feeling of misgiving. *Have I said too much?*

"Truth!" Lizzie snapped, taking a step closer to the woman as if daring her to go on. She roughly brushed Quon's restraining hand from her arm. "Truth about what?"

Ada looked the girl in the eye and tried to smile. "You're a woman now, not a child, Lizzie. Look at those old clothes and boots you're wearing. You don't even think about how you look, do you? We all know Mister Kratze and Clara made you several lovely dresses, I think it's high time you wore them!"

Lizzie's face clouded, hurt by Ada's stinging words. Her eyes glanced over at her partner. Thoughts flashed through her head. Ada was almost like a mother to her—certainly more interested and loving than her own had been in the first eight years of her life.

You're a business woman," Ada continued, "a power to be reckoned with, my dear. All of dockland's needy have their hopes set on you, but you're still acting like a street waif." She paused. "It's time to show those wicked devils you're a woman—that you've arrived!"

Ned, listening quietly in his corner, now pushed his chair back with a grating sound.

"Lizzie lass," he growled, "Ada's right. Yer a mighty fine young woman now. We need to see you in one of those nice dresses of yers, not just when something important is happening, but all the time. Those powerful men won't be expectin to be dealin with a lady of means and that's exactly how you'll appear when yer dress up."

Ada nodded in agreement pleased that Ned, usually a man of few

84

words, had come to her aid.

"You'll shock 'em lass, just like yer did to me!" he added, giving her a wink.

"My goodness, Ned, that was quite a speech," Ada chuckled, "but he is right, Lizzie. It does make a difference when you are in business."

Lizzie's eyes swung toward the door, her teeth biting hard into her lip as she felt Quon's hand slide into her own. Remaining silent, she gripped her partner's fingers and pulled him toward the door.

"Lizzie, come back," the bookkeeper called.

"Leave her," Ned growled, "she'll think it out for herself now."

Tossing her head defiantly, Lizzie walked quickly down the lane, pulling Quon along beside her. Thoughts raced through her head. Ada and old Ned were her friends, she knew they were trying to help and the brutal truth was plain to see ... she *was* a woman and they *were* right.

They turned abruptly into Pump Street and almost bumped into a mother breaking a small loaf of bread to share between her two hungry children. The woman's eyes held a look of bleak hopelessness. Her thin arms reached out to protect the sullen-faced youngsters as she shrank away in fear.

"Don't be afraid," Lizzie murmured, offering the woman two pennies.

Mistrust held the woman spellbound, but her urgent need forced her to find the courage to hold out a shaking hand and accept the kindness. Quickly pocketing the coins, she grabbed her children and hurried away up an alley, furtively glancing back as she turned the corner.

Frowning fiercely, Lizzie set off again, obviously expecting Quon to follow. Her mind was twisting and turning as she searched for an answer. She dearly wanted to help these poor people. *I must get on that council,* she thought, *no matter what it takes. If I have to be a lady, then a lady I shall be*!

They were soon in sight of Brown's Yard and could see several street urchins crowded around Daisy in the print shop doorway. As she handed each a bundle of newspapers, they scurried away.

Daisy looked up and saw them. "We found the *Black Otter*, they were loading gun powder and cannon balls. Billy says they're going after our ship and Captain Ben. Some of the lads heard the *Black Otter's* captain boasting while drunk last night."

"The *Restitution*'s a grain ship," Lizzie retorted angrily, "why would they want to do that?"

They followed Daisy into the newspaper office and suddenly Quon's hands began gyrating.

"I know what he says," Gabriel said coldly, "he says it's just to make trouble for the TLS shipping. Somebody's after your blood, girl."

"You're probably right," Lizzie agreed, "but they're in for a shock."

Silence settled over the shop as everyone waited for Lizzie's next statement.

"Ben's going out to meet the *Falcon* tomorrow," she announced, "and *Falcon*'s armed to the teeth. That old sea dog will welcome a little excitement—he just told us it's dull being captain of a grain ship!"

Concern laced Lady Sutton's voice, as she whispered, "But our ship carries no cannon. Captain Thorn will be in grave danger." Looking from Gabriel to Lizzie, she slowly added, "Perhaps he should stay in port."

"No," Lizzie replied, an evil smile curling her lips. "Ben will play cat and mouse with them, then lead them right into *Falcon*'s guns!" She fervently hoped he would be able to.

"Can I sail with Ben?" Gabriel asked eagerly, his voice rising with excitement.

"Yes," Lizzie replied, "if you can swim."

"Of course I can swim," he replied, the significance of her comment escaping him.

"Then, if Penny can spare you for a few weeks, be on our dock before dawn," Lizzie replied, turning for the door.

"Tomorrow?" he asked in surprise, looking over at Lady Sutton.

"You don't think I would spoil this for you do you, Gabriel? I wouldn't be able to live with myself knowing your disappointment!" Penny teased.

"Yes, my man, the *Restitition* sails tomorrow. Better get ready, Daisy," she said flippantly. "This story is going to shake up a few people!"

Chapter 9

In the public dockside area just beyond the East India Docks, Captain Roach was already setting his plans in motion as the *Black Otter* slipped her mooring lines. Topsail picking up the wind, she slowly made her way toward the sea. His plan was simple; attacking an unarmed merchant vessel posed no danger to him or his men. The stranger's gold would soon jingle in his own pocket. Having found out that the *Restitution* would be leaving almost immediately, they would head out to the channel and wait for it to show itself. Then all he had to do was follow it until there were no witnesses. It all sounded so easy.

"We go see Billy before supper," Quon announced, striding off down Chandler with Lizzie close behind him.

"Ther's a message for yer, Miss Lizzie," Billy called when he saw them approaching. "Willy Mutt says Walter wants to see ya."

"Fiddlesticks," said Lizzie, "we'd better go right away, it might be important. Better get a message to Martha that we'll be late, Billy."

"Velly late!" added Quon, rubbing his stomach and moaning.

A clock began to strike six o'clock as they set off at a run. Hitching rides on passing coaches and drays, they found themselves at the side gate of the Bishop's Palace about half an hour later. They made their way around to the back door and saw Walter sitting on a small liquor keg near the mouth of the tunnel—the entrance to his home in the cavernous basement of the large house.

Unnoticed, they sneaked through the gates and almost surprised their friend who turned and saw them just as a little brown and white spaniel raced out from the trees. Whimpering, it ran over to the cellarman; he knelt down to fondly rub its ears. A loud voice hailed them and Bishop Tide stepped into view.

"Hello Walter, am I interrupting? You have visitors."

"No, no, Your Worship," Walter sprang to his feet, "these are my friends, Lizzie and Quon."

Scratching his chin, the Bishop's eyes curiously moved from one to the other of the visitors, obviously deep in thought.

"I know who you two are," he said, "you're the children I met outside the tailor's shop in Water Street when I first took this position, a long time ago. You've grown and I hardly recognized you, but you're the one," he chuckled, looking straight at Lizzie, "who didn't want me as a friend. You said you already had one. Have you changed your mind yet?"

"No," she replied defiantly, although feeling slightly uncomfortable under the soft, warm gaze of the religious man.

"Some day we shall be friends, my children," he said, his voice hinting at a promise. He turned away, softly calling the dog, before climbing the stairs to the back door and disappearing inside.

"Does he always go in the back door?" Lizzie asked. "I thought only servants would go in that way?" Then without waiting for an answer, she continued, "You wanted to talk to us, Walter?"

"Yes," he replied, grinning. "He's been sent away."

"Who has?" she asked.

"He wor babbling about a ghost, now they're sending a new one."

Lizzie rolled her eyes in frustration, glancing at Quon who shrugged his shoulders.

"Hold it," said Lizzie. "Who's been sent away?"

"The minister at St. John's on Slaughter Lane near where you live."

"Right, right, now I understand what you're telling me, we have a new minister because he thinks he saw a ghost." She giggled.

"Yes."

"Good, is that all you wanted me for?"

"No," the cellarman gasped with excitement. "He's going to support the woman who's applied for a council seat, and that's you, Liz!"

Quon grabbed Lizzie's arm. Here was a turn of events they were totally unprepared for.

"Are you sure?" she asked. "Why the devil would he support me?"

"Bishop Tide says it's time for a change." Walter clapped his hands gleefully. "He said parliament were discussing changing the law."

"You heard all this on your speaking tubes?"

Walter nodded, pushing one of the barrels over and rolling it toward the tunnel entrance. "Tell Jessy hello when you see her," he said solemnly, before disappearing into the darkness.

"We in trouble," Quon muttered, checking his pocket watch as they went back through the gate and turned into the street.

"Walter seems to miss our Jessy. I imagine she was the only friend he had. We're so lucky to have found her for our angels. She's just like a mother to them."

"Wizzy their mother!" Quon exclaimed.

"Yes, they're pretty sure of that, aren't they, dumplin?" she giggled. "An our mother is going to be getting worried if we don't get home for supper soon!"

It was after seven when they arrived home, out of breath.

"Trouble, lass?" Martha asked with raised eyebrows. "One of the lads came to tell us you'd be late."

"No, we've been to see Walter over at the Bishop's Palace," Lizzie replied.

Everyone else had finished supper and sat back in their chairs waiting for Lizzie to give them more details. Martha slid two plates of food in front of them and they began to eat immediately.

"Lizzie, I'm sorry, I didn't mean to upset you this morning," Ada said quietly.

"Doesn't matter," Lizzie muttered between mouthfuls, "you were right."

Ada looked over at Mick and he merely grinned. The others looked on with inquiring expressions but dared not ask. Emptying their plates in record time, they handed them to Martha. Quon leaned back in his chair and groaned with satisfaction, holding his stomach.

Just then a sleepy cry of, "Granddad," came from the direction of the bedroom. Looking up, they saw Willie standing there in his nightshirt rubbing his eyes. Moving quickly, Martha went over and took his hand, leading him over to Joe.

"Has Ben's ship been unloaded, Charley?" Lizzie asked.

"Yes, and provided the fog doesn't roll in, he's leaving early in the morning," Charley chuckled. "Ben came and told us to switch the prisoner to the *Restitution* and we have word that Patrick and the *Golden Lady* are on their way here from Holland."

"Ah begorra, full of cheese, hoy hopes," Mick laughed, "just to make Nathan happy!"

"Lizzie," Ada murmured, "you're not still cross with me, are you?"

"Look Ada," Lizzie snapped in a quiet tone. "I know all about dockland and the people who live here, and not one thing about being a lady. Yes, I liked it when I dressed up for your wedding, but you can't make a silk purse out of a sow's ear."

"So, you're not willing to even try!" Ada flung back.

Instantly, a silence descended on the room. The only sound was from

Willie playing with a toy on the floor.

Quon's fingers burst into action tapping hard on the table.

"No!" Lizzie whispered harshly.

Crashing hard onto the table with his hand, Quon's eyes blazed as he rose from his seat.

"You turd," she hissed.

"He said you had to try, didn't he?" the bookkeeper ventured hopefully.

"No, he said if I'm not going to be a lady he was leaving!" A gentle softness not often seen in Lizzie's manner now crept into her voice as she reached for his hand. "I won't let him go, so I guess I'm going to be a lady!"

Willie had been listening intently and before Quon could sit back down, the boy got up off the floor and stood looking at him. His lower lip began to quiver and a tear silently rolled down his cheek as he ran around the table to Quon.

"You not leave me, Quon," he whimpered, taking Quon's arm and looking up into his face.

Quon reached down and picked up the boy then, without a word, he slung him over his shoulder and carried him outside, giggling happily.

"By gum," Martha sighed, dabbing at her eyes with the corner of her apron, "children can fair tek yer breath away."

No one spoke for an uncomfortable period of time until laughter suddenly came from the garden. Their eyes turned instinctively toward the door, as Daisy's high-pitched giggle reached them.

Shuffling nervously in his chair, Charley cleared his throat. "We could ask Daisy and her mother to help you, Liz," he suggested cautiously.

"Listen, Mister Mason, and all of you," Lizzie retorted, "I'll dress up and act the part, but underneath all that finery I'll still be Lizzie Short."

"Oh Lizzie," Ada sighed, "that's all we want, love."

The sound of Willie's laughter broke the tension as he led Daisy and Quon back into the cottage.

If anyone was watching, they would have seen the familiar glint of mischief in Lizzie's eyes. "Looking for Charley?" she asked the reporter.

"No, you *and* Charley!" Daisy smiled, settling onto the vacant seat that Mick had pulled up to the table. "The newspaper's growing and we need bigger premises. Mother and Gabriel would like to expand." The girl's eyes met and the smile slipped from her face. "And, mother thinks it would be better if Gabriel didn't sail with Ben."

Quon returned to his seat and began to tap out a message on Lizzie's arm.

"Dumplin says," she translated slowly, "that you can have the two empty shops next to the lampmaker." Daisy frowned as Lizzie continued, "They're just around the corner from Billy's bread shop."

"Perfect," Daisy agreed, "that would be ideal, but what about Gabriel?"

"He's a man and a former soldier," said Lizzie, "let him have a little excitement—two or three weeks at sea will be good for him."

Eyebrows raised, Ada nodded approvingly.

"Something's wrong," interrupted Charley, looking toward the door and frowning. "The Grim boys should have been here by now."

"I told them not to come," Daisy admitted. "Mother has arranged to have the carriage come for us."

"Why?" replied Charley, feeling the sweat begin to bead on his forehead.

"I can talk to you about the new press as we drive you home."

Ada, although interested in the progress of the *Dockland Observer*, stood up and began to gather together their belongings. "Time for home, love," she murmured to her husband, "it's been a long day and I'm tired. This being with child is not as easy as it appears."

Not knowing what to say, and being embarrassed by Ada's frank comment, no one ventured a reply as the O'Rourkes started for the door. Following them, Martha gave Willie a good night kiss, brushing the hair out of his eyes. Mick mischievously winked at the dockmaster, causing a blush of embarrassment to rush onto Charley's cheeks.

"Well, have you thought about it yet?" Daisy challenged Charley as the others left.

"Yes, but we'd need to draw it out first."

"Then let's get on with it," she urged, "it's an ideal time if we're moving to bigger premises and our sales are growing on a daily basis."

A smile spread across Lizzie's face as she listened to Daisy's urging. The shy, retiring upper-class girl had gone and a new fire was burning in her words as she pushed Charley for action.

Quon's fingers tapped a message on his partner's leg beneath the table. Nodding, Lizzie moved toward the door as the sound of a carriage was heard in the lane. Martha cocked an inquiring eyebrow at her departure.

The Sutton carriage stood by the garden gate and a smiling Lady Sutton displayed her pleasure by calling out to them. "Things are working wonderfully well," she chortled enthusiastically, her ink-stained hands reaching out to greet them. "Has Daisy talked to you about larger premises, my dear!"

"Yes, we have just the place for you," Lizzie replied quickly, "but I need a favour."

"Just ask, girl," Penny Sutton beamed, "and it shall be yours."

"I want to dress up and look like a woman," Lizzie exclaimed, blushing slightly. The words tumbled out as if she was afraid to stop them.

A pensive look of complete understanding crossed the highborn lady's face. "You want to impress someone," she whispered knowingly. "Well, brushed hair, dainty shoes, a parasol and lots of frilly petticoats will change your appearance immediately. That's the simple secret, my dear, and petticoats that show make most men into stammering fools!" she giggled.

"Mister Kratze made this one," Lizzie murmured, pulling up her soiled, black dress and exposing her old grey flannel petticoat. "I thought it was rather pretty."

"It was when it was new, but it says 'working girl'," explained Lady Sutton. Then she wagged a finger at the girl. "Snow-white petticoats under silk or satin, now that spells a lady!" Smiling broadly, she looked down at her own ink-stained smock and flinging her head back, roared with laughter. "Seems like we're changing stations, my dear—now I'm the 'working girl' and you're becoming the lady!"

"Mother," Daisy called from the cottage doorway, "we'll be out in a moment."

"Come on in and say hello, Penny. They're going to keep you waiting anyway by the look of it," said Lizzie, as she took her friend's arm and led her up the path.

When they all came outside 10 minutes later, Charley was looking visibly uncomfortable. Once inside the carriage, he settled back against the leather seats and Daisy continued to bombard him with questions. Her mother appeared, giving the coachman who stood waiting by the open door, directions to Charley's home in the Poplar District. Then he closed the door behind them. Climbing up into his seat, he clucked at the horses and flicked the reins.

A heavy mist floated up from the river as dawn broke on Sunday morning. Cursing under his breath, Captain Ben moved noisily about the deck, shoulders hunched as he stared out at the grey wall that dulled all sound. He listened to the muffled sound of arriving dockworkers and strained to hear the rattle of Charley's cart as he stomped down the gangplank.

The early start he'd planned was lost. Danger of collision and disaster lurked as several vessels, eager to be off, stayed tied to the wharf. There was nothing to be done save listening to the bells of incoming merchant ships searching through the gloom for their moorage.

Lizzie and Quon were almost at the bottom of Water Lane when they heard Charley's odd conveyance rattle onto the docks accompanied by the Grim boys who shouted a warning to those going ahead of them.

Crossing Dock Street, Quon grabbed her arm pulling her violently backwards as a coach rumbled past.

"That was close!" she muttered as the wheel brushed her leg.

Unaffected by fog, the rhythmic thumping and the loud hissing of the stream engine guided them to Charley's cart and, ultimately, to Ben. Lizzie smiled ruefully when she heard Ben grumble about the weather.

"It'll lift in an hour," Charley predicted. "Has Gabriel arrived yet?"

"I'm here," called the familiar voice as he materialized in front of them. "I was here before dawn."

"He's going with you, Ben," Lizzie answered the question in the captain's eyes. "Harry Roach is waiting out there for the *Restitution* and he thought he would be able to help."

Ben's back straightened, his hands doubling into fists.

"Mischief's afoot, lass," he growled. "Roach doesn't have the brains for it, he's workin for gold."

"Maybe we should attack him before he attacks us," Gabriel muttered.

"Who are you?" Ben snapped.

"Captain Gabriel Flood, formerly of the King's Own Light Cavalry."

Ben snatched his cap from his head, flinging it to the cobblestones.

"We don't have horses on ships, captain!" he exclaimed. "We travel on water!"

"Ben," Charley interrupted, "he's a fighting man. You'll need him if Roach catches up to you."

Stooping, Gabriel picked up Ben's cap and a slow humourless smile spread across his face. He dusted it off on his leg, punched it back into shape and handed it to the captain.

"I've faced cannon before, captain," he hissed through his teeth.

"Right then," Lizzie piped up interrupting their debate, "now that's settled, let's get on with it." She paused as Ben's eyes swung to face her, "Yer running light and fast, Ben. You wanted some excitement, well this trip won't be dull as dishwater. Use yer wits, man, and pull the *Black Otter* under *Falcon*'s guns. Jack will enjoy sinking this one."

The scowl lifted from Captain Thorn's face and, at the same instant, a call of, "Fogs lifting!" echoed along the dock.

"Get aboard, lad," Ben chuckled ominously, "and pray for a fair wind."

Lizzie and Quon stayed to watch as the *Restitution*'s topsails quickly filled with wind and damp sea air, then took the ship out into the river. Headed for the sea, now visible from the crow's nest, Ben moved the grain ship into the line of eagerly departing vessels.

"I hope he knows how to find *Falcon*," murmured Lizzie.

Quon looked at her with a worried frown.

8003

Out in the English Channel not far from the mouth of the Thames, *Black Otter* was also waiting for the fog to lift so he could see the ships exiting the great river. Having lived many years on the dark side of the law, Harry Roach knew how and where to hide.

Captain Ben Thorn was fully aware of the possibility of danger lying in wait for the *Restitution*. He knew the *Black Otter* was well ahead of him, having left the Thames the previous night. As they entered the busy seaway, he gave Gabriel Flood his first watch and the former cavalry officer now found himself high atop the main mast in the crow's nest— getting up there had been an exciting experience in itself. Now, from his vantage point, he could easily watch the shoreline for the *Black Otter* and the view was spectacular.

As the sun went down, the *Restitution* reached open sea, and Ben Thorn called for more sail. Pushing the grain ship into the blackness of the channel, Ben felt sure the villainous captain lay waiting for them not far away. The word on the street was not often wrong.

Roach waited until his quarry was well out in the channel; the gathering darkness and convenient line of ships, allowed him to slip unnoticed into the swelling seas behind the *Restitution*.

Out in the darkness, the two vessels plotted different courses. Ben fearlessly sailed due east into the wild waves, cutting sail as the wind whipped through the rigging. The mighty masts bent and groaned with an eerie, foreboding warning. Down in the belly of the ship, the icy chill of disaster swept down Gabriel's spine as he huddled in his cold bunk. This wasn't exactly what he'd been wanting for excitement.

Slyly, the *Black Otter* turned north, intent on providing a blockade before the Restitution reached the Humber River and the port of Hull.

ဆါၒၛ

Lizzie sprang suddenly awake. Premonition or night sounds? she wondered, listening to the bawling of cattle in the nearby paddock. Closing her eyes in the darkness, Ben Thorn, Captain Davis, Sam Benson and Judge Harvey slowly passed through her thoughts before sleep overtook her once again.

Hours later, early sunshine shot slivers of bright light through the low haze as the two partners made their way down Water Street.

"Any news, old friend?" she called to the tailor.

"News, girl!" Abe snapped harshly. "You're the news these days, you and that council." The old tailor shuffled his feet, watching the young woman as he wiped his mouth with the back of his hand. "Rumour says you're going to fail," he growled. "They say powerful men are plotting your downfall." Turning, he reached for the door latch and stared for a moment at the door. Then chuckling evilly, he continued, "And I'm going to be there to see you tear 'em to pieces!"

"But the public isn't allowed into the council meeting."

"Yes, they are," Abe snorted, "the law clearly defines the rules. It's the council members who vote for it to be private."

"You mean," she began as Nathan's buggy pulled in beside them, "we can fill that room with our people?"

"What room?" the trader interrupted as he leaned out of the buggy's window.

"Yes, you can," Abe replied, ignoring his cousin completely, "but it won't do no good, girl."

"Why?"

"What blasted room are you talking about?" Nathan's voice rose as he climbed out of the buggy.

Bombarded by their questions, the tailor threw up his hands, snapped his door open, stepped inside and slammed it behind him.

"Nathan," Lizzie whispered menacingly, walking up to him and wagging her finger under his nose. "One of these days …."

Grinning, the gypsy driver watched as Nathan stepped away from her

J. Robert Whittle

in surprise, banging against the buggy.

"What room?" he whined.

"The council chambers, Nathan!"

"They never allow spectators," he bleated, his fingers searching behind him for the door handle. "I tried it once, soldiers threw me out."

"But Abe said …."

"Yes, yes, my dear," he replied. Now eager to be away, he scrambled back into the buggy, quickly tapping his driver to move off. "You shouldn't believe everything my cousin tells you."

She stood still and watched, as if in a daze, as the buggy departed. Abe had always been right, there had been no reason to question his knowledge, but she had to be sure. Help came in the form of Clara hurrying toward them from across the street carrying Abe's breakfast tray. Following her into the shop, Lizzie slid quietly into the chair facing the tailor.

Fork hovering in mid-air, Abe watched her through eyes hooded by his frowning brow and bushy eyebrows.

"You're in need of proof, little missy," he hissed, "then read."

He pushed a legal-looking page of carefully formed handwriting across the table toward her. His fork pointed to one of the sections. Leaning over her shoulder, Quon followed her finger as she silently read.

"You're right," Lizzie grinned, carefully following the text. "It says here that every meeting is public; it's the council who vote for having no spectators."

"You doubted me, girl?" he whispered, putting his knife and fork down. He looked directly at her. "Well, you should, rules are like swords, they serve you well if you know their limitations." Chuckling to himself, he picked up his fork again and stabbed at his egg. "Take that paper with you, girl, and study it carefully," he ordered, flicking his fork to accentuate his command, sending spots of egg yolk across the paper. "Now go, I have work to do!"

Still uncomfortable with the tailor's bad temper, Clara backed toward the door.

"Not you woman," Abe bellowed, "get back to your work!"

"Take no notice of him, love," Lizzie whispered, as she passed the seamstress. "His bark is much worse than his bite."

Clara hurried back to her worktable grateful for Lizzie's friendship. She was beginning to understand her employer and his fierce loyalty to this beautiful and intelligent girl.

Leaving the store, Lizzie led the way over to the horse trough. She knelt down beside the trough and, taking a section of her dress, wet it in the water. Very carefully, she wiped the splotches of egg from the paper trying not to smudge the writing. She dabbed it with another section of her hem, stood up, folded the papers, and tucked them into her pocket. She heard her name called and looked back up the street to see Daisy waving to get their attention.

"Billy told me to warn you there was a new minister preaching at St. John's yesterday," she announced, continuing down the hill with them.

"I know, have you met him?" Lizzie asked.

"No, but Billy has and so has Mister Kratze."

"Busy little devil, isn't he?" Lizzie commented, thinking it strange Abe hadn't mentioned it.

"He's coming to the shop at three today if you want to meet him." Daisy grinned mischievously as they reached the TLS dock area and Charley's contraption appeared from out of a warehouse. "He told one of the delivery lads he wants to run an ad in the *Observer*."

"Selling what?" asked Charley, but Daisy only smiled and shrugged her shoulders. "I hope you lot haven't come by just to make a nuisance of yourselves this morning," he snorted irritably. "I have a lot of work to do today." The Grim boys moved him forward leaving the girls open-mouthed and Quon giggling.

"Charley not happy today!" he said quietly.

"Everyone has work to do today, it seems," Lizzie grumbled. "Well dumplin, we better find some work to do, too."

Daisy hesitated, not hearing their comments but listening with interest as Charley cracked orders at his men.

"You go," she decided. "I need to study the steam engine's flywheel."

Heading off, Lizzie glanced back and could see Daisy had gone over to stand near the steam engine. She appeared to be writing notes in her notebook.

"What she doing?" Quon asked his partner.

"Trying to figure out how to make a steam engine work their printing press, I think," retorted Lizzie. *Or is that what she wants us to think?*

Carefully crossing Dock Street, they started back up the hill, noticing a fancy carriage outside Abe's shop. Lizzie went over to the open door and peeked inside.

"Look who's visiting today!" she whispered as the harsh voice of Judge Harvey reached their ears. "Do you have Penny's letter?"

Drawing the copy of the damning letter containing information about Aurelius Harvey's past military service from his pocket—kept safely for such an opportunity—Quon's hand trembled as he handed it to her. He wondered what she was going to do but knew she had been waiting patiently to get even with the judge who had sentenced her friends to deportation so many years before.

Sneaking unnoticed into the shop, she moved stealthily until she came up behind the judge. Hiding behind a display, she cautiously placed the letter on the floor behind him, then stood upright and cleared her throat. Judge Harvey turned around.

Waiting until his eyes had settled coldly on her, she bent and picked up the piece of paper. As the judge's eyes narrowed, following her every move, she opened the folded sheet.

"Oh my," she exclaimed, pretending to read. "This must belong to you, sir."

Wheezing slightly, he snatched the paper from her hand. His pipe drooped in his mouth as he began to read the shocking, and familiar, words. *How the devil did this letter get here?* he thought, his mind screaming as his knees began to buckle. He moved closer to the counter for support. *This is the letter I wrote to my sister from Ireland many years ago—one she told me she had destroyed!* "Did you read this, girl?" he asked, trying to keep his voice even. His eyes bored into her.

"Well yes, most of it, sir," Lizzie said matter-of-factly. "It does belong to you, doesn't it?" She looked up at him innocently.

Stunned by the realization that his past was no longer a secret, his conscience screamed a warning and he held the letter gingerly in his fingers, as if it would burst into flames at any moment. Oh, how he wished … if this information about him being a member of the Irish Rebel Army ever became known, he knew his days as a judge would be over. *Compose yourself,* his mind shouted, *you can find a solution to this.* Sweat, balanced on his brow, began to run down his face in tiny rivulets, soaking his tight collar as he fought desperately to remain calm.

"You are Judge Harvey, aren't you sir?" she asked, breaking into his tormented thoughts.

Abe watched with fascinated fear as the girl toyed with this powerful man. *What is she doing and what was that piece of paper?* he wondered.

"You picked my pocket, girl!" the judge accused her unconvincingly. "You're a thief and I shall call the military immediately."

Peeking between the stacked bolts of cloth, Clara bit her lip. A cold finger of fear touched her spine and she began to tremble.

"Good day to you, sir, and ma'am," announced a new soft-spoken voice, indicating the arrival of a robed minister. "I'm Percy Palmer, your new vicar. You must be Judge Harvey."

"*My* new vicar?" the judge sneered, ignoring the minister's extended hand. "She picked my pocket!"

Eyebrows raised, the minister's expression seemed to demand an explanation as he turned to face Lizzie.

"I only picked a paper up off the floor," she explained innocently, "and handed it back to him."

"Commendable," the minister muttered, "hardly stealing, sir."

"She read it!"

"How else would I know who it belonged to?" Lizzie purred, "but I shall never reveal its damning contents."

The judge's jaw sagged, his teeth losing their grip on his pipe stem. It crashed to the floor breaking in several pieces spreading burned bits of tobacco and broken clay all around.

"Damning contents you say, girl," the minister interrupted, "perhaps you should …."

Pushing past them, Judge Harvey staggered toward the door, pocketing the letter; his feet crunched the remnants of his pipe underfoot. Sighing with relief, Abe took a deep puff of his pipe.

"Who are you, young lady?" the minister asked, cocking an inquiring eye on Lizzie.

"Why, kind sir," she laughed, pointing at Quon, "that's him and this is me!"

With their laughter ringing through the store, they walked out of the tailor's shop and disappeared into the crowd of shoppers. Frowning, Vicar Palmer turned to face the tailor.

"Who is that girl, Mister Kratze?" he demanded.

Abe dropped his eyes to the floor leaving the question unanswered as he shuffled over to his old wooden chair and flopped gratefully into it. He closed his eyes. *What is she up to now? And why has this new minister come into my shop—meeting him on the street yesterday was quite sufficient!*

Once again, the new minister felt the cold, unfriendly hand of dockland. He had arrived only two days before to his first parish calling and, the harsh code of silence, suspicion and distrust left him feeling helpless. Gaining the confidence and friendship of these people was going to be harder than he'd initially thought.

J. Robert Whittle

Chapter 10

The *Restitution* sailed hard through the night but was almost brought to a standstill by the thick bank of fog which again shrouded the channel at first light.

Cursing to himself, Captain Ben paced up and down the deck, occasionally stopping to listen for the sound of a ship's bell. Now running with main sails furled, he peered into the fog and shouted orders to his crew to be vigilant. *If we find Falcon, we certainly don't want to be sailing into her!* he thought nervously.

Not far away to the east, two other vessels found themselves in a similar situation. Ben had guessed right, the course he had set would have led him straight to the government ship now wallowing helplessly half a mile away. Unknown to both of them, Captain Patrick Sandilands aboard the *Golden Lady* was, true to his nature, slowly pushing on, his ship's bell clanging eerily in the mist as he approached the *Restitution*.

"SHIP AHOY TO STARBOARD!" yelled the lookout aboard the *Falcon* upon hearing the faint sounds of a bell through the gloomy haze.

"There are two vessels out there," Ben thought, listening intently. Quietly, he ordered his men to remain silent, and the helmsman to steer toward the sound.

The three vessels crept closer and closer together.

On the *Falcon*, guns were manned and ready and One-Eyed Jack had his crew standing at battle stations as everyone's ears strained to hear into the eerie stillness. Jack grinned evilly. He wasn't about to be caught unawares by any enemy gunship.

Silenced by fearful anticipation, Jake Newton's breathing was laboured, coming in short gasps, as the actor stood at the *Restitution*'s rail and peered out into the swirling mass of clouds. Eyes widening, his body began to shake as his imagination took over. He visualized roaring cannons belching flames and the anguished screams of wounded men blending with the horrifying crash of shattering timbers. His knuckles turned white as he gripped the rail. He turned to look behind him to see if the sailor who had been guarding him was still there. He was. *Do they think I might jump into the sea to escape?* his tortured mind demanded.

Trying to wipe this tormenting picture from his mind he drew himself up taller and passed a hand over his face. *Well I suppose this is better than being locked in the brig or tied to a steam engine*, he thought, shuddering as the memories returned. *I'll be lucky if I get out alive and get paid for this job. I was mighty foolish to think I could cross Lizzie Short.*

Suddenly, the bow of a vessel slid silently out of the fog immediately in front of him, narrowly missing the *Restitution*.

"HOLY HADES!" he yelped.

"JACK, YOU DOG!" Ben's relieved voice thundered from behind Jake, startling him. "TAKE A LINE ABOARD!"

Eager hands sent ropes flying between the two vessels, quickly lashing them together.

"Who the hell is that?" One-Eyed Jack asked, leaping over the side to greet Ben. He pointed to the uniformed figure of Newton, still standing at the upper deck rail.

"QUIET!" Ben yelled, waving his arms to cover both the ships. The crews understood perfectly and all eyes silently turned to the captain of the *Restitution*. Ben went to the rail and put a hand to his ear, straining to hear. *Yes, there it is again, another ship closing in fast, but is it friendly?* "It could be the *Black Otter* searching for us," Ben muttered to Jack who had followed him to the rail.

However, the sound moved away as the *Golden Lady* sailed by unseen, her warning bell soon fading in the distance. Jack scratched his head and turned to Ben.

"You say Harry Roach is searching for you?"

"Aye lad, and paid to sink the *Restitution*."

"Don't be stupid, Ben," Jack frowned, "this is a grain ship, somebody's foolin yer."

"No lad, apparently not and we're taking no chances."

"Who the devil is that, Ben?" Jack pointed again to the figure at the rail. "He gave me quite a turn," the hardened mariner admitted. "Is it his ghost? Is Davis dead?"

"Dead or alive, he's all yours now, mate," Ben chuckled, slapping his friend on the shoulder.

"Oh no he ain't, I don't want him."

"Lizzie's orders, lad. He's an actor she hired."

"What on earth am I going to do with him?"

"I don't care, just make sure you stand him on deck when you come into port. Everyone will think it's Captain Davis."

"What good will that do?"

"It'll protect the captain's job."

"All right, we'll take him," Jack grumbled, motioning to one of his men, "but ah tell ya mate, our Liz will get us all hung one of these days!"

"FOG'S LIFTIN, CAPTAIN!" the lookout shouted.

"CUT THE LASHINGS AND SET BEN ADRIFT. I WANT THAT SHIP THAT PASSED US," Jack screamed at his crew, as they quickly returned to the *Falcon*. "Set course for Hull, Ben, we'll watch yer back."

€❦❧

Leaving the tailor's shop, the partners crossed the road and turned up Mast Lane. They hadn't gone far when they heard the long, squeaky call of young Olivera hailing them. Like a charioteer, he stood in the middle of the bread cart, one foot resting casually on the empty cider barrel and the reins held firmly in his hand.

"Going to Bill's? Ah'll give yer a ride," he called, bringing the pony to a stop.

Pleased to see the young lad back to his happy self, the partners looked at each other and happily jumped onto the front corners, legs dangling over the side.

"Not there!" he ordered sternly, "over the wheels! Flash doesn't need your weight on his back."

Shuffling backward to the required position, Lizzie grinned at Quon and grasped the edge of the cart. Oly clucked his tongue and the obedient pony moved off. Gathering speed, the boy whooped with delight sending people leaping for the sidewalk as he sent the cart thundering down the ally.

"Damnit, Oly," bellowed Bill Johnson as they careened into the yard. "Slow down, yer goin ta kill somebody!"

Lizzie and Quon watched in amazement as the lad dropped his reins and raced into the bake house, emerging seconds later with half an apple pie and three plates. Setting them down on the table, he beckoned for them to join him as Clem quickly changed the empty barrel for a full one. Bill, his arms loaded with bread, began filling the cart. Oly quickly stuffed pie into his mouth, washed it down with a drink of buttermilk, and waved to two of the Johnson children who came out of the house to feed apples to the pony.

As the last armful of loaves was secure, Oly jumped to his feet and raced round the table to give Lizzie a quick hug. Within moments, he was leading his pony and cart out into the alley again. Bill and Clem, sweating profusely, came over to the table and collapsed onto the bench.

"Ah know, ah know," Bill gasped, answering Lizzie's inquiring eyes, "he's bin watching that steam engine of Charley's and now he thinks we should be loadin as fast as that thing does!"

"He's going to kill us," Clem laughed, wiping the sweat from his face with his apron.

"Bless his soul," added Bill, breathing heavily, "the lad's magnificent!"

Reaching over the table, Lizzie patted the baker's huge hand.

"And so, are you, Bill Johnson," she said softly, "now read this paper for me, will you?" Her hand slid the page of council rules across the table.

"Na what's this all about, lass? Yer can read it yer sen."

"No no, it's not that I can't read it, I just want you to tell me what you think it means."

Frowning, the baker flattened the paper out and, with Clem looking on, began to read.

"Looks clear enough to me, lass," the baker snorted, "though I never knew it before. Ah thought the public were barred from council meetings."

"And now?" asked Lizzie.

"Appears we can go," Clem chuckled, "but they'll have us voted out of there as sure as shootin, you can bet on that. It'll cause a mighty ruckus though."

"Are you sure?" she asked, looking over at Quon and raising her eyebrows.

The baker's eyes twinkled with devilment as he stared at the girl. "Yer want us ta fill all them public seats, don't ya lass?" he chuckled. "Well ah wouldn't miss this scrap for all the wheat in Hull. Leave it ta me, Liz. Ah'll 'av them council chambers full for ya tonight, you mark my words."

"Oh gosh, thanks Bill, but haven't you heard the meeting's been changed to Wednesday?"

"When did they do that?" he asked.

"Last week and they tried to keep it from me, but Nathan heard about it." Lizzie smiled ruefully and then changed the subject. "Have you met the new minister yet?"

"No lass, but 'av heard lots about him."

"From who?"

"Oly!" Bill grinned. He began to chuckle as he conjured up a picture in

J. Robert Whittle

his mind. "He told us he's seen this minister man walking around with a long stick. He said he looked pretty funny. You can't say that lad is a meek one anymore!" He came slowly to his feet and the two bakers made their way back to the bake house.

Lizzie and Quon shouted goodbye and headed up the street toward home. At the cottage gate, they stopped to listen to the sounds of cattle moving down Drover's Lane and heard the familiar sounds of Jeb and his men.

"The gypsies are back!" they said in unison, grinning as Quon opened the door.

"How's Captain Davis?" Martha inquired as they came inside.

Lizzie's eyes flicked to the clock on the mantle. "Haven't seen him today but we're going there after we've eaten. We think Jeb is back, too," she replied.

After lunch, Lizzie and Quon left the cottage with Willie and his gypsy friends running ahead of them toward the camp. But, when they arrived, they found the camp unusually quiet with no sign of activity, except for the old granny sitting beside the fire. She grinned, her toothless smile, and beckoned them closer. The children had disappeared.

Something's wrong, thought Lizzie. Following the woman's pointing hand, they moved between the wagons.

"Well, would you believe it?" she whispered, stopping abruptly and grabbing Quon's arm.

There, sitting on his bed-like seat was Captain Davis talking animatedly to a group of gypsy women and children. Willie and his friends were there, too. She couldn't hear what he was saying and was about to move closer when she heard a noise behind them. They pulled back into the shadows and found themselves face-to-face with Daisy and Ben, the young gypsy who had taught the highborn girl to ride bareback.

"What's the captain doing?" Lizzie whispered.

"He's telling them stories of strange, foreign lands across the sea," Ben whispered in an exaggerated awe-filled voice. "They can't seem to get enough!"

The sound of galloping hooves and the rattle of a cart sounded on the lane and Quon grabbed Lizzie's arm.

"It's Oly," announced Ben, as the cart stopped. "Watch."

The Portuguese boy ran over to Captain Davis and dropped on his knees beside the older man. The look of pleasure on the captain's face, as his one good arm gently hugged the boy, told Lizzie that Oly was the

104

medicine he needed. At that point, his audience moved away and Davis saw Lizzie and the others.

"So you finally found time to come see me," he growled. "Where's Jack, I need to see him. Have they caught the dog who ran me down? I need some answers, girl."

"Slow down, captain," Lizzie chuckled. Not wanting to get onto this subject with him, she tried another tactic. "Looks like your investment is already paying off."

"Investment?" he growled.

Daisy looked perplexed as she glanced over at Lizzie. Her mouth dropped open when she heard the girl's answer.

"Aye lad, investment in a family!"

His eyes softened as his arm tightened over Oly's shoulder. A smile lit up the boy's face and he looked adoringly up at his guardian.

"Wait, wait," Daisy squealed. "What family?"

"Me!" exclaimed Oly, wriggling free of the captain's grip. "Miss Lizzie means me, Tom, and Billy."

"Will somebody please tell me what you're all talking about?" Daisy asked, frowning with annoyance. "This is all very mystifying to me."

"Be quiet, girl," Davis snarled. "The lads are mine. Do yer hear me? They're mine."

Stunned by Davis' outburst, Daisy bit her lip and said nothing. Instead, she watched Oly's reaction as he jumped to his feet and grabbed the captain's beard in both hands. Staring into the old mariner's eyes, he planted a quick kiss on his nose and raced back to his cart.

Turning away, the captain wiped roughly at his eyes. "They're mine, Lizzie," he exclaimed emotionally.

"Yes, they are, captain," she agreed, dropping to her knees beside him. Daisy turned away, embarrassed and bewildered. Stopped by Quon's hand pulling her back, she sighed and stood watching.

"Listen, old lad," Lizzie whispered, "dumplin wants to have a handcart made for you, a bit like Charley Mason's, then you can move around as you want."

Captain Davis' head jerked up.

"Me? On a cart?" he muttered.

"You could visit the docks."

"T'ain't decent, lass."

"Why not, it'll only be for about a month then you'll have your strength back."

J. Robert Whittle

The gypsy woman had been watching and now walked over and also knelt down beside him. "Do it, sir," she whispered. "Will be good medicine to see your friends ... to show them you're not beaten."

Daisy blinked back a tear when she saw his determined look.

"Beaten, lass?" he hissed. "NEVER, not while Lizzie's by my side. I'll do it!"

"Right!" Lizzie exclaimed, jumping to her feet. "Come on, dumplin, let's get on with it. Oh Ben, I see the men are back from the farm. Where's your Uncle Jeb?"

"He's gone away again," Ben replied, looking apologetic.

"Already?" she asked, sounding a bit perplexed.

"He got an urgent message from my aunt over in Otford. He hopes to be back in a fortnight. He said to tell you they had a safe journey with the children."

Lizzie sighed with relief, thanked Ben, and followed Quon out to the road. Ben also excused himself and Daisy found herself alone and staring at the injured man. This heart-wrenching experience had made an indelible imprint on her mind and she felt indeed humbled. She'd seen Lizzie's power and strength giving hope and determination to the injured captain and she wished she possessed such power. She was so glad to be a part of Lizzie's plans. She quietly said goodbye to the captain who was now watching her curiously.

Before she turned the corner out of sight, she looked back and saw that the gypsies had returned to their places beside the mariner. She knew in her heart, that between Captain Davis and those wide-eyed youngsters, Lizzie's magic was at work again.

"It half past two, Wizzy," said Quon, checking his timepiece as they neared the cottage. "Let's see if mom cooked those meat pies she was making at lunch."

Shaking her head, Lizzie followed him through the gate.

Daisy, meanwhile, remembering that Lizzie and Quon may be going to the print shop to meet the new minister, hurried to catch up to them, but found they had disappeared.

Inside the cottage, Quon was delighted to find a dozen freshly baked, small meat pies, cooling on the counter, but Martha was nowhere in sight.

"I wonder where she is?" Lizzie murmured, not sure if they should help themselves.

"We have to go, Wizzy," he reminded her and, gingerly picking up one of the hot pies, he headed toward the door.

106

Deciding she wasn't hungry enough to raise Martha's wrath, she followed after him empty-handed. At the entrance to Brown's Yard, they stopped, watching the printing shop for the arrival of the new minister. As expected, it was a few minutes to three when Vicar Palmer appeared.

Following as closely as they dared, they mixed with the shoppers and watched. Appearing to look inside, instead of entering, he clutched the door frame and hesitated. Lizzie hurried to get closer. The object of their attention finally went inside and walked slowly to the counter.

"Brother Frederick?" he asked softly.

Lizzie and Quon had by now come up silently behind him just in time to hear his question. Quon gripped Lizzie's arm as they waited for Fred to respond.

Fred stared at the man of the cloth as if seeing a ghost. His hand dropped from the heavy lever and brushed sweat from his brow as the machine ground to a stop.

"Tip, is that you?" Fred asked, not taking his eyes off the stranger as he moved around the printing press toward them.

The men both moved slowly forward, hands reaching out.

"You two know each other?" Penny asked in surprise, seeing Lizzie and Quon near the door.

The minister also noticed the young pair and a quick flash of recognition passed through his mind as he hugged his old friend. Daisy moved closer, already smelling a story. Here was someone who could unravel the mystery of Fred Monk, a man who didn't often talk about his past.

"Who did you say he was?" she asked eagerly, charcoal and pad ready.

"We were brothers in the monastery," Vicar Palmer murmured, "simple novices, searching for a pathway to heaven."

"And you both came here to dockland?" Lizzie giggled. "Well, this sure ain't heaven, mister!"

"I've met you before, haven't I, girl?" said the minister, eying the outspoken girl curiously.

"Her name is Lizzie Short," Lady Sutton intervened, "a name you'd do well to remember, sir."

That name, thought the vicar, then a sudden realization struck him and he gasped. "You're that woman who's taking a seat on council, b-but you're only a girl! You were in the tailor's shop earlier today."

"Wrong," Fred growled. "She's an angel, Tip. She's dockland's princess."

Already shocked at seeing Fred Monk and finding him working in a printing shop, the sudden outburst of his old friend now surprised him even more. Percy Palmer turned away from the counter to compose himself.

"You have need of our services, sir?" Penny Sutton interrupted his thoughts and turned the conversation back to business.

"Yes, yes, dear lady," replied the vicar. "I need you to make a statement in your newspaper." He paused allowing his eyes to rest on Fred who waited expectantly. "That I, Percy Palmer, am the new vicar at St. John's on Slaughter Lane."

"Well done, Tip," Fred chuckled. "I'm proud of you, a stipend at last."

"Hold it, hold it," Daisy squealed, "why do you keep calling him Tip?"

Grinning, the men's gaze locked for an instant and they began to chuckle.

"It's a name we gave Percy at the monastery," Fred explained. "He's clumsy, tips everything over—milk, cream, communal wine! You name it, he'll spill it!"

Both men laughed heartily as memories returned. Percy's hand knocked the bell off the counter and when he grabbed for it, his elbow swept a stack of newspapers onto the floor.

"Ah told yer," Fred laughed, "ah told yer!"

By now, the shop was in an uproar and when one of the young street vendors poked his head inside, he quickly withdrew.

"Stand still, Tip!" Fred commanded. "Don't you move a muscle."

Jerking to attention, Percy backed into a corner while the others picked up the papers. Watching them, he noticed a change had taken place. These people had accepted him—laughter had destroyed their suspicions.

"I-I asked to come to dockland," he announced suddenly. "I want to help these people, but someone has to show me how. They're not very accepting of me it seems."

Fred glanced over at Lizzie and their eyes met. "We'll do all we can to help, Tip." He shook his head and turned back to his beloved press. "He's a nuisance," he muttered, "but his heart is in the right place."

"We'll show you dockland, Mister Minister," Lizzie grinned mischievously. "We'll show you the people who need helping and if they see you with us, it might help you."

Confusion filled Percy's mind—a guarded life in the monastery had hardly prepared him for this girl. He had a feeling he was going to find more than he had bargained for in dockland.

"We can start right outside this door," Lizzie snapped. "Come, let's meet the newspaper lads."

Ten dirty-faced, ragged-clothed urchins watched suspiciously as Lizzie and the minister came outside. She nodded and her partner produced an armful of newspapers, handing them to the minister.

"Right mister, the boys need 10 each," she stated, eyes flashing. "Then watch how they run to earn their supper."

Curiosity aroused, Percy complied, handing newspapers into the grubby, yet eager, outstretched hands. His heart beat wildly as he watched the thin, trembling fingers and the hopeless expression in their eyes.

"But they're only children," he said emotionally.

"They're street urchins," Lizzie hissed fiercely, "and that's their only means of existence apart from stealing. You can start by changing that, Mister Minister!" Old frustrations rising to the surface, she shook free from Quon's reassuring hand and stormed off toward the bread shop.

Standing in the doorway, Penny Sutton watched the reaction of the confused minister as Quon ran after Lizzie.

"Come back inside, vicar," she coaxed, "we should explain a few things to you."

Lady Sutton gently took him by the arm, leading him inside where she urged him to take a chair at her work table. Daisy placed a cup of hot, sweet cider on the table and joined them.

"Drink, you'll soon feel better," she murmured encouragingly.

Glancing over at his friend, Fred wiped the sweat from the end of his nose. *Tip, old friend*, he thought, *you'll be a much wiser man once you get to know dockland.*

His thoughts were shattered by Cuthbert Dunbar's squeal of pain behind him; his fingers trapped under the bedplate of the press—a situation which happened far too often. He rushed over to help the old man. Released from his trance, Percy looked up at Penny Sutton.

"Listen, Tip," she urged, glancing over at Cuthbert who was nursing his sore fingers. "We're an odd bunch of people that surround Lizzie Short. Every one of us owes her a debt of gratitude for a second chance at life."

Relaxing a little, Percy listened carefully. He knew he had experienced a strange feeling about this girl right from the start. Now, he was beginning to understand.

"I'm Lady Sutton, Penny to my friends, and this is my daughter Margaret, or Daisy, as everyone calls her. We were bankrupt and at our wit's end when Lizzie stepped into our lives earlier this year. Oh my, it seems like years ago, doesn't it, Daisy?" She paused to brush a lock of hair from her face. The minister's eyes twinkled with interest, eager for her to continue. "Unlikely as it might seem, my friend," she said softly, "Lizzie rescued us and set us on the road to prosperity. She gave Fred his dream of being a printer and resurrected Cuthbert's interest in life."

"But how can this be?" Percy muttered. "She's only a girl."

"Tip!" Fred growled from behind the press. "You don't know it yet but you're a lucky man. God sent you to help an angel."

"Oh? Yes, I will, I will," Percy said haltingly. "Bishop Tide himself told me he felt Lizzie Short held the key to dockland."

"Then support her on council," Penny encouraged patiently. "Help her bring good things to dockland; she knows how to go about it and she was once a street waif, too. Now go, we have a business to run."

Confused and unsure of himself, the minister rose. "We haven't discussed my notice in your newspaper," he muttered.

"Fred and I will write your notice," Daisy called, "mother will take your money."

"Money?" he repeated. "You're going to charge the church?"

"One penny, please, sir," Lady Sutton insisted brusquely. "We can't run a business on charity."

Two halfpennies clinked onto the counter. His will to argue had gone, though normally he would have resisted the charge. A half-hearted smile tugged at his face as he left the print shop to continue his walk through the parish.

Penny went back into her office and Daisy followed, wanting to tell her mother about her visit to the gypsy camp. While they were talking, a stranger with an unusual moustache entered the shop. Knowing Fred was there, they didn't give it any thought.

Engaged in conversation by the genial printer, Fred noted the man's faint Irish accent. He was not visiting as a customer but indeed was an admirer of Lizzie Short and wished to leave some gifts for her friends—the men who worked in the shop. Fred watched curiously, as the stranger quickly extracted three small tins from a cloth bag, explained they were a special blend of tobacco and hurried from the building.

"They're here!" called Daisy, hurrying to pick up her shawl and bag as a horse and carriage arrived outside. "Ready, mother? I don't want to keep Charley waiting."

"That's all she thinks about these days," Lady Sutton grumbled, as she, too, picked up her belongings and followed her. "Charley Mason, steam engines and printing presses."

"Get off with ya, girl," Fred grinned, "you love every minute of it."

"Yes, I do," Penny replied quietly, "I guess I do!"

Going outside with them, Fred held the carriage door open, offering Penny his arm.

"Thank you, Mister Monk," she murmured, as he closed the door behind her. She waved goodbye and quickly raised her parasol against the late afternoon sun.

Half an hour later, they had picked up Charley and were on their way to the Sutton mansion. As he and Daisy discussed the new printing press, Penny settled back into the soft leather seat of the open coach and let the events of the afternoon slowly move through her mind. In the background, she barely noticed that Charley and her daughter were arguing good-heartedly about their plans to add steam power to the printing press. She smiled contentedly and thought how different her daughter's life was from her own ... beginning in business as an aging adult. Daisy's raised voice calling instructions to the driver, broke into Penny's thoughts as she heard the words, "Billy's bread shop."

"Why are we going to the bread shop?" her mother asked.

"I need to get the latest gossip before we go home," Daisy giggled. "You two can take a look at the new print shop while we're here."

Charley's eyebrows raised as Penny Sutton shook her head in amusement.

"I'm sorry, son," Penny said in her soothing tone. "She's not quite the lady I taught her to be."

"She's fine, I like her just the way she is," Charley replied.

"Oh you do, do you?" Daisy whispered moving closer to him, her eyes sparkling with mischief. "Well, that's the first time you've admitted you even like me, Mister Mason!"

Cheeks glowing with sudden embarrassment, Charley edged away from the girl muttering, "Damn, you're a frustrating woman!"

"Steady, Charles," Lady Sutton admonished with a grin, poking him across the coach with her parasol, "remember you're a gentleman."

J. Robert Whittle

$$\mathcal{C}hapter\ 11$$

Tuesday morning after breakfast the partners first set out for the bread shop to see if there was any news on the *Restitution* or the *Falcon*. Lizzie hurried ahead of Quon, but she slowed when she heard Billy's voice up ahead. Stopping across the street in a doorway, they watched the shoppers milling around jostling for bread and sweets. Suddenly the imposing figure of an older man wearing a top hat and swinging a cane, strode toward the front. Even from the back, this man had an evil familiarity about him.

The buzz of voices quickly dropped to a whisper as people leapt from his path. Mothers clutched their children and scurried for cover. All knew Judge Harvey's fearsome reputation.

Stopping abruptly in front of the young barker's barrel, he pointed his stick menacingly at Billy. Lizzie burst into action. Jumping from the doorway, she raced to the young man's assistance.

"YOU AGAIN!" the judge boomed. An evil glint passed across his eyes as he noticed Quon.

"ARREST THAT LAD!" he yelled at two passing soldiers.

Before they had time to react, the soldiers grabbed Quon and held him fast, but he wasn't going without a fight. As they began to drag him away, he lashed out kicking wildly.

"Lock him up!" Judge Harvey snarled maliciously, then turned quickly and strode away.

"NO!" Lizzie screamed in desperation, running to bar the soldier's way.

Suddenly, Billy's ear-shattering whistle rang through the streets. It was the rallying call of sailors in battle imitated to perfection. Naval men of all ages jumped to attention, hurrying toward the sound. Street-vending urchins cocked their heads. Holding tightly to their newspapers, they raced toward the bread shop.

Vicar Palmer also heard the call as he walked through a back street a short distance away. He noticed many people stop what they were doing and begin to run. Clutching his staff and, increasing his pace, with robes flying, he curiously followed the growing crowd. A small group of shoppers and passersby who stood ready to confront the solders, joined

112

Lizzie and the bread lads.

"GET OUT OF THE WAY, GIRL," snarled one of the soldiers, roughly pushing her aside.

Hands reached out to catch her as Percy and others arrived on the scene.

"STOP THAT, YOU OAF," Percy roared, rushing forward. Taking up his staff, he began to twirl the long stick in a threatening manner.

By now, a large crowd of shoppers, sailors, street vendors and dirty-faced urchins had gathered around them.

"Get away from us," snapped one of the captors, "or we'll arrest the lot of you!"

Lizzie again ran forward pulling at the soldiers who looked furtively around at the tightening circle of working-class people.

"LET HIM GO!" Lizzie screamed, attempting to pull her partner free, before another violent push sent her careening into the crowd.

"STOP!" Percy's authoritative voice cut through the noise. "By whose authority are you arresting this young man?"

"Judge Harvey's authority."

"And for what reason?"

"Not my place to question, sir."

"Then set him free, I shall vouch for him."

"Not possible, sir."

As Lizzie accepted Billy's hand and was pulled again to her feet, she frowned. *This new minister has courage.*

Suddenly, a quick movement drew their attention when Olivera shot out from behind Tom Day, viciously sinking his teeth into the rear end of one of the soldiers.

"OWW!" the soldier screamed, releasing his grip on Quon and aiming a fist at the elusive youngster.

Quon jerked himself free, going to Lizzie's side, as others pulled Oly out of the soldier's reach and he was swallowed up by the crowd.

A smile crept across the new minister's face as he stepped between Quon and his would-be captors. His staff again went into motion twirling with lightning speed between his fingers.

Lizzie stared in fascination at their unlikely champion and Billy leapt back onto his barrel. His cheeky wit caused a ripple of laughter to run through the crowd and a quick hand movement sent the street urchins melting unnoticed into the labyrinth of shadowy alleyways and safety.

"RUN, SOLDIER BOYS, RUN," he boldly taunted, "OR FRIAR

TUCK'S GOIN TA GET YA!"

Backing away from the still-whirling staff, one soldier grabbed hopefully at the fast-moving weapon. Percy grinned and a flick of his wrist brought the staff cracking over the man's knuckles.

"FIRST HIT TO FRIAR TUCK!" Billy yelled enthusiastically.

The soldier nursed his sore fingers and exchanged a look of frustration with his partner. Shrugging their shoulders, they quickly retreated in a wild dash for freedom spurred on by a loud cheer from the spectators.

Lizzie walked over to the vicar feeling a new sense of admiration and respect for the man. *Is he the ally we've been searching for?* she wondered. Percy turned to face her and she was surprised to see a warm, mischievous twinkle in his eyes.

"THREE CHEERS FOR FRIAR TUCK!" the young barker called, raising his arms to encourage the spectators to join in.

"Young man," said Percy tapping the barrel with his staff, "may I use your dais for a moment?"

"Ain't got one, guvner."

"I mean your barrel, lad."

"Well, why didn't yer say so!" Billy's eyes found Lizzie. She nodded and he leapt to the ground turning to assist the vicar.

Climbing up cautiously, the minister first looked around at the small crowd that remained. Stretching his arms out wide, he began to talk about the Ten Commandments. No one seemed the least bit interested and many walked away. When an impish young lad hurled a dry horse dropping, narrowly missing his target, his voice faded to a whisper.

"Come down, vicar," Lizzie ordered gently, "nobody wants to hear it right now."

"But I really want to help."

"How?"

Her simple question, made Billy giggle as he again offered the minister his arm and quickly returned to his rightful place. Frowning, Percy listened for a moment to the boy's witty chatter. Shoppers began to return and came to listen to the advertised bargains he offered at the butchers, lamp makers and the bread shop. Dock workers hurried away to secure a job, when he called out the time a ship would be arriving, which dock and what cargo it was carrying.

"How? How, you ask?" the minister muttered over and over to himself.

Quon tugged on Lizzie's sleeve and began to tap on her arm. She nodded. It was time to go. As they slipped away, Lizzie puzzled over the new minister's reactions. He was obviously out of place in dockland as the poverty and misery seemed to bother him, and she'd seen him cringe at the squalor and filth of the alleyways. And yet he'd bravely challenged the authority of the law.

She had no way of knowing that Bishop Tide had personally selected Brother Palmer for this troublesome parish of East London. Ten years behind monastery walls teaching self-defence with a staff to young monks had made him an expert with the ancient weapon, but it had also left him sadly out of touch with the everyday world.

"I need a brave man," Bishop Tide had said, "a simple man whose devotion to God and his parishioners could never be swayed by money or power."

But the ways of dockland were confusing to Percy. He felt isolated and confused in this strange world of rough sailors, ships and street urchins. He wondered about Lizzie Short and her Chinese companion, about Fred and so many things.

Walking back along Chandler, Lizzie and Quon called in at the printing shop, now surprisingly quiet with no sign of street vendors. Peeking inside, they found Lady Sutton and Fred Monk in deep conversation, their backs to the door as they worked.

"I knew you'd come," Fred chuckled, glancing over his shoulder when he heard their footsteps.

Lizzie came straight to the point.

"Tell me all you know about that new minister, Fred," she demanded.

"Tip's a good man," Fred mused, "well-educated and kind." He paused, his eyes dancing with amusement, "But he's never dealt with many women and none like you, girl!"

"Or a place like dockland," Penny added quietly.

"Mister Tip good man, he be big help," Quon muttered.

"He's right you know," replied Fred. "Give the man a chance. Don't judge a horse by the blanket it wears."

Ada sat in her office gazing through the open bay window as she sipped on a glass of lemonade that afternoon. A soft breeze rustled the curtain and out of the corner of her eye, she saw a movement. Turning, she was just in time to see the young partners disappear into a building up the lane.

Entering the rag yard and not seeing anyone, Lizzie let out a yell. "MICK, ARE YOU HERE!"

The Irishman appeared almost instantly from one of the buildings.

"And now what be yer problem, moy darlin?" he asked, the usual sparkle of devilment in his voice.

"We need a handcart."

"Take that one then," he pointed across the yard. "Put it back when yer dun with it."

"No, no, we need a four-wheeled one that's lower to the ground. It's for Captain Davis."

"Hmm, you mean a builder's cart," Mick frowned. "We don't have one, lass. Ask yer dad at the brewery—they have some."

It was almost five o'clock when they reached the brewery and found Joe and Angus.

"We're looking for a four-wheeled cart, Dad," she called, looking down the row of barrels. "Mick said you would have one."

Angus grinned at the strange request. He watched Joe scratch his head with the stem of his pipe as he was often wont to do when Lizzie posed him a problem.

"Oh Mick did, did he?" said Joe. "Whatever do you need that for?"

"To carry the body of a man."

"A body?" the brewery manager gasped, staring at her in alarm.

"Aye, the body of Captain Davis!"

At that moment, Quon dashed forward catching Joe's pipe which threatened to fall on the floor. Angus ripped the cap from his head, standing stiffly to attention.

"Rrrest in peace," he mumbled, looking very solemn.

Chuckling, Lizzie glanced over at her partner who had turned away to hide his own amusement.

"Ach, show some rrespect, lassie," Angus growled. "The poorr man is deed."

"No, he ain't," Lizzie giggled, "we just want to get him out and move him around a bit."

"Ach now, yerr scarred me half to death, lass. It's noo a thing ta be jestin aboot," the brewery manager muttered before he stormed off.

A smile slowly spread across Joe's face as he reached for the pipe that Quon held out to him. "Come on," he chuckled, "let's find ya that cart."

Eagerly searching hidden corners with Joe directing their efforts, Quon finally found a cart that looked to be ideal. Pulling it out, they moved it back and forth over the warehouse floor. Its still-greased wheels moved with ease and hardly a squeak.

"With a bit of padding it will be perfect," Lizzie chuckled. "Jump on old lad, we'll ride you home."

Martha was out in the garden and heard their laughter as they came running up Goat Hill. Going to the gate to see what was happening, she frowned when she saw their passenger bouncing about like a bean bag as he clutched his pipe with one hand and held on for dear life with the other.

"By gum," the housekeeper sniggered, "yer need some padding on that thing or yer backside will be flat as a pancake!"

"One ride on that," Joe chuckled, as the youngsters helped him out, "could put a man in bed for a week. Is supper ready, Martha? These young'uns have got me home a mite early and I just realized how hungry I am."

"The mutton stew is boiling on the hearth, all I have to do is dish it up," she replied, winking at Lizzie. They all knew mutton stew was one of Joe's favourites.

Following supper, Lizzie and Quon returned to the rag yard and shouted for Mick.

"You missed him," a warehouseman told them, "he'll be down at the cottage by now."

Leaving the little handcart by an empty stable, Lizzie and Quon tore back to the cottage. Sure enough, Ada and Mick had arrived and Martha was just serving them. They slipped onto their chairs noting that Charley's remained empty.

"Joe told us you rode him home," Ada chuckled, "that was very nice of you two."

"Aye an they near killed him, too!" the housekeeper muttered, moving to the fire to give the stew pot an extra stir. Replacing the lid, she glanced over her shoulder and frowned at Lizzie.

"You two just ate half an hour ago, you're not looking for another helping are you?" asked Martha, also knowing how much they loved her mutton stew. They both grinned sheepishly and she dished them out a smaller serving.

The conversation stopped when Charley appeared at the doorway.

"Yer late, son," Martha sighed as the engineer limped to his chair.

"We were waiting for a ship to come in."

Ada tapped her spoon on her plate. "Eat first, business later," she reminded him sharply.

Thus, there was hardly a word spoken around the table until the last morsel of food was eaten and Joe moved labouriously over to his armchair.

117

Wiping his mouth, Mick casually broached the subject again by asking, "And who were you expectin, Charley?"

"*Golden Lady.*"

"Fog," Joe growled, "big bank of it in the channel, I heard somebody say. They been havin problems with it all week. It's that season."

Quon's fingers tapped rapidly on his partner's leg. Ada caught the girl's slight nod and her eyes flicked from one to the other.

"Have you had any word on Ben, Charles?" Ada asked quietly.

Nodding, Charley remained silent, his thoughts on the *Restitution*. He knew the ship could be in grave danger if Ben didn't locate the security of *Falcon* and the protection her guns afforded. He was only vaguely aware of the conversation around him and soon excused himself saying the boys would be returning for him any minute.

As the conversation continued, Martha noticed an unusual tension had developed in the air, particularly in Lizzie's conversation and Ada was being extra careful how she phrased her questions about council and tomorrow's meeting. Joe nervously fiddled with his pipe, then raised a question that was in all their minds.

"Do you need any help, love?" he asked quietly.

"Yes, I believe I do, Dad," Lizzie sighed. "I need some men to get the old shops next to the lampmaker's ready for Charley's new invention."

"What new invention?" Mick sat bolt upright. "I have two men workin there already."

"Is that what he and Daisy are always talking about?" asked Ada. "She called at the office today and mentioned Charley had eaten with them last night. I thought they were ...."

"Well they are," Lizzie cut in, "they're both courting a steam engine!"

Mick's eyes flashed wildly between the two women.

"New invention?" he muttered. "Walkin out with a steam engine? Ya ain't makin any sense, lass."

"Then talk to Charley."

"Leave it, dear," Ada patted her husband's hand. "I'll explain it to you at home."

"Evening folks," Angus McClain's voice called through the open doorway, "can ah be havin a worrd with yerr, Miss Lizzie."

"Is something wrong, Angus?" Ada inquired.

"Ach 'am not quite sure," Angus replied, frowning deeply, "but it's botherrin me somethin fierrce."

"What is?"

The brewery manager's eyes flicked between the young people, then settled on Lizzie. "W-we werre busy; he must have walked rright past us," he began.

"Who did?"

"A man drressed like a monk," Angus muttered. "We found him sitting next to a vat of whisky."

"Did he have a staff in his hand?"

"Aye, an drunk as the orrgan man's monkey, but how do ye know aboot the staff?"

"Interesting day," Lizzie chuckled, ignoring the brewery manager's question. "He got to the brewery mighty quick."

"You know this man?" Ada asked, her face growing pale.

"Tell them, dumplin."

"Him minister man."

"Ach, yerr have ta be mistaken, lassie," Angus frowned. "Yon drrunk's nay a minister, ah reckon he could'a tamperred wi the brrew if he had a mind."

"Sure he tampered with yer brew all right, Angus," Mick chuckled. "He drank a bellyfull!"

"Where is he now?" asked Lizzie, trying to keep a straight face.

"Outside in a wheelbarra sleepin like a baby!"

"Then you had better bring him in," she replied.

Joe, who had paid little attention to the conversation, now snored noisily in his chair, his arms wrapped around the little boy asleep on his knee.

"Grab Dad's pipe, Martha!" Lizzie squealed as the old man's pipe began to droop between his lips.

The housekeeper's reaction was immediate, reaching out and catching the pipe before it fell. She put the pipe down and went over to the table.

"Mick, that lad of yers is gettin mighty big for his granddad."

Mick looked over at Joe with Willie on his lap.

"Begorra, yer right, Martha. Willie is goin to slide right off!" He got up and hurried over to them. Gently removing the boy, he lay him down on the couch and covered him with the blanket handed to him by Martha. Neither Joe nor Willie woke up.

Meanwhile, a red-faced Angus arrived back at the door indicating the wheelbarrow at the bottom of the steps. Quon went out to help and Mick joined him. Together they lifted the wheelbarrow with the sleeping minister over the doorstep and into the kitchen.

"Now what are we going to do with him?" Mick asked.

The brewery manager straightened up and rubbed his back. Then, with hands on hips, he glared at Mick. "'Am away ta ma home, laddie," he hissed defiantly. "Ah'd be obliged if yer returrned ma wheelbarra when ye've dumped him!"

"Angus," Ada frowned, "don't be so uncharitable. The man needs help."

"Not frrom me lassie, ah'v done all 'am doin. I have me own lads to look after!" The Scot tipped his cap to the ladies before stepping outside and striding away.

"Well bless my soul," Martha groaned, "yer can't leave him here."

"Ah sure, hoy'll move him," Mick volunteered, "hoy'll wheel him on to the church." Quon helped him lift the wheelbarrow again, back to the bottom of the steps.

"It's amazing he doesn't wake up," said Ada, as Mick wheeled him down the garden path. "Listen to that rattling wheel, it's enough to wake the dead."

In a few minutes, Mick was back, grinning broadly as he strode through the doorway.

"Hoy gave him to the sexton," he reassured them. "I met him on the lane. He said it would give him great pleasure to find the minister a resting place."

Quon giggled.

Martha swung around to face the Irishman. "He's the grave digger, Mick. I hope he doesn't bury the poor man!"

Everyone began to laugh, quickly stifling their reaction as Ada pointed to Willie. Still chuckling, Mick went over and picked up the lad and they silently waved their goodbyes.

Later, Quon and Lizzie saw Joe off to bed and went outside in the warm evening air to look at the stars, not often seen in London. They sat on the garden wall but neither felt like talking, immersed in their own worried thoughts for Ben and the *Restitution*. Unknown to each other they were both thinking the same thing completely unaware of the battle of wits which had taken place out in the channel that day.

Chapter 12

Nearing the mouth of the Thames, the *Falcon* silently moved through the darkness. Captain Jack appeared from his cabin and went to the rail. A smattering of lights was now visible and, pleased with himself, he was relieved to know that the worries of this trip, at least, were almost over. They had an interesting tale to tell this time, for anyone eager to hear what had befallen their prey, the *Black Otter* and Captain Harry Roach.

Earlier that afternoon, a Spanish gunship bent on destruction and carrying no flags, had crept up the coast in broad daylight under cover of the fogbank. *Falcon*, hearing the roar of cannon fire to westward soon after parting from the *Restitution*, altered course immediately, assuming a British ship was in distress. Their chase of the now-distant mystery vessel abandoned.

With barely a breeze to fill their sails, by the time they reached the burning hulk of the *Black Otter,* the Spanish marauder had long since disappeared.

Ben had also heard the cannon and cautiously ordered the *Restitution* to follow the *Falcon*, still shrouded by fog and only minimally visible. Meanwhile, aboard *Falcon* and petrified with fear, Jake Newton neither blinked nor moved as he held on grimly to the deck rail having received explicit instructions from Captain Jack to stay put!

Hearing cries of help, the crew of *Falcon* scoured the sea as the lifting fog gave way to pounding waves in which the inevitable wreckage was found. In water littered with debris and bodies, they could only imagine the story of the attack until two sailors were spotted moving feebly in the water. They were brought aboard quickly but little hope remained of finding others who had been able to survive both the bombardment and the frigid waters.

"TWO SURVIVORS PORTSIDE," a lookout yelled, pointing toward the stern of the ship where a man and a boy, no doubt a cabin boy, still clung to the *Black Otter*'s name plate.

Eager sailors threw lines toward the two figures as the rest of the crew waited to assist. Anger shot through Captain Jack's brain like a hot poker when someone recognized the man as none other than Captain Roach.

Tying the rope around his chest, Roach savagely kicked the boy hurling him into the waves where he disappeared beneath the foam for too long a time. Then, amazingly bobbing to the surface, his thin, flailing arms found another piece of wood and miraculously found the strength to hold on. Obviously using his last bit of strength, he looked up and saw the ship towering above him; his lips mouthed the words 'help me' before another wave crashed over the young lad.

"GET THE BOY FIRST!" Captain Jack's voice boomed down to the sailors on the rope ladder as they pulled in Captain Roach.

Obeying orders, they left Roach who cursed feebly as waves battered him against the hull of the *Falcon*. One of the men managed to snag the lad's clothes with a grappling hook and slowly reeled him in where eager hands heaved him upward.

"BRING ME THAT NAME PLATE," was the next order and then, as they turned to the drowning captain and began to pull him in, another order was shouted out. "LEAVE HIM! LET HIM TASTE THE OCEAN AS HE WOULD 'A DONE TO US."

When the *Restitution* arrived on the scene, Ben was the first one over the side sprinting across the deck to join Jack at the rail as the men lashed the ships together once again.

"We've managed to save four survivors but I can't decide whether to spare the courts the sight of that one!" announced Jack, pointing to the familiar figure of Captain Roach floundering at the end of a rope. His cursing had grown weaker and he now desperately needed his strength to reach the ladder, where waiting sailors sneered down at him.

"Let him drown!" Ben said casually.

Behind them, Ben's enthusiastic crew leapt the rails and cheered when one of the *Falcon* sailors held up the *Black Otter*'s name plate.

"Right, now what are we going to do with Harry Roach?" Ben asked with a frown, peering over the side.

"Arrest him."

"What for, being shipwrecked?"

One-Eyed Jack glowered at his old shipmate. His fingers fiddled with his eyepatch as he struggled for an answer.

"Damnit, Ben," he muttered, "we both know he were gunnin for ya."

"But who sent him and why?"

An evil smile lit up Jack's face. "You go on yer way, lad," he chuckled. "Ah'll find it out and then deliver him to a fate worse than death. Ah'll give him to our Lizzie!"

Sailors scrambled back to their stations as whistles conveyed orders and the *Restitution* was set free. Sails unfurling, Ben worked his crew like demons and masts creaked under the strain of a freshening wind.

Gabriel sighed with disappointment as he stood at the rail with Captain Jack watching the grain ship sail away toward Hull. The excitement was over, a raiding Spaniard had robbed him of the thrill of action.

"I should have stayed home," he muttered under his breath.

Captain Jack ordered Roach pulled aboard.

"We might be able to make yer trip interesting yet, m'lad," Jack announced.

Gabriel looked quizzically at the captain and noticed Jack's one eye was shining mischievously as his sailors obeyed the order. Captain Harry Roach's nearly lifeless body was pulled over the side and sneering sailors dumped him unceremoniously onto the deck. Barely conscious and shaking uncontrollably, he moaned for mercy, obviously believing the Spaniards were his captors.

Teeth chattering with cold and his will to lie now gone, his speech was slurred as he truthfully answered Jack's shouted questions. Gabriel watched with interest as the captain dug out the facts from Roach's weakened mind.

"Who sent yer on this mission?" Jack yelled in his ear.

"T-t-twer A-A-Admiral J-J-Jones," the shaking man stammered, his eyelids twitching with pain from the salt water. He struggled to right his bearings.

"Blindfold him!" Jack snapped and a sailor whipped his neckerchief off and wrapped it around Roach's head.

"Ask him who his contact is?" Gabriel eagerly interrupted, but was silenced by a withering stare.

"Where did you meet?" the mariner hissed through clenched teeth.

"A-a-at Th-The K-K-Keg."

Barely were the words out of his mouth when Roach seemed to regain some of his strength. Shaking himself, as if from a dream, his senses began to return and he raised his hands to his face.

Anticipating the action, Gabriel leapt forward grabbing Roach's arms.

"Tie him to the main mast," Jack growled, "we've all we need for now."

Fred was working alone in the print shop that evening when he remembered the tobacco which he had put away on a shelf. He decided to open one of the tins and try the new blend, leaving the others for Gabriel and Cuthbert. Upon opening the lid, a sweet-smelling aroma assaulted his nostrils. His suspicions aroused, he remembered an experience he had had many years ago in the monastery. *There's opium in this tobacco!* he thought. His first reaction was one of anger, and then he smiled. He reached for a charcoal stick and drew a perfect likeness of the man on a piece of paper. He'd tell Penny and the men about it in the morning.

Chapter 13

Waking after a fitful sleep, Lizzie lay in bed and looked over at her clothes cupboard. *They want me to be a lady, do they? Well, if there's a council meeting tonight, I guess I had better start getting used to it!* Deciding to put on the pretty blue one with the rows of lace down the front, she took two petticoats from her drawer. *It's going to be awfully warm in all these clothes,* she thought frowning at herself in the mirror. *I hope this being a lady is worth the trouble!*

Turning this way and that, watching the fascinating transformation in the mirror as each layer of clothes went on, she noticed how the style of the dress made her shape look different and she smiled. *Now where did I put that boot hook?* She opened her top drawer. Finding it, she sat down on the side of her bed and bent to pull on one of the shiny mid-calf black boots with the fashionable heels. She giggled. *Maybe Penny is right,* she thought, *I need some dainty shoes and these certainly can't be called that! Oh well, they'll almost be hidden underneath all these layers.* When she finished the tedious job of lacing the high boots, she brushed her long, soft curls and tied them back off her face with a matching ribbon. Clara had thought of everything.

Her eyes lingered on the mirror. *I am a lady,* she thought, *but what a bother!* Twirling around once, she bumped into the bed and giggled. She opened the door and took a deep breath. As she walked slowly down the stairs, she knew Ada would approve. She even felt like a lady.

Joe looked up and grabbed the pipe from his mouth. Martha set down the pan she was drying with a clunk and Quon's fork clattered noisily onto his plate. Willie dashed through the door, skidding to a stop as he peered at the strange new look of his Aunt Lizzie. He walked slowly over to her as she twirled around for them. He leaned over, standing almost on his head, as he tried to touch the soft frills of her petticoats.

"You look wonderful," Ada cried from the doorway, "doesn't she Mick … everyone? Her voice trailed off as she noticed Willie. She began to giggle. "What are you doing, son?"

"She's a sight for sore eyes, is our lass," sighed Joe.

Mick stood absolutely still and grinned, watching his two favourite young people. It wasn't very often they saw Lizzie dressed up in her finery and his eyes flicked over to Quon. The boy stood up, but there was a puzzled faraway look in his eyes, as he stared at his idol.

"Well, say something ya little turd," Lizzie giggled.

Unable to put his thoughts into words, Quon shook his head and sat back down. Just then, Charley arrived. He complimented Lizzie on her outfit but they could all tell he was still worrying about Ben although he didn't say anything,.

"You need a parasol and a hat now—that would complete the transformation," he added.

"But I don't have a parasol," she moaned.

"Yes, you do," said Martha. "Daisy Sutton left one here last week. I'm sure she won't mind you using it." She went over to the door and looked behind it, producing a frilly yellow and blue object.

Lizzie giggled as she took it from Martha and examined it.

Willie sat down at the table but toyed with his breakfast, still not able to take his eyes off his aunt. Quon reached out with his fork pretending to steal a piece of his ham and the little boy reacted instantly.

"NO!" he ordered. "Grandma, stop him."

"Eee!" Quon squealed, jerking his hand back when the housekeeper's wooden spoon crashed onto the table beside his hand and her voice sternly warned him to behave.

"Patrick should be in soon, shouldn't he, Charley?" Mick asked, standing up and going toward the door.

"Should be here later today, *Golden Lady* was sighted yesterday near the coast."

Mick called a greeting to someone outside and everyone heard the familiar laughter of the Grim boys. Handing Joe his cap, Quon helped the old man on with his jacket. Lizzie ran upstairs and returned with her straw hat.

"We'll walk you to the top of Goat Hill, Dad," she said giving him a hug.

The morning sunshine broke through the thick cloud cover as Abe Kratze watched Charley and the Grim brothers go past heading down to the docks. Then his attention became riveted on a Dawson vessel slowly manoeuvring into a position near Charley's machine. So engrossed was he, that he didn't notice Lizzie and Quon quietly come up beside him.

"What yer watching?" she asked quietly, trying not to startle him.

Abe jumped and staggered backwards, his spectacles slipping from his nose. He caught them with a bony hand but, unable to see clearly, he squinted at the unfamiliar, hazy, shape of the lady.

"Can I help you, my dear?" he whined.

Quon touched her elbow and his hands began to spin wildly.

"Oh fiddlesticks," exclaimed Lizzie, "we need two cushions for the cart, Mister Kratze. Have you any cushions we could use?"

"Lizzie …?" the old man mumbled as he fumbled to get his spectacles back on his nose. "My gracious, I thought you were somebody else, my dear," he said, peering at her in surprise.

Turning, he shuffled back into his shop and they followed.

"Well, do you?" she asked more loudly.

"Do I what?" the tailor muttered absent-mindedly.

"Have any cushions?"

Obviously confused, Abe shuffled over to his table sitting down heavily on his chair. Lizzie watched him carefully, feeling her partner's fingers spelling his concern on her arm. When the old man reached for his kettle with his bare hand, she rushed forward.

"NO!" she said sharply. "It's hot, Mister Kratze!" She looked over at Quon and frowned, then found a rag to wrap the handle and quickly made his cup of peppermint tea. She set it down in front of him and her eyes searched the old man's face. Abe stared back at her with an unusually vacant look in his eyes.

Quon's hand touched her back and she turned to find him sniffing the air. *Yes, there is a peculiar sweet smell in here,* she thought as she followed her partner's pointing finger to Abe's smoking pipe balanced on the edge of the counter.

"What is it, dumplin?" she asked.

"Good morning, Mister Kratze," Clara Spencer's voice rang through the store as she entered carrying the tailor's breakfast. "Oh, hello Miss Lizzie and Mister Lee," she continued cheerfully. "My, don't you look smart this morning, miss, your dress fits you nicely." She stopped suddenly, glancing from one to the other as she also sniffed the air. "Oh good gracious," she groaned, "he's smoking that stinking stuff again."

"Stinking stuff?" Lizzie snapped.

Quon pushed past her. Picking up the pipe, he walked to the door and flung it out into the street. Setting her tray down in front of the tailor, the dressmaker shook her head sadly.

"Where did he get it from, Clara?"

"A foreign gentleman gave it to him yesterday afternoon," Clara whispered, "it fair gave me a headache and Mister Kratze went quite funny in the head when he smoked it." She paused and her finger pointed to a small square tin on the shelf. "It's there, if you want to look for yourself."

"He not eat his breakfast so best take Mister Kratze for walk, please Missus Spencer," Quon ordered. "Take down see Charley on dock."

"But sir," Clara murmured, "he'll be cross, and I've work to do."

"It's all right, love," Lizzie coaxed gently, "he's not well and the fresh air and walk will do him good. Keep him out until lunch time. I think he will go quite willingly right now. Coming home may be a different story."

Concern clouded the dressmaker's eyes but she soon found Lizzie was right and Mister Kratze allowed her to take his arm and they left the shop. Clara now wondered if she'd done right by telling Lizzie of the strange tobacco. She would have a lot of work to catch up on and she feared he would be very angry with her.

Lizzie sat at the table and began to write something in large letters on a piece of paper. "What is it?" she asked, watching Quon pick up Abe's tobacco tin and open it.

"Don't know yet," her partner grunted.

She picked up the paper and beckoned him toward the door. He moved slowly after her, putting the tin closer to his face and cautiously sniffing the container. Well ahead of him, her long skirt rustled as she walked quickly to the door. He made a face, replaced the lid, and slipped the tin into his pocket. She had already gone outside but stopped just outside the door. He held the door open wondering what she was doing.

"You can close it now," she said, from behind the door, indicating the paper which she had pinned to it. It advised customers that the tailor would return after lunch.

Quon glanced at the notice then turned toward the street.

"Do you know what sort of tobacco it is, dumplin?"

"Not sure, but we find out mighty qlick."

She raised her parasol and took Quon's arm. Heading toward the bakery, heads turned to watch them. They didn't immediately recognize her as she strolled confidently arm-in-arm with Quon Lee, who had always been a bit more concerned with cleanliness than she. After they had gone a block, she remembered why they had stopped at Abe's that morning. They still didn't have the cushions for the handcart.

There was no sign of Oly or the bread cart as they made their way to Bill Johnson's. People hurried along intent on their shopping and drays rumbled by as they turned into the lane. They were almost at the gate when they heard a call from behind.

"Miss Lizzie, Mister Quon!"

The new minister waved from his carriage as it trotted toward them. "I have a message for you."

"Oh, who from?" Lizzie asked.

"Fred at the printing shop."

Before they could say anything further, the baker saw them as he crossed the yard calling out at the top of his voice, "LIZZIE, OLY LEFT A MESSAGE FOR YA!"

Following them into the bake house yard, Percy nodded at the two bakers as Missus Johnson came closer to investigate the stranger in the long brown robe. Her eyes registered her approval of the girl's new dress.

"Are you a monk, sir?" she whispered reverently.

"Yes, I was, dear lady," Percy smiled pleasantly, "but now I'm your new minister."

"We call him Tip, Missus Johnson," Lizzie chuckled, "he's a clumsy one, knocks everything over. His real name is Vicar Palmer."

Bill stopped and eyed the minister suspiciously. He set down the fruit loaf in the middle of the table and moved the tankards of cider as far away from the minister as he could.

"It's no good inviting disaster then, is it luv?" he chuckled.

"Am I invited to partake, sir?" Percy inquired.

"Of course you are," Missus Johnson assured him, "'elp yerself."

"Oly sez Patrick's in the Thames," Bill growled, "should be in on't late tide."

As Percy reached for a tankard, he bumped Bill's elbow, spilling cider down his shirt front.

"I warned you," Lizzie giggled.

Missus Johnson sighed, hiding her amusement behind her hand as Quon's eyes met Lizzie's across the table and his fingers went to the tin in his pocket. He extracted it and set it on the table.

"You have one of those tins, too?" Percy spluttered, showering crumbs all over the table. "The message from Fred is about those tins."

"'Av got one of them, too." Bill muttered. "A well-dressed foreign gentleman, Spanish ah think, gave me an Clem one yesterday."

Lizzie's eyes narrowed. "Why would he do that?" she asked.

"He said he was an admirer of yers and wanted to give us a gift of some special tobacco."

"Exactly what Fred was told by their visitor," added Percy.

Frowning, Quon took the lid off and standing up, waved the tin under their noses. Clem took a deep whiff and grimaced. Bill followed suit and turned his head away.

"Let me see." The minister reached into the tin, feeling the texture of the tobacco-like substance in his fingers. Then he brought the tin closer to his face and sniffed liberally. He scowled fiercely at the familiar sweet aroma. His mind flashed back to the monasteries and the monk's use of this substance to enhance their dreams.

"What is it, Tip?" Lizzie whispered.

"The same as the others … opium."

"What is opium?" she asked.

"It makes men foolish, steals their brains and causes them to do things they wouldn't normally do. Have you smoked any of it?" asked Tip, looking from Lizzie to Quon.

"Oh no, but Mister Kratze has."

"How do you know?"

"He was acting very strangely and his pipe was full of it," she replied.

This startled Connie Johnson and she watched her husband as he walked slowly back to the main bakery building. In less than a minute, he returned with two identical tins and placed them on the table in front of the minister.

Rolling his eyes, Percy shook his head. "This is wicked, wicked. Who is the man who would do this?"

Lizzie bit into her lip as her anger rose. She watched Quon beat a rapid tattoo on the table before he came to his feet. She nodded. As he hurried away, she called after him, "Meet me at Ada's office."

"What about Captain Davis?" Bill asked.

"He's safe," murmured Lizzie, deep in thought. "He's supposed to be aboard the *Falcon* but the gypsies won't let a stranger near him anyway. Tip, go tell Fred at the print shop."

Without waiting for an answer, she turned and ran out of the yard. Frustrated when her skirts got in the way, she grumbled, picked them up, and continued on, as her mind conjured up pictures of disaster. Puffing heavily by the time she reached the top of Pump Street, she skirted around the heavy Slaughter Lane traffic, and through the door into Ada's office.

"Ring the bell, Ned," she gasped, collapsing onto her knees.

Startled first by the banging door, Lizzie's actions brought fear to Ada's eyes. Ned followed her order then rushed around the desk toward her.

"What is it, love?" he asked with a concerned frown, wanting to help her up but she waved him away.

Unable to speak, she pointed to the small square tin on Ned's desk.

"This?" Ned asked, picking up the unopened tin and holding it out to her. Lizzie nodded her head. "But it's only tobacco, lass."

Lizzie shook her head emphatically, snatching the tin from his hand she tried to pull the lid off.

"Poison!" she said hoarsely, shaking her head in dismay.

"Poison!" Ada murmured as Mick came through the back door. "Mick, Lizzie says that man gave you and Ned poisoned tobacco."

Lizzie held out the tin to him and, with one mighty twist, Mick's strong fingers tore the lid off. He smelled the contents and his face twisted in anger. He handed it to Ned and offered a hand to Lizzie gently lifting her to her feet.

"It makes men go crazy, Mick. Where's your tin?"

The Irishman's face drained of colour. "Tiny …!" Leaping for the door, they guessed he was on his way to the stables.

∞⊂⊃∞

On the Thames, just passing the East India Dock, Patrick Sandilands stood on the deck of the *Golden Lady* watching the hubbub of activity along the mighty waterway. He chuckled to himself as he anticipated the reunion with friends and supper at Joe's cottage. Although it had not been long since he had been with them, for Lizzie's birthday only about three weeks previous, he was eager to see them all. They were like family to him, especially Lizzie. A family away from Aberdeen—the life of a seafaring man did not leave a great deal of room for such a luxury.

∞⊂⊃∞

In his office, Joe listened to the thump of running feet on the stairway as he casually stuffed his pipe with tobacco from the fancy tin—his sense of smell impeded by the aromas of the brewery.

The match burst into life and he prepared to take the first puff.

"NO!" Quon gasped, bursting into the room. "DON'T DAD!"

131

Startled, Joe stopped. Quon blew out the flame and sat down opposite the old man and began to explain. Joe's face turned dark as he listened. Hands shaking, he emptied the pipe back into the tin and banged the lid on.

"You better go find John Watson, lad," he said hurriedly. "He's over at the Corn Lane warehouse. Ah'll get hold of Angus. Go quickly."

Grabbing Joe's tin, Quon left, running noisily back down the stairs. He knew John Watson would be harder to find amongst the buildings of the old corn mill. When he arrived, there was not a soul in sight. He ran from building to building, yelling for the whisky distiller in every doorway.

Finally, a distant echo led him into a dimly lit room where a workman pointed out his quarry. Pipe belching smoke, Watson sat on a small barrel in a corner. His unseeing eyes stared straight ahead. Quon coughed at the pungent, sweet aroma. *Too late!* he thought. *He already smoking it!* Snatching the pipe from the brewer's mouth, Quon crushed it under his heel while his eyes searched the room for the distinctive square tin.

Watson grinned at him foolishly, slobbering spittle down his chin. Locating it, Quon slipped the lid off and discovered only a small amount of the tobacco missing. He breathed a sigh of relief.

"Walk him 'round yard for hour," he called at two gaping workmen. "Bacco bad, velly bad!" They looked at him with a puzzled expression but the young man raced out of the yard without more explanation. Ten minutes later, he ran through the front door of the TLS office. Mick had just come in the back door and Lizzie was waiting for them. The foreman grinned as he waved his tin in the air.

"Hoy caught Tiny before he lit the darned stuff," Mick chuckled. "How is everyone else?"

"Joe all right, but Mister Watson, him smokin," Quon gasped, his chest heaving from the long run. Sliding the two tins onto Ada's desk, he glanced at Lizzie reading the question in her eyes.

"Dad getting tin from Angus."

"Seven tins," Lizzie whispered. "How many more can there be? Can you describe the man who gave you the tobacco?"

Ada's blood raced and her heart began to pound as she watched this girl, whom she had known since a child, go into action. She could almost feel the fire burning in Lizzie's soul, no longer the mischievous genius, now a woman—a woman with power and purpose.

Standing beside Ada's desk, Mick and Ned described the stranger to

Lizzie, each man adding pieces of the puzzle.

Ada suddenly gasped.

"Has anyone checked on Charley?"

Turning pale, Ned sat down on the corner of his desk, and Mick strode for the door.

"Stop!" Lizzie snapped, her eyes squinting in thought. "Nobody could get past the dock guards. Charley's safe." Thinking hard, she moved toward the door and Quon followed. Mick stepped aside to let them pass. "You mentioned a scar on his cheek," she murmured, "but did he have a beard?"

"No, he didn't," Ada said quickly, "he had a thin moustache."

"Sure yer right, luv," Mick agreed, "and twisted at the ends."

"Waxed," Ned corrected him, "like an army man."

The St. John's clock struck three as they walked slowly toward the cottage. Lunch time had passed and hunger gnawed at their bellies.

"We ain't got time for eating right now, dumplin," Lizzie sighed, hearing her partner's stomach rumble.

Hands on hips, Martha called to them from the garden, sending Willie racing out to meet them. His playmates followed along behind.

"Grandma cross," he moaned, "you better come and eat."

Quon grasped her arm and pointed.

"Lefty come," he said urgently. "He in big hurry."

"Charley's all right!" the old mariner panted when he reached them, stumbling tiredly on the uneven surface as he handed the tin to the girl.

Lizzie's eyes flashed as she passed it to her partner. Quon's fingers quickly checked the unbroken seal and raced off back toward the office.

"You saw Charley, Lefty?"

Her question brought an instant nod from her old friend. "Y-yes, miss," he struggled for words, "but they'd forgotten ta give it ta him. One of the warehousemen still had it. It were unopened."

"How did you know about it?" asked Lizzie, helping him over to the grass.

She sat down also and breathing heavily, Lefty began to relate the story.

"I-I were at the print shop this morning when th-that new minister c-c-came in talking about the tobaccy. I-I told it to some of the lads when I got back to the dock and-and one of them remembered the tin," Lefty said breathlessly.

"You've done well, old lad," she complimented him. "Now rest a bit until you get your wind back."

"What's the occasion, Liz?" he asked, looking at her curiously.

Staring down at her high-topped boots and the clean, white petticoats that peeked out from below her skirt, she grinned.

"I'm becoming a lady, Lefty, but I think I've had about enough of it for this day and these boots are too hot! Fiddlesticks, I'll have to dress up again for the meeting tonight," she mumbled. She suddenly came to her feet and picking up her skirts ran off leaving him open-mouthed.

Halfway back to the cottage, Quon, returning from the TLS office, saw her disappear through the garden gate.

"Wot's wrong, luv?" the housekeeper's voice inquired with surprise as the girl bounded through the door and ran upstairs to her room. Then Quon appeared at the door; he was smiling.

"Wizzy change, me eat," he stated solemnly. His eyes roamed onto a plate of meat sandwiches on the table.

"Then eat!" Martha snapped, now having some idea of what was going on. "Ah made 'em for the two of yer. I sent Willie out to tell yer, but yer never came. Yer just leave me here wonderin wot's happenin." Finished her ranting, she sat down heavily in one of the chairs and watched Quon devour several of the sandwiches washing them down with a glass of cider.

"Right, that's better," Lizzie exclaimed, running back down the stairs some minutes later.

Sighing, Martha passed her the nearly empty plate while she looked the girl over. Gone was the fashionably dressed young woman, now back into her chequered-top work dress and well-worn boots. Her old, floppy cap dangled in her hand and Martha was sure that the devil-may-care twinkle in her eyes spelt trouble for someone.

She hastily put on her hat and took a sandwich in each hand. Leaning forward, she startled the housekeeper by giving her a quick kiss on the cheek.

"We'll be home at six, mum. Don't you worry now, the council meeting is not until eight and then I'll get dressed up again." She sighed, making a face.

Chapter 14

Falcon and One-Eyed Jack were sailing for home with Captain Davis' double now tied to the main mast—the only way they could persuade him to stay in that position. The deception worked well as passing ships saluted the government vessel in their usual manner. Ahead of them, *Golden Lady* docked in the early hours of the morning. Reporting to Charley a few hours later, he handed over the manifest for their cargo of cheese and the dockmaster supplied the Scot with some of the local news and events which had taken place since his last visit.

"Ach yerr jesting man," Patrick chuckled, when told of Lizzie's application for council. With a grin, he added, "Grracious me, she'll torrment 'em all ta death!"

80C8

Arriving at Brown's Yard at half-past four, Lizzie frowned when she saw Tip hurrying toward them.

"Have you found out who the tobacco man is yet, Miss Lizzie?" he bleated. "I think authorities should be informed."

"You have done so?"

"Oh, no miss, I only thought to suggest it."

"It's all right, Tip. I'll deal with it, for the time being," she said in a voice which dismissed him.

This excited exchange just outside the doorway brought Fred, Daisy and her mother to the counter to listen. They watched with amusement as the new minister's expression changed from concern to surprise as he experienced Lizzie's confident approach.

"Lizzie, Quon, this is the man you need to find," interrupted Fred, raising his voice to get their attention. When they stepped into the shop, he grinned broadly and beckoned them to come to the counter. He showed them his drawing saying, "This is your opium man. He's tall, slim and I also detected a slight Irish accent."

"That's very good, Fred. Can you do a few more of these?"

"Of course," said the printer, cocking an eye at her, "will 10 more do?"

"Five should be plenty and, add an incentive, offer a ten-guinea reward for information, but distribute them cautiously. We don't want to alert him. You may need to explain it to your newsboys if they can't read."

Penny Sutton smiled. Here she was again, listening to a general deploying her troops, and it sent a thrill up her spine.

"Daisy, tell Billy to enlist the newspaper sellers. We need this man found quickly," Lizzie was saying. "Only the eyes and ears of the street urchins can do that!"

The minister could hardly believe his ears. This girl's orders were being followed with enthusiastic urgency.

"Daisy," Lizzie called after the girl who was hurrying toward the door. "Take Tip with you, he might learn something!"

Quon tugged on her sleeve, pointing at the clock on the wall.

"Yes, you're right, dumplin. We have to get ready for a council meeting."

"Bill Johnson is rallying your supporters. We'll all be there," announced Penny, looking over at Fred and Cuthbert who nodded enthusiastically. "It's a shame Gabriel is going to miss this! I do hope everything is going well with his adventure," she added, but Lizzie and Quon had already departed.

Outside, the partners ran into Lefty as he crossed the yard and breathlessly stopped them.

"Miss Lizzie," he mumbled, holding out an official-looking sheet of paper.

"What is it, lad?"

"A notice, miss. Charley said to bring it straight to ya. I've been trying to find where ya was."

Frowning, Lizzie read the notice as Penny and Fred came out of the print shop to see what was going on. A sudden apprehensive silence awaited her comment.

"They've cancelled the meeting!" Lizzie hissed.

"What!" snapped Penny. "Why?"

"They say," she continued sarcastically, looking at the paper, *'due to unforeseen circumstances, monthly meetings will resume on the 27th of July.'*

"It's only a month," Penny offered, "and by that time you'll be better prepared for them."

"They're scared of you, lass," Fred chuckled, "you're a woman and a challenge to their whole way of thinking. They're scrambling for time to find a way of dealing with you."

"And of course they're missing several of their principal players," Lizzie added with a chuckle.

"Wizzy." Quon looked at her seriously then broke into a grin. "When front door close, go in back. We not beaten yet!"

"Right then," she sighed, "it's time we attacked them where they least expect it."

Up at the gypsy camp, Captain Davis viewed the hard, wooden bottom of the handcart with obvious displeasure, grumbling fiercely to the olive-skinned lady who had been his nurse through the worst days of his recovery. Shouting orders in Romany, she quickly produced a grain sack padded with rags and had one of the men help him into the odd conveyance. Willie and four of his friends gathered around giggling and whispering as the captain got settled.

"There, I'm mobile again!" he chuckled gleefully, straightening the gypsy hat on his head. "Wheel me down to the cottage, children."

Squealing happily, the three boys and two girls went around behind the cart and pushed. They got it out onto Drover's Lane but it wobbled and bounced into the ruts making it almost impossible to steer. Sheer determination, with encouragement from their passenger, finally overcame the problem and they managed to get the contraption moving again. With a valiant effort, they pushed Captain Davis down the lane and through the garden gate at Joe's cottage.

"You can go now," he announced. "It's all right to leave me here."

Inside the cottage, supper was being served to a noisy group as Patrick and Charley had recently arrived. Everyone was glad to see the popular Scot and were all talking at once. Martha banged two lids together demanding quiet.

Out in the lane, Davis sat quietly listening, not having realized how much he missed his friends. But the one sound he was hoping to hear was the tinkle of Lizzie's laughter and that was noticeably absent.

Meanwhile, Lizzie and Quon were approaching the cottage along Slaughter Lane. Deep in conversation, they were almost at the gate when Lizzie noticed the conveyance but couldn't see the captain for the trees.

"That look's like …?" she whispered to Quon in a puzzled tone.

"Cap'n Davis' cart!" he grunted.

She cast her partner a withering look of doubt and her curiosity now aroused, she quickened her pace. They were almost at the gate when they heard voices calling to them and two gypsy women ran around the corner.

"We sorry, Miss Lizzie!" they cried in unison, gesturing frantically with their hands and pointing to the cart. "The children bring him here, they do anything he asks."

"GO AWAY!" boomed the captain's voice from behind the shrubs.

"Leave the old goat here!" Lizzie called back to them as she went to see the captain. "He's doing fine. We'll see he gets back."

"Old goat, am I?" grumbled Davis. "Ah'll have the skin flayed off yer back, girl!"

"Not today you won't," she replied with a grin. "Windbag!"

Patrick and Mick interrupted them as they came outside to investigate the voices.

"Ach arre ye nay glad ta see me, girrly," the big, red-bearded Scot roared, striding toward her.

"PATRICK, you're back!" she cried, running into his open arms.

Patrick put the girl down slowly and stared at the figure of Captain Davis over her shoulder.

"What on earth?" he whispered, walking around the cart. The men had told him of Davis' accident but the withered-looking captain, with his mud castings on leg and arm, was a sorry sight from the foreboding-looking ship's captain he had seen only weeks before. "My worrd, lad," he frowned, as a sparkle lit up his eyes, "arr yerr noo lang furr this world?"

"LIZZIE," growled Davis, "GET THIS DAMNNED HEATHEN AWAY FROM ME!"

"Bring that noisy devil inside," Joe commanded from the doorway. "His bellowing is enough to wake the dead. I thought you wanted his whereabouts kept secret."

As the captain grumbled loudly, Patrick picked him up and carried him inside with the help of the others to hold his bad leg and arm. They made him comfortable in Joe's chair, turning it to face the table. Then, Quon returned outside to move the handcart out of sight behind the house.

Davis was uncomfortable with the situation at first but once he caught his breath and relaxed, he looked all around and noticed young Willie watching from behind cook's wide expanse ... a humourous picture as she held her big wooden spoon in a threatening gesture.

"Quiet now, the lot of yer, and sit down," Martha shrieked, displaying a seldom-seen flash of temper. "This is my time and my rules apply."

An uneasy silence came down upon the cottage. Hidden by the table,

Quon's fingers tapped on Lizzie's leg. She smiled, glancing across at the captain.

His eyes had lost their hardness and in the stillness they were surprised to hear the battle-hardened mariner whisper, "I'm sorry, Martha."

"Can you manage to cut your food, Mister Davis?" Ada inquired as she pulled her son's dish in front of her and attacked it with fork and knife.

"No, ma'am, I'm afraid I can't," he replied rather sheepishly.

"Sure hoy'll do that for yer, lad," volunteered Mick, sitting nearest to him.

Nodding grimly, the captain looked around the table at each of them. Then, his eyes settled on Lizzie.

"We can't leave *Falcon* tied up too long, lass," he sighed with concern. "I need to take her out."

"Captain," Martha scolded, "we eat first in this house, and then you can talk business."

He doesn't know, Quon's fingers tapped on her leg as the dejected captain kept his peace.

Patrick winked at her and took his first mouthful of food.

Later, as the last empty plate was cleared from the table, Mick posed the first question.

"Did ya find any more tobacco, Liz?"

"Yes, we got three tins from the printers."

Listening intently, the captain's eyes clouded with annoyance. Unable to comprehend the importance of this subject, his temper began to rise again.

Ada intervened. "Be patient, captain, we have a grave problem on our hands …," she began.

"Tobacco, a grave problem?" Davis interrupted.

"Poisoned tobacco, sir."

"Poisoned toba…?"

His sentence was cut short as Lizzie interrupted. "Yes, and another bit of news. Judge Harvey has cancelled the council meeting tonight."

"I think we've all heard about the council meeting," Ada sighed. "Lefty was desperately trying to find you. Maybe it's better this way, love."

"Looks like they've beaten us, lass," Joe muttered, "ah knew they'd have something up their sleeve to stop yer."

Scratching his beard with puzzled amusement, Patrick could no longer contain his inquisitiveness. "Ach lassie, ah'd be mighty obliged if ye'd tell me what arre ye all talkin aboot!"

"An excellent idea!" Davis growled sarcastically.

Lizzie stood up. Standing barely five foot four inches tall, she tossed her head defiantly. Her eyes began to glow as mischievous thoughts raced through her head. Slowly, she detailed the events of the day. When she finished, she looked around at the faces of her friends. They were silent, knowing there had to be more. They knew their Lizzie well.

"I can see you want to know just what I plan to do about all this," she added in a subdued voice, trying to look serious.

There was a soft murmur of 'ayes.'

"Well I'm not through with them by any means, no matter what they might want!" With that, she laid out an audacious plan to take the opium-laced tobacco to the next council meeting and give them to the council members. "It's possible we could turn their grumpy, miserable outlook to one of laughter and lunacy, don't you think?" she chuckled. "And that's only the beginning," she added, a twinkle in her eyes.

Ada and Mick looked at each other. Is she serious? Their eyes asked each other.

"Ach, ah just might stay arroun awhile!" grinned Patrick. "Ah've an inkling ye might be in need of some assistance, an ah would'na miss this ferr the worrld."

This broke the serious mood and Mick was the first to move. Standing up with his now-sleeping son lying against his shoulder, the foreman murmured goodnight and urged his wife to hurry.

Ada put on her shawl and went over to the captain.

"Now you can ask her about the *Falcon!*" she whispered.

Davis looked at her curiously and was going to say something but she hurried out of the door. Instead, he turned to Lizzie.

"Take me to the *Falcon,* girl. I must see my ship!"

Winking at her partner, Lizzie snapped a curt reply. "Can't captain, she's at sea."

"AT SEA!" Davis exploded, then seeing Martha's stormy expression, he lowered his voice, "under what master?"

"You!"

Davis' jaw dropped open and he stared at Lizzie.

The rattle of wheels outside interrupted their conversation. Then the unusual sound of Nathan's laughter grabbed their attention.

"Nathan!" Quon yelped in alarm. "Wizzy, we forget Nathan!"

Supported by Wick and Dan, the trader staggered drunkenly into the cottage babbling incoherently. Frowning fiercely at the interruption, Davis sniffed the air.

"Opium!" he snarled.

Dashing out to the buggy, Quon returned with two familiar-looking tins and Nathan's still-smoking pipe.

"Greedy turd!" Lizzie snorted. "I should have known he'd have two tins."

"Walk him 'till he drops!" advised the captain.

"You know about opium?" asked Lizzie, as the gypsies turned around and led Nathan back outside. "Why didn't you say something?"

Ignoring her question, he stated emphatically, "I know everything, girl, and who supplies it!"

Quon reached inside his pocket for Fred Monk's drawing. Opening the paper, he gave it to Lizzie.

"Is this him?" she asked, handing the paper to the captain.

As he studied the picture, Nathan's voice faded away down the lane. Davis scratched his beard and he began to mutter incoherently, struggling with his memory. Finally, he spoke so they could all hear.

"Van ... Van," he began. "Captain Albert Van Bloom. He said he was Dutch when we stopped his ship out in the channel, but he lied. We turned his vessel away later." Captain Davis' memories seemed to flood back now. "I also heard those Chinese from under Tower Bridge were after him for stealing their opium trade."

Lizzie and Quon's eyes met. Could it be the Tong were the secret allies they needed in the struggle against this new threat? Her almost imperceptible nod sent Quon racing for the door, snatching the picture from the captain's hand as he passed.

"Where's he going?" Charley asked.

"For a mud bath," she replied, shaking her head sadly.

"A mud bath!" asked Charley, who had been very quiet so far that evening.

"Yes, a mud bath." Lizzie retorted. "And that's all I'm telling ya, so go home Charley, I can hear your cart arriving."

"Are you staying with me, Patrick?" he asked, coming slowly to his feet and grimacing at the pain.

"Nay, lad, ah'll be stayin aboarrd ma vessel."

As the engineer moved slowly toward the door, Lizzie glanced over at the Scot and, with twinkling eyes, she winked at him. Patrick's heart skipped a beat. This was the Lizzie he had always known and loved, the feisty young woman whose courage had made so many good things happen to the people around her. Her fight had also become his fight and he silently vowed this would never change. For years now, Lizzie had been like a daughter to him, the daughter he had never had. *Och aye, perhaps one day one of me strrapping lads will prroduce a spirrited little girrl just like Lizzie!*

Growing more irritated with each passing second, Davis tried to get up but, failing to do so, simply glowered at the girl. In frustration, he banged his fist on the chair, found his cap and flung it wildly at Lizzie.

"LIZZIE SHORT," he bawled, "where the hell is my ship?"

"Jack took it out."

Keeping a stern face, Patrick retrieved the captain's cap and held on to it pretending to smooth out the wrinkles.

"Traitor!" exclaimed the captain.

"He saved yer job, I'll have you know, sir!" snapped Lizzie, standing up and leaning over the table toward him.

"And what about the admiralty spies?" Davis exclaimed. "What happens when they don't see me on board?"

Lizzie sat back down and took a deep breath.

"They will see you, we have it covered," she said calmly.

Intrigued, Patrick glanced over at Joe and Martha for some clue to the severity of the situation. The old man was contentedly puffing on his pipe and Martha was happily tending the fire. He knew then that Lizzie had everything well under control, but what about Quon? Where had the lad gone?

Chapter 15

Quon peered over the parapet wall into the gloomy darkness under Tower Bridge and tried to locate the Tong guards. He had made good time here, using the ancient tunnels from dockland and hitching rides whenever possible. The Tong had given their assistance to him twice before but were savagely protective of their master. Would they remember him? Would they care, or would they try to kill him once again?

He understood the risk but took a deep breath and squared his shoulders. It was a necessary risk and he thought ahead to the soothing bath which would be waiting on his return. He took the first faltering step down the well-worn stone steps to the river below. It was getting very dark under the bridge and he gingerly stepped off the last step into the mud. Fighting back his fears, he moved forward, eyes darting to left and right. Two figures emerged instantly from the darkness on each side, moving quickly to intercept him. He began to speak but a quick blow to the back of the neck knocked him senseless.

The guards dragged him through the stinking refuse-strewn silt to a small house built near the outer wall of the bridge. Here they dropped him unceremoniously onto the floor at the feet of the Tong Master. The cold of the cobblestones against Quon's face helped to clear his head and his senses began to return. He could taste blood but he remained still and listened.

His knowledge of the Chinese language was minimal having little use to communicate with those of his race since the age of seven or eight—he could only guess as Chinese calendars were different. At any rate, it was the year his evil uncle, Won Su, entrusted with his training as a cabin boy and seaman by his parents, had taken him off the ship when he was asleep one night. Stashed in a barrel, he was left on the Thames dock. By the time he awoke, the ship had sailed away and he would never see his family again. Quon had often wondered what would have happened to him if Lizzie had not become his friend.

Frustrated with the quickly spoken, strange words, he realized it was no use. He could feel the pain of his position now and knew he had to move soon. Realizing this would cause a reaction from the guards, he prepared himself. Very slowly, he moved the muscles of his left arm. Nothing happened. The voices droned on. Next, he slowly moved his other arm, groaning slightly. The two guards were at his side instantly, grabbing him in a vicelike grip. He opened his eyes and realized he could not make out the face of the Tong men. Only one small candle burned in a corner.

"Leave him," the faceless voice of the Tong Master, sitting on a chair in the dark corner, said in their language, "he has been here before. He asks only for others, never for himself."

The guards let him go and Quon, sensing a new development, raised himself to his knees and faced the man in the shadows. He tried to talk but his mouth was caked with mud. He rubbed his dirty hand across his face and tried to spit it out with little success.

"Th-this man," he began, reaching slowly inside his shirt and producing the picture, "bring opium to dockland."

One of the guards seized the paper from his hand. A light was struck some distance away producing a faint, wavering glow. The rustle of paper told him it was being passed around. Angry comments in Chinese broke the stillness, then again an ominous silence.

A small round object was thrust into his hand and he realized it was a cup—which he put to his dry lips. *Tea! It will help make the mud taste better.*

Suddenly the voice spoke again, this time in English.

"You have a need, young man?"

"Yes sir. Wizzy need help."

"The girl named Wizzy who we helped before?"

"Yes."

"Go, she will be contacted."

"She need you qlick, sir!" he added in desperation.

"GO!" the voice boomed, indicating the door with an arm encased in a beautifully embroidered garment which shone in the dim light like a fine cloth of silk.

Slipping with each step, Quon went in the direction indicated until he came out from under the bridge and into the growing dusk. Looking for a pool of water, he stopped to wash his face of the caked-on mud. *No time for swim, river too dirty anyway!* "I hope Lizzie have bath ready!" he mumbled aloud.

He found his way back to the steps and soon he was on the roadway again. Passersby stared curiously at the strange sight but he ignored them in his eagerness to get home.

જીજ્રજી

Captain Davis was becoming more and more frustrated over the fate of his ship as he stared inquiringly at Lizzie.

"But I'm here!" he exclaimed. "What has Jack done with my ship?"

"I put an actor on board," Lizzie chuckled. "He looks just like you. Everything is working according to plan. Don't worry."

"Don't worry!" Davis growled, appearing confused.

Patrick, listening intently, had to once again stifle his urge to laugh. Lizzie slipped off her chair and walked around the table, settling onto her knees beside the captain. She took his hand and looked up at him.

"Nobody could ever replace you," she whispered, "you old devil. Everything will be all right and you will soon be on *Falcon* again. Patrick, can you take him back to the gypsy camp, please?"

"Ach aye, lassie," the Scot replied, "if ah nuw weerr it was ya werr talkin aboot!"

"Oh my gosh, I forgot," Lizzie grinned. "You didn't even know he was hurt!"

"Noo ah didna until Charrley told me sum of it."

"Come on then, let's get him outside and into his cart. I'll tell you all the news as we go."

Once they were moving up the lane, the girl chattered on, relaying the news of the past weeks to the Scot. The captain grumbled loudly at first, and then strained to hear what she was saying as they pulled him slowly over the ruts and bumps.

Upon arrival at the camp, two of the gypsy men came to greet them, helping them get the cart over to his tent and lifting the captain out. As Lizzie and Patrick turned to go, Davis suddenly burst into laughter.

"We fooled 'em again, lass!" he chortled. "We fooled 'em again!"

"It took him long enough to see the funny side of that situation," Patrick muttered, as they walked back toward the cottage in the fading light. He asked for more details of the council meeting, listening attentively before quietly making a suggestion.

"How would you feel if ah asked ma Uncle John Hope ta be therr for you."

"What do I need him for?" she asked cheekily.

"Weel, he is a lawyer noo, isn't he?"

Before she could reply, a long whistle sounded from the direction of the slaughterhouse and she began to run.

"Dumplin's back," she called over her shoulder. "He's at the slaughterhouse."

"WHY IS HE AT THE SLAUGHTERHOUSE?" Patrick asked, hurrying after her. Not receiving a reply, he was totally unprepared for the sight which awaited them. "What happened to you, lad?" Patrick gasped when he saw the mud-covered figure waiting in the killing shed doorway. "You did have a mud bath!"

"Did you see him, dumplin?" she asked eagerly, wrinkling her nose at the repulsive smell and taking a step backwards. Then seeing the bruise on the back of his neck, she stepped closer and lowered her voice. "What did they do to you, dumplin? Did they hurt you again?"

"He said you would be contacted," her partner assured her, trying to grin through still muddy, blood-stained lips. He walked quickly over to one of the hog barrels and turned on the water. "Feel better with bath," he mumbled.

"Whew, what a smell! Who's going to contact you?" asked Patrick, waving his hand in front of his face.

"Quon need bath, qlick!" he said, becoming aggitated. "Get towel and clothes, Wizzy. Hurry!"

"Right away," she replied, beginning to feel slightly concerned. "Stay with him, Patrick." She turned and hurried outside.

The Scot turned back to see Quon climb into the water, clothes and all. He produced a cake of yellow tallow soap and rubbed it all over himself splashing muddy water everywhere. Curious, but deciding this necessitated standing well back, Patrick laughed as boots, stockings, shirt and finally pants were scrubbed and sloshed out onto the floor at his feet. Lizzie returned with an armful of clean clothes, shoes, and two sackcloth towels.

"Wherre the devil has yon lad been?" Patrick demanded, as they waited outside for him. "He stinks worrse than the hogs. What's going on Liz?"

"He's been to see some friends of ours," she said secretively, "powerful friends."

"Frriends he can well do without by the look of that ugly bruise on his neck. It looks like someone hit him over the head. Did he tell you what happened? Who arre they, Lizzie?"

"Men who live on the river bank," she said resignedly.

"Who?" the Scot persisted.

"Mister Sandilands," Lizzie finally snapped, "you ask too many questions!"

"Ach, then ah'll bid ye a good nicht, ma'am," he growled, recognizing the ring of stubbornness in her voice and being too tired to argue. He turned on his heel and strode off into the fast-falling darkness.

ঞঞঞ

Across the heath, a shadowy figure prowled the property of the Benson Estate, puzzling at darkened windows and lack of activity. Stealing into London secretively by night, this man often conducted his business in this manner, avoiding the law with cunning brashness.

No rumour of Sam Benson's arrest had as yet touched his ears and the purpose of his visit this night was for the conclusion of a business arrangement. Gold was to change hands but the darkened mansion caused a knot of apprehension to twist at his innards. Something was wrong; his animal instincts screamed a warning, yet his greed drove him on. A debt was owed to him and he meant to collect … tonight.

Albert Van Bloom, a long-time associate of Sam Benson's and an opium dealer, was also known to some of London's gentry. Moving quietly on the dark side of the law, he was Sam's connection between foreign governments and armies, though he bore no allegiance to anyone. Profiteering and gold were his sole motivators.

Born to an Irish-rebel mother, Van Bloom called Holland his home. His father, a Dutch sea captain on the East India run, had long ago introduced his son to the popular Chinese opium weed and its profits. Openly plying his trade on London's dockland until a few years before when he was chased out of town by the Tong who controlled its illegal import.

Sam Benson, who shared in the profits while introducing the opium dealer to his highborn clientele, had carefully planned his return. With his crew of Irish rebels usually nearby, Van Bloom had learned to move cautiously through the shadows eager to alert no one of his activities. Tonight, anticipating no trouble, he was alone, having sent the men on ahead to a nearby tavern to await his return.

The plan of the foundry owner was to create havoc amongst the TLS management, thus taking Lizzie's attention away from her effort to join council. However, thanks to Fred Monk's memory for faces and his artistic ability, Sam Benson's plan for the Dutchman was already going awry.

Knowing that Sam's son-in-law, Arthur Miller, who was also part of the conspiracy, lived next door, Van Bloom walked down the long avenue to the Miller residence and brashly knocked on the heavy door. Answered by a stern-faced butler to whom he briefly stated his business, he was informed that Arthur Miller and his father in-law were indisposed. The butler suggested he should inquire at Highgate Hall, Richard Byrd's home at the top of the lane. So he set off back up the drive the way he had come. Finding the house and seeing lights on inside, his spirits lifted. Going boldly to the front door, he had difficulty locating the knocker in the darkness—finding it, he let it fall briskly, several times.

This time it was the Byrd's butler who answered the door. Again stating his name and that he had business with Mister Byrd, the butler left him standing outside, closing the door.

"There's a gentleman to see the master, madam," the butler announced to Alyse Byrd.

"Show him in, Barnsby. I'll be in the sitting room," she informed him.

At ease with the gentry, the visitor bowed as he entered, obviously surprised to see a lady and the conspicuous absence of a gentleman. His eyes observed the woman's jewellery as she introduced herself.

"My husband is not at home. May I help you, Mister ...?" she asked.

"Actually it is your father whom I have need to see, ma'am," he said, somewhat haughtily, ignoring her question.

"A business matter, sir?"

"Yes ma'am, I'm owed a tidy sum of money."

"You're a debt collector, sir," Alyse replied.

"No ma'am, it's a debt of honour, a service I performed for your father."

"And your name, sir?"

"Albert Van Bloom."

Alyse turned the name over in her mind. It did have a familiar ring to it, but why? Suddenly, the memory became clearer. *It was at a Kensington party where Sir Tomas Kromer mentioned his name. This is the man who supplies the illegal opium Sir Tomas smokes! s*he realized in surprise.

"You're the opium man," she sneered.

Astonished at being so readily identified, Albert reverted to his natural instincts and reaching under his coat, he drew a knife.

"I intend to be paid, ma'am," he hissed, moving a step closer, holding the knife at his side.

Alyse took a sharp breath and told herself to remain calm knowing her staff were closeby. "And the amount you deem you're due, sir?" she asked trying to appear calm as she noted the snakelike eyes and vicious curl of his lips. "You shall be paid and I may also have a use for your services."

"The amount is fifty golden guineas, ma'am."

"And for what service do I pay such a high price, sir?"

"Goods and services, ma'am," Albert leered, "and the destruction of Lizzie Short."

Oh, her again, thought Alyse. *Father and his friends are simply obsessed by that woman. Well, he can't have been very successful because she's apparently seeking a council seat. I wonder ....*

"My gold, ma'am," Van Bloom's voice interrupted her thoughts, "then we'll continue our business."

Calling loudly for the butler, Alyse moved toward the door.

When he arrived, she didn't allow him to enter but urgently hissed, "Get the shotgun, Barnsby." The butler pushed the door shut and hurried off.

Not able to hear what had been said, Van Bloom suddenly had a feeling that all was not as it seemed. *Has she sent him for the money or for assistance?* he thought. Unsure and, too late realizing he was being foolish to trust this woman, panic struck the opium dealer and his throat went dry. He didn't need any trouble, he thought to himself. He put the knife away and looked around for the quickest way of retreat should it become necessary. He found none, save for breaking a window, or the door through which he had entered. Remembering the boys had wanted to come with him, he fleetingly wished he had taken heed. In near panic, he bounded across the room pushing past Alyse.

"STOP HIM, BARNSBY!" she screamed, grabbing for a nearby chair to keep her balance.

As he threw open the door, the butler was waiting, gun at the ready. Aimed at his chest, Van Bloom threw up his arms and retreated. Barnsby pressed forward until he had forced the man to sit down.

Looking over at the highborn lady standing stoically by the door, Van Bloom was shocked to hear her next words.

"If he moves Barnsby, shoot him!" Then she left the room.

Cold rivulets of sweat began to run down the Dutchman's back as he stared into the barrel of the shotgun only inches from his face. Held tightly in the slightly dithering hands of the sour-faced butler, Van Bloom was quite sure the servant would be most willing to carry out the order should the necessity arise.

Lizzie watched the Scot disappear down the darkening track, knowing she had angered him but not wanting to divulge her thoughts just yet. She waited impatiently for her partner, her mind going over and over their problem. *Who sent the opium-laced tobacco and why? It could be Benson or his hot-headed son-in-law, Richard Byrd, or even Judge Harvey, Admiral Jones, or Josiah Cambourne, the newspaper owner. They've all threatened to use violence and they're all powerful men, readily demonstrated by the cancellation of the meeting.* She sighed. *The only clue to his identity is the man with the moustache who delivered the tobacco.*

"Wizzy," Quon's voice broke into her thoughts as he came to stand beside her, dirty clothes wrapped in the towel.

"We have to find him, dumplin," she muttered, "but where do we start?"

"Tomorra, Wizzy, tomorra," he said wearily.

His fingers found her hand as they walked silently toward the cottage. Lizzie squeezed his hand. She was now very concerned about his head injury but as he seemed so tired she decided to leave her questions until the morning. He squeezed her hand back.

Joe had already gone to bed and Martha was just finishing up. She noticed their worried expressions and Quon's wet hair and couldn't help wondering what they had been up to tonight. But she asked for no explanation as they quietly said their good nights and went straight to their rooms.

Chapter 16

At the breakfast table the next morning, Joe and Ada wanted to discuss the cancellation of the council meeting but Lizzie would have nothing to do with it shaking off their penetrating expressions.

"I told you, I have plans and that's all I'm going to say about it," she retorted defiantly, shovelling porridge into her mouth.

Voices sounded at the door. It was Patrick, with Captain Jack, who had arrived in port that morning. Jack was eager to tell the rollicking tale of the demise of the *Black Otter,* thankfully changing the mood of the room. He related how the *Falcon* had come upon the wreckage shortly after they had been surprised and sunk by a Spanish gunboat in the fog. Only Captain Roach, a cabin boy and two sailors had survived and were found clinging to the wreckage.

"We turned the sailors free when we reached port," he explained, at the bookkeeper's inquiring look. "We also managed to find the cabin boy a job aboard a coal freighter and our friend, Captain Roach, was turned over to the military," he added the last bit sarcastically and grinned broadly, displaying several missing teeth.

"Did you find out who sent him after Ben and the *Restitution,* Jack?" Lizzie asked eagerly, as Charley came through the door.

"Aye lass, it were Admiral Jones, but you'll have a hard job provin it."

"Did you see Gabriel?"

"Aye, we met up with Ben while rescuing the survivors and brought Gabriel aboard with us. Gabe went straight over to the print shop this morning and Ben has carried on to Hull."

Martha hovered over the table after distributing plates of bacon and eggs, not wanting to miss a word, and seemingly forgetting about her house rules.

"And Jake Newton?" Lizzie asked, as Joe finally banged the table for quiet.

"Locked in our brig, lass," Jack whispered as the old man's stormy expression brought silence at last to the table.

Only young Willie's voice was heard above the clinking of silverware on tin plates until the meal was finished. Lizzie helped Martha clear the table and conversation eagerly resumed.

Grey Grim appeared at the door and Charley, whose quiet demeanour and puzzled frown had been bothering Ada all through breakfast, stood up and began to move toward the door.

"Are you all right, Charley?" she asked her brother-in-law. "You're very quiet this morning and you can't be worried about Ben anymore."

"I'm sorry, I guess my mind is elsewhere," he replied, glancing over at Lizzie. "We need another steam engine."

Patrick swung around to face the engineer, his interest now peaked but, before he could speak his mind, Mick intervened.

"Sure and begorra yerr not trryin to double yerr output are yerr, lad?"

Charley had no time to answer as Grey swept him off his feet and carried him outside.

"Time we went, too," said Ada pushing her husband toward the open door. Turning to the Scot, she added, "Charley wants a steam engine for the new printing press, Patrick."

The Scot, now totally confused watched the couple leave, and then turned to Lizzie with questioning eyes.

"The printing shop is moving to larger premises," she murmured, only half paying attention as her eyes were on Joe who seemed to be staring into the fire. "Charley's trying to make a steam engine work the printing press." She rose from the table and went to kneel by the old man's chair, gently taking his hand. "Are you all right, Dad?" she asked.

"Aye lass, I'm fine," he sighed, removing his smoking pipe. "It was just a flood of memories that came over me for a minute watching you so all growed up. Remember when there were just you an me in this old cottage?" He put his arm around her and she moved onto his knee. They wrapped their arms around each other and Lizzie put her head on his shoulder. Joe let out an audible sigh. "It seems so long ago, lass."

Rattling wheels told them a carriage was drawing up at the gate and Lizzie gave Joe a kiss on the cheek and came to her feet. Hearing the sound of Nathan's grumbling voice, Patrick and Jack decided it was time for them to leave also. Joe quickly followed suit taking the sandwiches Martha handed him, tied in a red and white neckerchief. Puffing fiercely on his pipe, he went outside greeting the trader gruffly as they passed on the steps. He was finding it all a bit too confusing these days.

Quon left his chair to intercept the trader at the door.

"Leave it, dumplin," Lizzie snapped, moving to the door herself. "You stupid, little man, I thought you of all people would have known better!"

Martha cringed as the trader wilted under Lizzie's barrage of biting words. She took Willie by the hand, leading him out the back door into the garden away from the confrontation.

"How was I to know it was opium?" Nathan muttered, groaning as thoughts of the near-disaster still tortured his mind.

"We have enemies, Nathan, you know that," she admonished him. "You're important to me, so please be careful. Now go."

Squaring his shoulders, Nathan touched his hat with his cane, silently vowing to find the rascal who caused him this humiliating torment.

After everyone left and Martha and Willie came back inside, the boy got out his wooden toys and began playing ships on the floor, showing Lizzie the two new ones Patrick had brought him the day before. Martha noticed that Lizzie was very quiet this morning and seeing that they weren't leaving in a hurry, she joined them at the table.

"C'mon love," she coaxed, "put a smile on yer face, there's a whole world of answers out there and you're the one to find them." She pointed her wooden spoon at the door.

Grinning mischievously, Quon's fingers beat a message on the table.

"Tell her yourself," Lizzie responded, jumping off her chair and making for the door.

"Whatever did he say?" the housekeeper called after her.

"He said you were lovely," she giggled, as her embarrassed partner shot past her.

As they walked toward Abe's shop, they searched every face they passed hoping to find the man Fred Monk had drawn. Too late to catch the tailor outside, they gently pushed his door open and listened. Abe was busy at his work table. He appeared to be talking to himself.

"Hello, come in," the seamstress encouraged from just inside the door. "Mister Kratze has been expecting you," she said, then more softly, "Lizzie, that stuff he smoked, it's changed him."

"Changed him?" whispered Lizzie. "How?"

Looking up from his work, Abe grinned showing his black teeth. Lizzie watched with growing interest.

"You heard the news, girl?" he snapped.

"What news?" Lizzie asked.

Reaching for his cup of hot peppermint, the tailor's eyebrows bounced up and down his forehead as she took her seat.

"They're laughing at us, girl, they think we're beaten," Abe hissed. "They think cancelling the council meeting will be the end of it and you'll

J. Robert Whittle

change your mind." Lowering his voice, he leaned toward her. "They want to play games with old Abe, do they? Bring me their names, girl, and I'll twist their tails!"

"See miss," Clara whispered, "he's been acting strange and not making much sense since I got here this morning. I ain't never heard him talk like this before."

"Come, Missus Spencer," he chuckled, "make yourself a nice warm drink."

"He's gone off his rocker," Clara sighed.

Abe dropped his eyes back to the garment in his hands and continued working with renewed energy.

Quon tapped a sharp message on her arm bringing a cold smile to her lips. Did Abe have a secret? Quon asked. Clara was right, the change in this usually grumpy old man was obvious and remarkable. His surly frown had disappeared, replaced by an impish grin.

"Humour him, Clara," Lizzie whispered. "It might not last very long."

"Go girl!" Abe dismissed them, without looking up from his work. "You have much work to do."

Back out on the street they stood for a moment as Lizzie searched her mind for a clue to the tailor's behaviour. Then, walking slowly down the hill, they watched the feverish activity on the TLS docks. They heard the rising voices from the drinkers at *The Robin* as they passed, and noticed the arrival of Nathan's buggy turning onto the dock area.

She felt Quon's urgent fingers on her back. She followed his pointing arm to two Chinese men in traditional garb moving quickly through the crowded forecourt of the coaching inn. They appeared to be searching for someone as they stopped to look at each person's face.

"They searching for tobacco man," Quon whispered excitedly.

"Who are they?"

"Tong men."

"I hope they find him," she replied, frowning as the searchers disappeared among the coach passengers in the stableyard. "Perhaps this means we won't need to hear from them," she mused.

With a picture of the face Fred had drawn in their minds, they hurried past the hissing steam engine—their eyes, too, automatically checked each face they met.

"What are you looking for?" Charley asked, interrupting his conversation with Nathan.

"The tobacco man."

"Oh, we'll soon have him apprehended," Nathan chuckled. "I told the printers to put his picture in the newspaper, somebody is bound to know who he is."

"YOU DID WHAT?" Lizzie screeched, then lowered her voice to a whisper. "You fool, now he'll know we're after him."

The trader looked bewildered, grasping his silver-topped cane nervously as he backed toward the buggy. Charley shook his head and smiled.

"So now, you'd better get over there and stop the press," she said coldly.

Scrambling into the buggy, he shouted an urgent order to Dan then settled back into his seat. *Can I never do anything right for that girl?* he thought, glad to escape.

She watched the trader's buggy thread its way along the dock, through the congested tangle of drays, until it turned into the heavy morning traffic and disappeared. A loud bellowing of her name brought a smile to her face and she turned to see One-Eyed Jack coming toward them.

"Victuals, lass," Jack panted. "We need Captain Davis' signature on the order."

"Have you written an order out?" she asked.

"Ah don't write so good," the mariner admitted with a serious expression. "It's me missin eye, lass, ah can only see half the letters."

Spontaneous laughter erupted as they all reacted to the mariner's excuse.

"Well, it's sorta true!" Jack chuckled sheepishly.

"All right, Jack!" said Charley. "Get me an admiralty form and I'll write it out for you."

"Ah got one here," Jack replied, producing the appropriate paper from his pocket. "But you can't sign it, lad, it needs Captain Davis' signature."

"And he's a broken arm," Charley replied. "Now what do we do?"

The men both looked at Lizzie.

"You list the victuals," she replied, "and we'll get it signed."

"How?" Charley demanded.

"Just wait a minute, Charley, and I'll tell ya," she snapped. "Give him that form, Jack, and go to the *Falcon* and get me a sample of the captain's signature. But first, I want you to help Charley make out the list of what you need."

The men got their heads together and soon there was a list on Charley's writing board.

J. Robert Whittle

"There, now go get that signature, Jack, and send it back with Lefty. We'll look after the rest. Don't just stand there, do it!" she insisted when he hesitated. After he had gone, she turned to the dockmaster. "Now write me out a duplicate which will go to Ada."

Charley watched Jack disappear in the direction of the *Falcon* and began to write out the duplicate list; his mind was still puzzling out how Lizzie was going to achieve her objective. By the time he finished, Lefty was running toward them. He handed her a piece of paper and she gave him instructions to take the second list to Ada. Without so much as a question, Lefty pocketed the list and ran off.

Lizzie thanked Charley as Quon carefully put the papers inside his shirt and they also moved off. Taking the longer route to the print shop, the young partners continued checking the crowds for the opium man.

As they climbed the hill, they went past several taverns where men sat at outside tables. Their eyes darted about but they soon realized that someone else was doing the same thing as they were. It became obvious that there were a lot more Tong men than the first two they had seen earlier. They scurried silently amongst the shoppers, darting into shops and staring at groups of business men.

It was almost lunch time when they turned into Brown's Yard and saw Daisy talking to an excited group of street urchins as she loaded them with newspapers.

"They've seen him!" Daisy gasped excitedly after the street lads had hurried away. "He was eating breakfast at an inn about a mile from here."

"Oh fiddlesticks, they should have followed him," Lizzie groaned.

"Come inside," the reporter urged.

Following her, Lizzie stared at the four grinning faces that lined the counter to greet them.

"Our boys found that man for you," Penny stated eagerly, "and you needn't have worried, Lizzie. We didn't even consider printing his picture; it would have been foolish. We don't take our orders from Nathan Goldman!"

"Our boys, Lady Sutton?" Lizzie whispered.

"Yes, *our* boys," Gabriel interrupted, "we've all agreed. They came and slept here when we thought the fire starters were coming. They're the best information service in dockland and it's time somebody besides Lizzie Short gave them a hand."

Lizzie thanked them as Penny handed out the pennies. Dismissed, the boys ran hurriedly outside.

Quon's arms began swinging like pendulums.

"Yes, that's right, Quon. Those boys might be the winners of our reward when this is over." Seeing him take the victual order from inside his shirt and lay it on the counter, Lizzie carried on. "Fred, can you copy this signature, then write the *Falcon*'s victual order onto this official admiralty order sheet? I need it signed with Captain Davis' signature." She looked at him without expression waiting for his answer.

Fred studied the paper for only a moment before looking up. Smiling, he took the paper and went over to his work table. "Inkpot and new quill," he said to Cuthbert, grinning as if he was about to fulfil a lifelong dream. He sat down at the table. Holding out his hands, he spread his fingers, opening and closing them several times. He picked up the pen Cuthbert set down in front of him. Then they all watched in fascination as Fred painstakingly began to copy each word. You could tell that old Cuthbert viewed Fred's talent as an extraordinary one by the way he silently watched his every movement.

"Did you enjoy your voyage?" Lizzie inquired of Gabriel.

"No, he didn't," Daisy giggled, "he was glad to get back to his beloved printing press!"

"Daisy, behave yourself," her mother chided.

"The truth of it is," Gabriel sighed, "she's right, there's a lot more excitement right here in dockland!"

"So who was the opium man they found?" Lizzie asked. "Where is he now?"

"We don't know yet. He's moving around, but it's the man in Fred's drawing all right. The boys are sure of it," said Daisy.

"Where was he when you last heard?"

"North of the slaughterhouse about a mile, in a hansom cab leaving *Black Sheep Inn*," replied Gabriel. "He seemed to be with several other men. The boys said they talked funny."

Quon's fingers danced on the counter, his silent comments causing Lizzie to frown as she hissed through tightly draw lips.

"Benson!"

Lady Sutton and Gabriel looked sharply at each other. Benson was the name of the traitor—why would Lizzie be talking about him. Daisy, now the inquisitive reporter, scrambled for more details.

"Who's Benson? It seems I've heard that name being talked about around the docks."

"Here you are," Fred interrupted, bringing his latest creation to the counter and liberally sprinkling it with drying powder. He turned to Daisy. "Sam Benson's a foundry owner, he was the traitor caught last week with the guns hidden in his ship."

"No, that's not it," Daisy puzzled, searching for a thread of memory.

"His son in-law, Arthur Miller, had the wool ships," Lizzie added, "he's locked up in jail, too."

Just then, two street urchins who had sold their newspapers crept nervously through the door and up to the counter.

"My, but your hands are dirty," Daisy murmured as they held out their hands filled with pennies. "Is that soot you've been into boys?"

"No miss, it's boot blacking," the taller boy said proudly as they dropped their pennies on the counter. "It's near the Hungerford stairs, we sell 'em newspapers."

"That's it!" Daisy squealed, frightening the boys so much they moved backwards toward the door. With wide, frightened eyes, they looked ready to make their escape even without their money. "Don't run away," she called. "Please come back, you don't have your pay."

They stopped, looking fearfully at each other, ready to escape onto the crowded sidewalk if they deemed it necessary. Talking quietly, Daisy held out their pennies toward them, trying to coax them to come back in.

"Is there a wharf at the boot black works?" she asked quietly, as they moved forward and took the money.

"No miss, it's a mud bank. Can we go now?" they asked eagerly, edging away again.

"Yes, all right, off you go."

Daisy turned back to grin at the others.

"I heard the name Benson coupled with the boot black works yesterday," she said. "Two men were saying that a man named Benson had been planning to buy it. Could this be the same man, Liz?"

"Maybe."

"But why would a man like that want to buy a dirty, boot black factory," Penny snorted. "I think you've eavesdropped on one too many conversations, daughter. You've got things all mixed up."

Watching quietly as the print shop staff resumed their work, Lizzie listened to the thoughts of her partner's fingers tapping on her arm. *Good place to hide opium man*, his message silently conveyed.

Late that afternoon, after a fruitless day of searching the streets for the opium dealer, they located the boot black works. Built out over the river, the roughly constructed wood-and-stone building looked dark and foreboding, its open windows regularly billowing black dust into the air.

Looking for a way down to the river, they crept between neighbouring buildings and found themselves on the muddy river bank. A rickety walkway led them to a small dock where they found two small rowboats.

"Low tide," Quon announced.

"They could bring a small ship in here at high tide," Lizzie mused, "and nobody would know."

Her partner nodded and she grinned triumphantly. Confident they had found the tobacco man's hideout and that Sam Benson was also involved, they made their way back to the bread shop to enlist Billy and the street urchins to help watch the boot black works.

A strange silence filled the streets as they neared the bread shop. The everyday noise of horses and iron-rimmed wheels rattling over the cobble stones and the frustrated cursing of drivers battling heavy traffic, were all normal; yet something was missing. Billy's voice was absent.

Quickening their pace, they darted down a snicket and hurried through back alleys. Abruptly, Lizzie and Quon found their way blocked by three Chinese men wearing a type of dress Lizzie had never seen before. However, Quon recognized them immediately. Their costumes were like those of the guards he had encountered under the bridge. He moved quickly in front of Lizzie.

"No need, boy!" one of the men said in a well-cultured voice. He wore a wide-brimmed hat which hid his face. "We come to speak with Miss Wizzy, we mean you no harm."

Glancing over her shoulder, she saw more Chinese men standing near the entrance to the alley. Quon's hands spun wildly, telling her the rickety stairs on their right ran onto the rooftops, and a knife suddenly appeared in his hand. She looked furtively about but the man began to speak again.

"You are Miss Wizzy?"

She nodded, but before she could even consider why he had asked this pertinent question, he spoke again.

"The opium dealer will cause you no more problems."

Her racing pulse began to settle down as her brain recovered its composure and questions formed in her mind.

"Who was he?"

"Captain Albert Van Bloom," the voice replied without emotion.

"Who gave him his orders?"

"Sam Benson was the only name he uttered before he departed this world."

J. Robert Whittle

Turning to leave, the man glanced back over his shoulder, his face still hidden. "My master wishes you well, Lizzie Short," he said quietly, bowing to her. As he turned to leave she noticed the others had already disappeared.

Quon stood stone-faced as Lizzie slipped her arm over his shoulder. She could feel the tension in his body as it slowly subsided.

She sighed with relief as the words of the Tong man sunk into her brain, adding her own thoughts. *The danger from the opium man is over and Sam Benson will surely be a dead man when the law takes its course on this new, treasonable act.*

Walking slowly arm-in-arm out of the alley, they looked sideways at each other and grinned as Billy's loud call resumed—music to their ears as it reverberated through dockland's streets.

Chapter 17

Billy was teasing the crowd with his usual small talk and jokes about the establishment as Lizzie and Quon arrived, causing titters of laughter from usually serious-faced shoppers. Tip stood back watching with undisguised admiration, trying to learn the young barker's magical fascination.

Over in front of the butcher shop, Tom Jackson was in deep conversation with Daisy and Sid the butcher, when Billy called for quiet. A second high-pitched shout rippled over their heads as Olivera and his loaded pony cart came trotting down the incline.

Quon went over to help the bread lads unload as Lizzie talked to Tom and Daisy.

"What brings you over here, Mister Jackson?" she greeted the architect.

"A steam engine. Nathan Goldman said the newspaper office needed one and I came to see Lady Sutton."

"You have one, sir?"

"Don't rightly think so, young lady, but I know who has. It's broken though."

"How much will it cost us?"

"Fifty guineas."

"For a heap of junk!" Lizzie snapped. "You seek to turn a profit, sir."

"But Lizzie," Daisy pleaded, "we need it."

"You cheeky, brat," the architect fumed, "to accuse me…."

His sentence was abruptly cut short as Lizzie's eyes blazed with annoyance and Quon Lee stepped between them. Quietly menacing, the Chinese lad's eyes became mere slits staring intently at the man.

"I know where there's one." Billy's voice cut through the growing tension from atop his platform. "Want me to get it for ya?"

His voice was drowned out by the arrival of the trader's buggy as it pulled up in front of the butcher's shop.

"DID YOU TELL HER ABOUT THAT BLASTED MACHINE?" Nathan shouted to Tom Jackson who walked over to the conveyance. "I heard they're eager to get rid of it."

"Yes," the architect muttered, nodding in the affirmative as his face turned various shades of crimson. "I told her fifty guineas."

"You did what!" Nathan cried, causing the architect to wince and step back.

Scrambling awkwardly out of his buggy and over to Tom Jackson's side, Nathan waved his fancy cane in the architect's face as a crowd of inquisitive onlookers gathered around. To the delighted amusement of his dockland audience, Nathan enthusiastically berated Tom Jackson. Arms waving dramatically, he loudly proclaimed the virtues of friendship and fair play to the municipal councillor.

Standing to one side, Daisy clutched Lizzie's arm and watched intently until Billy came to the rescue brilliantly exploiting the gathering.

"GET YOUR BREAD, MEAT AND CANDLES AT 10 PERCENT OFF, FOR THE NEXT FIFTEEN MINUTES," he yelled, "FIRST COME, FIRST SERVED. Come on now, push to the front and save yer coppers, missus."

Squashed by shoppers eager for a bargain, Nathan and the architect endeavoured to push their way out of the large crowd.

"Damn, that kid's smart," Nathan gasped as he came up beside Lizzie. "He turned that crowd into eager buyers in an instant. I could use a lad like that." He went back to his buggy and climbed inside.

"Mister Jackson, sir, I repeat," Lizzie purred as the trader drove away. "Were you attempting to make an inordinate profit at my expense? I would tread very carefully if you want TLS business in the future, my friend!"

Taken aback once again, Tom Jackson was growing more uncomfortable by the second. *It was not wrong to make a profit*, he told himself stubbornly, *that's business*. Turning to escape, he glanced over his shoulder. He could hardly believe that this beautiful young woman was so hardened in business matters.

"And if I don't vote for you at council?" he called back.

"Wouldn't it be easier to simply work together, Mister Jackson?"

Daisy Sutton shuddered. She really admired this girl who was five years younger than her. She knew she would never have the nerve to deal with issues as Lizzie did but certainly wished she was more able. Her mother had become much more confident with Lizzie around and was doing a wonderful job with the printing shop. Nathan had proved she was right in being suspicious of Mister Jackson's offer. *Perhaps I will grow more like my mother, and Lizzie, one day.*

Tom Jackson had stopped and now swung around to face his tormentor. He was furious at this girl for embarrassing him and making him feel inferior.

"You bi….," he hissed under his breath, taking several strides toward her. "I shall …."

"No you shall not, sir!" stated a young seaman who stepped forward from his position by the butcher shop from where he had been watching. He smiled coldly. "If you move even one more step, I'll kill yer, mate."

"Why thank you, kind sir, although I doubt that would be necessary." Lizzie acknowledged the young man, dressed in sailor's clothes, with a questioning smile. There was something familiar in his features, perhaps the way he cocked his head, or the cheeky grin. "Do I know you, sailor?" she asked. There was definitely something about this young man with the twinkling green eyes that held her attention.

"Are you Lizzie Short?" he asked bluntly, moving toward her.

Quon moved quickly to block the seaman's path.

"Yes, I am," she slowly replied. Taking Quon's arm and gently moving him aside, she continued to study the young man's features.

Daisy was watching the scene very closely, her disappointment of the steam engine forgotten for the moment. She felt a new mystery unfolding and her attention remained riveted on this tall, good-looking, muscular young man with skin tanned to a deep brown.

Tom Jackson, seeing they were otherwise occupied, took this opportunity to move away and disappear into the crowd. He would have liked to eavesdrop but he didn't want to raise Lizzie's ire anymore. They had business to finish but she would find him if she wanted the engine bad enough.

"Who's he?" the sailor asked, pointing to Quon, "your protector?"

"None of your business," she snapped. "Who are you?"

"Haven't really changed much, have you, Liz? Think back about eight years, girl," he whispered, "you and I stole a pie from *The Robin* and it was my last!"

Spinning out of control, Lizzie's mind took her back to her childhood, to the days before Joe Todd and Quon Lee—that fatal day when four young street urchins, her very best friends, were caught and sent away to Australia leaving her alone and so lonely.

"Willy? Willy Dent?" she gasped, covering her mouth with her hand. Her knees suddenly felt weak and her heart began to race. She moved a step closer and looked at him, tears forming in her eyes. "Is it really you, Willy?" she whispered.

"Aye Liz, it's me all right," he replied softly, his voice catching momentarily. "We docked yesterday. I'm a deckhand on board the East India *Goose.* It's a spice trader out of Sidney, Australia. The colony needed other supplies only found here. It's my first trip back."

Quon and Daisy looked on in shocked amazement as Lizzie moved forward and hugged the stranger, tears wetting her face as the young seaman reciprocated holding her gently.

"Who is he?" Daisy whispered to Quon.

"Me think he's a memory."

"Where are you staying, Willy?" Lizzie asked eagerly, as they separated. "You can stay with us."

"No, I have to stay aboard the ship," Willy replied, frowning. "I'm owned by Captain McHoule for five more years."

"You're a slave?" gasped Daisy.

"We hide you," Quon offered eagerly. "They never find you."

"No, no," the seaman shook his head. "I'm not a slave, Captain McHoule owns my penal sentence—he bought it from the government agent. I must work for him until my sentence is over."

A sharp call from the bread shop doorway stopped further conversation, as Billy called out, "Miss Lizzie, these two lads," he pointed to two young urchins of about 10 or 11 years, "they've found you a steam engine!" Turning pale under his tan, Willy Dent fought back his emotions. He was about the age of these two when the law had dragged him away from here. Some of the streets and alleys near here had once been home to him, too. He understood their fears and he watched them nervously approach the girl.

Jingling two half-pennies in her hand, Lizzie gently coaxed them over to her. "Tell me where the steam engine is, lads?" she asked gently.

"It's on a ship, miss," one of the youngsters gabbled, "at the East India Dock, but it's dead."

"What's the ship's name?" she asked, handing over the coins.

"Don't know," one called over his shoulder as they began to move away, "ah can't read, miss!" They were around the corner of the building so fast, Lizzie had to smile.

"We were like that once, Lizzie," Willy reflected sadly, "and I'm still a prisoner, but sailors tell me you run this part of dockland now." His eyes settled firmly on the girl he had once known so well. "How did you do it?" he asked, with an awefilled voice.

"First things first, lad. I've a hundred questions for you too, but what happens to you now?"

"We're getting some repairs done, so we're here for about a month. Then we return to Australia."

"But why," Daisy interrupted, "when you could stay here and be free?"

"No miss, ah couldn't. The law would send me back if they caught me, and it wouldn't go good for me, and anyway, there's Kate and the Smith boys still out there. They need me."

"You know where they are, Willy? Are they all right? You must come home with us for supper? We have so much to talk about," she pleaded.

Lizzie's expression caused a smile to light up the seaman's face but he shook his head resignedly.

"I have to be on board by eight bells, them's the rules for indentured seamen."

"We can have you back by eight," Lizzie assured him grabbing his arm. "Come on!"

Racing through the streets, she heard Willy shout from behind her, "WHERE ARE WE GOING, LIZ?"

"UP NEAR THE SLAUGHTERHOUSE!" she yelled back.

He knew of an old slaughterhouse, but not near here, remembering its grizzly product and smell when, as youngsters, they'd ducked inside the building to hide from the law.

"This is like the old times," he called, catching up to her.

Slowing as they reached the cottage, they heard an excited young voice shouting from inside.

"Wizzy coming, Grandma! Wizzy coming."

Willy Dent looked at her curiously.

Before we go in Will," she said, stopping abruptly, "let me introduce you to these two. This young lady is the Honourable Margaret Sutton, we call her Daisy. She's a newspaper reporter and, my protector is Quon Lee, also my business partner and best friend. I met him soon after you left."

"Are ya staying for supper, Daisy?" Martha called from the doorway.

"Yes, please Martha," she chuckled, following the others through the gate.

"We have another guest tonight, Martha," Lizzie announced softly as she went by the housekeeper.

Daisy quickly slid into the seat next to Charley and whispered, "We found another steam engine, but it's dead."

"Dead!" He looked at her and frowned, but his attention fastened on the stranger who had followed them in and now stood uncomfortably inside the door.

"Ah sure you can be sittin there, son," said Mick, pointing to a chair. "Patrick's not comin, he's visitin with his Uncle John."

Quickly introducing everyone, Lizzie held their rapt attention when she told them who the seaman was.

"You mean he's one of the children, your friends, that were sent to Australia," Ada asked, "the ones you used to have nightmares about?"

"Yes, there were five of us," said Lizzie looking off into space. "Willy here was … is a few years older than me, Kate was about my age and the Smith boys were quite a bit younger."

"Little Peter and Eddie barely survived that voyage," said Willy taking up the story, between mouthfuls. "They made me into a cabin boy and I sneaked extra food to them all. We were nearly there when they caught me."

"That's a serious offence, lad," Charley interceded. "I'm a former naval officer, they could have hung you for less than that."

Willy's eyes turned hard and a shadow passed over his face. He glanced around the table, his memory reliving the pain. "I got ten lashes, sir, and the brine bucket slopped over me."

"Hurt like hell, didn't it, lad?" Joe Todd growled sympathetically, spitting angrily into the fire, "my back's felt them lashes, too."

"Oh my," Ada sighed, "it's too cruel to think about. What happened when you got there?"

"We were put out to work, missus, on government work gangs."

"But you must have been billeted with a family," the bookkeeper continued, overcome with curiosity.

"No!" he hissed bitterly. "We were chained to a tree at night and when winter came they let us sleep in a woodshed!"

Twenty minutes later, iron wheels were heard in the lane and, young Willie shouted to them from the garden that Mister Nathan was here.

"I shall have to go, Lizzie," the seaman whispered, glancing at the mantle clock and making a face. "It's almost half past seven!" Willy rose quickly from his chair turning apologetically to the others. "Thank you for dinner, it was good to meet Lizzie's friends." Then pushing his chair in, he turned back to her. "I really have to go, Liz, or ah'll be in big trouble."

"Come on," she replied. "Nathan will ride us down to your ship."

Quon sprang into action. Grabbing the trader's arm, he rushed him back down the garden path, complaining bitterly as they all piled into his buggy.

"EAST INDIA DOCK," Lizzie shouted to the driver, "AND FAST!"

Moaning, Nathan covered his eyes as they tore down Water Lane. Sparks flying from the horse's iron shoes, they swung wildly into Dock Street. Wick used all his expertise to thread them through the traffic at breakneck speed.

"Holy kangaroo, what a ride!" Willy exclaimed when they turned the corner onto the East India Dock.

"WE WANT THE *GOOSE*," Lizzie again shouted to Wick.

Willy leaned out the window and pointed to a three-masted bark on their right. "THAT'S THE *GOOSE!*" he cried.

Pulling the sweating horse to a stop beside the vessel, the gypsy jumped down and flung open the door.

"Fast enough, Miss Lizzie?" he asked with a wink as Willy ducked under his arm and ran for the ship.

Getting to the bottom of the gangplank, Willy turned back to face them. At the same time, a voice roared menacingly from up on the *Goose*'s deck.

"GET ABOARD, SAILOR!"

"I'll come find you again," Willy assured her as she stood sadly watching him. Beginning to walk backwards up the gangplank, his voice full of emotion, he continued quietly, "We don't leave until the 31st of July. I'll see you again."

Lizzie finally smiled, then waved as he quickly ran the rest of the way. She suddenly got a strange look on her face and turned to look upwards. "WHAT CARGO ARE YOU CARRYING, MISTER?" she shouted to the bearded figure above her.

"Iron, barrels of nails, axe heads, building tools and lamp oil bound for the Australian Colony," he growled, stamping down the gangplank toward them, "and a prisoner or two. Why?"

"And your victuals, sir?" Nathan inquired eagerly from the carriage. "TLS offer the most value for your money in this area."

His question went unanswered as the dark figure moved through the shadows toward the buggy. Even in the shadows, they could see his fierce expression. He removed his pipe and spat a long stream of tobacco juice onto the cobblestone dock.

"Captain Caleb McHoule," he rasped, "Master of the *Goose*." His face, deeply wrinkled and tanned dark by weather and sun, held piercing black eyes under long, bushy eyebrows framed by a full, curly grey beard.

"Ah'll not take it lightly if yer plannin to steal one of my men, sir," he hissed ominously at Nathan.

"You could always buy yourself another," Lizzie interrupted.

"Damnit girl, yer talkin from ignorance," the captain sighed. "Ah bought four of 'em off a road gang in Australia—burnin heat and starvation kills men quickly out there." He paused, sucking hard on his pipe stem. "Ah gave 'em a chance to live, fed 'em and trained 'em to be first-class seamen. They'll be free men when their time's up—free men with a trade."

"It's an investment captain, admit it. You get your crew for a bowl of victuals," she taunted.

"You're a strange one, girl," Caleb McHoule growled, "what would be your interest in a convict seaman?"

"He's a man with a price on his head. I thought to buy him," she said, brushing Quon's tapping finger from her arm.

"Ten guineas and he's yours," he growled, thinking to call her bluff.

"And the price for all four?"

Taken by surprise, McHoule snapped eagerly, "Thirty-five guineas!"

"We have a deal, sir," Lizzie purred, "but I insist on secrecy. No one must know of this night's work. Have them all on the dock at noon tomorrow for my perusal."

The captain stood open-mouthed at the speed of their business negotiations. *Am I actually doing business with this young woman? Well, I guess we shall see tomorrow at noon.*" he thought. "Yes, ma'am, noon tomorrow," he replied aloud, retreating back up the gangway.

Nathan, shocked by the negotiations in human lives, twiddled his cane nervously as he watched the captain stride away. His mind was in turmoil as he struggled to understand her purpose.

"You've gone too far this time, young lady," he whined. "I want no part in slavery."

"Don't judge me too hastily, sir," Lizzie countered tiredly, putting her hand on the buggy door. "Now take me home."

"No, Wizzy!" her partner insisted, grabbing her arm. "This East India Dock, we find dead steam engine."

Her eyes strayed over the vessels lining the long wharf and she shook her head in dismay.

"But which one, dumplin?" she asked. "We can't search them all before dark."

"We try Wizzy, we try," Quon urged eagerly. "Nathan has a light!"

Glancing up at the setting sun, Lizzie's nimble brain quickly formed a plan. There was a note of urgency in her voice as she cracked out an order to the gypsy driver.

"Wick, take Mister Nathan and Dan up to the end of the dock. You stay with the buggy; they can each search a side. We'll start here, now go!"

"What are we searching for, miss?" asked Wick.

"A steam engine like Charley's," she called, "but this one is quiet."

"I'm not looking for any steam engine," Nathan pouted, "it's an exercise in futility. No, I won't," he grumbled to no one but himself as the buggy moved off along the dock.

Shadows were lengthening and the sun had gone behind the rooftops far to the west when 15 minutes later, Dan spotted the engine on a deck. One lonely seaman stood guard. Dan's whistle brought the buggy and Nathan to his side and Lizzie and Quon came running to meet them."

"That's it?" she gasped, following Dan's pointing arm.

Pushing to the front, Nathan stared into the shadows, his eyes just able to see the large silent machine on the deck.

"Probably not worth a widow's groat," he growled.

"Is it dead?" Lizzie shouted to the guard.

"Aye lass, dead as a doornail!" a voice rasped from the upper deck as a man in a captain's hat appeared out of the shadows. "Ah rue the day ah bought it. The dang thing's been nothin but trouble."

Quon's fingers beat a rapid tattoo on her arm, insisting she try to buy it. But Nathan presuming himself in charge again, shouted to the shadowy figure.

"Are you the captain?

"Yes, Captain Wendel Oscar, at your service, sir."

"You would accept an offer, captain?"

"It's already sold!"

"Too late, Miss Lizzie," the trader muttered, "we can go now."

Climbing back into the buggy, Nathan sat impatiently tapping his cane on the floor and held the door open. As he waited for the youngsters, he heard Lizzie's voice.

"It's paid for then, captain?"

"No lass, it ain't."

"You have a deposit?"

"No, ma'am."

"Then you have no deal at all," she chuckled. "I have gold, sir, and would match the offer if you told me his name and would agree to lift it onto the dock."

"Tonight?" he replied, surprised at this change of events.

"At this very moment, sir! Listen to the clink of gold that could be

J. Robert Whittle

yours," Lizzie teased. Rattling several golden guineas in her hand, she tempted the man until his heavy, booted footsteps sounded overhead hurrying across the hard wooden deck, then banging down the gangway.

"Show me five guineas in gold, lady," he wheezed excitedly, coming toward them, "and ah'll fulfil yer conditions."

Quon raised the lantern. Holding it over Lizzie's open hand, the gleam of gold coins caused the captain to gasp. He reached for the money.

"Not yet, sir," Lizzie warned quietly, closing her fingers around the coins, "the conditions first, please."

The captain called up to the watchman on board. His orders caused some immediate action above them. Lanterns hung from rigging blazed anew casting their eerie light as seamen scrambled to work the hoist, lifting the steam engine off the edge of the ship and slowly lowering it down beside them.

"The gold now!" snarled the captain.

"A name, sir, you owe me a name." Lizzie smiled in the near darkness.

"Tom Jackson, lady. It was a man named Tom Jackson," he muttered.

Lizzie held out her hand and the captain did the same. The sound of clinking coins told everyone the deal was complete.

The lanterns above were snuffed and the noise of sailors coming down the gangway told them they were off to the nearest tavern. The captain joined them and the sound of voices quickly faded.

"Now what are you going to do with it?" Nathan called angrily. "I'll go get Mick and a dray."

"No need, we'll take it with us," Lizzie announced, surprising them all. "Find a rope dumplin, we'll tow it. We can't do much damage to it and it should slide quite nicely if we go slow enough."

Quon and Dan soon located a rope and secured the iron monster behind the buggy. Nathan continued to rant, his temper obviously stretched to the limit as they set off with the steam engine skidding noisily over the cobblestones. They met with few obstacles as they made their way very slowly along the mostly deserted waterfront road. Twenty minutes later, they turned onto the TLS dock—Nathan had almost lost his voice from shouting abuse at the laughing partners.

"What have you got there, Mister Nathan?" asked the TLS night watchman, recognizing their buggy. Scratching his head, he raised his lantern to illuminate the iron monster.

Tiredly, Lizzie ordered the gypsies to untie the rope right where it was.

"You'd better put a cover over it until Charley can deal with it in the morning," she suggested. "Now please take us home, Wick."

A light still burned in the cottage as the buggy stopped and they climbed out. Nathan had been finally quiet in the ride from the dock but now, as they slowly walked to the door, he sat up and leaned through the window.

"You've cost me an evening's work, girl," he grouched after them, "pulling junk through the streets at this time of night. I shall be the laughing stock of dockland tomorrow." Impatiently, he tapped his driver on the back, sending the buggy disappearing into the darkness.

Two glasses of cider, a sandwich and a slice of apple pie stood on the table, speaking volumes of the housekeeper's motherly concern. They silently shared the sandwiches, had a quick drink and climbed the stairs together. On the landing, they stopped in the darkness and hugged each other.

$$Chapter\ 18$$

The old determination was back in Lizzie's eyes the next morning when she came down for breakfast dressed again in her blue dress. Her worried expression had gone and the tinkling, happy laughter had returned.

"Something special on today, Liz?" Ada asked, when they arrived.

"No, I just decided to dress up today," she replied casually.

Ada and Martha both looked at each other and frowned. They knew their Lizzie better than that, but she ate quickly, and she and Quon left even before the others dispersed.

She had been making some important plans in her mind and Abe was to be the first to hear of them. *Even Quon only knows a part of what I'm planning,* she giggled inwardly, feeling the excitement of a new adventure.

Abe was on his step when they arrived, but sensing she wanted to talk, he moved quickly inside.

"We're not beaten yet, old friend," she murmured, putting her hand on his thin arm. "It's court day today and we've decided," she began, her eyes unwavering as she watched the tailor's building anticipation and felt Quon's hand on her shoulder, "to ruffle the judge's feathers!"

Clara had entered with Abe's breakfast tray just in time to hear Lizzie's last word. She quickly put down the tray and covered her mouth to stifle a gasp. No one had ever dared challenge Judge Harvey; his power was absolute, striking fear into the hearts of those who came before him.

"Careful girl," Abe hissed, picking up his fork and beginning to eat. He used the back of his hand to wipe some egg off his beard, "He's a dangerous old devil, you know."

"Court starts at ten," said Lizzie, unable to contain her grin. *Yes, we're going to do it,* she silently vowed. "I want the place full of docklanders," she instructed, displaying her excitement. "Be there early and I want you both to bring anybody you can find!"

Lizzie's last order was called over her shoulder as she hurried toward the door. Quon followed as he planned his own next move—spreading the word to the nearby coaching houses, and then to Bill Johnson's, as they had discussed in her room earlier this morning.

"I'll go to the office and the print shop," she called. "Meet me at

Billy's."

Ada looked startled at first when Lizzie arrived and made her request. Remembering the morning conversation, her thoughts were now on Lizzie's safety.

"Why love," she asked, "what are you going to do?"

"Never mind, just get everybody there," Lizzie panted, racing off again.

Outside the printing shop, Tip watched as Lizzie and Quon raced up the street, passing him, and entered the shop.

"We need everybody in the courthouse at ten," she gasped.

"Hold on!" Daisy leapt up from the work table. "I'm coming with you."

"What's this all about, Penny?" muttered Fred Monk, looking up from the printing press as the girls disappeared out of the shop.

"I don't know," replied Penny Sutton, "but we're going to do as she asks. I've a strange feeling it's going to be a wildly exciting day in our friend Judge Harvey's courtroom! Come on men, finish up what you're doing. We're closing the shop for awhile."

"C-can I go, too?" asked Tip, who had been standing just outside the door as the youngsters left. Although not quite sure what was going on, he wasn't about to be left out.

⟡⟡⟡

In another part of dockland, a secret meeting was taking place in Judge Harvey's office on Naval Row. Three powerful men raised their glasses of rum and laughed uproariously as Joshua Cambourne waved the notice of the council meeting cancellation in his hand. Sam Benson's situation had been thoroughly discussed and quickly dispelled from their minds. They would be offering no help to their former friend and deny any contact with the traitor.

"Rest easy, men," announced Judge Harvey. "I'm the chairman of this assembly and no upstart woman will ever take a seat on my council." He felt pleased with himself—his legal mind having worked long into the night, many nights, to find a loophole in the Municipal Act. Strutting pompously around his chambers in wig and gown, he flaunted this simple manoeuvre of suspending council meetings until further notice. "Gentlemen," he continued, "be assured Joshua Cambourne will soon take our vacant seat. Lizzie Short is beaten, now drink up, I have court to convene."

"Court, Algenon? Anything interesting today?" asked the admiral.

"Mostly street thieves and young rascals," the judge elaborated flippantly. "The jail is full. I shall make it a transportation day. Australia suffers from a shortage of workers and I have a quota to fill."

"You will sentence everyone to the colonies today?" Admiral Jones spluttered, his knees feeling weak. He worried that one day he might be standing in Harvey's court, accused of associating with rogues and privateers.

⊱✠⊰

The sound of Billy's voice kept Lizzie moving toward the bread shop.

"T-tell everyone t-to meet at the courthouse, Billy," she announced, gasping for breath.

The young barker instantly understood the urgency of her order and his nimble mind conjured up the words that sent the crowd scurrying in that direction. His neighbours, the butcher and the lampmaker, came to their doorways and cocked an ear to see what was going on. Quickly shedding their work-stained aprons, they too, followed the crowd.

"Can I go, too?" Billy asked, grinning expectantly at Lizzie.

"Not yet, you keep 'em comin, lad," Lizzie laughed as Quon arrived also panting for breath.

"You've brought that Judge Harvey letter haven't you?" she asked, watching her partner nod. "Then come on or we'll never get in!"

As they approached the large, coal dust-stained, stone building which housed the dockland courthouse, Lizzie's thoughts were solely on what would take place in the next half hour. Her stomach began to churn slightly but she and Quon pushed through the crowd and entered the building. William Toppit, the clerk, looking totally confused as he sat at his desk in the foyer, watched the crowd of people descend on him. He hadn't been informed of any special trial going on today. He knew only that his normally quiet world was being destroyed by the eagerness of these working class people excitedly pushing their way past him.

Ada, Mick and Nathan were already seated in an ideal position, about halfway back on the middle aisle.

"Let's join them," Lizzie whispered tugging on her partner's arm and sliding in at the end of the row.

Joe, John Watson, Abe Kratze and Bill Johnson were three rows back with the huge frame of the baker covering the two seats at the end of a row. As the partners took the seats next to Ada, whispers ran through the crowd—no one really knowing why they were here.

"What the devil is going on out there?" Judge Harvey growled aloud upon hearing the din in the outer room. There being no one nearby, he cautiously opened the chamber door and peeked into the courtroom. He blinked in surprise, immediately shutting the door again. "Highly unusual," he snorted, going to his desk to gather his papers. He looked at the clock on the wall and waited. It was five minutes to ten.

Uniformed jailers manned the doorways as 10 whimpering young street urchins in leg irons were herded into the room. Pushed into the prisoner's box, a hush fell on the crowd as the heart-wrenching proceedings began.

When the hour hand moved precisely to the 12, Algenon Harvey grasped the handle of the courtroom door and opened it wide. Palms sweating, he entered the courtroom where he had presided thousands of times. Already he had the uneasy feeling that this day was going to be different.

"All rise for Judge Harvey," the clerk's voice droned and everyone came noisily to their feet.

The judge's morbid expression, coupled with the dark wig and gown, made Lizzie quake a little as she remembered the first and only time she had been in this room. *So long ago,* she thought. She bit her lip with firm resolve. *There's no turning back now.*

"Who prosecutes for the Crown?" asked the judge as people settled back into their seats.

"I do, Your Honour," replied a bespectacled, sour-faced lawyer from a table near the judge.

"And who will defend?" the judge muttered flippantly. Not expecting a reply, he prepared to carry on.

"I DO," Lizzie cried, coming to her feet.

Heads turned and a murmur ran through the crowd as the slim, sophisticated-looking woman stood up to defiantly face the judge. Known to all as the man who doled out the most ferocious and unfair penalties of any court in London, the audience waited expectantly.

Glaring with fierce animosity, he banged the oak desk with his gavel. "SIT DOWN, YOU FOOL!"

"No, I will not, sir!" she replied calmly.

"THROW HER OUT!" he screamed, jumping to his feet and banging his gavel again.

Several women in the audience began to titter softly, causing a ripple of giggling to begin.

The clerk banged his gavel. "Silence, there must be silence in the court!"

At that moment, two soldiers came forward and every TLS man in the courtroom rose to their feet. The young soldiers, dressed in red tunics, moved nervously toward the girl. Despite his size, Bill Johnson quickly got out of his seat and blocked their way.

"Don't try it boys or yer'll get yersen killed!" he growled menacingly.

Seeing their dilemma, Judge Harvey quickly intervened. "Bring that woman to me, now!"

"Don't go, Lizzie!" Joe whispered loudly, looking like he was going to stand up, but John Watson whispered something into his ear and he settled back down.

Meanwhile, Ada looked up at the girl's stormy face and knew there was nothing anyone could do. She passed her hand over her heart, feeling like she was going to faint.

Stepping across Quon Lee, Lizzie took the piece of paper Quon pressed into her hand as he began to rise.

"Not this time, dumplin," she whispered, pushing him back down. "I might need you on the outside."

Moving slowly past wellwishers who whispered their concern, she turned to look at Bill Johnson, standing just behind her.

"One yell, lass, and we're all ready to help yer," he muttered.

Lizzie nodded solemnly, took a deep breath, and allowed the soldiers to escort her to the front. Facing the judge, she stood calmly, deliberately looking straight at him and waiting for his next move.

"Into my chambers, young lady!" Judge Harvey ordered, glaring at her.

The soldiers, warming to their task, each took her by an arm and, followed by William Toppit, led her forward. Coming to his feet, Judge Harvey swept around the large oak desk and charged toward his private office, leaving the door open for the procession to follow. When they were all inside the room, he issued his next demand.

"Leave, I want to see her alone," he said testily.

The soldiers quickly moved to the open door; the clerk followed.

"SHUT THE DOOR, GIRL!" the judge bellowed, sitting down at his desk.

"SHUT IT YOURSELF!" They all heard Lizzie's snarled reply before the court clerk quickly closed the door and came back to sit at his desk in the courtroom.

In the outer office, Harvey, still holding the gavel, crashed it onto the desk, beginning a new tirade. "One more word out of you, girl," he threatened, "and you'll be bound for Australia."

"Remember this?" she asked coyly in a slow deliberate tone holding out the letter. "I have the original in safekeeping and there's a copy of it on its way to the Bishop of London at St. Paul's. Only I can stop its delivery."

Afraid to think, he snatched up the letter, realizing immediately it was a copy of the same one she had purported to give him in the tailor's shop.

"It's a forgery!" he growled unconvincingly, looking at the girl with hateful eyes.

"I repeat, I have the original," Lizzie tormented him. "I could easily ruin you … or shall we discuss my terms now?"

"Damn you, girl, you're intent on blackmail."

"No sir, I am not. I'm about to make you into the most compassionate judge in London."

"Go to hell!"

"Not me," Lizzie chuckled evilly, "but I can assure you it's your destination if you don't comply with my wishes."

"Who are you that you dare speak to me in this manner?" he asked almost inaudibly.

"Lizzie Short," she replied calmly.

To hide the chill that had run through his body, he pulled his robes about him and glowered at the girl. "I suppose you want a relative released from prison," he said venomously.

"No, I want you to discharge the people I select, into my care."

"Murderers and cutthroats, never!"

"No!" Lizzie snapped. "Street waifs, mothers who steal bread for hungry children and old sailors too proud to ask for help." She paused to study his face and a smile formed on her lips. "Oh yes," she continued, "and you must support my application for council."

"It was cancelled!"

"The next one, sir, in one month's time," she whispered, her eyes flashing a warning. "Those are my terms. I trust you understand your secret will only remain hidden, if you comply with all of my wishes."

Sighing heavily, he sunk down into his chair. Judge Harvey had suddenly found a new, grudging respect for this clever young woman. She had somehow bested Sam Benson and other members of the council … and now she had him trapped … or did she?

A girl, he thought, *could never match wits with a man of my standing. Why she'd already made her first mistake by leaving his power as a judge*

J. Robert Whittle

intact. "Come," he said quietly, "the court list is here." Taking a sheet of paper from his desk he handed it to her. "Show me who you want."

A few minutes later, silence again swept over the courtroom when the door creaked open and first Lizzie emerged. She smiled at Quon and Joe and began to walk toward her seat. The judge entered right behind her, looking very stern-faced.

"You will sit here, girl," he instructed sternly, pointing to a chair at the lawyer's table, "and no more interruptions."

Everyone waited anxiously as they watched the hated judge take his seat. What he was about to say would stun the crowded courtroom.

Turning to the clerk, he announced, "Put a notice on the outer door, Toppit," he growled. "The next council meeting is on the 27th of July." Then, as his eyes searched the desk for his gavel, he surprised the prosecuting lawyers by whispering to Lizzie.

"Get my gavel, girl, it's in my chamber."

Ada's fingers bit deeply into her husband's arm, as she watched the little performance being played out in front of them. Her hand sprang to her mouth when she heard the judge's next order.

"AND YOU," he roared at the prosecutor, "get those damned shackles off those children!"

"Good grief, she's done it!" Lady Sutton gasped aloud as Lizzie returned, handing the judge his gavel and sitting down again. Penny turned to Daisy and whispered, "Lizzie has the noose around his neck, it looks like she has tamed him with our letter."

The clerk began to read the charges on this group of prisoners.

Lizzie rose as each name was called and the prisoner stepped forward. She answered each charge with the same words. "Their only crime, your honour, was being hungry and homeless," she said. "I ask that you release them into my custody."

To the amazement of the spectators each time Judge Harvey's gavel banged, he dismissed the charges, setting free another ragged street urchin or young mother into Lizzie's custody.

Relieved that his partner was safe, though a deep-seated suspicion remained in his mind, Quon quietly stood up and went to take control of their new charges. Penny Sutton quelled the urge to follow, and then noticed the brown-robed figure of the vicar move in behind Quon Lee.

Two more cases passed under the judge's gavel, each one a tearful mother with an infant in her arms. They, too, were speedily dismissed into Lizzie's care.

Banging his gavel again, the judge called a recess for lunch and left the room quickly. The spectators filed noisily out of the courtroom, their whispered conversations growing louder as everyone talked of what they had just witnessed.

When Lizzie came outside, they bombarded her with questions.

"Yes, we've finished our job here. You're all free to leave and thank you," she said, turning to face the confused minister. "Take them all over to the church, Tip, we'll be back as soon as we're able."

"Me big hungry, Lizzie," Quon complained as his stomach growled.

"No time for eating right now, dumplin," she laughed, "we have to be at the East India Dock at noon."

A nearby clock began its noontime chimes, as they raced in and out of back streets, raising the ire of drivers by darting through heavy traffic. The last of the church clock chimes were just fading when they arrived at the *Goose*.

"Stand to attention, men!" a surprised Captain McHoule hissed at the four young sailors standing stiffly on the dock.

Trying to set Willy Dent at ease with a wink, she walked slowly down the row, noting the strong firm muscles on the tanned young bodies. She couldn't help but wonder what they thought of being sold like cattle but she supposed this was not the first time.

Quon frowned at Lizzie and his hands made a sudden movement.

"Shirts off!" Lizzie said firmly. "I want to see their backs."

Amused by the request, Captain McHoule gave the order. As each young man removed his shirt a criss-crossed pattern of scars was revealed. These lads had suffered bitterly for their crimes.

Willy's shoulders sagged at Lizzie's next words.

"It would suit your plans, sir, if they worked their passage back to Australia aboard your vessel?"

"Yes it would, ma'am."

"Then so be it," she replied, reaching into her pocket she took out a handful of coins. She held out her hand to the captain. "I will take their papers now."

"Have them back before dusk on the day prior to sailing which is the 30th of July," he ordered, taking the money.

Handing her the Assignment Papers, Captain McHoule felt pleased with himself and smiled as he stuck out his hand to shake on the completed deal. He had fared well in this dealing. However, his elation was short-lived.

J. Robert Whittle

"I'll not shake the hand that puts the lash to a man's back," Lizzie snapped. "Follow me, boys."

Sailors all along the dock looked up with interest at the little procession—four strapping young men with kit bags on their shoulders following the well-known TLS couple.

"Where are we going, Liz?" Willy inquired.

"To church."

"Church?" the sailors chorused, looking at one another and shrugging their shoulders.

They walked in silence for a while until Quon pointed up ahead to the *Swans* ale house. Once again, he grumbled that he was hungry. Grinning, she ignored him. Quickening her pace, she led them through the narrow back streets to Slaughter Lane, and then eastward to the little church of St. John.

Looking through a wide-open window, Lizzie stared with surprise when she saw the street urchins sitting on the altar steps. The minister was sitting amongst them talking to them rather seriously. They entered and Lizzie instructed the sailors to sit down. She and Quon moved to the front and were just in time to hear Tip end his lecture on the evils of stealing.

This was the first time Lizzie and Quon had been inside the little neighbourhood church. Her eyes followed the broad aisle lined on either side with seating that led to an altar table. Above it on the wall was a large wooden cross and, above that, the sunlight filtered through a large stained-glass window with colourful pictures of angels and people.

"Welcome to the House of God," Tip's voice boomed.

"Where are the two mothers and their babies?" Lizzie asked.

"In the manse, my dear," Tip apologized. "I thought they would be more comfortable there. Shall I get them?"

"No, but have they been fed?"

"Billy sent Oly with donated food for everyone, even milk for the babies," the minister chuckled. "The mother's drank it instead! Miss Sutton has been here, too. They're going to give free advertising to anyone who offers a job or apprenticeship to a street urchin," he explained. "Everyone is talking about you."

"Well ah'll be damned," said Lizzie, looking a bit startled, "people do care after all."

"You'll never be damned in this house, young lady," he sharply admonished her. "Now what have we here, who are these young men?"

"They need some schooling—reading and writing. Talk to Charley, he might be able to find them work during their short stay. I say, Mister Minister—show your metal, you wanted some responsibility—now you have it. These boys leave in less than three weeks; the others could be here forever. See what you can do for them."

"What about the ladies?"

"Them, too!"

Percy's expression changed from one of surprise to determined acceptance when he realized Lizzie was throwing him a challenge. All along, he had desperately wanted to become involved and now here was his chance, but he realized that people's futures were at stake. *But how am I to house and feed all these new charges?* he wondered.

As if reading his thoughts, Lizzie walked over to him and put her hand on his arm.

"You can feed them at the rag yard cook shack until you find them a suitable job and homes," she said. "The women can stay where they are for now, unless they have a place to go."

"Can I make a suggestion, Liz?" asked Willy.

"Yes, what is it Will?"

"Women are scarce in Australia," he explained. "If you could find a way and they wanted to go, them ladies would find husbands out there and have a fresh start," he broke off, blushing with embarrassment.

"They wouldn't be ill-treated?"

"Not if they are free settlers, no. They'd be in great demand."

Lizzie turned to her partner and watched him shrug his shoulders. She smiled as she followed the quick movement of his arms.

"Quon says you lot must be hungry."

"No Liz, we're not," Willy grinned. "We only get fed breakfast and supper onboard, we're more interested in what you have in store for us. The lads don't want to go back to Australia."

Lizzie beckoned the four sailors to follow her and they went out of the church to a quiet corner of the churchyard. She motioned them to sit on the grass around the gravestones and, with Quon hovering close by, she told them of her plan.

"I'm going to offer all of you your freedom," she began, "but first you all have to agree to help find Kate and the Smith boys for me."

"We'll still be prisoners if we go back," groaned one of the boys.

"No, you won't," she said. "This trip will be as free men. I'll give you the papers to prove it before you leave."

The boys stared at her with disbelieving eyes.

"Thanks Liz, but it may not be so easy to find 'em," Willy finally muttered, speaking for all of them, "in our absence they could have been moved or bought as indentured servants, but we'll give it a try. Only one thing bothers me though," he paused, poking at the ground with the toe of his boot, "how the devil will we get back here?"

"How far away is it?"

"It's usually a four to five month sail, but the winds are unpredictable and if we are becalmed or run into a storm, the trip could take much longer. We also must stop in various ports for provisions and water."

A wild idea flashed through her mind. *Would TLS dare send a trade vessel to Australia? What cargo would it carry?* Her mind was already pondering the details.

"I don't know yet, but I should have an answer for you before you leave. We need to see Charley, Quon," she muttered, "they must be put to work. Let's go, men."

Hardly a word was spoken as they made their way through the streets that Willy Dent vaguely remembered from his boyhood. He shuddered inwardly when they turned into Water Street and he saw the place where he and the others had been caught stealing that meagre pie from *The Robin*. It seemed a lifetime ago.

Hurrying through the heavy traffic, she led them onto the TLS dock. She saw their looks of amazement when they passed the steam engine unloading a grain ship.

"What is that, Lizzie?" asked Willy.

"It's a steam engine, my friend. They're a marvellous new invention."

Aware of their approach, Charley watched them coming. His eyes roamed with interest over the four strong-looking young men, obviously sailors.

"I hope these lads are for me?" he growled. Then, recognizing Willy, he added, "You've not jumped ship have you, lad?"

"I bought them," admitted Lizzie, before Willy could reply.

"You did what?" asked the dockmaster, not believing what he had heard.

"I bought their penal papers from their captain."

"I'd heard about that before," he said thoughtfully, "but I thought it was a fallacy." His eyes strayed past them up the dock. "Careful, there's a coach coming."

Polished to a perfect shine, the smart coach pulled slowly to a stop beside the dockmaster's cart and all eyes turned to watch the occupants alight.

"Patrick!" Lizzie exclaimed, going over to meet him. She stopped suddenly as a silver-tipped cane protruded from the open coach door. She watched suspiciously as a distinguished-looking man of tall stature, slightly bent with age, stepped out. He stared at Lizzie, his eyes twinkling from behind the bushy red beard streaked liberally with grey. A beaver skin top hat was set firmly on his head.

"So you're Lizzie Short are you, young lady," he chuckled. "I'm John Hope, Patrick's uncle. He tells me you may have need of me."

Lizzie grinned mischievously, glancing at her partner and reading his silent message.

"You're right, Patrick, m'boy," the old man chuckled. "He is talking with his hands. What did he say, girl?"

"He said to ask you if these papers are legal."

Producing the Assignment Papers for the four sailors from her pocket, she handed them to Patrick's uncle.

Unfolding his spectacles, John Hope's face turned serious as he quickly scanned the documents. Glancing at the sailors each in turn, he read their names aloud, each one nodding in turn.

"Willy Dent from London ... John Burton from Hull ... Tom Shaw from Plymouth ... and you must be James Cumes from Bristol." When he finished, he took off his glasses and with a deeply troubled expression said, "Yes, young lady, these papers are legal."

"Put them to work, Charley," Lizzie demanded with a frown. "They can sleep on our training ship and eat with the rest of the men."

The old lawyer's face had turned into a mask of stone as he turned toward the carriage.

"We can go now, Patrick. You know I don't approve of the English and their transportation laws. This sort of business turns my stomach."

"Then go, sir, and be damned!" Lizzie snarled. "You've judged me by your own yardstick. You're a man and it's to be expected."

Patrick blinked at Lizzie's insult. He knew his uncle had jumped to conclusions and she had not hesitated in using street logic to attack him. He thought to intervene, then noticed the amusement in her eyes. The hint of a smile tugged at the corners of her mouth. *You little devil*, he thought to himself, *there's a calculated reason behind your abrasiveness.*

Slowly the lawyer's hand fell from the coach door. John Hope was seething with controlled anger as he turned to face Lizzie, his courtroom instincts strangely screaming caution.

"You hold those men in shackles of paper ma'am—revolting, yet legal," he growled.

"I'm a woman, sir. By whose law do you hold me in contempt? Yours?"

"I make no laws, girl."

"Men make the law and men enforce it," Lizzie argued. "Would you not agree these four men are bound by your law, not mine?"

Patrick smiled at the sharpness of the girl's mind and tongue, her streetwise logic driving home her point with subtle cunning. He knew his uncle would accept the verbal challenge.

"Laws are made for the good of the people," he stated, his voice having lost some of its intensity.

"You would dare to suggest that you care about ordinary people, sir? Look around you at the war crippled you see. These are men you've thrown on the scrap heap with no thought for their welfare. Women are mere chattels in your world and children are allowed to go hungry," she continued relentlessly, then finally paused as Quon fingers gripped her arm. "Yes sir, hungry children and street urchins. You choose to exterminate my class of people."

"That's the most eloquent speech I've ever heard," replied John Hope frowning deeply, "but you're still holding those men in bondage."

"No sir," she whispered. "I have bought their freedom."

"I believe I have misjudged you. I proffer my apology, young lady."

Charley's eyebrows raised, his attention riveted on the lawyer. Like Patrick, he'd heard Lizzie's strange logic and arguments many times.

"I don't need your apology, sir," Lizzie replied. "I intend to be the first woman councillor in dockland and for that I may need your help."

"My time is limited."

"As is your conscience."

Ignoring the barb, Mister Hope glanced at his favourite nephew, then over to Charley on his cart. He realized the two men were smiling at his discomfort even though they were trying to hide it. Patrick had warned him that Lizzie's charm would be like a magnet, that her hard logic would be impossible to ignore. His fighting Scottish spirit had been stirred by her fearless, acid comments. This was a girl like no other he had ever met.

"Can yer noo get the council meeting put back on, Uncle John?" Patrick asked.

"Aye lad," the old lawyer nodded, "but it will take a while."

"It is back on," Lizzie snapped. "Judge Harvey already ordered it for the 27th of July."

"You talked with him?" Patrick gasped.

"We were in his court this morning!"

Patrick and his uncle looked at each other in surprise. As a lawyer, John Hope was familiar with Judge Harvey's reputation. The stiff sentences he imposed and the many unfortunate souls sent to the penal colonies of Australia were well talked about.

It was also common knowledge, in legal circles, of his grip on the borough council in East London's dockland. Its old blackened buildings and stinking back alleys where poverty and misery were commonplace and treated like his own personal empire. They knew he was a man who was greatly feared, and rightly so.

A sudden call from far down the dock told them Charley's helpers were on their way. Before he left, he called to her. "Lizzie, Dan Duffy's working on the steam engine. I'll explain more at supper."

"Who was that man?" the lawyer asked watching Charley's cart leave.

"Best dockmaster on the river," replied Lizzie.

"You were in court," Patrick pressed his question. "What happened?"

"We caused a ruckus."

"In Harvey's court!" John Hope snapped, looking doubtful. "I'm surprised he didn't lock you up."

"He couldn't."

"Why?"

"The court was full of people. He'd have had a riot on his hands."

"And why do I think that you actually planned it that way, my dear lady?" John Hope muttered sarcastically.

"Well sir, I had to get him alone; it was the only way I could think of."

"My God, what gall you have, girl. Some would call it courage!" the lawyer gasped. "Yes, I'll help you all I can. You have me intrigued."

Still shocked at Lizzie's description of their day in court, Patrick smashed his fist into his hand.

"ACH DID YER NOO THINK YER WERR IN DANGER, GIRRL?"

"Quon keep Wizzy safe." Quon Lee's voice rang with sincerity, his eyes narrowing to slits of black fire which held a menacing intensity.

"My Lord, he means it, too!" John Hope muttered. Although his nephew had told him quite a bit about these two young people, he certainly had not been prepared for what he had witnessed this afternoon. He suddenly felt very tired. "Come Patrick, you can take me home now."

Chapter 19

It was almost three o'clock when Lizzie and Quon landed at Bill Johnson's and Quon was finally able to satisfy his hunger on Bill's crusty bread and apple pie. Missus Johnson was there too, rushing around to make sure they got everything they needed and rambling on about the court-room scene.

"By gum, lass," she giggled, "ah thowt Judge Harvey wor going ta explode when yer jumped onta yer feet. If looks could av killed, ye'd be dead now."

"Did Lefty find yer, Liz?" the baker yelled from the bake house, "he wor here lookin for yer."

"Did he tell you what he wanted?" Lizzie tried to shout, showering her partner with crumbs.

"Yes, he did," Bill laughed, walking partway back toward them. "Tip, that new minister, has lost all them street lads you saved this morning."

"Lost 'em?"

"Aye, Lefty said they'd just disappeared."

Grinning, Lizzie finished her pie and glanced over at her partner's tapping fingers. Their eyes turned toward the gate at the sound of a carriage approaching.

Nathan's gray swept into the yard, snorting at the strange smell of the bake house. Sitting perkily inside, the trader waved his cane in greeting as Wick brought the buggy to a halt. Making no attempt to step down, Nathan leaned out the window and waved a piece of paper at Bill.

"Quickly now," he urged impatiently. "I'm a busy man."

Ambling over, Bill took the paper. "It's a bread order, Nathan. Why didn't yer give it to young Billy at the bread shop? Oly takes all the deliveries with his pony cart."

"This order must go to the vessel right away," the trader snapped irritably. "I personally guaranteed its immediate delivery to the captain."

"But Nathan," Bill argued, "the lad just left here loaded. He'll do it when he gets back."

"You take them, on that handcart over there," Nathan persisted, pointing his cane at a rickety old cart in the corner of the yard. "Or send him." He pointed haughtily at Clem.

Quon's fingers suddenly began to rapidly beat on his partner's arm. Their eyes met and held for a moment, then Lizzie winked mischievously.

"NO, NATHAN," she yelled across the yard, "YOU TAKE THEM!"

"I will not!" the trader fumed. "Smelly cheese is one thing, but bread I will not transport."

Hearing the argument, Connie Johnson loaded her arms with long ship's rolls and headed toward the buggy.

"OH NO YOU DON'T, WOMAN!" Nathan screamed, as he tried desperately to block her depositing the bread into his transport.

Galloping hooves were heard in the lane and Oly's cart came flying into the yard. Skillfully missing the trader's buggy, he drew to a sudden stop.

Climbing out of his buggy, Nathan quickly steered Connie over to Oly's cart. He stepped back and let out an obvious sigh of relief at not having the ignominy of a buggy littered with bread crumbs. Reverting back to his pompous self, Nathan stormed over to Lizzie but was confronted by Oly blocking his path.

"Out of my way, boy," he snapped at the youngster.

Missus Johnson had just about had enough of the trader and his high and mighty ways. She scooped up a long roll of bread and swept into the attack, chasing a fast-retreating Nathan back to the safety of his buggy.

"Go away with yer, silly little man!" she screeched.

His unsympathetic bodyguards laughed uproariously as he climbed back into the carriage and they quickly drove him out of the yard.

"Ee by gum she's a vicious woman is my Connie," the baker chuckled. "Ah think you should tek her to't next council meeting, Lizzie. She'd beat the hell out'a them stuffed shirts with a crusty roll of bread!"

"Na thar's an idea," Connie laughed, "are we allowed ta be there, Lizzie?"

"Of course," Lizzie replied, joining in the laughter as they walked toward the gate.

"Right then, me an Bill will be there."

Still laughing, Lizzie and Quon made their way up Baker Lane to the brewery. Her arm resting on Quon's shoulder, they walked in silence contemplating the day's events. Even before turning into the yard they could smell the distinctive odours of vinegar and cider. Joe's voice came from somewhere behind the long rows of barrels.

"Hey kids, come smell this," he shouted excitedly.

Following the sound of voices, they also found Angus and John Watson, eagerly tasting the contents of a freshly tapped barrel.

"It's whisky," John chuckled, "the first of our own brew. Taste it, lass."

"No, thank you," Lizzie grimaced.

"Ach yer right, lassie." Angus sloshed the contents of his tin cup down his throat, then burped. Smacking his lips to savour the taste, he added, "It needs a wee bit longerr ta age."

Hammering the bung back into the barrel, Joe dismissed the two managers with a friendly comment before turning his attention to Lizzie.

"I want to talk to you, young lady," he muttered, waving her to follow him. Leading the way up the flight of stairs to his office, Joe slowly reached the top stopping to wheeze and puff before entering and collapsing into his chair.

"You almost gave me a heart attack in court today," he grunted, "won't yer give up this notion of being a councilman?"

"Councilwoman, Dad!" she corrected him.

"But what good is it goin to do, ye?" the old man argued. "We're doin well and we don't need the trouble yer stirrin up."

Surprised at his reaction, but realizing he just didn't understand, she hugged him. "It will be all right, Dad. You'll see, it will all work out for the best."

"Ask dad about Aus-rail-ya, Lizzie," Quon said slowly.

"Right," she giggled, turning back to Joe. "I have a question for you. Have you ever been to Australia?"

"No," Joe replied. His interest aroused, he cocked an eyebrow. "Why would you want to know that?"

"Do we have a captain who could make that long voyage? And what would we take as a cash cargo?"

"Hold on, hold on," Joe laughed, "yer going too fast. Ben could do it, but I've no idea what yer cargo would be." The thought of another adventure gripped the old man's imagination. He knew he was too old to even consider the thought, but still he could feel the warm, south sea breeze on his face and see the white sand and palm trees in his mind. He'd heard about the large and wild country in that unknown world to the south. His blood raced with excited enthusiasm and he felt his cheeks grow warm with the old anticipation he had felt as a young sailor. Then feeling very tired, he leaned back in his chair. "It's after five," he growled, glancing at the wall clock, "are you going to walk me home?"

"We've a call to make yet, but we'll walk you home first," she replied, going to plant a kiss on his forehead. She helped him out of his chair and together they went down the stairs.

"Tell Martha we'll be late, will you love?" she asked, waving goodbye to Joe at the gate.

She and Quon headed off toward the gypsy camp, but this time they didn't stop, continuing out onto the common heathland. With only sheep and cattle to observe their movements, the partners sat down on a wall to catch their breath. Hidden in the shadow of the shrubbery, the Benson mansion could be observed quite unobtrusively.

All seemed quiet, though Quon pointed to a gardener working on a large and colourful flower bed.

"They're gone," Lizzie whispered. "Let's check on the Miller place and the Byrd's."

Standing in front of the closed iron gates of the Miller residence, Lizzie stared up the driveway at the imposing and heavily curtained windows of the large stone mansion. She took Quon's arm and they moved cautiously, looking for the gardener's gate. Finding it, they slipped stealthily inside.

"Stables," he whispered. Taking her hand, he led her through the tangle of bushes to the stable block where they found a door slightly ajar.

"Horses gone," Quon muttered, poking his head inside and sniffing the stale air. "Nobody here."

Moving down the lane to Richard Byrd's large mansion, the youngsters noticed a coach and horses standing in the driveway. The coachman and a stablehand were talking quietly.

Sneaking around the back of the property, Lizzie and Quon found a way into the garden and keeping under cover of the lush plant growth, they worked their way up to the house. The sound of harsh voices were heard above them, coming from an open window.

"You were my father's friend," a woman was screaming hysterically, "and now you come to steal his business."

"Damnit woman, I'm thinking only of your welfare," replied a familiar male voice, "but I see you're more demented than that stupid husband of yours!"

"Missus Byrd," mouthed Lizzie to Quon.

The insult added fuel to Alyse's rage and, as she vented her anger on the man, Lizzie and Quon quietly slipped away.

"You know who that man was dumplin?" Lizzie chuckled, when they reached the road. "That was Joshua Cambourne and it sounds like he's up to his usual no-good tricks. I hope she can stand up to it."

As they crossed the heath and neared the gypsy camp, the guard dogs warned of their arrival.

Threading their way through the wagons to Captain Davis' tent, she stopped in surprise when she came face-to-face with a figure balanced on two sturdy crutches.

"Don't stand there gawking, girl," Davis roared. "I'm not a ghost!"

"But your arm …?"

"We took the mud plaster off."

"Who did?"

"Me and my new crew," he laughed. "Want to meet 'em?"

Nodding, she winced as the captain bellowed.

"BOSON, TEND TO YER DUTIES, MAN!"

Lizzie poked her partner in the ribs and smiled as a young gypsy lad raced out from behind one of the wagons and skidded to a halt in front of the captain. Jerking up straight, he stood stiffly to attention and saluted.

"Assemble the crew, lad, and bring the vessel alongside," Davis ordered.

Turning, the gypsy boy sent a shrill whistle echoing through the camp, and several more young lads, including Willie, arrived at a run. The rattle of a cart interrupted them and the builder's cart trundled into view, pushed eagerly by two small boys and two slightly bigger girls. Pulling the cart up in front of the captain, they formed into a straight line and stood waiting, their arms at their sides.

"Thank you, crew. Well done, boson. You're dismissed!" the captain growled.

Shaking her head in amazement, Lizzie walked over to the captain, noticing the wicked twinkle in his eye.

"You old devil," she whispered, "you're enjoying yourself."

"Yes, I am," he snapped, "and I don't want you interfering."

Wobbling unsteadily, he made an effort to move but, seeing the danger, the partners each took one of his arms and assisted him over to his seat. Gently, they lifted the leg encased in the heavy mud cast into a comfortable position.

"You're quite a man, Mister Davis," Lizzie whispered.

"You know, lass," he quietly replied, "this leg has given me a great respect for Charley Mason."

Lizzie smiled. "Have you ever been to Australia, captain?"

"Aye lass, a long time ago."

"Could Ben find his way there?"

"Ben Thorn's a good sailor, but what do you want to go there for? It's a penal colony," he snapped irritably.

"A premium cargo could bring a good profit," Lizzie persisted.

"Strap iron, nails and glass," Davis rasped. "Now go away and ask somebody else yer foolish questions."

It was almost seven as they walked down the track toward the cottage. Her questions about Australia had been answered. What had started as a wild idea was quickly becoming an obsession. Chuckling together that their enemies were fighting amongst themselves, which could have far-reaching consequences for the Benson Foundry, Miller and Byrd, Lizzie and Quon strolled up the garden path.

"Come eat, loves," the housekeeper pleaded as they came into the kitchen. "Joe told me you'd be late, where have ya been?"

Furtively glancing at each other, they took their places. Ada and Mick watched them suspiciously, unable to see Quon's foot tapping on Lizzie's foot.

"Now what are you two up to?" Ada asked, inquisitiveness getting the better of her.

Lizzie's eyes levelled on the bookkeeper as she took a mouthful, then she lay down her fork.

"We went to check up on a few of our enemies," she said, smiling shrewdly.

"And who would that be, moy darlin?" Mick whispered, leaning across the table.

"Benson, Byrd and Miller."

"A driver told me this afternoon, that their houses are closed and they've gone," said Ada.

"The Byrds are still in residence," Lizzie replied, "at least Missus Byrd is."

"You didn't go to the house, did you?" Ada asked in alarm.

"Yes, we heard a wild argument between Missus Byrd and Joshua Cambourne.

"You were in the house?"

"No silly, we walked around by the garden and there was a window open. We could easily hear them."

"Mother of Murphy," Mick chuckled, "you've more nerve than a steeplejack on a windy day!"

The conversation stopped abruptly, as loud rattling sounded in the lane and they heard the sound of Daisy's voice as she ran up the path.

"Charley, Charley, are you ready?" she called, throwing open the door.

Martha looked up from her washing in the sink and glanced over at the sleeping child on Joe's knee. Disturbed by the noise, he whimpered sleepily but settled back down again.

Daisy mouthed the word 'sorry' and went over to help Charley.

"Where are you two off to in such a hurry?" asked Lizzie.

"The new print shop to work on a new press," he replied.

"Daisy's going with you?"

"Yes, we're going on the cart," he replied, his face going crimson as he took Daisy's arm and wobbled toward the door.

"This I have to see!" Lizzie laughed.

Crowding into the doorway, they watched the Grim brothers heave Charley into his seat, then assisted Daisy up onto his knee. Everyone was grinning as they set off down Slaughter Lane.

"By gum," Martha giggled, "nar that's wat I call riding in style."

"Now, young lady," Ada's tone was gentle yet commanding as she turned to Lizzie. "You made us so proud today when you defended those homeless children in court; and again when Charley told us about the four sailors from Australia, and buying their freedom," she paused, reaching for Mick's hand. "You're planning something aren't you, something much bigger than a seat on council? I'm worried sick for you, love."

"Council comes first, Ada," Lizzie tried to reassure her, "that fight is not over yet, so you can stop worrying about anything else."

Later, as the lamps were snuffed out and Lizzie closed her eyes in sleep, she began to dream of Kate and the Smith boys. Her mind wandered through the old streets of London—the area they used to know intimately—with its oppressive laws that sent starving children to penal colonies. She tossed and turned feeling the hopelessness, then opened her eyes to see the moon shining through the curtains.

She thought of them in Australia, so far away, and wondered if their lives were any better there. Was it like dockland? Did the old and infirm and, particularly the mothers, still have a desperate existence trying to eke out a living for their children? She suspected they did despite what Willy had said about finding husbands for young women. Striking out at her pillow in the darkness, she moaned in anger and turned her back to the window.

Chapter 20

Daylight streaming through Lizzie's open bedroom window and Martha downstairs getting breakfast, finally brought an end to the girl's tormented dreams. Stretching, Lizzie smiled as the fierce stink of the slaughterhouse filled her nostrils and her fertile young mind began its inevitable scheming.

Wrinkling her nose, she jumped up and closed the window. Deciding to dress in one of Clara Spencer's new creations—the one that had a green satin tunic with long sleeves and a pretty muslin skirt—she took it from its hanger and lay it on the bed. *I should only need one petticoat with this one. Perhaps it won't be so hot today!* Sitting on the edge of the bed, Lizzie laced her feet into the uncomfortable black boots. *I hope they feel better today,* she grumbled. She stood up and checked her image in the mirror.

Uncharacteristically fussing with a few strands of hair that refused to stay in place, she looked over her new hats. Deciding on a small cloth creation with a few summer flowers sewn into its narrow brim, she took it from its peg and set it on her head. Taking one last look at herself, Liz smiled coyly at the figure in the glass. *No one would believe you were once a poor street waif, Lizzie girl!*

Kneeling on the floor lacing Joe's boots, Quon first noticed the long dress and black boots coming slowly down the stairs. Without raising his head, his eyes followed her across the room. Joe also noticed and smiled. He was glad for Captain Davis' comment for he liked Lizzie's new image a great deal.

"Me change, too," Quon muttered.

"What did yer say lad?" Martha chuckled, stirring the eggs in the large frying pan.

"He said he's going to change his clothes," Lizzie giggled, watching Quon take the steps two at a time.

This brought a louder chuckle from the housekeeper as she straightened her back and glanced over her shoulder.

"By gum, lovey," she whispered, "yer lookin quite fancy this mornin."

"Thank you, Martha," she replied demurely.

Things were late starting in the cottage that morning and by the time

J. Robert Whittle

Mick and Ada arrived, Willie was already pestering his grandfather and had extracted a firm promise that he could accompany him to the brewery.

"You certainly look like a lady of means this morning, Lizzie," commented Ada. "I think you need a ribbon to tie your hair back though, and a parasol … do you still have Daisy's? You won't need a shawl, it's warm out today, oh, and some dainty shoes! We should go shopping one day. Now you're ready to show dockland you're a lady to be reckoned with."

"Hoy smell somethin burning," Mick frowned from the doorway. "I trust it's not breakfast, Martha!"

"Oh be quiet, Mick," his wife admonished, "it's only the pitch in the wood. My, my, look at Mister Lee, he's certainly looking the prosperous businessman today! What a sight this couple will be today."

Quon stood still at the bottom of the stairs. He felt quite out of place in his tight breeches, shin-high boots, patterned silk waistcoat, tailed coat, and a tightly knotted cravat around his neck.

"Boyo," called the Irishman, as Quon went and sat beside Lizzie, "all yer needs is a Johnny hat now."

"Top hat," Lizzie whispered to her partner then, with a giggle added, "a beaver skin with the smell of power in its brim!"

Lizzie got up and disappeared up the stairs. She quickly returned with Daisy's fancy parasol, which she had forgotten to return, and a spanking new beaver skin top hat for Quon. Hanging from her finger was a wide, green ribbon for her hair.

Ada went over to her. "Here love, let me do that for you," she said, taking the ribbon. "You are so lucky to have such beautiful hair."

Watching with lessening interest from the doorway, Willie tugged on Joe's hand to get going.

Joe grinned. "Come on Willie, these folks are too fancy for us, lad."

The Yorkshire housekeeper went to the door and watched the old man and boy walk hand-in-hand down the garden path. "Ain't that a picture? Ah loves them two rascals," she said softly. Closing the door and, returning to the fire, she poked fiercely at the burning logs. Lizzie quietly came up behind her and slipped her arms around Martha's ample waist.

"Mum," she said soothingly, "this cottage would be an empty place without you. We should be home for lunch."

Mick and Ada watched them in silence knowing these special moments did not happen often and not wanting to spoil it. Martha continued staring into the fire until their footsteps faded down the path, then she turned around and glanced at Ada and her husband.

"I'd give anything to be that girl's mother," she sighed.

"Ah sure, yer mother to us all," Mick chuckled. "If you weren't so bad-tempered hoyd be calling yer mother meself by now!"

Ada laughed as Martha sprang to the attack, bustling around the table after the fast-retreating Irishman, brandishing her wooden spoon.

Partway down Water Street, Lizzie stopped and sniffed the air.

"Funny smell, Wizzy," commented Quon before she could say anything.

"Yes, I just noticed it, too. Something's burning, somewhere," she said, starting out again. "That must have been what Mick smelled."

Just before they reached Abe's, they saw Nathan's buggy pull up to the tailor's. Climbing out, he stormed to the door, banging his cane on it.

"Who is it?" Abe's panic-stricken voice came from just inside. "What do you want?"

"OPEN THE DOOR, COUSIN!" Nathan cried impatiently, looking up the street and seeing the two figures coming toward him.

"G-good morning, M-Miss Lizzie, Mister Quon," he stammered, looking them up and down.

"We go see Mister Tip, Wizzy," Quon suggested.

"You mean the new minister?" the trader frowned. "Why the devil is Abe's door locked?"

"It's not locked, you fool!" The tailor's voice cackled from the slightly ajar door and his head peeked out. Seeing Clara Spencer heading across the street with his breakfast tray, he quickly disappeared.

"Shall I come back later, miss?" Clara whispered hesitatingly.

"No, you'd better feed him," Lizzie laughed, "we're just leaving with Mister Goldman."

"Where are *we* going?" Nathan pouted in annoyance.

"*Observer* office," Lizzie smiled, "they'll know if there's been a fire."

The distinctive smell of burning hung in the air as the buggy turned into Brown's Yard. Slowing to a walk, Wick avoided the newspaper lads who were scurrying in and out of the print shop.

"Wait for us," she ordered, trying to climb out of the carriage too hurriedly and meeting Quon in the doorway. She let him go ahead and he held the door open and offered his arm.

"I have urgent things to do, girl," Nathan snapped irritably. "I can't spend all my day chaperoning you here and there at your whim!"

Spinning around so quickly she knocked her hat askew on her head,

Lizzie pointed her parasol angrily at the trader. Then, just as suddenly, her mood changed and a winsome smile curled her lips as she gently tugged her hat in place.

"You may go, Mister Goldman," she purred. "I'm not sure it would be appropriate for us to be seen riding with a common salesman!"

Lady Sutton looked out the shop window and, although she hadn't heard what had been said, she knew Nathan had upset the girl. She chuckled to herself and moved to the open doorway just in time to hear the last words of Lizzie's cutting comment. Nathan's expression now quickly changed to one of dismay. This was the Lizzie she knew and admired.

"Not appropriate!" Nathan declared. "Not appropriate!"

Knowing that he would wait, Lizzie beckoned to Quon and they moved into the print shop. The noisy printing machine was working at top speed and Fred and Gabriel merely raised their eyebrows in greeting as printed pages flew out onto a holding shelf.

"We can't keep up with the demand today," Penny exclaimed. "The Benson Foundry has been taken over by the government and there's been a riot down at the Miller dock. Now it seems there's a fire, didn't you notice the smoke?"

"Yes, we did smell something. What is burning?" Lizzie asked.

"We don't know yet, but Daisy's out there trying to find out," added Penny.

"Mick said he smelled burning this morning when he came for breakfast," she said, going outside.

"What was that you said?" Nathan poked his head through the door. "There's a fire? Where is it?"

"Come on, Nathan," Lizzie called as she moved quickly toward the buggy. "Billy might know."

Skilfully avoiding the heavy traffic, Dan sent the high-stepping gray trotting smartly into Chandler Lane where they soon heard the call of Billy's voice ringing through the streets. Listening carefully, they quickly caught the note of excitement in the lad's voice.

"FIRE ON THE DOCKS, RIOTERS LOOTING THE TRAITOR'S OFFICES."

"Dan, you can leave us here," Lizzie called out the window, seeing Daisy standing listening to Billy.

Breathing a sigh of relief, Nathan pulled the door shut once they were out and quickly ordered his buggy on. He wanted no part of the trouble on the docks. Although he had the gypsies to protect him, ever since the event several years before when he had been attacked, he feared the angry reactions of people, especially crowds.

"Where's the fire, Daisy?" asked Lizzie.

The older girl's eyes floated admiringly over their clothes. Grinning, she gave an exaggerated curtsy.

"On Miller's wool dock, my lady."

"A bad one?"

"No ma'am," Daisy curtsied again, "the military have it under control."

"Stop that, you brat!" Lizzie snapped, poking Daisy with her parasol.

"Hmm, I thought I recognized my parasol at the courthouse yesterday," Daisy declared. "It goes well with your dress, Lizzie. You can have it!"

"I'm sorry Daisy, I did mean to return it. Martha found it when you left it behind last week and Ada said I needed one."

"Don't worry yourself about it, I have plenty more at home!" she said, then with eyes twinkling, added, "no posh young lady should be without one!" She quickly put her own parasol up in the air and opened it, winking at Quon.

"Daisy?" Lizzie asked quietly, not sure how to approach the subject.

"Yes, Lizzie, what's the matter?" Daisy asked, looking alarmed.

"Oh it's nothing really, your mother said I should wear dainty shoes and Ada mentioned them, too. I hardly think these are what your mother meant!" she replied, holding up her dress to reveal the heavy winter boots.

"Oh my, you're right. Let's see, do we have the same size feet?" She moved to stand beside Lizzie placing her foot beside her friend's. "Oh look, we do, or close at least! I'll bring you some tomorrow and hope they fit, no problem at all."

"I'll only loan them for now; would you take me shopping one day, Daisy?" asked Lizzie. "I've never been shopping before."

"I would love to introduce you to the art of shopping," she grinned, noticing Quon's look of dismay.

"Thanks Daisy, it may have to wait until this council meeting is over though."

"Mister Tip coming," Quon muttered, stopping the girls' banter as they turned to watch the brown-robed figure hurry toward them.

Billy jumped down from his barrel to see what was happening.

"He's coming!" the minister gasped as he ran up to them.

"Who's coming?" Billy asked in alarm, looking up and down the street.

"Bishop Tide," Percy moaned, "he sent a message but he didn't say when he would arrive."

"Oh stop yer moaning," Lizzie snapped, "you've better things to do than worry about him. He's not going to bite you! Those boys, have you found them a job yet?"

"They left, but I heard from one of your men, they ate at the rag yard yesterday."

"Then let them be, they'll come back when they trust you."

"Oh Lord, help me understand," Percy muttered, looking upward. He walked off shaking his staff in the air.

Saying goodbye to Daisy and Billy, they continued on toward the waterfront road. Walking more slowly in her less comfortable shoes, Lizzie soon became aware of the well-attired strangers who were tipping their hats to her in silent greeting. *It's working*, she thought. *They're treating me like a lady!*

Smoke hung heavy in the air as they approached the wool merchant's wharf. Quon's hands talked furiously when he saw the soldiers dispersing the last of the rioters and a captain talking to a woman in front of the broken office door.

Hiding behind Lizzie's parasol, the partners moved closer and closer until they could hear most of the heated conversation.

"No madam," the captain snapped, "my orders are clear, every bale of wool will be searched. The crown has confiscated all of Mister Miller's possessions."

"But they can't," Alyse Byrd whimpered, "my sister will be destitute."

"Please ma'am," the captain's voice softened. "I can be of *no* help to you and my advice would be to seek the advice of a lawyer."

Lizzie's concern was apparent as her fingers tightened on Quon's arm, but she pensively watched the officer reluctantly assist the distraught woman to her carriage.

"She broken, Wizzy," Quon whispered.

"Can I help you, ma'am?" asked the captain, approaching them.

"Tell me, sir," Lizzie asked. "Was that Missus Miller?"

"Oh no, ma'am, that was Missus Byrd, a close family member."

"And the vessels, sir, can they be leased?"

"All inquiries are to be directed to Admiral Jones, ma'am, at his office on Dock Street. I have given the others the same information."

"The others, captain?"

"Yes ma'am, Dawson's man *and* the East India Company representative."

Quietly discussing the new information as they walked back along

Dock Street, Lizzie pointed toward the Dawson shipping offices.

"We eat first, Wizzy," Quon objected.

"Tell you what, lad," she grinned mischievously, "we'll eat at *The Robin* after we've visited Minnie Harris."

"*The Robin?*"

She could hear the doubt in her partner's voice and a rush of air as he repeated the name of the old coaching inn. Many times, when they had cause to find Tom Legg in the ale yard, they had seen the fancy ladies and gentry making their way from a coach to buy a meal at the inn. Never in his wildest dreams had he ever thought he would be allowed to eat there. Glancing over at his partner, and looking down at his own clothes, he chuckled.

Folding up her parasol, Lizzie stepped into the Dawson office and saw Alexander leaning over his mother's shoulder. They were studying an accounting book and Alexander was shaking his head.

"You can't quite afford it can you, Alexander?" she asked, smiling coyly.

"Hello Lizzie!" Minnie squealed, beaming at their visitors. "Do come in, you both look wonderful."

"Thank you, we will. It's so nice to see you, Missus Harris. Answer my question, Alexander," Lizzie prodded. As she spoke, she looked sharply over at her partner. "Take your hat off, Mister Lee."

"You're quite the lady now, Miss Short," Alexander said softly, looking at her with searching eyes as if she was a stranger. "You must be a mind-reader also, because you're quite correct." He paused to adjust his spectacles. "We could use another vessel. The situation is so opportune, we had to investigate."

"And if TLS helped you?"

"Then I'd put my bid in and hope for the best."

"Your competition would be the mighty East India Company, my lad. However, if you gave me a better reason than simply helping you make more money, I would check with my advisors to see what could be done."

"You would want a partnership?"

"Oh, I need much more than that, my good man."

"You propose to take our business?"

"No," she chuckled, "if that were in my thoughts, Mister Harris, I would have already done it. Remember Alexander, TLS owns the only unloading machine on the river and we allow you to use it."

"I know what you want, my dear," Minnie whispered knowingly. "You

J. Robert Whittle

want all the men who worked for Miller to have jobs with us."

"Not quite all of them," Lizzie replied, smiling, "just the ones who are not involved in Miller's treason. And, by the way, Alexander, I shall want you to bid on both vessels—there are two you know."

Smiling at her son's puzzled expression, Minnie gently patted his hand in a motherly rebuke. Then, when Quon began tapping out a message on the desk, drawing everyone's attention, she began to giggle.

"Mister Lee would like to know if you've talked to the admiral yet?" Lizzie translated.

"No, I only just received the information," Alexander replied.

"Well move your arse, lad, and get over there! Opportunity doesn't knock very loud in dockland and make sure you tell all the members of the board."

"Why?"

"Wake up man and use your brain!" Lizzie snapped. "Admiral Jones is your enemy, he knows your mother supported me for council."

"Oh, what's the use," Alexander whined, slumping into his chair. "Admiral Jones won't approve us because of our association with you, and the East India Company will get both ships."

"Listen to me!" Lizzie's temper exploded. Pushing her parasol into Quon's hand, she went to stand in front of Alexander. With her now taller stature, due to her high heels, she was almost nose-to-nose with him. She began to spell it out for the inexperienced young businessman. "If you tell every last one of them, the admiral won't be able to hide your application."

"But the East India Company?" he moaned.

"We're going to talk to them, they won't make an application. We'll make sure of it!" She paused, adjusting her hat as the colour rose in Alexander's face. "Now can you see? With no other applications they would have to lease the ships to you."

"That's cheating." Alexander pouted.

"No, it's not, it's the way you men do business and I'm applying a woman's logic to it. Instead of trying to bully the opposition, I'm appeasing them!"

"Don't worry, Alex, Lizzie knows about these things," Minnie gently assured him, patting his arm. She turned to Lizzie. "We'll do it your way if you think that is best, dear. Dawson Shipping will be guided by your decisions."

"I'm sorry, Miss Lizzie," Alexander muttered self-consciously.

"Me eat now!" Quon demanded, jamming the top hat on his head and making for the door. "Wizzy can starve, Quon eat now!"

Giggling, Lizzie followed him and arm-in-arm they set off along the waterfront road. Shoppers and sailors often stepped from the narrow causeway to let the well-dressed couple pass. Quon caused Lizzie to smile when he tipped his hat to several ladies and received a courteous nod in return.

At a distance from the TLS dock, she stopped to watch Daisy scamper across the busy road. Lizzie smiled when one of the dray drivers stood up and shouted at her, obviously cursing her actions. She raced down the wharf and found Charley by his cart. Even from a distance, they could tell from his actions that he was pleased to see her. *He's finally accepted their fondness for each other*, Lizzie thought, with a touch of envy as Quon jerked her to resume walking.

"We go to bakery," he muttered.

"Oh no, we won't," she hissed through gritted teeth, as Tom Legg's drunken laughter rattled above the chatter of the forecourt drinkers. "We're going in *here*."

Leading the way, with head held high and carrying her parasol as she had seen other ladies do, she walked through the door of *The Robin,* but this time she was acting the lady, and enjoying it. Greeted in the doorway by the beaming landlady wearing a sparkling white apron over a garish dress, they were quickly ushered to a quiet table off to the side, no doubt kept for their higher-bred clientele.

Very quickly a young waitress appeared.

"Drink, my lady?" she whispered, through tear-stained eyes. She was no older than 14 years.

"Two flagons of local cider, please."

"GIRL!" the landlady shouted, making a scene as she called harshly to another waitress. "Come here!"

Quon's fingers flew into action wildly beating a message on his partner's hand. Lizzie struggled to keep her emotions in check. Here was another facet of dockland—the harsh treatment of working children by oppressive employers.

Their serving girl edged nervously toward them, aided brusquely by a push from the owner.

"Go 'way woman!" Quon snarled, leaping to his feet. He waited until the landlady had turned and walked away in a huff.

"Don't be afraid, love," Lizzie whispered. "Tell me your name. Why do you work in such a place?"

"No ma'am, if ah talk to the customers ah'll get into trouble. I need this job," she quickly replied.

"Then bring us each a flagon of local cider and a bowl of stew with bread."

"Yes, marm, right away," replied the waitress, turning quickly and walking away.

For the first time, Lizzie examined the interior of *The Robin*—its ornaments, pictures, darkly panelled walls and the huge stone fireplace with its chimney that disappeared into the ceiling. This room held no warmth, no happiness, no heart. It was a resting place for the weary traveller soon to be forgotten.

Is this the place I've always longed to see? Well if it was, she thought, *it's another of dockland's cruel disappointments.*

Quon stared fiercely at a table of patrons by the door who seemed to be enjoying yelling orders at one of the hard-working young waitresses. Their girl brought their order and, while Lizzie paid for it, Quon gratefully began to eat. Lizzie, however, picked at her food. Quon knew something was bothering her but he was too hungry to be concerned at the moment.

Deep in thought, Lizzie's mind had gone back many years to her days as a street urchin. It was here she had cheekily stolen food from the kitchen while posing as a waitress and pinched pies from the windowsill with Willy Dent and the others. It was the only way they had to keep their young bodies alive. Their parents were poor and had done their best.

She looked over at Quon and realized he had finished his meal and was watching her. Silently, she finished her stew, washing it down with a long swig of cider. Picking up her parasol, she stood up. Passing their waitress as they walked to the door, Lizzie slipped two pennies into her pocket.

"Wizzy," Quon muttered, grasping her arm when he finally caught up to her on the street, "you can't help everyone!"

She silently continued walking until they reached Abe's door. Inside, she drew up sharply when she realized the tailor was talking to someone. It was Bishop Tide.

"I shall use my influence," she heard the bishop say. "Someone at Westminster must listen."

"It won't do any good," Abe growled, "you are wasting your time."

Neither man realized they had company until the dressmaker's scissors slipped from her hand, clattering noisily onto the floor.

"Sorry sir," Clara whispered, looking fearfully up at Lizzie and Quon.

"Well, Miss Short, we meet again," said the bishop, his eyes running over Lizzie's beautiful clothes. "You look charming, my dear."

"Thank you, sir."

"You have business with Mister Kratze?"

Still preoccupied from her thoughts, Lizzie snapped out an unexpected reply.

"No sir, my business is with you. Your influence might better be directed at your orphanages and the pigs who run them!"

Completely taken aback by the girl's sudden and fierce outburst, Bishop Tide stepped back and surveyed the girl he barely knew. He had however, heard much about Lizzie Short in the few years he had been in the area. He had also found it quite difficult to believe all that he heard. This girl was certainly bothered by something today and he desperately needed to find adequate words to make a response. He was saved from further discussion by the dressmaker's scissors, once again disturbing the poignant stillness, as they slipped from Clara's shaking hand.

Grinning with delight at Lizzie's attack, Abe stumbled to his chair in the corner. His eyes were now sparkling and he banged his tin cup on the table in an unusual gesture.

"GO MAN, OR SHE'LL TEAR YOU TO PIECES!" he ordered the bishop who looked at him with startled eyes.

"Yes, yes, I should go," mumbled the bishop, his robes rustling as he hastened toward the door. It shut quickly behind him.

Beginning to laugh hysterically, Abe's spectacles flew off his nose when he flopped over the table. He tried hard to control himself, lifting his head and wiping the spittle from his chin with the back of his hand.

"It's started, it's started!" he chuckled.

"What's started?" asked Lizzie, surprised at her friend's unusual mood.

"You have!" the old man chortled. "You're all grown up now and those clothes I made for you certainly give you the appearance of a lady." He paused to wipe his mouth. "Men think you're a woman of genteel breeding, until that wicked tongue of yours goes to work!"

"What on earth is he talking about, Missus Spencer?"

"He's right, love," Clara whispered nervously, "you scared the bishop half to death. Aye, and gave me quite a fright, too, ah might add."

"When you've finished making fun of me," retorted Lizzie, trying to look serious, "I have a question."

"Ask it and begone," Abe snapped, his eyes pinching into slits as his hands began their incessant rubbing and folding, "there's work to be done."

Settling into her usual position at the table, she felt her partner's hands gently holding her shoulders, giving her strength and assurance. She reached up and caressed his fingers. As always, Clara watched with fascinated interest.

"How long will the government take to dispose of the Miller wool ships?" she asked, noting the lack of surprise on the old tailor's face.

"I didn't teach you to ask foolish questions like that!" he growled. "How would I know?"

"Will they be leasing those vessels?"

"No girl," he frowned. "Miller's a dead man, caught in the act. They'll use an agent and try to find a buyer for the whole blasted wool business."

"Would the East India Company buy it?"

"East India Company?" Abe repeated, suddenly becoming very attentive. "What the devil have you heard out there?"

"I heard they've shown an interest."

The old man's lips twitched involuntarily. His hands slowly unfolded, one reaching for his pipe. Lizzie recognized the signs that Abe was thinking. Actually, he was wondering how much he should tell her as he applied the flame from a lighted splinter to his pipe.

"They're a powerful company, girl," he muttered through the wispy smoke that rose from his lips.

"Where are their offices? Are they in dockland?"

"No, their main office is in Westminster."

"I'll find 'em," she murmured, standing up. Sensing Abe's reluctance to feed her the information she needed, she hesitated and stared at the old man.

"N-Nathan knows them," the tailor volunteered resignedly and Lizzie sat down again.

Quon's fingers sent a sharp message through her shoulder. He, too, had noticed the old man's unusual attitude. Usually eager to help, Abe had suddenly become evasive.

"You're hiding something," Lizzie hissed at her old friend.

Wincing at the obvious sign of Lizzie's rising temper, Abe dropped his eyes. His pipe wobbled nervously as his lips dithered in anticipation of an outburst. But it never came.

"You're involved with the East India Company, aren't ya?" she whispered accusingly, leaning across the table toward him. "That's what yer trying to hide from me."

Listening intently, the dressmaker's needle stopped and her ears strained to hear the conversation.

"So Nathan's in this, too, is he?" she continued.

"But we're only small investors," Abe whined.

"Tell me!" she demanded, pounding the table.

The startled tailor's spectacles jumped from his nose, clattering onto the table. His hands clasped together so hard, his bony knuckles shone white through the thin covering of flesh. Clara's heart began to pound even harder as Lizzie berated her employer.

"It's t-the b-brotherhood," he stammered. "W-we own 30 percent of the company."

"What brotherhood?"

"The Jewish Merchants' Association."

Lizzie sat back in her chair. Bringing her hands to her lips, she let out a deep sigh. "And both you and Nathan are in it?"

"Yes."

Suddenly, the sound of the trader's voice snapping an order to his driver, floated into the store. Quon's hands left her shoulder and she looked back to see Nathan bustling toward them. His eyes quickly assessed the situation and he spun on his heel intent on retreat. But Quon was quicker and hurried to block his path. Nathan stopped and cursed under his breath.

"Come in, my dear Nathan," Lizzie invited him menacingly. "I have a few questions for you."

"I'm in a hurry, young lady. Perhaps we could do this later."

"NOW, Mister Goldman! Now!"

"But it's almost half past five and I still have calls to make."

"Tell me about the East India Company."

"There's nothing to tell," replied the trader. "Their main trade is spices from India and the East."

"You know them well."

"Maybe," he said slowly, now eyeing her suspiciously. "What business have you with them?" His eyes moved stealthily to his cousin but Lizzie was on him in a flash.

"Listen, you turd, I know the brotherhood owns 30 percent of them and you and Abe are investors," she paused watching the astonished expression on the trader's face. "I need to talk to them."

"They won't talk business to a woman," he said, a sly grin twisting his lips, "but I could represent you."

"When?"

"Monday the 18th of July at their next meeting."

"And we go with you?"

"And my fee, madam? I trust you will be generous in my reimbursement."

"Ten guineas, of course, the same fee I'm going to charge you for the use of the buggy and drivers." She smiled coldly, watching the crimson shadow slide up his fat neck and onto his cheeks. "I think that fair, don't you, Mister Goldman?"

"But-but," Nathan stammered as he began to back toward the door. "I think …."

"STOP!" Lizzie interrupted. "Don't you start thinking, my dear. You wouldn't want to hurt yourself, would you? Now, off you go!"

Nathan rushed out of the shop, muttering to himself. Lizzie turned her attention back to the tailor.

"Now, Mister Kratze," she whispered, "why all the secrecy?"

"We're Jews," he growled through the haze of his tobacco smoke. "We do things quietly. We're not welcome in your halls of power." He paused to take a puff on his pipe, then slowly his hand reached out and covered hers. "You, Quon, and old Joe are the only gentiles I ever felt a fondness for."

"What's a gentile?" she asked, squeezing his hand.

Abe sighed, then stood up and looked over at Quon.

"Take her home, lad. I'm fair worn out."

Chapter 21

The weather changed and, for the next 10 days, rain often soaked the streets while storms raged at sea. Everyone was getting frustrated with the summer dampness, although it was helping Joe's garden and he was able to brag about a bumper crop of almost everything.

Ben Thorn arrived home two weeks later from his trip to Hull with tales of meeting the *Falcon* in mid-channel. He also talked of the mountains of grain being stored at the Yorkshire port.

Now walking with the aid of a stick, after the Chinese doctors had removed the mud cast from his leg, Captain Davis caused a reaction of surprise when he shaved off his beard and dressed like a gypsy. He told everyone he was planning a tour of the docks with his young friends.

"It seems I can't go anywhere as myself these days," he chuckled when Lizzie questioned him.

Whispered rumours said Sam Benson and Arthur Miller were tried and sentenced in secret; however, no word of their fate had so far reached out to the gossipmongers of dockland. Shunned by her former friends and, abandoned by the business community, Alyse Byrd tried to cope with her husband's failing lumber business after having him committed to an asylum. Some assistance finally arrived by way of a distant relative and a lawyer.

Watching from a distance, Lizzie and Quon began to admire Alyse's determined resistance. *This lady has courage*, thought Lizzie, though her intuition stopped short of offering any help.

"Things have gone awfully quiet around here," Ada remarked after supper on Sunday the 17th of July, adding quietly, "Only 10 more days before the next council meeting."

"I hear the Benson Foundry has a new owner," Joe remarked.

"Daisy heard that, too," Charley confirmed, "and she also said Alexander Harris of Dawson Shipping thinks they'll get one of the Miller vessels. Now I wonder who put that idea in his head?" He grinned, looking over at Lizzie.

Mick raised his head and sniffed the air.

"What is it, lad," Martha asked in alarm, copying his action. "Fire?"

"Sure it's no fire hoy be smellin, me darlin. It's the smoulderin of someone's schemin brain!"

"Lizzie!" said Ada in a warning tone. "What are up to now?"

"Me?" Lizzie smiled innocently. "I'm dressing up and acting like a lady, that's what you wanted me to do."

"Those men you sent me," Charley interrupted, "do they have to go back to Australia? They're good workers and bloody good sailors. Why can't we keep them?"

"All I'm going to tell you, Mister Mason," she said, frowning at him, "is they do have to go back, but they will be returning some day. How they do all this may change."

"It's that Australia trip you're planning," Ada sighed, as the rattle of Charley's cart drew up in the lane. "I know it's on your mind, love. We all understand your concern, but please talk to us before you make any decisions."

Expressionless, Lizzie nodded and reached for Quon's hand. She squeezed his fingers as she tried to swallow the great lump that had formed in her throat at the thought of that faraway land. A tear wet her eye, as for the thousandth time, she heard young Kate's pitiful cry of despair which had haunted her thoughts through the years.

Swallowing again and biting her lip, she watched Charley hobble to the door and leave. Ada motioned to her husband to get their sleeping son, then she walked around the table and placed her hands on Lizzie's shoulders. She bent to kiss the top of the girl's head.

"God bless you, Lizzie Short," she whispered before following Mick outside.

Later, as dusk began to creep over the city, Lizzie and Quon chatted quietly as they walked to the gypsy camp. The familiar flashing white teeth and low growling chuckle of the hunched figure sitting by the fire told them that Jeb was back at last. Quickening her step, she called to him and he leapt to his feet. She walked into his open arms.

"Things have been happening around here," the gypsy leader growled. "Captain Davis damn near killed and you in Judge Harvey's court causin a riot. What else have you been up to, girl?"

"They cancelled the council meeting."

"That were to be expected. They'll never let a woman onto that council. Give it up, Liz, it will only be more trouble for you."

"Don't you dare!" hissed the voice of Captain Davis, limping out of the shadows. "Too many people are relying on you."

"It's true, Jeb. I can't stop now," she exclaimed, turning on the captain, "but first I want some information from you, you miserable old coot!"

"And I want my ship back!" Davis roared.

"Not yet, that leg's not strong enough," Jeb interrupted their banter. *It's mighty nice to be home,* he thought, *I certainly missed this girl and the excitement!*

"I won't be stopped," Davis growled.

Glancing over her shoulder, she winked at Quon as his fingers tapped a message on her arm.

"Quon says you can't go back yet," Lizzie chuckled, "without yer whiskers nobody would recognize you!"

Davis' hand grabbed for his stubbly chin muttering to himself as he turned and limped back to his home, followed by the gypsy leader's laughter.

"Hey, wait a minute," Lizzie called after him, "you haven't answered my question yet."

Enveloped in shadows, the captain stopped. "What question?"

"What do you know about the East India Company?" she called.

"Ruthless, greedy … don't you go near 'em, girl!" he snapped.

"He gone, Wizzy," said Quon, hearing the rustle of his footsteps.

"Our children, Jeb?" asked Lizzie, turning to the gypsy leader. "Tell us they're well and you had a safe journey."

"Aye, they're well, lass," his voice whispered with a soft gentleness. "You're their mother, so you bide well the captain's warning. It would break their hearts if anything happened to you."

"Don't go soft on me, Jeb," she replied, dabbing at a tear as Quon's arm slid over her shoulder. "There's so much to do yet before they've a future to look forward to … then we can bring them home!"

"We win, Wizzy," Quon assured her. "No worry, Quon help you."

"That goes for me, too, lass," Jeb whispered, "you're very special to all of us."

Monday's dawn brought the usual activity to their part of dockland. No one at the cottage had mentioned knowing of their meeting with the brotherhood today, which could only mean that Nathan, for once, had kept their secret. As they neared, they could see Abe outside his shop watching the vigorous morning hustle down on the docks.

"Nathan said he will meet you here at ten," the old tailor muttered without turning his head. "Rumour has it," he continued, scratching at his wispy beard, "that the judge has found a way to keep you out of the next council meeting."

"How?" she demanded.

"I don't know!" Abe muttered angrily, disappearing into his store and banging the door.

They set out for the dock and joined the curious crowd watching Charley's machine unload Ben's ship.

"It's unnatural," a top-hatted gent declared loudly, pompously tapping the wall with his cane.

Puzzling over the tailor's statement, Lizzie absentmindedly led them back across the busy waterfront road. With her parasol raised to slow the traffic, as she had observed other genteel ladies do, they stood for a moment listening for Tom's raucous laughter.

Hearing it, they followed the sound and found him sitting on his barrel. The old mariner's eyes bulged with surprise when he recognized his visitors. Sober and loud, he pointed his empty tankard at the girl.

"A drink for an old sailor, lass?" he bawled.

"Certainly," returned the girl, nodding to her partner who slipped a penny into his eager, waiting hand. "You have news for me, Mister Legg?"

"Aye lass, news of an admiral who hates yer," he whined pausing as one of his mates slid a fresh drink into his hand, "but it's worth another drink."

Quon flew into action, snatching the shepherd's crook from Legg's hand and raising it high above his head.

"No miss," Tom screamed, cowering from Quon's expected assault. "Ah'll tell yer, call him off."

"Well ger on with it," she said, placing her hands on her hips and frowning at the old sailor as Quon lowered the shepherd's crook.

"Old Billy Tom's braggin you ain't going to never be on council."

"Billy Tom who?"

"Admiral Jones."

"Well, we'll have to change his mind, won't we?" she replied. "Give him his stick back dumplin, it's almost ten."

Watching the young couple thread their way through the drinkers before turning up Water Street, the one-legged mariner felt a chill run down his back. Lizzie's reaction gave him the impression she had everything under control and heaven help the admiral if he got in her way. *But how could that be possible?*

Nathan's empty buggy waited in front of his cousin's shop. Wick and

Dan stood nearby. They waved a greeting when they saw the partners and Wick went to announce their arrival.

"Let's get this over with," Nathan grumbled, hurrying outside and climbing into the conveyance. "At least you look respectable now," he commented aloofly as the two joined him and they set off.

The buggy moved briskly down the back streets in an effort to avoid the tangle of mid-morning traffic. They went past grey, smoke-stained buildings and alleys littered with trash until they entered a better class district. The road gave way to a wider thoroughfare of sidewalks with nannies pushing baby carriages and several top-hatted gentlemen walking with ladies on their arms. Slowing the horse to a walk, the driver drove through an archway to a hidden stableyard.

"We're here," announced Nathan. A stable lad raced across the yard to hold the horse's head, and a man, appearing to be a butler, arrived at the buggy door.

"You are expected Mister Goldman, sir," he murmured, "would you please follow me?"

Leading them in through a freshly painted door, they went along a well-lighted, wood-panelled hallway and on into a room where a group of men in dark suits sat around a long, highly polished mahogany table.

"Mister Goldman, gentlemen." The butler made the lone introduction and left.

"Sit down, Goldman," a voice boomed from the head of the table. "I take it this young lady and gentleman are the principals you represent. This is most untraditional, sir. Please take a seat."

All eyes watched with interest as Lizzie handed her parasol to Quon and demurely settled onto a chair. Quon Lee accepted the folded parasol and took his usual position behind her. He gently lay his right hand on her shoulder.

"Your servant, ma'am?" asked one of the men, in a cultured voice.

"No sir, my partner, Mister Lee," she replied.

Heads rose to stare at the expressionless, young Asian with black, burning eyes.

"Mmm, yes, most odd," the chairman mused almost under his breath. "Gentlemen, your attention please. The brotherhood has a business proposition, I believe. Mister Goldman, the floor is yours."

Suddenly realizing he had no idea exactly what Lizzie wanted, Nathan rose to his feet and improvised.

"Gentlemen," he began, "it gives us great pleasure to have the honour

J. Robert Whittle

of an audience with …."

"Nathan," the chairman hissed, "don't waste our time with your blather, please come to the point."

"Sir," Lizzie interrupted sharply, "it is I who have a proposition, one that should bring a large profit to each of our companies."

"MADAM," the voice from the head of the table shouted. "WE DO NOT DEAL WITH A WOMAN!"

"Gender has no bearing on profit, sir," she continued. Various heads nodded in agreement. "Only a fool would refuse gold," she concluded.

"Women have no place in business," the chairman flung his words out angrily albeit, a bit less enthusiastically.

Nathan hung his head not daring to look at the stern faces of his powerful colleagues.

"You think women are born with empty heads, sir?" Lizzie continued, "or is it merely fear which forces you to keep them out of your business circles?"

"FEAR, GIRL?"

"Yes sir, fear of what we have to say."

Several of the men began talking at once, disputing her allegations.

"Let her speak!" growled a white-haired, well-dressed old gentleman.

Two others softly grunted their agreement and the room went silent.

"Then out with it, woman," said the chairman. "State your business and quickly."

"Our company has the possibility of an empty ship leaving Australia bound for London, an empty ship which needs a cargo." She paused to look around the table at the attentive faces. "Think of it, gentlemen, spices could be delivered to your warehouse in London with no capital cost to yourselves."

A silence settled over the room, broken only by the heavy breathing of men under stress whose minds were labouring. Disturbed by the silence, Nathan chanced a peek at his fellow members' faces. He was surprised to find them smiling and nodding at each other.

"And the cost of transportation, young lady?" asked another white-haired gentleman with a kindly smile.

"Equitable, fair and by negotiation," Lizzie said slowly and deliberately.

"Withdraw, we'll vote," said one of the businessmen.

Ringing the bell on the table beside him, the chairman silently waited until the butler entered.

212

"Would you both withdraw to the hall momentarily?" he said, somewhat more kindly than he had earlier. "The gentlemen will vote on your proposal."

Lizzie and Quon were ushered outside of the room to a dimly lit, dark-walled ante-room, and then the servant left them. It was barely a few minutes before the bell rang again and he returned, ushering them back to the main room.

"We accept your offer," announced the chairman, smiling warmly. "Of course, you would be willing to sign papers of commitment."

"Yes sir, but I also need a commitment from you."

"Oh yes, we will certainly send your ship home loaded."

"No sir, I want a commitment that you will withdraw from any attempt to acquire the Miller vessels."

"Give it to her," said a stout, grey-haired man. "We have no need of them now."

"Done. You have a deal, young lady," vouched the chairman, "and incidentally, I am Sir Nowles Compton. May we know the name of the person with whom we are doing business?"

"Lizzie Short, sir."

"Lizzie Short," he repeated, raising his voice slightly. The room went quiet again. "You're the young lady from dockland who is raising a ruckus with Judge Harvey and council, are you not?"

"The same, sir," she replied, smiling coyly. She offered her hand. "Shall we shake on our deal, sir?"

Gallantly, he took her hand and raised it to his lips. "Your name has been mentioned to us before," he murmured. "Rumours about the city say you're both a genius and an angel—a force to be carefully reckoned with."

"No, sir," Lizzie laughed, reaching for her parasol. "I'm simply a businesswoman and this little man is my able partner. Nathan Goldman is a very dear friend of ours."

Restored to favour, Nathan brushed off his despondent mood. Before taking their leave, he rushed around to each of the board members shaking hands and loudly declaring his loyalty to Lizzie.

"Take us to the newspaper office, Wick," she ordered, as they returned to the buggy.

They were soon moving out of the East India Company's stableyard and onto the road again. Hardly noticing the trader's babbling chatter, Lizzie and Quon sat quietly looking out of the windows, each deeply engrossed in their thoughts. Today, they had put the first stepping stone in

J. Robert Whittle

place for a successful trip to Australia … and the ultimate rescue of her old friends.

Arriving at the print shop, she smiled at the row of street lads waiting eagerly for their bundles of newspapers.

"Wait for us," she said to the trader, following Quon and taking Dan's offered arm.

"I've a living to earn," Nathan grumbled. "All morning I've given you my valuable time and support. I can't waste my entire day!"

Quon's arms swung wildly, expressing his anger.

"I know, love," she giggled, stopping his flailing arms, "but do we really want to be seen with a common salesman?"

"You've said that twice," Nathan ranted, "after all I've done for you."

Ignoring him, Lizzie stepped inside followed closely by Quon Lee.

"He's fuming," said Lady Sutton, watching the trader through the window as they entered her office. "What did you do to him this time?"

Lizzie simply shook her head and raised her eyebrows. "Any news of what the judge is up to?"

"No, not a word," Penny frowned, "but something is going on."

"Well, we shall soon find out." Lizzie sighed and turned to leave.

The trader gave her a fierce glare when they appeared. Unwillingly, he had waited, strutting around importantly and banging his cane on anything nearby. Seeing them, he moved quickly toward the buggy.

"Are you sure you want to be seen with this common salesman?" he snapped sarcastically.

We could leave you behind, my friend," Lizzie purred, "if you don't mind your manners." She twirled her unopened parasol in her hand then climbed into the conveyance. She called an order for Wick to take them to Billy's bread shop and the scowling trader scrambled in behind them. They were soon within range of the young barker's voice.

"Bread for the hungry! News for the nosey! Half price for the first 50 loaves!"

"LET US OUT HERE!" Lizzie shouted to the driver.

Nathan sighed with relief and the buggy picked up speed again leaving them on the street. Glancing over his shoulder, Nathan had to admit, she looked quite a lady under her parasol.

Avoiding eye contact with Billy, the partners skirted around the building to stand watching the workmen busy on the new *Observer* offices. They could hear Daisy's laughter coming from inside.

"Lizzie!" she called in surprise as her friend stuck her head through the open door. "Come look at our new invention."

Carpenters were busy erecting work tables against newly painted walls. Daisy pointed proudly to a strange-looking steel drum balanced on a cast-iron frame. It had a shaft running through it.

"What the devil is it?" Lizzie asked as Quon moved a bit closer and peered suspiciously at the contraption.

"It's a steam-driven printing press," Daisy eagerly explained. "Charley says it's going to print a hundred times faster than our Stanhope Press."

"How?" asked Lizzie, a doubtful look clouding her face.

"You'll see when we get that steam engine working. Oh, by the way, did anyone tell you that the new minister caused quite a stir in church yesterday morning?"

Quon's fingers wrapped around Lizzie's arm and tugged her toward the door. But she brushed his hand away focusing her attention on Daisy as her excited chatter continued.

"Tip gave a powerful sermon on charity and having concern for others. He caused many a blush from the congregation. I think he'll probably lose some support from the wealthy who attend that little church after that sermon. He also had those two mothers and all the street urchins you saved from prison all sitting in the front row! I do believe some of those uppish ladies will have had something to say about that, too!"

"They came back!" Lizzie said softly, almost to herself, then louder, "maybe he's the man we've needed to help our cause in dockland. God knows they can use some hope and someone to lead them out of this misery. *We'll* fill his church next Sunday." Tapping irritably at the floor with her parasol, Lizzie made her way to the door. Stepping outside, Billy's voice burst through the din.

"FRESH NEWS," he called. "PROMINENT MAN HELD BY MILITARY!"

Daisy came up behind them and all three made their way out onto the street toward the barker, eager to hear more about this latest rumour.

Several coaches and drays pulled to a stop as a crowd began to gather filling the roadway. Top-hatted businessmen hung out of coach windows, all straining to catch the young barker's revelations. Cleverly, he teased his audience with scant details of destruction at a store on Water Street, then he delivered a stunning sales pitch for the *Dockland Observer*, causing Daisy's fingers to tighten on Lizzie's arm.

"READ ALL ABOUT IT IN TOMORROW'S *OBSERVER*," he yelled. "THE *OBSERVER* WILL NAME THE CRIMINAL TOMORROW!" His eyes flashed a mischievous wink at the girls. "COME GET YOUR BREAD, MEAT AND CANDLES RIGHT HERE IN THE MORNING. WE'LL HAVE THE NEWSPAPER LAD WITH ALL THE NEWS!"

Frustrated speculation rumbled through the crowd, while heated discussions erupted amongst the men. Billy jumped down from his barrel grinning with satisfaction at the suspense he had caused.

"What have you heard?" Daisy asked, when the wily barker had pushed through the crowd to join them. "Who are the military holding?"

"It's old Captain Curly, miss. Two newspaper lads saw it all. He wor dragged off by two soldiers screaming that he wor crazy!"

"When did all this happen?" asked Lizzie, shaking her head.

"Just before the lads came back for more papers," he replied.

They followed Billy into the bread shop and Daisy raced off to inform Gabriel and her mother of the strange turn of events.

"I want the church on Slaughter Lane filled with people for the six o'clock service on Sunday, Billy," said Lizzie. "Can you do it?"

"Don't know, miss." A wistful look spread across his face. "I don't have ter go, do ah?"

"Yes, you do!" she replied, knowing how much the boy hated churches. "You know better than most how important friends can be. Tip helped us and we're going to help him."

Quon tugged gently on Lizzie's sleeve then quietly led her back outside and over to the new print shop.

"How can round drum print flat paper, Wizzy?" he asked, pointing at the new printing machine.

"I don't know dumplin," she sighed, slipping an arm over his shoulder. "That's Charley's problem!"

Once again, Billy's voice rang through the streets behind them as they walked down toward the river. They hesitated for a moment when they noticed people stopping and heads turning toward the sound.

"CHANGES ARE COMING TO DOCKLAND!" Billy yelled. "NEW MINISTER PLEDGES HELP FOR POOR. HEAR THE NEWS AT SIX NEXT SUNDAY IN ST. JOHN'S CHURCH ON SLAUGHTER LANE."

Snatches of conversation caused a frown to crease Lizzie's brow as they passed a group of rowdy sailors.

"That minister must be a fool," one seaman jeered loudly. "Who would want to help the poor? There ain't no profit in that!"

His friends loudly agreed as they quickly crossed the street and ducked into the coaching house.

Chapter 22

All week, Quon and Lizzie listened as rumours raged through the streets of dockland. She was surprised to overhear wagers being made and gloomy predictions regarding her own future. They also finally heard the story of how Dan Duffy the local blacksmith, was enlisted to help them with the new steam engine, rising to the challenge of Charley and Daisy's new invention.

On Saturday afternoon, they made their way over to the Dawson shipping office. When Quon opened the door, they could hardly believe their eyes. Sunlight streamed through the old multi-paned windows allowing them to gain a much better look at the once dingy interior. Walls had been painted, office furniture gleamed with polish, and a vase of spring flowers stood on Minnie's desk.

"Alexander, come see who just walked in!" his mother called, beaming happily. "My word, you look grand, my dear." She said these last words almost in a whisper.

"And so does this room, Minnie!" Lizzie retorted, keeping her voice low.

A chair scraped on the bare wooden floor in the owner's office and heavy footsteps sounded. There was a gasp of surprise when Alexander appeared, his hand slowly reaching up to remove his spectacles.

"Miss Lizzie and Mister Quon," he exclaimed.

"Well, don't just stand gaping, son," Minnie chided. "Get them a chair."

"No, we're not staying," said Lizzie. "We need a favour. Would you please go to the Slaughter Lane church tomorrow for the 6 o'clock service? We'd appreciate it if you took some of your friends as well."

"We don't have any friends, love, but if you would like us there, we will certainly go. What's the special occasion?" asked Minnie.

"Tomorrow then," Lizzie murmured. Leaving the question unanswered, she turned quickly and moved toward the door. She stopped and turned, winking at the Harrises as they stood watching her with puzzled frowns. Seeing these kind people had just caused a new thought to cross her mind—another way to help the unfortunates of dockland.

217

Sunday was much like any other day at the cottage, but today Charley didn't appear for breakfast. As a result, Lizzie steered Quon down to the TLS dock later that morning. It was bristling with activity as vessels prepared to leave on a late tide. Schedules had to be kept and Sunday was no different from any other day. Not knowing what Lizzie was up to, although she had appeared quite agitated this morning, Quon watched her out of the corner of his eye. She finally stopped, looking all around. She appeared a bit puzzled. Then her face brightened as the dockmaster's cart, atop the shoulders of the Grim boys, came into view.

"I saw you coming," said Charley, his head still down concentrating on his writing board.

"Supper's early tonight," she announced.

"Why?"

"We're all going to church."

Charley's head jerked up, his writing board slipping from his hand and dropped onto the cobblestones with a crash.

"Who is?" he asked, as Quon retrieved it. *I'm not going to any church,* he told himself.

"We're all going!" she snapped, spinning around and marching away.

Halfway up Water Street, providence provided her with a solution. Up ahead she noticed a group of women standing outside the door of Clara Spencer's home. As they got closer, one of the ladies beckoned to them and Lizzie realized it was Clara.

"Blimey, yer look every inch a lady, m'dear," the dressmaker chortled, aware of the sighs of envy from her black-aproned companions.

"Hello, Clara ... ladies. Will you be at the church tonight, Missus Spencer?" Lizzie asked pointedly, not sure if she was aware of what was going on. "I trust you are bringing all your friends along."

"Eeh, ah haven't been to church for years, deary," Clara whispered with embarrassment. "Ah'd feel right out of place, love."

"My man works fer yer dad at the brewery, Miss Lizzie," one of the women interrupted. "He's only one leg, but Mister Todd gave him a job. Ah heard about the goings on at the church. Ah'll be there if yer want me to."

"Aye and so will I," the rest of the women chorused.

"You want it filled do you, deary? All right then," said Clara, "I'm curious enough to see what you're up to. We'll all be there and I'm sure some of the ladies will bring their husbands as well." She looked around the group and several of the ladies nodded.

Lizzie smiled her thanks. "We'll see you at 6 o'clock then."

Leaving the women behind, the partners cut through an alleyway to Baker Lane. Shading his eyes, Bill watched as the two stylish figures entered his yard.

"By gum, lass," he muttered, "yer gave me quite a turn. I didn't expect to see yer today. Is somethin going on ah don't know about?"

"Yes Bill," Lizzie grinned. "I would like you and the family to go to church tonight at six."

"Can't do it lass," he shook his head. "I have a large order to bake for early tomorrow but the Missus will go."

"Go where?" Connie called, striding across the yard to join them.

"I want to fill the church for the new minister tonight," explained Lizzie.

"You'll fill it, girl," she replied, "after that performance in Judge Harvey's courtroom every woman in dockland is talking about you."

Word spread like wildfire through waterfront streets, urged on by yelling news vendors and gossiping housewives. All afternoon, as they walked the streets of dockland, they heard the rumour spreading.

Supper ended with subdued conversation, word having arrived that Charley and the Suttons were eating at the tavern and would meet them at the church. Leaving the cottage at half past five, they met Clara, her sister, and several of her friends on the way.

Vicar Palmer stood on the steps of the little church watching with disbelief as the steady stream of people came toward him. Half an hour ago, he had been informed that Bishop Tide would be attending his service. He was wondering how he was going to explain his new charges, the street urchins, and the two young mothers he had installed in the manse. As he greeted each person in turn they entered the church and went to take a seat. Hearing a coach, he looked up to see the Bishop arrive, the churchgoers out on the road giving way to let it by.

"Save us a seat," Lizzie whispered to Ada as they entered the gate.

Helped respectfully by a footman, Bishop Tide stepped from his coach and adjusted his robes. His eyes ran over the crowd before centring on Lizzie Short waiting at the gate.

"So, my dear," he murmured, approaching her, "the new vicar has impressed you?"

"He'll do," she replied, smiling, "if he learns the ways of dockland!"

The bishop cocked an eyebrow. He could hear the harsh note of argument in her voice. As he made his way cautiously inside the church, he wondered at her hidden meaning. Inside, he went up to the front of the church and took a seat reserved for dignitaries.

Almost full to capacity with still more waiting to find seats, the little parish church was abuzz with whispered voices as the bishop surveyed the frowning faces through hooded eyes.

Suddenly, when it seemed that not one more person could enter the crowded nave, the verger moved to close the doors.

"LEAVE THEM OPEN, PLEASE," Percy's voice commanded, surprising Lizzie with its power as it bounced about the rafters and high ceiling. "THOSE DOORS SHALL NEVER BE LOCKED AGAIN. THIS IS A HOUSE OF GOD AND SHALL REMAIN OPEN TO ALL IN NEED."

Quon's fingers played a silent message on Lizzie's arm as the organ came to life. Its bellows squeaking from age and leaking air made it difficult for the organist to hold the tune.

Bishop Tide grimaced at the sound, though Percy hardly appeared to notice as his voice rose alone with the beginning words of the popular hymn. Lizzie glanced along the row of solemn faces and opened her hymn book. From beside her, Ada's voice quietly joined in and, slowly the others around her followed until row upon row were singing haltingly, many never having sung the words before.

Gradually, heads lifted with enthusiasm, and the mismatched voices grated on the bishop's eardrums although he was well-practiced with hiding his discomfort. The vicar's own enthusiasm grew visibly as the noise increased. Beaming, he flung his arms wide and moved down the aisle to encourage greater participation.

The hymn came to an end and Tip moved quickly back to his pulpit stumbling on the raised step and spilling his notes onto the floor. Stooping to recover the papers, he banged his head on the lectern. A titter began to run through the church and the Bishop closed his eyes, no doubt praying for God to mercifully intercede with one of his miracles.

Light footsteps were heard and, then a murmur of surprise, as Fred Monk came purposely down the aisle. The bishop's head jerked sideways and the eyes of the congregation swung around to watch. In total silence, he slowly collected the sermon papers from the floor, grinned at his friend and tore them to shreds.

"Say it from the heart, vicar," the printer responded loudly to Tip's horror-struck expression. "We want to hear the man, not the minister."

Lizzie felt Ada's fingers touch her hand as an air of tension crept over the congregation. Percy sighed deeply and watched Fred return to his seat.

"Well, friends," he said facing his congregation, "you can see I'm a clumsy, incompetent excuse for a vicar."

Red-faced and angry at the display, Bishop Tide sat rooted to his seat wondering how best to recover the situation while vowing to remove Percy Palmer from the stipend as soon as possible.

The uneasy silence continued as Percy removed his cassock and regalia, letting his items of office drop to the floor at his feet.

"You see," he said, raising his head, "I'm just like you, a fool who needs a leader, a leader who is a driving force with the courage of a lion and the heart of a saint."

Ada squeezed harder on Lizzie's hand and the bishop's eyebrows slowly climbed up his forehead. From the stillness, a whispered comment thundered through the air.

"You need our Lizzie, lad!"

Both Lizzie and Ada recognized Martha's voice and smiled.

Suddenly, more murmuring voices took up the chant.

"We need Lizzie Short! WE NEED Lizzie Short! WE NEED LIZZIE SHORT!" With each phrase, the volume increased as more voices joined in.

Smiling, Tip raised his arms for silence.

"I agree," his voice boomed. "No greater courage have I ever seen, when only last week, she tackled Judge Harvey in court and saved eight souls from the rigours of slavery and deportation."

During the whispering that followed, Bishop Tide stepped forward and went to stand beside Percy, his angry expression now replaced by a smile of admiration. *Percy's simple eloquence and Lizzie's wild determination could very well make this little dockland church a centre of hope and change*, he thought. Raising his arms, Bishop Tide brought an end to the whispers. "I pledge the support of the Church of England to The Reverend Palmer," he announced with a flourish of his arms. "God be with you all."

Immediately, the sound of shuffling feet was heard and, attention was turned to the side of the room where two well-dressed families were making a hurried exit. The men's faces displayed their displeasure and one of them mumbled Lizzie's name.

Her jaw set tightly, Lizzie gently freed herself from Ada's hand and stood up, moving past Quon Lee. Eyes twinkling with devilment, she adjusted her hat and with her parasol under her arm, marched confidently up the aisle to the front, stopping at the first pew.

"Come, my dear, tell us your plans," said the smiling bishop, standing and extending his hand.

"No sir," Lizzie hissed. "I belong down here with the people of dockland."

"Does she fear no one?" whispered Clara's sister, Lena.

"No, no one!" Clara whispered back, emphatically shaking her head.

"You, sir, are a powerful man," Lizzie began, standing so both the congregation, Tip and the bishop could hear her. "We would like to hear what you intend to do to help the poor of dockland!"

A hush fell over the congregation. This young woman had suddenly placed the bishop in a very awkward position.

Only slightly surprised at her forthright manner and clever use of words, Bishop Tide felt the pressure of intimidation. He gazed out at the sea of waiting faces—mothers holding hungry, dirty children to their bosoms, crippled sailors hardened by the harshness of an uncaring society, and Daisy Sutton scribbling furiously on her notepad ready to report the proceedings in the *Observer*. All were loyal to Lizzie Short—he had no doubt of that.

"I shall think long and hard on the matter, my child," he smiled condescendingly.

The words had hardly left his mouth when the girl's stinging reply lashed out at him.

"And how will your thoughts satisfy their hunger, sir?" she hissed.

"I must be given time to think," the bishop replied softly, so only she could hear.

Old Joe, sitting beside Martha, frowned, then reached for his pipe. Martha took it from his hand. "Not in church, sir," she scolded quietly.

"Quiet, you two," Ada snapped. "I want to hear. Lizzie's in a fighting mood and she has the bishop trapped."

"Food!" declared Lizzie, pointing her parasol at the bishop's rotund middle. "Your gold timepiece, sir, would feed half of dockland for a week!"

"M-my w-watch?" the bishop stammered. He looked up and winced as a murmur of approval ran through the congregation. There was no way out and he knew it. His fingers groped beneath his cassock for the valuable timepiece.

"Get the collection plates, vicar," he snapped, "but first get yourself dressed!" He turned back to Lizzie. "How will YOU aid this cause, young lady?" he growled testily, after carefully placing his gold watch on the plate.

"Like this," Lizzie purred, dropping five golden guineas onto the silver tray, "and I'll collect from the congregation."

Shocked at her generous action, the bishop watched her take the collection plates and hand one to Quon. Together, starting at the front, they sent the plates across the rows as he watched their every move. He heard the clink of coins as Lizzie carefully selected her donors by giving them a penetrating glance as the plate came their way. But he totally missed the whispered instructions she gave to Quon as the plates reached the back of the room and they met near the door. Her partner hastily departed and she moved to one of the side aisles slowly completing the process.

Quon returned breathless, minutes later, joining Lizzie behind the last pew. In his hand was a small canvas bag. Under the watchful eyes of Bishop Tide, her slow stride had never faltered and now she tipped the tray of gold coins and the watch into her partner's open pocket. With her hands hidden from view, she handed the plates to Quon and took the bag of pennies from him.

It was an easy matter now to place a small number of pennies on the tray and, starting at the back of the church, she offered two coins to each of the harassed mothers with clinging children, stooped widows, and crippled, grey-bearded sailors. Whispering them a goodnight, she smiled at their startled faces as she placed the coins in their hands and assured them they could leave. As they eased self-consciously from their pews, not daring to look right or left, she turned to the next person repeating the process, each leaving the church as quickly as they were able.

Confused at Lizzie's performance, Bishop Tide scowled at the plate as they passed him. His watch had gone and so had three-quarters of his congregation. The plate held only a few pennies when she handed it to the vicar.

Suddenly, as Tip announced the last hymn and the organ droned its off-key notes, the bishop sighed as he realized he'd been tricked. Strangely though, he felt no anger at Lizzie's unusual demonstration of caring. She'd made her point that these people needed help and had not been afraid to do it on his turf. He saw a future for this young woman. She could very well change the future of dockland causing concern in the halls of power. He felt sure his watch couldn't be in safer hands. However, he knew not all would be as understanding as he, as demonstrated earlier by those who had left early.

"Stay," he whispered to her, moving down the aisle as the service ended and Lizzie stood to leave.

"No, sir," came her soft-spoken reply as she smiled impishly over her shoulder. "I'll not repair your damaged conscience."

Slipping quietly away, the partners hurried out through the back gate.

Sighing, she gazed up at the heavy, smoke-laden air swirling upwards toward the golden streaks of magnificent sunset.

"It looks so peaceful, dumplin," she murmured. "It's hard to believe there's so much suffering and heartache all around us."

Quon put his arm over her shoulder and they walked slowly toward home.

Chapter 23

The next day, Lizzie and Quon visited the gypsy camp, skirting the heath to approach from the east. Barking dogs and children advertised their arrival and the booming voice of Captain Davis shouted a welcome from his seat under the trees.

"Spit it out, girl," Davis growled as they came closer. "Yer puzzling over somethin, I can see it in yer eyes. Is it that Australia nonsense?"

"No I'm not!" she replied belligerently, "and it isn't."

"Well, there's something bothering you, out with it!" But the captain's voice had lost its harshness and his eyes softened to a gentle glow.

"We need to raise money to feed and educate the street kids," she told him softly, the speed of her words increasing. "Somehow we have to find a way to provide shelter and homes for the crippled sailors and the women with young families that have no income. They all live in such poverty and squalor." She stopped to catch her breath.

"This really has got you all fired up. All right, let's think about it. We could donate some of the money we took from that blackguard, Stroud," Davis suggested.

"You mean you'd give your own money?" she asked mischievously.

"If you asked me I would." Captain Davis dropped his eyes from Lizzie's gaze.

"You're a gentleman, sir," she murmured, dropping down beside him and reaching for his hand, "but that's not the answer I'm looking for."

"Then tax the rich!" he snapped, snatching his hand away. "Why on earth are you askin me?"

"I can't tax anybody," she chuckled, "though I would if I could."

"Council can," Davis laughed evilly, "if you can convince 'em."

"THAT'S IT!" Lizzie shouted, jumping to her feet. "That's the answer I needed. Thank you, Mister Davis!"

Hearing the noise and laughter, some of the gypsy children came running, surrounding the captain as the partners began moving away.

"COME BACK HERE, LIZZIE!" Davis roared.

She stopped and walked slowly back, her eyebrows arched with inquisitive mischief as their eyes met.

J. Robert Whittle

"You look wonderful," he whispered. "You *are* a beautiful young lady Lizzie Short. Now be off with you!"

She winked at him, pushed her shoulders back and opened her parasol. Spinning it over her shoulder, she took Quon's arm and, giggling quietly, strode away, her mind already churning over this new information.

After supper they returned, walking up Slaughter Lane toward the slaughterhouse. Seeing the TLS night watchman making his rounds, they waved a greeting and carried on past the stables.

Mick, sitting in Ada's chair at the window, waved. Lizzie turned and dashed into the office.

"Where's Ada?"

"Holding a woman's meeting over at the church."

"A woman's meeting?"

"Aye lass, ah think you've opened a few eyes to the possibilities."

"You mean they're ready to help others in their fight to live a normal, decent life?"

"Sure and begorra!" he grinned. "Ah think they're ready to follow you."

The conversation was interrupted as Ada walked through the door.

"Well, my girl," she began, slipping her coat off, "it's started."

"What's started?" Lizzie returned, frowning.

"A movement for women's rights and we voted you as our leader."

"There'll be trouble," Mick cautioned. "Who's in it, luv?"

"Me," Ada smiled, "Penny and Daisy Sutton, Connie Johnson, Minnie Harris, Clara Spencer and her sister, Lena Robinson, Missus Brown, the butcher's wife, and many others including our Martha."

"Hold on, me darlin," Mick chuckled. "Yer with child, lass!"

"I know love, but I'll be fine. The baby won't be along until near Christmas and it's only July. We won't be doing anything strenuous."

Mick looked at her doubtfully.

Lizzie and Quon watched as Ada slipped her arm around her husband's waist and lightly planted a kiss on his cheek.

"Sure hoy've a feelin, Colleen, you'd be doin it even if I were to forbid ya," Mick groaned.

"Forbid ya!" Lizzie snapped, her eyes flashing. "You're thinking just like the other men. We women are human, you know? We're people just like you are ... we've arms, legs ... *and brains!*" She paused, watching the grin spread across Mick's face. "The only difference is, Mister O'Rourke," her tirade continued, "we use our brains more than you men do!"

226

Mick burst out laughing and threw his arms around his wife and swept her onto his knee. Giggling, he held her until she stopped trying to wriggle free.

"Lizzie, hoy'd follow you to hell and back, lass," he laughed, "and if I were a woman hoy'd join yer meself!"

Lizzie and Ada looked at each other and laughed.

"I'll make sure she behaves, Mick," Lizzie giggled.

"I'm sure I don't trust you anymore than I trust her," he objected.

Quon tugged on her arm so she blew Mick a kiss and allowed him to lead her outside. Lizzie was extra quiet on the walk home that night and Quon knew she was mulling over her plan for the council meeting, only two days away. He had no doubt there would be surprises; he just hoped Lizzie was going to be able to overcome any obstacles thrown in her path. They knew well how dangerous and determined Judge Harvey could be.

Wizzy know he bad man; Quon need to be ready for anything, he thought, making his own silent plan.

It was almost 8 o'clock the next evening when they made their way home after another busy day. Lizzie felt very tired but when they walked up the garden path and saw the lights in the window, she remembered how her life had changed again when she met Joe.

She had been so happy nursing Joe and helping him recover from his injuries—he had replaced her missing friends. He slowly recovered and got stronger and her bread route had brought them the much-needed money for food when there were no more vegetables to barter. Joe was not able to work for a long time and she had to use all her ingenuity to feed them before Ada arrived to help take care of them. She remembered the warm feeling she got when Joe lit the lamps and they sat down to a simple meal beside the small fire. Life had been hard but times were good—she had a family again.

Tonight, when she and Quon came through the door, Martha was lighting the last lamp and greeted them with a smile. Joe was awake and they had been quietly talking about tomorrow's council meeting.

"Are yer ready, lass?" he asked, concern in his voice. "It's going to be quite a night, you know."

Lizzie nodded and hoisted her dress to her knees, kneeling on the floor at his feet. Resting her elbows on the seat of his chair, her chin cupped in her hands, she gazed fondly into his eyes. She was worried about this old man she called dad, having recently noticed he was looking older and getting a lot slower in his actions. Martha and the men at the brewery looked after him well and she was thankful for that.

Joe reached out and stroked her hair. Removing his pipe, he brushed a tear from his eye with the back of his hand.

"I'm scared fer ya, lass," he whispered almost inaudibly.

"Stop yer worryin, Joe," Martha interceded. "Ada and Lady Sutton are organizin the women of dockland. We'll be standin right behind her and we'll fight if we have to! You mark my words, lad, there are changes comin to this part of London."

"Aye, and high time," Lizzie hissed, "but it won't be easy."

Quon was removing his boots and silently watching the scene he knew so well. He realized Joe worried about Lizzie and he also knew Lizzie was just a bit worried, too, although she would never admit it.

Suddenly, he shrugged his shoulders and sighed. "I wonder what Mister Byrd doing?"

"What bird, lad?" Joe asked.

Lizzie leapt to her feet and went over to sit facing Quon. Joe watched the two come alive as if they were reading each other's minds again. He hadn't seen this happen for awhile and he sat up straight in his chair and put his pipe down. "What bird is he talking about, Lizzie?"

"Richard Byrd," she replied, "he's a councillor and he's dropped out of sight. I wonder ...."

Heavy footsteps sounded on the garden path and they all turned to look at the door and wait for the knock. Instead, it opened.

"Ach are yerr noo in yer cot, lassie?" Patrick chuckled, as his head and red beard poked around the door frame. "And you aboot to make history tomorrow, too!"

"Patrick!" Lizzie rushed over to greet him.

"Stop!" He grinned, holding his arms out so she could come no closer. "Stand still noo, lassie, and let me feast ma eyes on yerr. Ach aye, yerr do look everry inch a prrincess!"

Blushing, she moved into Patrick's arms and received his hug.

"Ah have news for yerr, lassie," he said secretively. "Ma Uncle John will be at yerr council meeting tomorrow."

"Aye and so will we!" Martha exclaimed sternly, standing with her hands on hips near the now-crackling cook-fire, ready for the pot of soup she was going to cook all night. She waved her wooden spoon at Patrick. "Every woman in dockland will be there."

"Ach noo," Patrick wailed, "yerr not plannin another rriot are yerr lass?

Yerr could rruin Uncle John's plans."

"This is our fight, Patrick," Lizzie snapped. "It's dockland and the rules are simple—win any way you can or you don't survive."

"This is not a rraid on Zarauz, lass. It's London, England, wherre laws must be obeyed."

"So you think I should act like a lady and ask them nicely if they would please let me sit on their council?" Lizzie said sarcastically, her eyes hardening as she confronted him. "Well, let me tell you the way it is, lad. Underneath this fancy dress I'm still Lizzie Short, a street kid who knows the harsh ways of dockland."

"Ach, I'd be the last one to doubt yerr ability, lass," Patrick shook his head in frustration, "but these arre powerrful men, and they'll do anything to keep ya out of theirr worrld."

"Oh, they've tried," Lizzie replied solemnly, shaking her head as the memories made her bristle. "They ran Captain Davis down, arranged to burn the newspaper office, tried to poison my friends with opium tobacco, and then they even called the meeting off just to spite us."

"She's determined, lad," Joe growled.

"Yes, I am, Patrick!" Lizzie snapped defiantly. "I'm mad now and it's high time somebody stood up for the women and the poor folk."

Patrick glanced around their faces before settling on Quon. "Weel laddie, what have you to say aboot this mess?"

"Quon will protect Wizzy!" he stated menacingly.

The tall red-bearded Scot stood up straight and squared his shoulders seeming as if he would touch the ceiling. "Ach lassie 'am with yerr all the way, don't yerr worrry yerr pretty head. Ah'll be therre ta see ye win. Now ah'll bid ye all a good nicht."

Turning, he lifted the latch and stepped out into the night. His footsteps quickly faded away.

"Bedtime," Martha reminded them. "We've a big day tomorrow, all of us."

Sleep didn't come easy to Lizzie this night as her mind charged haphazardly through the events of the past month. Finally, sleep did overtake her weary body, and there would be no bad dreams to wake her.

Morning came and Martha's out-of-tune singing finally got through to Lizzie's brain. Rising quickly, she pulled the curtains back and stared outside. The sun was shining for the first time in days and she lifted her window higher and breathed in the morning air. Although filled with the obnoxious odours of the slaughterhouse, she also got a whiff of the smell of cooking bacon, no doubt from downstairs.

Closing the window with a thud, she went over to the dresser and picked up the jug pouring water into her washbowl. When she was finished, she selected her clothes and lay them neatly on the bed. *This being a lady sure is a nuisance!* she grumbled to herself.

Dressing slowly, she stepped into her petticoat before slipping the brown satin dress over her head. She quickly checked her image in the cracked mirror, smiled, combed her hair, and tied it back with a yellow ribbon. She chose her shawl and hat and started downstairs.

Mick and Ada had arrived and Willie ran over and hugged her when she got to the bottom of the stairs, before running back to his chair beside Joe. A few minutes later, Joe's chair scraped on the floor as he pushed away from the table.

"Work time," Willie yelled, wiping the crumbs from his mouth with the back of his hand and leaping off his chair.

"Not today, son," Joe growled, going to the back of the door and getting his cap and coat. "Yer shipmates are waiting for you at the camp."

"Oh," the boy sighed and turned sadly away. "It's more numbers and writing."

"What did you say?" his mother asked, looking at him curiously.

Joe stopped at the door also wanting to hear the boy's explanation. Lizzie hid a smile behind her hand and Martha's pans stopped rattling as everyone watched Willie.

"It's Captain Davis, mum," Willie whispered with uncertainty, "he says we have to learn to read and write to be his shipmates."

"Just you, lad?" Joe growled from the doorway.

"No granddad, Benny, Ziggy, Shirma, Luke, all of us."

"Captain Davis is teaching all the gypsy children to read and write?" Ada gasped. "Well, I declare."

"Yep," Willie answered casually, going to find his shoes. "Ah'd better go or he'll give me a punishment."

"A punishment?" asked his father.

"Yes, dad, if we don't learn good, the captain won't tell us any more stories."

"Ee by gum yer don't want that to happen, lad," Martha chuckled. "Come and give yer grandma a hug, then off ya go."

"Na what do yer make of that?" asked Joe, grinning at the serious faces as Willie scooted off down the garden path. "Captain Davis teaching the youngsters, well I'll be danged."

Quon's fingers tapped out a thought on the table, then jumped as Lizzie slapped his hand.

"Say it, Quon!" she snapped.

He pushed his chair back from the table. "Captain Davis is teaching us," he said slowly. "He show us that education should be interesting and fun, then even gypsies will learn. So why wouldn't street kids do it?"

"Well, I guess Lizzie taught me, didn't she?" Joe laughed, waving his hand as he disappeared outside shaking his head.

"I learned at the village church school," Martha volunteered blushing.

"We thought it was you teaching him, Martha," Ada whispered, "why only yesterday he was chalking Quon's name all over the outhouse door."

"Sure, it's a great way to learn," Mick snorted. "Fred Monk taught all the stablemen with a piece of chalk on barn doors!"

"I would never have thought Captain Davis had the patience," said Ada.

The rattle of fast-moving buggy wheels on the slaughterhouse track sent Mick racing for the office as Lizzie dashed to a window.

"It's Nathan," she grinned, "do you want me to come with you, Ada?"

"No love, I can deal with Nathan. What I want to know is did you realize what the captain was doing?"

"Well let's say, I'm not as surprised as you are," said Lizzie. "He's trapped, unable to move around on his own. The old warhorse would go mad if he didn't invent something to do with his time. We saw him telling stories to the gypsy youngsters and he's organized those kids into his own personal crew. He's used to dealing with rough men and handling unexpected situations. He tries to get what he wants by ranting and raving, but under all those whiskers, Ada, he's a good man, one of us. I'd trust him with my life."

Nodding, Ada sighed and a tap on the door interrupted any more conversation.

Martha's broad Yorkshire accent called, "Cum in."

There was no movement so the housekeeper moved quickly to open it.

"What is it, lad?" she asked the wide-eyed boy standing on the doorstep.

"Miss Daisy said to give you this," he said hesitantly, dropping a small bundle of *Observer* newspapers on the doorsill and backing away.

"Thank you, lad. I'll take one of them with me," commented Ada, scooping them up, pulling one out of the bundle and handing the rest to Martha. "There must be something she wants us to see."

"Let me look at one." Lizzie's voice trailed off as her eyes read the glaring headline, DOCKLAND WOMEN IN REVOLT. Slowly a grin spread across her face. "This should put a thistle in their britches!"

Quon tugged on her sleeve indicating he was eager to be off.

"What time is the council meeting?" Martha shouted as they left.

"SEVEN," Lizzie yelled back, "we'll be home for supper."

"Don't forget to leave enough time for you both to wash and change into clean clothes," called Martha.

"WE WON'T," Lizzie called back.

Standing on his doorstep, Abe watched them approach. His hands had already begun their excited rubbing.

"Are you ready?" he growled, turning to open the door.

"Yes I am, are you?"

"They're beaten, lass," Abe assured her, shuffling back into the store.

"How are they beaten?" Lizzie asked, walking past Clara and throwing her hands into the air in a puzzled gesture. Clara smiled as the girl settled into the chair facing him.

"I told yer, lass," he slobbered, wiping the excited drip of spittle from his mouth with the back of his hand. "I twisted their tails."

Quon's fingers tapped urgently on her shoulder, remembering the threat Abe had earlier made. Glancing up at her partner, Lizzie frowned, then nodded her understanding.

"Whose tail have you twisted, old friend?" she asked.

"I called their money in."

"What money?"

"Mortgage money," Abe chuckled humourlessly, "the brotherhood financed them."

Sighing with frustration, Lizzie glanced at her partner. Clara spoke quietly from behind a mannequin.

"I think he's gone off his rocker, Miss Lizzie," she said. "He's been talking like that all morning."

A light of understanding suddenly flashed in Lizzie's eyes. Swinging back to face Abe, she repeated, "Tell me Mister Kratze, whose tail have you twisted?"

"Judge Harvey and the admiral's," he hissed venomously. "They won't poison old Abe again."

"But I don't understand," she muttered, "you say they owe you money?"

"No, not me," Abe snapped in annoyance, "the brotherhood!"

"We go Wizzy," Quon whispered, sending a message through his fingers on her shoulder to tell her to stop questioning the old man.

"Good luck tonight, Miss Lizzie," Clara murmured as they passed her on the way out of the store.

"Do you know what he was talking about?" Lizzie snapped when they reached the street.

"No, but Gabriel's a banker's son, him know."

Today they avoided the back streets, walking confidently and no urgency in their step. *Ada was right*, Lizzie thought to herself as shoppers and workmen quickly stepped out of their way and businessmen tipped their hats. Hearing snatches of conversation from street corner gatherings, she smiled when the council meeting seemed to be the main topic.

Arriving at the printing shop, they noticed the eager row of newspaper lads lined up at the *Observer* doorway waiting as Cuthbert handed out their newspapers.

"Hello Penny, where's Daisy?" asked Lizzie, smiling at the dishevelled figure. *She's working so hard and even enjoying it!*

"At the new shop with Dan Duffy. They're setting up the steam engine and Charley's new invention," Penny replied tiredly.

"Is it working?"

"It will be tonight, thank goodness," Gabriel groaned, stopping to straighten his aching back. "We can't keep up with the demand here."

"Charley and Daisy say their invention will print both sides at the same time," Fred chuckled, peering over the top of the printing press.

"Have they tried it?" Lizzie asked suspiciously.

"Aye, they have," Fred giggled. "They did a few by hand."

"Care to share our lunch, my dear," Penny inquired, turning to Lizzie as she opened a sewing box full of sandwiches. "Call Cuthbert in, Fred. It's time we all had a rest."

"Cider?" asked Gabriel, pouring several foaming tankards half-full.

As they ate, Lizzie questioned Gabriel regarding the conversation with Abe.

"Oh that's easy," he replied, "it's the Jewish merchant brotherhood he's talking about, they're bankers and Abe must be a member."

"He is, but what do they do?"

"They loan money to influential people and merchants."

"And would Abe wield any power?"

"He certainly can," Gabriel snorted. "He could make life absolutely miserable for anybody who's done him a wrong. The brotherhood won't

J. Robert Whittle

stand for any nonsense, they're extremely powerful people."

"So that was the other half of the old devil's secret," Lizzie chuckled.
They were just about to leave when Daisy arrived out of breath.

"We're ready, we're ready!" she squealed. "I need Fred straightaway to
set the type trays into the drum."

"You will sit and eat first, young lady," her mother ordered.

"But mum, I don't have the time," Daisy pleaded. "Charley's expecting
it to be ready for printing tonight."

"Charley Mason, is that who gives the orders now?" her mother's voice
raised shrilly. "I'm your mother and I want you to eat!"

Lizzie reached for Quon's hand as the confrontation between mother
and daughter exploded. Daisy's face went red and she looked as if she was
going to cry, then she went over to her mother and hugged her.

"Don't fight me, mum," she whispered, "my Charley's worked night
and day for this moment and he's never asked for a penny piece. He's
done it for us. We're all tired but please don't cause me to let him down."

"But you have to eat, love," Penny whispered, taking her daughter by
the shoulders and holding her at arm's length. "Take two sandwiches with
you and promise you'll eat them as you walk back to the shop."

"I'll make sure she does, Penny," Fred assured her.

The women hugged again and Penny kissed her daughter's cheek,
shaking her head as they separated. A handcart was loaded with print
trays; quick goodbyes exchanged and Daisy bit into her sandwich as she
waved goodbye to her mother and hurried after Fred.

"A Sutton eating in the street!" Lady Sutton retorted disapprovingly. "I
really don't know how to deal with that girl anymore."

"I do," Lizzie chuckled, "you can be proud of her, like I am."

Penny turned to the girl who had become like a second daughter to her.
Holding back her emotions, she replied, "I am proud of her, Liz, and I'm
proud of Charley, too."

"And I'm proud of you," added Gabriel, gallantly slipping a comforting
arm around Lady Sutton's shoulders. "You're a lady of character, Penny
Sutton, a woman of courage and foresight and I'm proud you're my friend
and partner. Lizzie knew what she was doing when she put us together."

"Dear boy," Penny blushed, "I think we had better get on with our
work. Come along, Cuthbert," she ordered, "you help Gabriel on the press
and I shall deal with the boys."

"Let's go, dumplin," Lizzie ordered, pushing her partner toward the
door. "I want to see this newfangled machine."

They walked quickly down Chandler and were soon in range of Billy's voice as they approached the new print shop. Moving slowly through the crowd, but avoiding contact with the young barker's eyes, she grinned to herself when she heard the hiss and dull thud of a steam engine chugging in the background. Following Quon, as he opened a pathway through shoppers and spectators eager for snippets of news, they went past the butcher's shop. Turning the corner, they found a group of sailors suspiciously looking through the window at the hissing monster.

Inside, Fred sweated and grunted from the effort as he followed Daisy's instructions getting the plates in position and making sure everything was right. Peering through the doorway, Quon shook his head. His tapping fingers asked a myriad of questions on Lizzie's arm.

"I don't know!" she snapped, brushing his hand away.

"COME ON IN," Daisy yelled above the noise when she noticed them.

The partners entered and slowly walked around the new invention. Its big steel drum looked oddly grotesque as Fred worked with feverish excitement on the print bed.

"HOW DOES IT WORK?" shouted Lizzie.

Daisy indicated to Fred he could stop and the room went deathly quiet.

"Here, let me show you," Daisy giggled. "Come look at this, then you'll understand." Leading them over to a worktable, she pointed to a tray of thick brown mud. "Watch this," she said patting the mud with a wooden paddle until it became quite flat, then slowly she rolled a small wooden roller over the mud, leaving the perfect impression of a leaf.

Frowning, Lizzie shrugged her shoulders.

"Don't you see," Daisy laughed, "if a wheel will print on mud, that drum will print on paper, except it carries letters."

"Oh," Lizzie grinned, "and as the drum rolls over the paper it prints your newspapers with ink."

"Yes, yes," Daisy bubbled enthusiastically, going to the door with them, "and tonight we're going to be able to use it—after the council meeting!"

"You think there's going to be something newsworthy happening tonight, do you?" Lizzie asked.

"I *know* there will be!" Daisy retorted with a grin.

As they moved off, Billy's patter caught their attention.

"SOLDIERS PATROLLING THE COURTHOUSE!"

Quon gripped her arm in alarm but Lizzie cocked her head defiantly and turned in the direction of the courthouse. Halfway down the street, he was still trying to stop her when Nathan's buggy pulled up beside them.

"Have you heard the latest rumour?" he asked abruptly.

"The one about the soldiers patrolling the courthouse?" she asked.

"No," he muttered, watching the violent twirling of the girl's parasol and wincing at the thought of a sudden outburst. "Missus Byrd is going to take her husband's seat on council."

Lizzie frowned. *Is this merely an idle rumour, I wonder?* she thought. *Would Alyse Byrd do this?*

"I could leave one of my men with you," Nathan offered. His bluster was gone and the silver-topped cane hung limply in his hand; worry had swept the red from his cheeks, replacing it with a cold, grey expression.

"No," she smiled coldly, "I shall fight them on their terms."

Nathan stared after her as she took Quon's arm and, with her head held high, turned her back on him and walked off.

Coming within sight of the courthouse, they stopped abruptly when they saw a group of curious onlookers had gathered to watch the soldiers at the entrance.

"Look," Quon whispered, "they're stopping people from going in."

Now what are they up to? she wondered gripping Quon's arm even harder. Together, they eased through the crowd toward the big doors.

People noticed and, recognizing her, stopped talking to watch. Suddenly, the rattle of a passing dray disturbed the poignant silence.

"STOP!" A young soldier came forward to block their path. "Sorry, miss," he said, looking rather embarrassed. "No one is allowed in today."

"On whose orders?" Lizzie snapped.

"The Crown, miss. It's a safety measure."

"A safety measure? Who *is* inside?"

"Judge Harvey, Admiral Jones and another man, miss."

"And they told you to keep everyone out?" she retorted.

"No, miss, it's my commander's order."

"MISS LIZZIE!" Tip arrived to join them. "It's no good, they won't let anyone through. I tried an hour ago."

Suddenly, a loud creaking caught their attention and they realized the great oak door had opened. Judge Harvey stepped out.

"Let her through, you stupid oaf!" he snarled irritably.

"No sir, my orders are ...," the soldier began.

"DAMNIT," the judge roared, swinging his cane wildly at the soldier. "I SAID LET HER THROUGH."

Taken by surprise, the guard took a sudden step back, allowing Lizzie,

Quon, and the minister to move through the doorway.

"NOT YOU," Judge Harvey screamed at Tip, jabbing the minister with his stick.

"Wait for us," she called, as the judge urged them through the doorway. They stepped into the great hallway and the door slammed behind them.

"This is not my doing, girl," the judge snarled. "Only council members will be allowed in until further notice."

"And the council meeting tonight, sir?" Lizzie snapped coldly.

"On as usual," he grinned evilly, trying to hide his delight, "but you're not a member as yet so will not be allowed to attend. I tried to argue on your behalf, my dear," he lied, "but to no avail."

"Well, sir," she purred, "I suppose desperate deeds require desperate solutions. We shall meet again."

Quon's face showed his displeasure, scowling as she turned back toward the door. His arms flailed crazily as he objected to her passive acceptance of the situation.

"Wizzy, he lie!" he hissed after the door had banged shut and they were outside again.

Unmoved by his comments, Lizzie reached for his arm and she pulled him toward Tip, waiting at the bottom of the stairs. Hurrying them across the street, she turned and looked back at the stately, yet small, smoke-blackened building. *What is going on inside those walls?*

Inside, Judge Harvey raised his glass of rum with Admiral Jones and Josiah Cambourne. The clerk looked smugly satisfied, as he listened to their conversation through the partly open door.

"I think we outwitted Lizzie Short this time," growled the judge to his co-conspirators. "There's no way past those soldiers. She'll never get into the meeting tonight."

$\mathcal{C}hapter$ 24

Lizzie bit her lip in frustration. Determination surged through her body as she watched the crowd and the soldiers guarding the courthouse.

"Tip," she said finally, "I want you to count how many soldiers are on duty here."

"But why?" he asked, "they're not going to let you in."

"Do it," Lizzie ordered, "then come tell me. We'll be at the bread shop."

News spread fast throughout dockland. Whispered rumours swirled around every street corner even as they made their way back to Billy's shop.

"COURTHOUSE CLOSED UNTIL FURTHER NOTICE," his voice rattled through the streets. "COME BUY YOUR BREAD, MEAT AND LAMP OIL. GET THE LATEST NEWS!"

"Just listen to that," Lizzie giggled. "That little devil knows already."

A few doors away in the new print shop, Fred stopped the machine.

"You had better go, Miss Daisy. I can smell trouble in the air. Look at all the people outside."

Hurrying outside, she pulled up sharply when she saw Lizzie striding purposefully toward Billy.

"What is going on?" Daisy asked.

"They closed off the courthouse," she snapped. "Tell Billy I want all the women in front of that building tonight at six sharp."

"How many?"

"Everybody we can get!"

"Where are you going?"

"To see some ladies!" a smile tugged at the corner of Lizzie's mouth. She was thinking of the day Connie Johnson chased Nathan across the baker's yard with a long loaf of crusty bread. She could still see his fear-filled eyes as he hurriedly retreated from the charging woman. "You can also tell Billy there's a free loaf of bread for everyone who comes. Go now and help spread the news."

Daisy turned to leave but swung back abruptly when she heard Tip's voice calling Lizzie's name as he ran toward them.

"Twelve!" he gasped, wiping the sweat from his face with a handkerchief, before continuing, "they're guarding the place 24 hours a day until further notice. We don't stand a chance of getting in there, Miss Lizzie."

A church clock somewhere in the distance struck two as Lizzie hissed her order. "Go Daisy, go, but be back here at six."

Excitement consuming her, Daisy hurried over to Billy, coming up behind him. She whispered Lizzie's instructions and moved on.

"M-Miss Lizzie, what am I to do?" Tip asked cautiously.

"You need to go and take care of your own business for now," she replied, abruptly dismissing him with a wave of her hand. "BUT BE BACK HERE AT SIX," she shouted, before he disappeared amongst the shoppers.

Quon grabbed Lizzie's arm pointing up the street to where Oly's cart was weaving through traffic toward them. Tom appeared at the shop doorway and Billy leapt from his barrel. As soon as Oly arrived, they began unloading the bread cart. Oly went over to Lizzie and Quon.

"Mister Quon, Miss Lizzie," he whispered in awe at the fashionably dressed pair.

"Don't I get a hug today, Oly?" Lizzie murmured.

"But you're a lady," the Portuguese boy muttered reverently, cautiously coming closer.

Bending over, she wrapped her arms around him. "Clothes don't change a person, Oly," she whispered in his ear. "Sometimes bad people are dressed in silk and satin and the good people have only rags to wear."

Wriggling free, he stood back and let his eyes wander over her. Then he looked up at Quon and frowned.

"You and Quon good people, you are my friends," he said solemnly.

"Come on, you lazy little brat!" Billy's voice interrupted them. He handed a delivery note to the boy. "Charley wants this order straightaway on the TLS dock. Better get movin, lad."

"We'll ride with you to the bakery," grinned Lizzie.

Climbing onto the bread cart to the amusement of the watching shoppers and carriage drivers, they sat as previously instructed by the lad, each on opposite sides directly over the wheels.

"Put legs on cart, please, we go quickly through many tight places," ordered Oly. Then frowning at Lizzie, he added, "Better hold onto your skirts, Miss Lizzie," and, as an afterthought, added with a giggle, "and your hat!"

J. Robert Whittle

Billy stood on his barrel watching as Oly arranged his passengers, then jumped onto the cart and scooped up the reins. Standing like a charioteer in the middle of his cart, he set the pony into motion. Laughing, Lizzie took her hat off and grabbed at her blowing skirts. Picking up speed as they went down the hill, they seemed about to be trampled or squished between the huge drays, but little Oly proved to be an expert cart driver negotiating the congested road with seeming ease. Skimming lamp posts and shoppers, the nimble pony thundered along Chandler to Baker Lane, swinging wildly into Bill Johnson's yard.

"Lord Almighty," Connie gasped, getting up from the table and coming over to meet them. "Yer riskin yer life ridin with that lad!"

"Yes, I think you're right, Missus Johnson," Lizzie chuckled, accepting Quon's help to climb off the cart and straightening her hair. "I don't think we'll make a habit of riding with Oly!"

"Are yer looking fer Bill, luv?"

"No, I think I'll put this order in with you!" she said mysteriously.

"Me?" Connie replied, a note of surprise in her voice as she involuntarily brushed breadcrumbs from her apron.

"I need 60 hard, very hard, crusty loaves," Lizzie giggled, "and I want them at the bread shop by six tonight. Can you do it?"

"Eh, whatever for, lass?" Connie asked.

"Weapons!"

Witnessing this girl's hair-brained schemes from the age of nine years, the Yorkshire woman merely shook her head and smiled. She took Lizzie's arm, leading her over to the table where Bill and Clem had joined Oly and Quon as they shared a pie.

"She wants 60 hard, crusty loaves for 6 o'clock tonight, Bill," his wife informed him.

"Hard, crusty loaves?" her husband repeated, turning to look at his helper. "Yer mean like the ones my assistant overcooked yesterday?"

"Oh come on, Bill," Clem whined, "ain't yer goin to let me ferget it?"

"YER RUINED A BAKE!" Connie shrieked, dashing toward the bake house. "So that's what ye were hiding!" she continued as she entered the storeroom and flung aside a sackcloth cover in the corner. She kicked angrily at the pile of burned loaves then gathered up a few. Going back outside, she continued her assault on the assistant baker. "I SHOULD BEAT YER OVER THE HEAD WITH ONE," she screamed, "JUST TO TEACH YER A LESSON."

With a loaf grasped menacingly in her hand, she returned to the table.

240

Clem jumped to his feet backing rapidly away.

"STOP!" yelled Lizzie, feeling Oly's hand grip her arm. "Don't you see, those are just what I need!" she laughed.

Connie stared at the loaf in her hand and, then at Clem, now keeping well out of her way. A twinkle of humour flashed in her eyes and her giggle quickly turned to body-rocking laughter.

"Oly, I want you to take Charley's order, then come straight back here and load all them crusty loaves. I need them at the bread shop before six," Lizzie urged.

"Well, ah guess we better get busy, lads," announced Bill, pulling his large frame to a standing position. "Ah don't know what these women have up ther sleeves but it looks like no good to me and they need our 'elp!"

Lizzie quickly explained her plan and they all roared with laughter.

"It just might work, luv," laughed Connie, "and we'll 'av fun doin it."

Lizzie and Quon linked arms, grinning with satisfaction as they waved goodbye, and left them busily carrying out her orders.

Down the street, they passed the brewery entrance and John Watson hailed them.

"Sorry lass," he growled, "we've all heard the news."

"What news?"

"That soldiers are guarding the council office and courthouse." He paused, removing his pipe, "You know, lass," he muttered, "it just might not be the right time for a woman to be on council."

"Do me a favour, Mister Watson," Lizzie replied, smiling coyly, "use the brains God gave you to make whisky and mind your own business!"

The whisky maker dropped his eyes and stammered an apology. Lizzie pressed home her advantage.

"I need your support, Mister Watson, not your doubt."

Quon tapped her arm and pointed up the street to the top of Goat Hill where a lone, hunched figure stood watching.

"Him big worried," Quon sighed as they hurried toward Joe.

"It's all over now," the old man mumbled as they joined him. "They've finally beaten yer, lass."

"Don't you believe it, Dad," she chuckled, "this day is not over yet!"

"But yer can't fight the military," Joe growled.

"GRANDDAD!" came Willie's voice, destroying any further conversation as he came tearing across the lane to meet them.

Sighing, Joe bent down to hug the boy then smiled gratefully as Lizzie helped him up and Quon chased Willie back to the cottage. As they entered, Martha announced that supper wouldn't be ready for about 10 minutes.

"Why don't you and Quon go and get dressed, Lizzie. You just have time," she suggested.

"Good idea, Martha. Let's go, Quon, I think we shall put on our very best outfits tonight," she murmured as she pulled her reluctant partner toward the steps.

Fifteen minutes later, Lizzie returned to the kitchen to find Quon and the others already at the table. She slowed to make her entrance.

Martha was the first to see her. Gasping, the housekeeper stopped, plate in hand, to watch with undisguised pride as Lizzie walked slowly down the stairs and stopped. Joe turned and smiled adoringly, looking as if he was going to cry. She walked over to him and, gathering the folds of the green skirt, trimmed with narrow white lace, curtsied deeply. Then, sweeping her rolled-brim, beaded hat onto her head, she sat down at the table.

Quon, dressed handsomely in his black suit and white shirt, seemed unable to speak as he gazed at his partner. By the time she sat down, he found his voice again.

"Wizzy beautiful," he whispered.

"Ee yer do look grand, luv," murmured the housekeeper, beginning to set plates of food in front of them. "And so do you, Quon."

"You look every inch a lady now, Lizzie," Ada smiled approvingly. "I can even smell the powerful aroma of authority!"

Daisy giggled and Charley nudged her with his shoulder. Willie jumped off his chair and ran around the table to stand beside his aunt.

"Mum," he cried, pointing at Lizzie. Willie's eyes spoke volumes as he continued to stare at the girl.

"What is it, m'lad?" Martha gently coaxed the boy.

"Aunt Wizzy going away." His voice trembled and a tear ran down his chubby cheek.

"Come here, you little rascal," Lizzie laughed, pushing her chair back and holding out her arms. "I'm not going away, come give me a cuddle."

Relief showed instantly on the boy's face and he brushed his tear away and scrambled onto her knee.

"Lizzie, don't let him do that," Ada admonished the girl. "He'll crease your dress. Get down please, son. Come on, your dinner is waiting."

"All right everyone, simmer down and let's get eating. We don't have a lot of time," Martha declared, passing out the last plate to Lizzie.

No one had yet mentioned the council meeting though Lizzie was sure everyone had talked about it during her absence. Remembering Martha's rule of no business during dinner, they ate quickly with only bits of casual conversation breaking the silence. Then, noisily scraping the last of his steam pudding and custard from his bowl, Quon's fingers reached out on the table and beat out a rapid message. Heads silently turned to watch Lizzie and saw her nod.

Mick pushed back his chair and grinned, folding his arms across his chest. Mischievously, he looked across the table as Martha scooped the dessert plates away and, uncharacteristically, returned to sit with them.

"Right," she said, "now you can tell her."

"Well, me darlin," the Irishman began, chuckling mysteriously. "You're going to need some help tonight!"

"I know. I've sent a call out for all the women in dockland to be at the bread shop at six," Lizzie replied.

"And I told all the rag men, dray drivers and stable hands," the Irishman countered, grinning back at her. "These were the men who helped us raid the Spaniards! It's been a long time since they had this much excitement in their lives."

Eyebrows raised, Lizzie listened intently. Her hand stopped Quon's fingers tapping on the table, as Mick continued, "They're marching on the courthouse tonight."

"That's good," Lizzie said softly, glancing over at the mantle clock. Pushing back her chair, she rose. "I don't want them *in* this fight, Mick. I just want them to be there."

"But me darlin," Mick pleaded, "ther ready and willin to fight for yer, girl!"

Lizzie looked at him solemnly. "Not tonight, Mick," she said softly.

"You'll need their help, love," Joe interceded, "if you're going to force your way in."

Daisy began to giggle and Charley looked at her sideways and frowned.

"I don't think so," Lizzie continued, raising her eyebrows at Daisy and now allowing a smile to light up her pretty face. "I have a plan. We're going to arm all the women with crusty loaves of Bill Johnson's bread."

"Bread ... to fight solders!" Charley Mason gasped.

"You've obviously never seen Connie Johnson swinging a crusty loaf of bread, lad," she giggled. "It's a fearsome sight!"

"This I have to see," Charley laughed, glancing over at Daisy. "You already knew about this didn't you, love?"

Daisy smiled back at him coyly.

A shrill whistle from out in the lane told them the Grim brothers had arrived.

"Come on," announced Lizzie, pushing her chair in and smoothing the wrinkles from her dress. "Let's get this evening started."

"Off you go, son," Ada directed her son. "You can stay with the gypsies and Captain Davis until your father comes to get you."

Chapter 25

Led by the Grim brothers pulling Charley's cart, with Daisy walking beside, the small cavalcade made its way down Slaughter Lane. They had not gone far when they met up with a large group of men. The TLS workers cheered when they saw Lizzie and quickly formed a line behind them. Shoulders squared and heads held high, they moved proudly off.

Almost instantly, the sound of a fife and drum was heard and Lizzie turned around in surprise.

"LIZZIE, LIZZIE," began the chant, as the group marched toward the bread shop. Along the way, more inquisitive men and women joined them, most not even aware of what was happening.

"It's like an army," Daisy commented to Charley.

"They're all good men who have been given a second chance at life by our Lizzie, just like you and me," the dockmaster replied, "and they'll fight for her if need be. You watch!"

"Listen to Billy!" Daisy called excitedly to Lizzie.

"LADIES, GET YER FREE LOAVES!" Billy shouted. "ONE FOR EATING AND ONE FOR BEATING! COME LADIES, GATHER AROUND AND SHOW YER FIGHTING SPIRIT FOR THE FIRST WOMAN COUNCILLOR OF DOCKLAND."

Crowds of sour-faced women now filled the street in front of the bread shop as Lizzie's little army arrived.

"How is she going to do this?" Penny whispered to Ada, as Connie helped Lizzie climb onto the barrel and face the crowd.

"I have no idea, love," the bookkeeper chuckled, "but I feel we're about to find out!"

"RIGHT," Lizzie shouted, "ALL THOSE WOMEN WHO WANT FREE BREAD, FOLLOW ME. WE'RE GOING TO TAKE OVER THE COUNCIL OFFICES."

"Soldiers are guarding it," a shrill voice bleated from somewhere in the crowd. "We can't fight 'em all!"

"OH, CAN'T WE?" Connie yelled back, taking a crusty old loaf from Billy and swinging it like a club. She pretended to bang it against the side of the barrel Lizzie was standing on. "WE'LL BEAT OUR WAY

THROUGH THEM LACKEYS, WE'LL SHOW 'EM!"

The stern faces of the women slowly broke into smiles, then grins, as they realized what was going to happen. First, Martha moved forward to take two loaves of the hard bread, handing one to Lizzie and helping her down from the barrel. Ada was next and then Penny Sutton, followed by Ada's church group with some of the more daring women egging on the others.

Before long, the women were all armed with bread and pushing Lizzie to the front the march toward the council offices began. Beside them, the men also fell into step, curious about this army of women and eager to see what was going to happen.

Arriving at the courthouse, sure enough, a group of about a dozen soldiers blocked the entrance, just as before. They noticed the women were carrying loaves, but as Lizzie had ordered them to hold the bread normally in their arms, the soldiers did not suspect anything.

"You can't go in here," the officer snorted. "be off with you or I shall have you all arrested!"

Connie raised her loaf and swung with deadly accuracy, crumbs flying in all directions as it crashed onto the officer's ear.

"Oww, what …!" he exclaimed in surprise, staggering backwards, his musket falling to the ground.

One of the TLS men rushed forward to pick it up and darted back into the crowd as the confused soldier moved toward the front of the building in an effort to escape the several other women heading toward him with upraised loaves. This gave courage to the other loaf-wielding women who, with excited shouts and screams, rushed in to attack the other soldiers who were all looking very puzzled. Urged on by Joe and Mick, the TLS workers yelled their support. The fight was quickly over and the soldiers, many now without weapons, were put to flight.

"FILL THE PUBLIC SEATS WITH WOMEN," Lizzie shouted to anyone who could hear. Then seeing Ada, she added, "Tell Mick to put our men on guard outside."

The women surged through the now-open doors, laughing and congratulating each other.

"Look Wizzy," Quon Lee tugged on her sleeve and pointed to an arriving carriage. "Patrick and uncle come."

Stepping to one side, Lizzie waited on the steps as Patrick and John Hope alighted from the carriage and strode toward her.

"Is this another of your tricks, girl?" the lawyer's voice thundered, looking her up and down. "I shall take no part in a riot!"

"Ach, therre's nay a rriot, Uncle John," the younger Scot assured him, winking at Lizzie. "Ah think it would be best, sirr, if you escorrted this lovely young lass into the meetin."

John Hope stood sternly looking from one to the other. Then, his face broke into a grin, and he held out his arm.

Inside, Judge Harvey and Admiral Jones stared dumbfounded as the public gallery began to fill with women, their clattering feet echoing on the bare wooden floor erasing the stillness. Albert Potter leapt to his feet and cheered, while Tom Jackson, stared at the table and hid a grin behind his hand.

"Good evening, gentlemen." The imposing figure of Sir John Hope walked to the front of the room and faced the councillors. When he spoke again, his deep baritone voice cut through the tension-filled air as he took his place near the table. "Arre yee rready to starrt yerr meeting?"

"The meeting has been called off," the admiral retorted. "Soldiers are outside and just who are you?"

"Therre arre no soldierrs outside this building, man," John Hope growled. "Rrule Number 24 of the Municipal Act states, sir, that it is illegal to cancel a council meeting without firrst inforrming the generral public! I am Sir John Hope, legal representative and Agent for the Crown, here to see that goverrnment rregulations arre followed!"

"Wait for me!" a brown-robed figure shouted as Tip rushed into the room and up to the table, quickly taking one of the empty seats.

"Toppit!" Judge Harvey hissed at the already edgy clerk, "clear this room immediately!"

"B-but sir," the court clerk stammered, "the soldiers are gone!"

Albert Potter leapt up from his seat and, with a sweep of his arm, beckoned to Lizzie and offered her a chair.

Judge Harvey and Admiral Jones scowled fiercely as she confidently moved toward the front and sat down at the table, calmly adjusting the folds of her dress. The shock of a Crown regulator and a woman in their midst was almost too much for Admiral Jones who had been assured by the judge that this could not happen. Gasping for air, his face turned beetroot red as he slumped back in his chair.

"Shall I read them your letter, sir?" Lizzie directed her request at the judge.

Eyes bulging with hatred, he slowly shook his head. With a shaking hand, he knocked his drink onto the floor spreading shards of glass everywhere.

"What did you just say, Miss Short?" asked Sir John scowling at Lizzie as the bedlam continued.

"Call a vote, Harvey," Admiral Jones gasped, "we must follow procedure."

"COULD WE HAVE ORRDER, PLEASE," thundered Sir John, waiting until quiet prevailed. "Therre are two empty chairrs to be filled before any vote may be called."

Suddenly, two figures entered the door at the front of the room and all eyes followed the newcomers. Missus Byrd was ushered to her seat by a tall gentleman in barrister's robes. Alyse was trying her best to keep calm having arrived in the middle of the mêlée outside and having to find their way to another door had made them late. Bound on vengeance, she had prepared herself for this night with the aid of counsel although she had absolutely no knowledge of who was to blame for her troubles. She looked around the table eyeing everyone with suspicion.

"Excuse the interruption, gentlemen," her counsel announced, gently pushing Alyse into a chair. "Richard Byrd is unavailable tonight and will be represented by his wife at this council meeting."

"NO!" the judge wailed dementedly.

"Humph," commented Mister Hope, frowning deeply. "This is highly irregular, but correct. You may continue with your meeting, gentlemen."

Labouring under intense anxiety, Judge Harvey called the meeting to order and quickly requested a vote on the acceptance of Lizzie Short as a new member of council.

"Are all her papers in order?" Tom Jackson asked smugly.

"Toppit?" the Admiral demanded, peering at the clerk.

"Y-yes sir."

"Then those in favour, show your hand," Judge Harvey growled angrily, scowling at the towering figure of John Hope watching them carefully.

Slowly, the judge raised his right hand, though his eyes never lifted from the table. Admiral Jones hissed in derision, his hands remaining on the tabletop. Tom Jackson, Percy Palmer and Albert Potter all signified their approval.

"Missus Byrd, pay attention!" the admiral snapped irritably. "Which way do you vote?"

Glancing timidly around the table, Alyse slowly raised her hand.

"That only leaves you, sir," Lizzie said coyly, leaning toward the admiral. "I'm sure Harry Roach, captain of the *Black Otter*, would expect *you* to vote for me, sir!"

"You must cast your vote, sir," Sir John reminded the admiral, but his legal mind had not missed the girl's comment which had visibly shaken the old naval man. Inwardly, the lawyer smiled with admiration for this dockland lass who was putting up such a hard fight for a place on council. What else was going on behind her confident acting?

"Roach is dead," Admiral Jones snarled.

"Oh no sir, he survived," she hissed calmly.

"Your vote, sir," the lawyer's voice thundered, "discuss friends later!"

"Methinks the cutlass at my throat, demands a 'yes'," the admiral snorted.

"Motion passed!" exclaimed the Chairman, none too eagerly.

"Thank you," growled John Hope. "This council has duly accepted Miss Short as a legal member."

Leaping to their feet, the packed public gallery burst into wild cheers and clapping led by Ada and Connie Johnson.

"ORDER, ORDER," the judge shouted. His gavel crashed onto the table. "Mark my words," he boomed, looking toward the gallery of women. "Miss Short's seat on my council will not be a comfortable one!"

The old Scottish lawyer watched solemnly and shook his head. Although getting tired, he was beginning to enjoy his part of this history-making moment. A second round of cheering sounded from the men outside and Quon was seen returning to his seat.

"Meeting adjourned," ranted the frustrated judge, smashing his gavel so hard the head broke off and whizzed down the table bouncing off Admiral Jones' nose and onto Tip's lap.

"EVERYONE, KEEP YOUR SEATS, PLEASE," Sir John shouted with fierce authority. "The meeting is *not* over. The Crown demands you complete the whole procedure, as required by law."

"What does he mean?" Martha whispered, as she and some of the other women stood to leave.

"I'm not sure," Penny murmured. "We'd better sit down and listen."

Slowly the room lapsed into an uneasy silence, as those remaining regained their seats. Only the sound of the admiral sniffling, as he dabbed at his bleeding nose, was heard.

"Now, sirr," John Hope waved some papers in his hand as he strode to a position behind the minister, "you will take a vote on the office of chairrman of this new council."

"Damn you, sir. I will not!" the voice of Judge Harvey wavered with a sudden uncertainty, "I am chairman."

"Procedure, sir," the lawyer insisted, waving the papers.

"He's right, you fool," Admiral Jones sniffled. "Get on with it, man."

"I PROPOSE LIZZIE SHORT AS CHAIRMAN," Tip shouted, leaping to his feet.

Lizzie glanced up at the wide-eyed faces of her friends in the public gallery. Her eyes skipped quickly along the rows searching for Quon Lee, finding him crouched at the end of a row near the back of the room. She smiled and he raised his fist.

John Hope glowered at the judge then slipped his wire-framed spectacles back on. He turned the pages of the document in his hand.

"You must accept the prroposal, sirr," he growled, concentrating on the paper in his hand, "but first you arre legally bound to dissolve the office of chairrman and offer yerrself for re-election—if you wish to rremain in the office, that is."

"Let me see those papers, sir," Judge Harvey snarled, holding out his hand. "I shall interpret the law in these matters."

"Hold your tongue, sir. I am charged to represent the Crown in all propriety matters of this jurisdiction."

"Who is that man?" Penny whispered to Ada.

"He's Patrick's uncle. He's an important Scottish lawyer."

Pouting under the lawyer's fierce stare, Judge Harvey put his hand down and shuffled nervously in his chair before finally announcing, "I hereby dissolve the municipal offices, and elect myself chairman!"

"NO, NO," Sir John snapped harshly. "You must call a vote. Will those in favour of Judge Harvey please raise your hands."

"This is mutiny!" the judge growled when the lone hand of Admiral Jones rose from the table.

Alyse Byrd, looking confused and lost, slowly began to raise her hand.

"Madam!" asked John Hope. "Are you voting for Judge Harvey?"

"No, NO!" Alyse whimpered, as her hand dropped limply into her lap.

"Now gentlemen," the lawyer hissed, a note of satisfaction in his voice, "all those in favour of Miss Short for chairman?"

Tom Jackson was the first to raise his hand, as he had promised Lizzie so long ago, followed quickly by Tip and Albert Porter.

"And you, madam?"

Alyse Byrd smiled in self-conscious confusion. She looked around the table, surveying each face one more time, then slowly raised her hand.

Chapter 26

A gasp ran through the public gallery. Lizzie had not only been accepted as chairman of council, but this tall, fierce government regulator had turned the tables on both Judge Harvey and the admiral.

"Miss Short is duly elected chairman," Sir John stated firmly. "Judge Harvey, you will be required to exchange seats with the lady."

Lizzie felt the firm hand of John Hope on her arm as he eased her from her chair and escorted her around the table, past a despondent and muttering, Judge Harvey. She caught the twinkle in the old Scotsman's eye when he leaned toward her.

"I grranted yourr wish, Lizzie Short, now do it weel!" he hissed into her ear. Moving away, before she could react, he once again addressed the council. "Miss Short and Council," he began, "you may now carry on with yourr meeting. I shall rremain as an observer and rreport this evening's worrk directly to the goverrnment ministerr."

Taking a seat against the wall, John Hope chuckled to himself. He had lied to the meeting but his plan had worked. That girl had impressed him at their meeting on the docks and with Patrick's insistence, her cause had stirred his appetite for adventure and justice.

Some years before, his nephew had told of how Lizzie had divided the spoils from a pirate's locker, returning to him the family ring and other Douglas jewellery discovered amongst the pirate's booty. Patrick's words again ran through his head. *She desperately needs your help, Uncle John.* He didn't often do favours for anyone. *Lizzie's exploits have intrigued me and, with just cause.*

Slowly, Lizzie rose to her feet, a magnificent sight in her green satin dress with her beautiful mane of auburn hair. When she turned to face the gallery of women, a snap of her fingers brought Quon Lee to the front, going to stand off to the side.

Ladies," she said loudly so all could hear. "I thank you all. We've made history tonight and if we all stick together, we'll make more tomorrow."

"I need food, not promises, girl," one voice wailed.

"There's a free loaf at the bread shop for every one of you."

"Bribery!" Judge Harvey snapped pompously.

J. Robert Whittle

The gallery came to their feet and cheered as many of them moved to the exit.

"You should know, sir. It's common knowledge you're a master of the art!" quipped the girl.

John Hope stifled a chuckle. *This girl not only has nerve, she's smart!*

"What's happening in there?" Mick called to Daisy as the women began to pour outside.

"LIZZIE'S BEEN VOTED CHAIRMAN OF THE COUNCIL," she yelled over her shoulder, eager to get to the newspaper office.

Inside, Ada, Martha, Connie, and a whole row of women had remained and were silently watching as Lizzie performed her first municipal duties.

"She seems so young and frail," whispered Minnie Harris.

"Frail!" Connie laughed. "In a pig's eye! Lizzie Short's the smartest and toughest woman you'll ever meet."

"She's also the best friend I ever had," Ada murmured. "Hush, I want to hear what they're saying."

"Mister Lee, would you bring the clerk in, please," asked Lizzie, but they all knew it was an order.

"We don't allow servants in council meetings, ma'am," Admiral Jones objected.

"Quon Lee, a servant?" she hissed. "He's a better man than you could ever hope to be and his watch chain holds his own timepiece, not that of another man!"

Penny Sutton gasped at Lizzie's audacity, flinging her own blatant accusation in the admiral's face. Recognizing another of Lizzie's taunting insults, John Hope half rose from his chair expecting a violent outburst from the admiral. Puzzled when none came, he settled back onto his seat churning the implications of her words over in his mind as he closely watched the naval man's reaction.

An icy cold chill of conscience had just touched the admiral's back as his fingers involuntarily felt for the timepiece, hidden from sight in his waistcoat pocket. The gesture did not go unnoticed by Sir John.

Shuffling footsteps disturbed any further conversation as Quon Lee escorted the clerk, William Toppit, into the room. Back bent in submission, his hands twitching nervously, he stood in front of the new chairman.

"From whom do you take your orders, Mister Toppit?" Lizzie asked gently.

"Admiral Jones and Judge Harvey," he replied nervously.

252

"Well, no doubt you've already heard, that a change has taken place here tonight." She smiled, looking squarely at him. "You will take your orders from me from now on."

"But miss, the judge said ...."

"Mister Toppit!" Lizzie's voice rang with authority, causing droplets of sweat to appear on the man's forehead. "Are you not intent on keeping your present position, sir?"

Sir John rose from his seat. Frowning, he watched as the vacant-eyed clerk shuffled past him, nodding his head continuously as he left the room.

"Madam Chairman," asked Sir John, "would you like me to guide you through the correct procedure?"

"Leave us, sir, we have no further need of your interference," Admiral Jones snorted, dabbing irritably at his nose. "I would remind you this is a municipal council."

"Bang the gavel and call for order," the lawyer prompted the girl.

"I can't, he broke it on the admiral's nose!"

Jackson and Potter snickered loudly.

"Then get another one girl, you're in charge!"

Lizzie smiled at the lawyer's abruptness. She looked over at her partner and winked. Quon stared at her for a moment, his face showing no emotion, then he quickly moved toward the inner doorway and disappeared.

"DON'T YOU GO NEAR MY COURTROOM, BOY!" Judge Harvey yelled, sensing where Quon was heading.

The sound of hurrying feet could be heard on the bare wooden floor of the great hall.

Mick, Joe Todd and Abe Kratze took this opportunity to enter the council chambers and join the ladies in the gallery. Their whispered conversation drew the stern attention of Admiral Jones.

"Toppit, clear those peasants from the gallery," he called angrily. When there was no sign of the clerk, he repeated the command even louder.

"Leave them be, Toppit," Lizzie announced calmly as the clerk's head appeared around the door, "these offices are open to the public from now on."

"Yes, miss," the clerk mumbled. "There's a military man to see you."

"Please show him in."

Quon returned to Lizzie's side, sliding the courtroom gavel onto the table, causing the judge to grow very red in the face. With eyes bulging, he leapt to his feet sending his chair crashing to the floor.

"THIEF!" he screamed at Quon Lee, just as the soldier entered. "ARREST THAT CHINAMAN!"

"Who sent for you?" Sir John's voice thundered as a captain and four soldiers in red uniforms marched into the council chambers. "You have no authorrity here."

"Captain Riley sir," the army officer identified himself. "We're here to restore law and order. My men came back to the barracks in disarray, many missing their rifles—beaten by rioters they said."

"Then arrest them, you fool," Admiral Jones blustered pompously. "The ringleaders are there." He flung his arm toward the public gallery.

"But they're women, sir."

"Vicious, evil rogues and thieves, I tell you, others are outside, arrest them all!" As he spoke, the volume of his voice increased giving the onlookers the sense they were listening to a madman.

Lizzie brought her gavel down with a resounding crash bringing a sudden silence to the room. Flinching, the soldier's moustache bristled in anticipation.

Smiling to himself, John Hope moved slowly back to his seat, intensely alert, as Lizzie took control. Her appearance gave others the impression of innocence, but he knew better. *Why is that Chinese man of hers standing right behind her ... very puzzling,* he thought. When he caught the movement of Quon's fingers on her arm, he saw a fire of determination flash in her eyes. *Yes, this was the girl who had berated him so eloquently on the dock. She's a leader born to the ways of dockland and well equipped to fight its evils. There! Mister Lee sent her another message just like Patrick described it!*

"Sit down windbag," she purred, looking straight at the admiral. She had an ominous threat in her voice. "And you, sir," she continued, turning to the army captain, "have a legitimate complaint. Your men were terrorized by an army of women armed with loaves of bread. Arrest them if you dare, for tomorrow you'll be the laughing stock of dockland!"

"Loaves of bread?" the captain muttered in dismay. "My men were put to flight by women armed with loaves of bread?"

"Come, son," Sir John interrupted the captain's thoughts, "let me enlighten you. I will show you Lizzie Shorrt's army. You will note that the majority of spectatorrs in the gallerry are women. Some have already left to tend to theirr families, but I can assure you that these women are merrely a small porrtion of Miss Shorrt's so-called arrmy. We'll go outside now and I'll show you the evidence of *yourr* rriot." He winked at

Lizzie as he picked up his papers and indicated to the soldiers to follow him to the back of the room.

When the group stepped outside, the first person they met was Patrick. "Uncle John, is everrything under contrrol?"

"Aye laddie," Sir John chuckled and, lowering his voice continued, "that wee lassie is the fierrcest thing in skirts I've ever encounterred!" As Patrick chuckled, Sir John raised his voice slightly and added, "Ah prromised this soldierr boy a peek at Lizzie's arrmy and evidence of theirr rriot." He rolled his eyes and sighed. "I'm getting too old and I put him in yourr capable hands, nephew. I'm away to ma bed noo."

He raised his hand for his carriage, parked across the street. His driver signalled his understanding, spoke to the horse and the buggy moved toward them. Patrick Sandilands watched as his uncle's carriage was brought around and he assisted the older man inside. As Patrick waved goodbye, he thought of the secret they held between them … a secret which would remain hidden forever. No one would ever know the truth of what his uncle had done this night in order to achieve their goal—a goal of utmost importance to dockland.

"Better send yer soldier boys back to their cots, laddie," Patrick laughed. "Lizzie's army is a fearsome sight!"

"B-but who are all these men standing around? Did they steal the guns of my men? I have been led to believe that her army is made up of women?" he asked, looking all around him.

"Well, you should look a wee bit closerr, lad," the Scot suggested, trying to keep a straight face. "They may be a fearrsome lot, but they do have you surrrounded! As for yourr guns, yourr poorr men dropped them when they were surrprrised by the women—I hope you won't be too hard on them!" Grinning, he indicated to the TLS men to step aside exposing a small pile of rifles. "I think you will agree, captain, that these men have no use for yourr guns. They will be only too happy to return them!"

Bristling with suspicion, Captain Riley stared at the large group of men and then to the rifles. He began to realize why this man was smiling, for the evidence in front of him was obvious. These men, young and old, were former soldiers—peglegs, hands in the shape of hooks, sleeves hanging devoid of a limb, and many with eyepatches. Despite their obvious injuries, he couldn't help but notice the still-cocky look of confidence which fighting men tend to have in their manner.

"They're all cripples!" Captain Riley gasped.

"Aye lad, they arre," Patrick sighed, "and everry one of 'em harrdened in battle."

"This is ridiculous, they can't fight in a riot."

"You lay one finger on our Lizzie, mister, and you will damn sure find that out!" one of the ex-sailors commented.

"You were going to show me evidence of this riot, sir," the captain, reminded him.

"Look arround you on the grround, captain," Patrick said solemnly. "That's not bird feed you see, ach aye, that is the rremnants of the rrioters' weaponrry—loaves of crrusty brread, to be exact, sir! It worrked quite nicely, or so you tell us!" Patrick smirked, looking over at the soldiers. "Now, you may want to dismiss yourr men before I take you to see the rrest of ourr lady's army—and please take yer guns away with you!"

Looking rather sheepish, Captain Riley gave a subdued order to his small troop who, appearing quite anxious to be away, retrieved the guns and marched off in all haste.

The captain straightened his tunic and squared his shoulders. "I'm ready, sir."

Leading Captain Riley quickly though the streets, they soon became aware of Billy's powerful voice breaking the stillness of the evening air.

"FREE BREAD FOR THE BATTLING LADIES OF DOCKLAND. LIZZIE'S ARMY WINS FIRST BATTLE. THERE'S NO STOPPING NOW, GIRLS!"

The atmosphere in front of the bread shop had changed dramatically from an hour previous. When Patrick and Captain Riley arrived, they found the usually sour-faced women—many from the backstreet hovels—shouting and laughing together, as they relived their exciting evening.

"Ach, therre's the other half of her army, captain!" Patrick chuckled. "Tell me soldierr boy, arre ye brave enough to tackle that lot?"

"This is most unusual," retorted the captain. "My men will not fight women and crippled ex-naval men," he muttered absentmindedly. "Just who is this Lizzie Short?"

Back in the council chamber, arguments still persisted as Judge Harvey and the admiral screamed abuse at each other across the table. Lizzie felt the steadying hand of Quon on her shoulder and glanced at the public gallery in frustration. There, sitting alone in the shadows off to one side, she found Abe Kratze staring in eager fascination at the noisy proceedings. She suddenly remembered the words he'd once said. A smile touched her lips as she crashed her gavel onto the table.

"ENOUGH OF THIS BICKERING YOU FOOLS, WE HAVE WORK TO GET DONE TONIGHT," she shouted.

"Now she's ready to take charge," Penny whispered, as the women leaned forward, eager to catch every word.

"We are going to pass a repair law," Lizzie stated to the startled council members.

"By-law girl, by-law," Abe's voice hissed from the gallery.

"All right, by-law then!" she repeated in frustration.

Tom Jackson jumped at the ferocity of her words and Alyse Byrd cringed in her seat. Hatred shone from the judge's eyes as he swung his gaze from the pouting admiral to their new chairman in the green dress, who had obviously found her voice.

"Every property owner of these backstreet hovels," she announced tersely, "will be required to begin repairs immediately. Dockland families have a right to decent homes."

"Property owners will ignore you and your bylaw!" Judge Harvey sniggered.

"Then, we'll take the property from them!" she replied coldly.

"Expropriate!" Abe's voice hissed again from the gallery.

"But this council has no money to furnish repairs, if we expropriate," Jackson interceded. "So what do we do then?"

"First things first, sir," Lizzie snapped, "but I mean to have my way in this matter."

"People should have decent houses to live in," Missus Byrd agreed, finally finding her courage.

"This discussion could go on all night," said the vicar. "I move that property owners repair their buildings or we expropriate." Tip inwardly chuckled to himself. These city men thought him a dolt—how were they to know that at the monastery he had served on many councils and committees. He knew the procedure well and was determined to support Lizzie's action.

"I second that motion," agreed Tom Jackson, "but do let's get on with it."

"Take a vote, girl," Abe's voice prompted from the shadows.

"ALL IN FAVOUR, RAISE YOUR HANDS," Lizzie shouted excitedly, scanning the table. "That's five of us, it's passed!"

"OBJECTION, you didn't count the nays," Judge Harvey growled.

"What's the point, there's only two of you left!"

Laughter broke out in the gallery.

J. Robert Whittle

"Now to the matter of money, Mister Jackson. How much are councillors paid?" she asked.

"The chairman," Albert Potter chirped up, "gets 10 guineas a month. The rest of us get a token amount of 10 guineas a year but, of course," he chuckled smugly, "the council covers all our refreshments and expenses."

"We should fill the coffers, sir. This council is going to need a lot of money," announced the chairman.

"Property taxes are at a premium," the architect muttered. "You'll need to be a genius, girl, to find more money in this borough."

"There's money here," Lizzie replied, now warming to her task, "but before I tell you where, I shall be generous and let you keep your stipend. However, the council will pay no more of your expenses or refreshments. If you wish to guzzle liquor, you should go to a tavern!"

"You'll never get that past a vote, madam," Jackson leered.

"She doesn't need to," the vicar informed them with a grin, "the chairman controls the finances!"

"Then I won't be staying," Tom Jackson snapped, leaping to his feet. "I'll not be ruled by a petticoat trying to imitate a man."

"Oh you'll stay, Mister Jackson." Lizzie smiled coldly. "You're a lackey, sir. You represent powerful masters and I'm sure they will want an accurate report from you."

The blatant insult brought a wounded growl from the architect's throat as a titter of laughter from Abe Kratze whispered from the shadows.

"She's not making many friends around that table," the butcher's wife proffered quietly.

Unnoticed, Quon's fingers tapped out a message on Lizzie's shoulder. Slowly, she raised her hand to his and tapped an answer.

"Gentlemen and Missus Byrd," Lizzie began, "the money this council needs is out there in the River Thames."

"There's gold in the river?" Admiral Jones interrupted greedily.

"Fool!" Judge Harvey flung his insult at the admiral. "She's going to try taxing the river and that, ma'am, belongs to the Crown!"

"No sir, not the water, nor the docks," she announced slowly, in a low voice. Every face turned her way, straining to hear. "It's the capstans we need to tax. They are 20 feet apart. Every ship will use as many as they need and pay accordingly. Cost will be on the shipowners, not our local merchants."

"BRILLIANT!" Penny Sutton yelped, hugging Ada before dashing off to write her own newspaper report.

"You're quite the tactician, girl," Judge Harvey muttered in sudden admiration. "This is quite innovative, quite innovative."

"It just might work," Jackson agreed, "but who would collect the fees?"

"Crippled ex-naval men who can't get a job," Lizzie replied, "for 10 percent of the fee."

"Hmm, could be too much," the admiral growled, "we don't want to be too liberal with cripples."

Lizzie's temper exploded again. The gavel in her hand whizzed down the length of the table thumping hard into the admiral's flabby chest and skidded on into the minister's lap.

"Want another try?" Tip chuckled, sliding it back down the table to her.

Women in the gallery jumped to their feet sending a resounding cheer through the building.

"Look out, she's mad now!" Joe grunted, calmly putting a flame to his pipe. He coughed through the billowing smoke. "The fires of hell couldn't stop her!"

"Joe, put out your pipe!" admonished Martha, but he didn't hear her because Lizzie was standing up and admonishing someone else.

"YOU EVIL TURD!" Lizzie screamed, at the admiral. "This meeting is over. I can't stand another moment of seeing your horrible face."

"You can't talk to me ...," the admiral's pouting objections quickly stopped and turned to a yelp of fear as Lizzie flung the gavel again. This time it narrowly missed his head. Moaning, he pushed his chair back, trying to hide his overweight body behind Alyse Byrd's thin frame.

Cheers erupted again from the gallery and the sound carried out through the slightly open doors to the men outside. Patrick and Captain Riley were just returning to the area.

"Ach, ah thinks we had better be checkin inside, laddie," the Scot muttered.

Mick grinned from his gallery seat when he saw Patrick come striding into the council chambers followed by the army captain. His urge was to join them, but Ada, sensing trouble brewing, held tight to his arm.

"ARREST THAT MAN, CAPTAIN!" Lizzie yelled through the confusion.

"ON WHAT CHARGES, MA'AM?" asked Captain Riley.

"STEALING!"

Silence suddenly settled over the room. The red-faced admiral, panting for breath, stumbled to his feet.

"Stealing from whom, ma'am," the captain demanded.

"From every battle-scarred and crippled sailor," she retorted tersely.

Captain Riley glanced at the Scot for direction and saw the twinkle of amusement dancing in his eyes. Riley looked around the room, then strode down to the front to stand near the councillors.

"And what did he steal, ma'am?" he asked only as loud as necessary.

"He stole their self respect and then questioned their ability to earn a decent living," she replied, slowly and deliberately. Her temper was now in check but her voice rang through the silent chambers. "Have you ever been wounded in battle, captain?"

"No ma'am."

"Then look around dockland, soldier. Men with no hope are everywhere, men on crutches or sticks, men missing an arm or an eye. They're heroes every one of them but who even cares?"

"But ma'am," Captain Riley whispered in embarrassment. "I can't arrest a man for not caring!" He turned on his heel and walked quickly to the door and outside.

Patrick could feel Lizzie's hurt, as Admiral Jones, now openly smirking, flopped back into his chair. Patrick pushed the small, swinging door to the inner council chamber open, and walked toward the table. Judge Harvey felt strangely insecure and cringed in his chair as the big, red-bearded Scot moved past him and clamped a hand on the admiral's collar.

"Ach, 'am nay a soldierr, lassie," he chuckled evilly, yanking Admiral Jones violently from his chair, "but ah'll be glad to drrown him ferr ya!"

The gallery waited in stunned silence as if each were afraid to breathe.

"No," Lizzie hissed, "take him out and give him to our crippled men. Tell them to take him down every garbage-strewn alley in dockland. Make him walk the lanes and back alleys day and night and see the pain of poverty first hand—poverty he helped to produce."

"Can ah noo drrown him then?" Patrick jested.

"No, just let the turd drop in the nearest gutter, Mister Sandilands!"

With the admiral whining and pleading for mercy, Patrick dragged him to the door. The hushed council room could hear Patrick repeating Lizzie's instructions as the door closed behind them. A roar went up outside and the admiral's protestations soon faded away.

Meanwhile, inside the council chambers not a word was spoken as everyone seemed to be alone with their thoughts. Had Lizzie gone too far this time? Was there big trouble looming ahead or had she struck the first blow for freedom and greater equality? Only time would tell.

Lizzie Series

by J. Robert Whittle

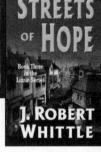

This popular multi-generational series begins in the year 1800 when a young English girl, Lizzie Short, finds herself alone following her friends' deportation for stealing food. Later, aiding an old man hurt in a street accident causes her life to be forever changed.

Set during a period of history when women were considered chattels, Lizzie, without a family to inform her of this system, begins the challenging and intriguing life of a young entrepreneur. As the years pass, Lizzie and her best friend, Quon Lee, aspire to change the face of dockland. Whittle traces the youngsters' rise to fame from the age of nine to young adulthood, during the Napoleonic Wars. They battle poverty, the establishment, jealous rivals and personal danger while seeking their goal.

The author, a Yorkshireman immigrating to Canada in 1971, first began writing while recuperating from a life-threatening illness in 1994 discovering a new passion—writing historical novels. Once a child entrepreneur, this former mining engineer/raconteur experienced many of the scenes in this series and knows the feelings of a child seeking a better life for his family during hard times—in his case, during the Second World War.

Available at your local bookstore

Visit author's website: www.jrobertwhittle.com

More books by bestselling author

J. Robert Whittle

"Victoria Chronicles"
2 Books

Take a journey back in time as author, J. Robert Whittle weaves a fascinating tale of friendship, love and adventure through real historical events and settings. Nancy and Dan meet in a Victoria orphanage as children but fate brings them together years later. Set in and around the beautiful Pacific Northwest, the story features actual whaling stations of the early 1900s, real rum runners and adventure on land and sea encompassing the coastal regions of British Columbia and Washington State. *Bound by Loyalty* became a Canadian bestselling novel in 2004.

"Moonbeam Series" by Joyce Sandilands

From an original concept by author, J. Robert Whittle, developed into a series of children's chapter books by his wife, Joyce Sandilands. These books feature their own grandchildren. Companion audio books narrated by the author are available on the website.

The delightful adventures of a leprechaun, parrot, and their Fairyland friends who become Moonbeam Riders—yes, by sliding down moonbeams! These Moonbeam Riders have a special mission to help Earth children solve their problems. Non-scary, fairyland characters. Gr. 2-3 vocabulary. Ages 4-9

All books are available at your local bookstore.

Whitlands Publishing: www.whitlands.com